PRAISE

'MOST OF US WOULD LIKE TO BE HARLAN
FOR AT LEAST A DAY.'

'IT READ LIKE I WAS WATCHING A MOVIE.'

'THIS IS A FANTASTIC READ, COULDN'T PUT IT DOWN!'

CHILD'S PLAY

HARLAN ACTION THRILLER SERIES

HARRY HUDSON

MICHIE LONDON LTD
71-75 Shelton Street
Covent Garden
London
WC2H 9JQ
www.michielondon.com

First published in the United Kingdom in 2023 by Michie London Ltd.

ISBN: 978-1-7393428-6-9

"When we are children, we seldom think of the future. This innocence leaves us free to enjoy ourselves as few adults can.
The day we fret about the future is the day we leave our childhood behind."

Patrick Rothfuss

MOTORCYCLE CLUB TERMINOLOGY

1%er - The American Motorcycle Association once said that '99% of motorcyclists were law-abiding citizens', implying the other 1% were not

Brother – A member of an MC

Charter – A local division of an MC where they have more than one physical presence

Clubhouse – Where MC members meet to discuss club business and to party

Cut – The leather vest worn by a member of the MC

Full Patch – A title given to a member who has passed their probationary period

Harley – A Harley Davidson motorbike

MC – Motorcycle club

Old Lady – The wife of an MC member

Patch – The club's livery as worn on the back of their vest/cut

Patch Over – When a motorcycle club becomes part of a different, often bigger, MC

Prospect – Someone serving their minimum 12-month probationary period before they become a full member

President – The elected leader of the MC at international, national or individual club/charter level

Sgt at Arms – An elected position and responsible for the discipline of MC members and the protection of the club

Vice President – The under-study to the President

SLANG

Bag or Bag of Sand – £1,000

Burner – A cheap mobile phone for anonymous use

Charlie – Cocaine

Monkey – £500

Readies – Money

Ton – £100

Trap phone - An untraceable, prepaid mobile phone used for making narcotics deals

Weed – Cannabis

1

Harlan ordered from the menu. It was nice enough; not trying to be anything that it wasn't. There were no frills on the menu, pub grub at restaurant prices. Low level lights in crimson-coloured shades over each table. Cheap sauces in ceramic pots. Silver cutlery that had started to stain. He asked for a burger with fries, no pickles and definitely no garnish. And a Coke. He wanted a ribeye but didn't trust the chef to cook it how he liked, whereas anyone with a half-ounce of tobacco between their ears could cook a damn burger. The minutes slowly passed, some of the time spent removing a piece of beef from his tooth with a pick. He wondered what he would be facing this time. Not that it mattered. Not really. Different pub, different part of the country. The same damn problem. A pub that was in trouble; an owner not knowing how to stop it. They would turn a blind eye at first, hoping that, whatever the trouble was, it would soon go away. Harlan knew that was seldom the case. They would then call the police, but that wouldn't work, in fact, it would probably make it worse.

They would be at their wits' end, not knowing who to turn to. But then someone, somehow, would hand over a number. It would be on a scrap piece of paper. They would be told, this is who you need, and this is how you get hold of him. They would sit on it for a day, maybe two. Not wanting the war to escalate, but they were in a war, and they were losing. Losing their business, their livelihood. Losing sleep and losing money. A downward spiral. Then whatever it was that was causing the sleepless nights and the anxiety attacks would happen again. And then they would go back to that piece of paper. They would unfurl it, smoothing it flat, trying to make it decipherable. They would type in each digit, slowly, checking it through, twice. Then they would add the three words. They would wait a second before sending. Breathing hard and heavy, their stomachs starting to knot. Then the confidence would come and they would press send. It would be done quickly, like ripping off a plaster. There, it was gone.

Those three words had been sent: *I need you.*

Michael wasn't sure. His friend showed him the money in his fake Gucci wallet, a wallet he assured him would be the real deal soon. The wallet contained a stack of twenties. Ten of them. Two hundred pounds. A lot of money for a fourteen-year-old.

'It's so easy, Mikey. You will be minted, mate, proper minted,' said Ryan. Michael, *Mikey* to his friends, knew all about peer pressure. That's what got him into bunking off school. Then smoking. Then smoking weed. But this was the next level. But he couldn't deny that the stack of cash was tempting. Very tempting.

Ryan was the same age but more streetwise, it helped of course having an old brother who had a rep for being a brawler, that earned him some kudos and some protection. But this didn't involve his brother, this was his own gig, and now he wanted to earn more by doing less. He knew how it worked; it had been explained to him. The art of pyramid selling. The more people you have underneath you then the closer you are to the top. He knew he wouldn't ever reach the top, but if he had Mikey working for him, he wouldn't be at the bottom, either. They were standing in an old shed on an all-but abandoned allotment. They didn't know whose shed it was, they didn't care. It gave them a roof and a closed door. The humble beginnings of an HQ. The shed was old. It had the smell of mould and the shelves contained pots with dead flowers in them and various boxes of stuff that would help make whatever was supposed to be growing, grow. The shed had two deck chairs. The type you find at the beach. A flimsy wooden frame with a piece of sagging cotton to sit on. It was perfect as long as whoever owned it didn't come in, but that hadn't happened in all the times they had been in there, so no reason to suspect that it would now.

'What do you say?' asked Ryan.

'I'm not sure.'

'Look, I can go into town tomorrow and get me what the hell I want. I don't even need to nick it, I can just walk up to the counter and put down dollar. Self-made, that's me.'

There was an air of swagger in his friend's voice. Michael envied that. He was tempted.

. . .

They left the shed. The padlock was placed through the clasp but not pushed fully home. They found it like this when they first started dossing in there, and saw no reason to change it. They fist bumped and got on their bikes. Michael had a mountain bike; a Christmas present from his parents. It had been wrapped and put under the tree and Michael couldn't tear the wrapping off quick enough to reveal its beauty. It had twenty-two gears. Soft grip handlebars and his dad had fitted the drinks bottle holder onto the frame. It was so cool, he no longer believed in Santa but he did believe right there and then that he was lucky.

Ryan's bike was different. It was an old-school BMX and it hadn't been wrapped up in Christmas paper and propped up against the radiator, next to the tree. It was second-hand and had been stolen for him by his brother. He may have had a second-hand stolen bike, but his threads were new, and expensive. He was wearing another North Face tracksuit and Jordan trainers. Typical clothing for a streetwise teenager, and he had a leather man-bag strapped over his chest. Inside was a half-smoked packet of cigarettes, some weed, some rizla papers, his fake Gucci wallet and 2 phones. One contract, the other a burner. The burner started to ring. The friend stopped pedalling and sat stationary pulling the phone from his bag, he knew exactly who it was. Only one person had his number. He answered and listened carefully. He didn't speak. He was told never to speak. He knew to put his hand over his ear to drown out the noise, he knew never to ask twice for a set of instructions.

'217A, Carlton Road. Pick up. 7pm. At 7.15 I'll call with

where to deliver.' The line went dead. He didn't mind the work. £200 for delivering packages across town. What could possibly go wrong...

The person who had made the call then made three more. Each one made from a different mobile. The room was full of them. Some charging, some still not yet set up. A tenner a time but the cost of anonymity was priceless. The other three guys were sitting around the table playing cards. The room was thick in fog from the joints that were either sitting in the ashtrays or hanging from mouths. There were posters of Bob Marley on the wall, but the corners dog-eared and curled from the smog. The carpet was stained and sticky and the blinds were drawn. They were always drawn. Three women were also there. Two in one bed, one in the other. Gangster groupies. They meant very little to the four men. They were disposable. Money was all that mattered. Money and merit. You earned both in this game. There was also something else on the table, next to the ashtray. A loaded gun. There were more stashed around the place, some of them bigger. Some more powerful, some had bits sawn off, some bits attached, but this one, unmodified and loaded, was there, lying in wait and close to hand. Four men; three heavies, two brothers. One leader. They were part of a much bigger plan. A much bigger problem. But in this room, they felt like kings. The CCTV cameras were high-tech but the safe, that was old-school. A big, cumbersome box that couldn't be lifted by one person alone and it was full of cash. Twenties and fifties, mostly. One thing that was missing was drugs. Aside from the weed in their joints, there was nothing else here that could land them a sentence for supplying. The guns, that would carry a sentence, but the thought process was that if they needed to use them, then a jail cell was the least of their impending problems. They were four very dangerous men but they weren't dealers, they were the facilitators.

'Pass me the smokes, man,' said the guy who was sitting alone surrounded by burner phones.

One of the men took the spliff from the ashtray and walked it over to him. His jeans were riding halfway down his butt and his underwear riding high above. He had a white wife-beater vest on and a thick gold chain around his neck, his hair in tight rolls. He was the smaller, scrawnier of the four but still had swagger and an air of arrogance. The leader, his skin asphalt black, wearing a white t-shirt with a Bulls basketball jersey over the top, took the spliff and inhaled slowly, holding onto the gathering of smoke that had accumulated, then exhaled it all through his nostrils. It was a menacing move from a seasoned smoker. He took one more long drag before going back to business. For him, it was *always* about the business.

Ryan used his smartphone as a GPS. The burner one not having the sort of technology. It made and received calls. Sent and received texts. And had a couple of games built in. That was it. Ryan knew roughly the area but not the street. He had his baseball cap on and his hood up over that. He was a fourteen-year-old boy riding his bike. Depending on their view of teenagers, some would think him a hoodlum, others would think him a sweet and innocent child, but no-one would know what he was really up to. He was riding one handed and holding his phone in the other. He was near, less than 600yds. This part of town was dog rough. Most of the houses had cars in various states of disarray and with bits missing, many with mismatched panels. There was a little green with kids playing football and he rode past remembering when he used to be that age and spending all day kicking a ball. He now spent his time riding his bike and earning his cash to then be out spending it. He put his bike down on the front lawn of the house and walked up the path to the door. Before he knocked, he always looked left to right, and then back to the left. It was something he'd taught himself to do. He once heard someone say that *prying eyes and inquisitive minds cause problems* and it had struck a chord with him. He felt sure no-one was paying him much attention. There was a guy across the street with his head under a bonnet. Behind him, a fair-haired woman had her head over his shoulder, both staring into the mechanical abyss of the engine. They weren't about to pay him any attention and the kids playing football were too invested in their match to notice him.

The coast was clear. He knocked on the door, three clear, crisp taps. Standard protocol for door knocking. No-one seemed to be forthcoming. He repeated the three-tap knock. The door didn't have any glass so he couldn't see in. He stepped away from the door and tried to see through the bay window but the nets were either too dark or too dirty, he wasn't sure which. He was about to abort when he heard the door creak open. It wasn't the sound of the door opening nervously, rather one that was sticking in its frame. Wood wasn't impervious to water and it had no doubt swallowed enough rainwater over the course of time to have swollen up and got itself ever so slightly out of shape. When it did open, it was only enough for an arm to appear holding a tan-coloured Jiffy bag. There wasn't a face attached to the arm, that was behind the door. There was just a pale-skinned arm with pockmarks and a cheap watch holding out a package. Ryan took the package and put it inside his man-bag and by the time he had zipped it up, the arm had disappeared and the wooden door had been closed. The entire physical transaction had taken less than ten seconds.

Ryan was back on his bike twenty seconds after that, and thirty seconds after that he was cycling past the kids playing football and was out of the street all together. He knew he would stop again shortly; he had the 7.15pm call to answer and he knew *never* to miss a call. He had been told what happens if you miss a call, or a collection, or a delivery. He hadn't seen it, but he had heard about it. That was enough.

The evening sunlight was holding on for dear life but it would be a losing battle. All his errands were usually done before 8pm. But never after 9pm. He wasn't sure why that was. He stopped off at the off-licence and treated himself to a Coke and a bag of Haribos. He would get some chicken later from the KFC on the high street, that would be his dinner. A well-earned treat. The phone call came dead on time. The person on the end of the phone was always precise. And it was always the same person. And it always scared him a little.

'Go to The Rise. Ring the buzzer for the penthouse suite. The door will open. Take the lift. Do the exchange and then stash the cash until I arrange to have it collected.'

Then the line went dead. As always. The Rise was one of the swankiest flats around, and by far, the tallest apartment block in town, hence the name. The GPS on his phone told him it was a good twenty-minute ride but for £200, that was £10 a minute, or £100 a mile at a slow pace. Not bad wages, he told himself. He knew he could earn more in a week than his brother did in a month. He downed the rest of his Coke and tossed the can onto the pavement and set off for The Rise.

Liam answered his burner. The person then told him what was needed. It was one sentence long. An address and a time. He grabbed his school rucksack from his bedroom floor, undid the toggles and removed most of the text books. He kept two in there just for the lie he was about to tell. His room was a mess. Clothes over-spilling from the wash basket. Dirty cups and plates on his computer desk from the dinners his mum had made, to which he had promised to bring back down as soon as he had finished, but seldom did. The waste bin was full of empty sweet wrappers and crushed up cans of pop. Liam pulled a clean hoodie from the wardrobe and slipped it over his head. He picked up the rucksack and slung it over his shoulder, the burner phone buried deep down inside. He left his room and headed downstairs ready to go out through the galley kitchen and into the shed.

'Just off out, Mum,' he shouted as he opened the back door, hoping to be out of the house before she could reply. No such luck.

'Where are you going, it's getting late?' His mum was in the living room, watching the news, a fag in her hand. Liam didn't fancy a face-to-face conversation so he shouted through his reply loud enough for her to hear.

'Off to Carl's, we have coursework to hand in tomorrow.' The lie now told.

'Oh, OK. Ride safe, honey.'

'Will do.'

Liam closed the back door behind him and walked down the garden to the shed. He lifted the hook from its eyelet and then stepped inside to manoeuvre his bike back out, an arduous task but it was a stipulation from his dad that if he got a new bike that it must be put away every night, "*you can never be too careful, son. And that bike of yours wasn't cheap. Money doesn't grow on trees you know*", but Liam now begged to differ. He now had his very own money tree and he could buy a new bike every goddamn day if he wanted. The bike was sandwiched between the lawnmower and his dad's Black & Decker workmate. As always, the handlebars or the pedals seemed to get stuck every time he pulled it out. After a cuss and a tug, the bike was freed but at the expense of the workmate falling over. Another cuss.

The bike was finally out and he pushed it back down the path and then along the side of the house and out through the side gate. He was then on his way to the destination he had been given and would soon be £200 richer.

The waiter came over with his bill, and with him, a card machine. He waited gracefully as Harlan read the bill and then, with well-trained timing, held out the machine in readiness for the card. Harlan didn't do plastic; never had, doubtful he ever would. He got paid in cash and paid in cash. He reached down into his pocket and pulled out a handful of notes. He opened up the neatly folded stack and thumbed off three ten-pound notes and handed them over. The waiter had already done the math; an eight-quid tip; nearly 40%. The waiter thanked him and started to clear away the table. Harlan had arrived in town just over an hour ago, and now he was fed, next up was finding a bed. He crossed the road over to his bike. It was a warm night, the sun wouldn't be setting for at least another hour, maybe two. It was quiet outside, empty except for a family that was on the same side of the street, a few hundred yards away. The family was made up of two adults with two young kids, and the guy seemed to be in a foul mood. From what Harlan could hear the guy was pissed that she hadn't got the cab to collect them on time although she was trying to say she had, and that it was just late, that's all and for him to calm down. Harlan watched, from the seat of his bike, both feet touching the floor, the bike still on its stand. The man was getting louder and more abusive. One of the kids had started to cry. Harlan was still watching, but it wasn't any of his business. Until it became his business. The guy grabbed her arm and forcefully pulled her towards him, as if to hiss in her ear rather than shout in it. Harlan had seen enough. You don't bully women, and you definitely don't do it in front of their children. He hung his helmet over the handlebar and headed over, it was time to get involved. The guy with the attitude didn't see Harlan approach, the first he knew of the biker's presence was when he spoke.

'Miss, are you OK?' asked Harlan.

The aggressor turned to face the voice, and noticed a guy with a beard staring straight at him, a little more than five feet away.

'Excuse me, who the hell are you?', he fired back, his

right hand still clutched tightly around his partner's bicep.

'I'm the person who is going to break your arm if you don't release hers right now.'

Harlan watched the man process what was happening, deciding on his chances against the stranger standing in front him, ignoring his child that was still crying. Harlan raised the stakes. 'Let her go right now, or I will snap your arm clean in two. Your call.'

The guy was now staring into darkness. The colour of Harlan's eyes had turned black, like coal. The guy suddenly lost all of his backbone and wilted right there in front of him.

'I don't want no bother,' he said, releasing her arm from his vice-like grip. She rubbed her arm for a second, then bent down on her knees to console her upset child. A true mum, putting her child's pain before her own. Harlan knew his mum would have been like that, too, when he was a child. God rest her soul.

'No, I bet you don't,' Harlan replied, taking a step forward to narrow the gap.

'Now you'll do well to remember me, as there are people like me. People who hate bullies, and will kick your ass all goddamn day if you give us a reason.'

Harlan let the words linger before turning to face the woman who was now standing up again and was holding one of each of her children's hands in her own. Trying to be strong for her kids. She was a good person; Harlan could see that. She deserved better.

'Have a good evening, Miss,' and with that, he walked back down the street to his bike. Harlan was glad he hadn't hit him, that the guy had seen the danger he was in and kept his trap shut. Harlan didn't want to have to break his arm in front of the children, but if pushed, he would have, no questions asked.

He watched again from the seat of his Harley as the cab pulled up and they got in and drove off. Harlan had heard her tell the partner she had booked it, that it would be there any minute but that wasn't good enough for him. He had dismissed her and called her stupid and then made the cardinal sin of putting his hand on her. There was no need for any of that. Harlan hoped he had taught him a lesson, and that he would change his ways, but he knew it was doubtful. The world was full of assholes. This guy just added to that headcount.

Harlan took the helmet that was resting over the handlebar and put it on, clicked the strap up under his chin, fired up the Harley and kicked away the stand. He was off to find a bed for the night.

He stood and watched as the two guys sat on opposing chairs, their thumbs a blur as they battled for the ball that was being kicked about on the huge TV screen that was fitted on the wall. Liam loved FIFA and if he was offered a game right now he would take it. But he wasn't, the guy came back into the living room with a package in his hands.

'Here you go. It's all there, no need to look inside.' A subtle warning.

'And you sure you don't want a beer or a smoke?'

Liam declined for the second time. And he didn't need reminding not to look inside the bags. He wasn't stupid, he knew exactly what was inside. He unzipped his rucksack and stuffed the package right down to the bottom; then fiddled around with the books that he had left in there to cover it and then zipped it back up and slung it over his shoulder. The guy walked him back to the door, he was six or seven years older than Liam. He had intricate tattoos on the backs of his hands and sovereign rings on a few of his fingers.

'Later, bruv,' the guy said as Liam stepped back onto the patio. He shut the door before Liam had a chance to turn around and reply. He pulled his bike off the wall and threw his leg over it. He was soon pedalling back the way he came, making a slight detour to get a bag of chips.

2

Ryan rode into the complex. There was a barrier for car access but for a kid on a bike, that was no bother. He slipped in the gap between the barrier and the wall to the left of it and rode up to the double doors. On one side of the doors, in big, shiny stainless-steel letters, were the words 'The Rise' and on the other side was an intercom system that listed the surnames of who lived at each number. He ran his fore-finger up through the labels until he reached 'Penthouse', there was no surname next to it, the title seemingly speaking for itself. He pressed the button adjacent to the label and the doors made a clunk as the mechanism unlocked itself. He pulled open one of the doors by the long, curved shiny handle and stepped inside the foyer. It was more of an atrium, floor to ceiling plants stood in waist-height pots and there was a giant marble effect coffee table in the middle with four different coloured sofas sitting around each of the four straight sides. Huge oil paintings hung on the walls, not of idyllic scenery or portraits, but four cream-coloured canvases that looked like a bunch of kids had been allowed to flick paint all over them. None of this interested him. He didn't care about designer décor, he just wanted to get to the penthouse and then get paid. He called for the lift. LED lights told him it was coming down. The glass doors opened and he stepped inside and pressed for the penthouse. The glass box took him up through the building and to the top floor. He was young but *now* he was impressed, whoever lived here had serious dollar. The Rise was *the* place to live and he wanted a slice of it, and who was to say it was beyond him, he was only fourteen and was already pulling in up to a grand a week. He knew though that he needed to start saving some of it if he wanted to ever live in a place like The Rise.

He knocked on the door. It was made from brushed aluminium and had two full-length narrow frosted glass panels running through it, so you could make out the silhouette of someone inside but not their distinguishable features. He waited and finally it opened. A guy was standing there, in a silk robe with wet hair and designer slippers on his feet. Ryan thought about what Tony Montana would look like if he, too, had just stepped out of the shower.

'Alright, son, you got something for me?' asked the guy in the robe. A local accent.

Ryan pulled the package from his man-bag and held it in his outstretched hand. He held out his other hand, too, making it clear this was a two-way street. The guy in the robe leaned back behind the door, the frosted glass taking effect, and then returned with a package of his own, and one that was considerably thicker than the one the teenager was holding. They made the exchange and the transaction was done. The ride in the lift up to him had lasted longer. They both said their goodbyes, although not by words, just by a nod of their head. Ryan took the lift back down into the atrium, then walked up to the heavy door with the long, curved, shiny handle, pulled it open and made his way over to his bike. His task was done, his employer would be happy. It was time to go get his chicken.

Liam was riding across town, sometimes on the road, sometimes on the pavement. Carefree yet careful. He had been there before. He had even been inside, well, only to wait for a minute whilst one of the guys went upstairs and came back down carrying what he had come for. His mum thought he was at Rob's. It was a lie, but only a white one. OK, not a white lie, a damn right big black one, but what could go wrong? He rode past a line of stopped cars that were waiting for the light to turn to green, knowing they would all be pissed with his nimbleness and then he cut through the park. He rode through the soft-play area; wood with its chipped base that housed the baby slides and swings. He went up and over the grass bank, in and out of the underpass, before finally joining the new spur road for the final five-minute leg. It was a good half hour trip each way, factoring in a few minutes to take the delivery and then stopping for some chips on the way back. It would be around an hour and a half before he got home, which would seem about right for a spot of studying with his friend. Believable, he thought. He checked his watch and knew he had to peddle a little bit faster.

. . .

Harlan had checked the internet browser on his smartphone for nearby B&B's. It was all it was good for. He didn't even like to think when the last time it was it had rung, or received a text. The screen had told him he wasn't too far away, fifteen minutes, tops. It was the other phone that had brought him here. The work phone. Nothing smart about it, if you forget the fact that it was merely a few inches big but could send and receive messages to other phones all around the world. The roads were quiet, which surprised him as it was a nice night. Bournemouth was a seaside town; picturesque postcodes and beach front apartments. He was heading into a part of the town called Boscombe, he knew nothing about it, which was how he lived his life as a whole. Minimum research but maximum results. He would find a place for around twenty-quid a night and then if it was decent enough, decent breakfast and a comfy bed, he would look to stay and do a deal on his laundry and evening meals. He would pay in cash, keep his room tidy and leave with his bill up to date. The perfect guest. Harlan pulled into the street he was looking for and rode slowly past the row of buildings. The first three were showing they were full, the fourth had vacancies but he didn't like the look of it, the next three were also taken but the eighth one had spaces available and had two hanging baskets either side of the front door which were full of flowers and rich in colour. He had to drive a few cars down to find a space. He walked his bike back into the parking space and put it up on its stand. He walked the few yards down to the B&B, lifted the latch on the little black gate, and then made his way to the front door. The light was on in the room to the right of the front door and through the blinds he could make out the television, it was some sort of early evening gameshow. He didn't know what it was called, nor did he care.

A bell rang when he pulled open the door, and Harlan turned his head to see it, laughing to himself that this was still a thing. He walked over to the reception desk and waited. There was another bell, this one was situated on top of the desk, with a little placard saying *please ring for attention,* and he was tempted to press it if someone didn't come into view soon. He didn't have to. An elderly-looking man came out of the room that had the television and walked past him before stepping behind the desk and speaking.

'Good evening, I presume you would like a room?'

The man standing opposite Harlan was maybe mid-sixties, Harlan thought, and he noticed the hearing aid. The man's hair was white, not grey, and he had big, bushy, black eyebrows. Harlan found that an amusing quirk, and his top lip moved upwards slightly. 'Yes, if possible.'

'Certainty – it is a two-night minimum stay though, I'm afraid.'

It wasn't the height of the season as that had passed but there would still be tourists milling about the town so Harlan could see the need to have the policy in place.

'That's fine, what's the damage?' he asked.

'£25 a night, breakfast between seven and ten.'

It was a fiver a night more than most places he had stayed but this was a seaside town so those same tourists would be a captive audience. Harlan pulled out his wallet and the white-haired man changed his mind on the pricing, 'Can do it for forty five if paying cash?'

Harlan liked him already, he saw an opportunity to keep all the money and deprive the taxman, good on him, he thought. He handed him the £45 and the old man reached over to the cork key rack, lifted a key off the brass hook and handed it over.

The green plastic tag said it was Room 4. Two keys. Front door and the room. Everything he needed in the palm of his hand. Harlan thanked him and started to walk up the stairs, thinking about who the old man reminded him of, and then it came to him, it was one of the old dudes sat up in the wings from The Muppets.

The room was smaller than most and it was minus an ensuite, meaning he would need to use the communal bathroom which was always fun. There was flowery wallpaper and recently painted woodwork and a double bed with starched linen sheets, plus a desk with a cheap kettle and an upturned mug next to a little wicker basket with sachets of coffee, sugar, sweeteners and teabags, and a solitary biscuit. He took out the handful of black t-shirts from inside his rucksack and the two spare pairs of jeans. They were also black. The wardrobe had a row of cheap, yellow plastic coat hangers and the kettle was also cheap and nasty, which he found out when he picked it up before stepping out onto the landing and walking over to the bathroom to fill it up. Whilst the kettle was boiling, he felt the bed. It wasn't as cheap as the kettle, or the hangers, and it felt like it was made from memory foam. Maybe the old guy from the muppets put a higher price on his guests' sleep than he did their other creature comforts. The kettle clicked off and some plumes of steam left the spout and made their way up to the ceiling but disappeared before they got there. The teabag and sugar were already sitting inside, waiting. Harlan added the water and with a quick anticlockwise swirl took the mug over to the bed and got comfortable. It had been a long ride down; close to five hours, and his shoulders were aching, as were his hands. He took a large swig from the mug; the heat never seemed to bother his gullet. He went through his phone and called up the number. He pressed down on the call button and waited for it to ring. The person on the other end already knew he had to answer it. If he didn't, Harlan would be gone. It would be as simple as that.

The phone was answered on the fourth ring, the person answering sounded out of breath, like he had run to get it before it stopped.

'Hello, Harlan?'

'Evening. I'm in town. Now tell me again why you need me. Start to finish, and you have the time it takes me to drink my tea to convince me to stay...'

Ryan was back in his room. He reached inside the wardrobe and pulled out the empty trainer box. It was red with a big tick on it, which Ryan felt suited what was inside perfectly, a sign of a job well done. He carried the box over to his bed, still unmade from this morning, or maybe yesterday morning, he wasn't sure which. He lifted off the lid and looked inside, it was full of fives, ten and twenties. His haul to date, minus his extravagant spending at the sports shop in town, extravagant for a fourteen-year-old that was. He added to the pile from tonight's wages. He knew he would be buying his first car himself, in readies, which was just as well really, as his mum was always skint - although she seemed to always have money for fags and four-packs of cider. Money had become his God, he knew the more you had, the better your life, and the more you had, the happier you were. It didn't matter that he was just a roadman, riding his stolen bike doing the donkey work for the bosses, because soon he would be a boss, and he would have his own crew, it would be him barking orders and taking the majority of the money for none of the risk. Ryan knew he needed Mikey on board; he was to be his first recruit. Ryan put the lid back on the box and put it back in his wardrobe, covering it once again in some old clothes and a stained pillow. He went back to his bed, and took out the can of coke, flicked the ring pull, took a long swig, belched loudly then went on his phone and started sending snaps to a few of the girls he was talking to. He knew he wasn't a proper G yet, but he also knew he was well on his way.

Liam put his bike back in the shed, the same arduous task but in reverse. He failed to see why his dad needed such a bloody big lawnmower, as he hardly ever cut the grass, the same could be said for the workmate, as his dad hardly did any DIY. It just seemed to be shit that men collected when they became dads themselves and Liam wanted no part of that. He was already making his own money and he had plans, big plans, none of which involved cutting grass or putting up a shelf. He loved his parents, they were decent people and gave him what they could, but he wanted more, and that's what this job gave him, more. A lot more. He walked into the kitchen, opened the fridge and took out the milk. He was just getting a taste for it when he heard his mum's voice from the living room.

'You better not be drinking whatever it is you're drinking straight from the bloody bottle.'

He was, and he stopped, cursing his mum's x-ray

vision, or her hidden camera, whatever it was that also seemed to stop him from necking a drink or helping himself to the chocolate biscuit stash. He put the lid back on and wiped the white ring from around his mouth and went into the front room to say hello, followed shortly by 'Goodnight,'. He made his way up to his room and opened the bag to check if the package was still there, which of course it was. It hadn't left his back, but when you had something as expensive as that in your possession and you knew that it belonged to proper players, it felt good to check. And to double check. He pushed the bag under his bed as far as it would go and then turned on his Play-Station and settled down to play some FIFA of his own.

Harlan had listened to the story, and it was told just in time, there was just a small mouthful left, not that he would drink it, he never did. The pub was called the Crossways, he had been told, and recently a crowd of football thugs had made it their own, turning the pub into their own little HQ and his car park into something out of the Brad Pitt film, Fight Club. The town's team had recently been promoted and Saturdays had become really good for business. Travelling supporters would arrive by the coachload. Many would descend into the boozer and a good time would be had by supporters both before and after the match. Harlan was told the doormen there never really had much work to do, it was a good pub, with good food and decent prices and the Saturday home games and the Sunday trade would more than make up for the quieter nights during the week. But that had all stopped, now it was like the wild west, with the gang arranging their punch-ups with the rival thugs there a little after 3pm, when the football would have kicked off and all the spare officers would be at the ground or directing the traffic. By the time the game had ended his pub would be in bits, with windows smashed, and bodies and blood on the floor. The local gang would rarely lose and would then go into the pub and celebrate their victory by getting tanked up and acting as vile and as abusive as the alcohol would allow and this would continue all night, with friends and associates coming to join them throughout the evening. It had first become their local, now it had become their pub. The guy on the other end of the phone was worried about his business, his customers safety and his wife's health. Harlan had heard enough. He told him he would help and he would meet him there tomorrow at midday. The guy on the other end of the phone had started to say how grateful he was for his help but was cut short when Harlan hung up, before setting the phone to silent and ending his day.

3

L iam's alarm went off, again. He snoozed it, again. Finally, his mum stomped into the room and told him to *'turn off the damn phone and get dressed. You're going to be late'* which got a grunt in return and the first stirring of movement towards getting up. He checked his phone for messages. There were a few texts, some snapchats and a few of the celebrities he followed in America had posted tweets and photos. He got up and took his uniform from the back of his desk chair and got dressed and then went to his rucksack to stuff it with the books he needed for today's lessons. He unzipped it and breathed a sigh of relief, the package was still there, he knew it would be, the bag had been pushed back under his bed when he got home last night and no-one had been in his room since, except him, playing his console. But still, it was a relief to know the package was where he'd left it.

He crammed in his text books and then with the curtains still closed, pulled the bedroom door shut behind him and made his way downstairs for some cereal before setting off for school.

Getting dressed for school wasn't an issue for Ryan, he had pretty much stopped attending the previous year and despite threats from the headmaster and governors to fine his mum, they knew she wouldn't pay and he wouldn't come, and when he did, it was always a shit-show anyway. His bed frame was pushed up tight against the far wall when you walked into his room and he had wedged the package right down the side of it. He was awake but not up, he had a call to wait for. The package would need to be delivered to someone, he just needed to know what time and where.

His brother banged on the door. 'Oi, it's your turn to do the dishes, don't forget, shithead.'

His brother was nineteen and nasty, he ran with a gang and they would often start fights in pubs for the hell of it and had started to attend football matches for the same reason. He looked up to his brother. Rob had a reputation and that meant something. But he also knew he was the smarter one, his brother may be a brawler, but he was only earning a couple of hundred a week, it was him that was earning the big dollar, he was earning the same as him on a single bike ride.

'Yeah. OK. Don't sweat it, bro,' he shouted back, loud enough for his brother to hear.

'Make sure you don't.' He then heard his brother's footsteps stomp down the uncarpeted stairs and the front door closed in its frame behind him. His mum would be asleep, she had insomnia and would stay up until all hours and then finally a sleeping pill would kick in, on the days when she wasn't immune to them, and she would get into bed and have her last fag of the day and then stay in there until the afternoon. The house was cluttered and damp clothes were always hanging from the curtain poles or on the back of door handles on the days she actually did the washing. There was a dog too, a Staffordshire Bull Terrier, it belonged to the pair of them, it was called Tyson and it wore a thick gold chain around its neck but he was knocking on now, he would be seven this year and he no longer wanted to snarl at dogs or walk the streets at night for hours. It fell to Ryan to walk him, his brother would often bung him a tenner every week or so to do it, he no longer needed the extra cash but he didn't like the punch in the arm followed by the choking headlock he would get if he objected.

His mind went back to Michael and his need for him to join his *firm,* a firm of just one. Himself. But if he could recruit Michael he could then do twice as many rides, he could take half of Michaels wages. Then if he got another one onboard, he would double his income for only one third of the work. He started to like the business brain he was developing. What could possibly go wrong. His empire building dream was cut short by the sound of his burner phone ringing. He took it from underneath his pillow and answered it, knowing his brother had left for work and his mum would be away with the fairies.

'Be at the McDonalds next to the BowlRink for eleven. Order a meal as a takeaway and then put the package inside the bag, then when you leave there will be a guy begging just outside, give him the bag. Carry on to the arcades, find the Walking Dead game and sit in there, someone will sit in there next to you and give you dough.'

The line then went dead. He had no opportunity to

talk or decline. The instructions weren't repeated and he was expected to remember. He decided this would be a good time to try and recruit Michael so with his own mobile, he sent a text.

Skip school. Meet me outside Maccy's at 11. Don't be late G.

He believed Michael would show, the weeks he had spent cajoling, teasing and enticing him would pay off and pretty soon he would have himself an employee. He decided to stay in bed a little longer and watch YouTube.

School hadn't started when Michael's phone buzzed in his trouser pocket. He pulled it out and read the notification. It was Ryan – **Skip school. Meet me outside Maccy's -**

The text was too long to read on the home screen, he needed to open up his phone and click onto his messages. He then read the rest of it – **at 11. Don't be late G.**

He knew if he peeled away now it would be before he had even set foot on the school grounds, and before registration that he would be marked as absent. Sure, his mum would get a text but she would be working all day and wouldn't check her phone until she finished and he could just say they had made a mistake. That he had been there all day, ask anyone.

He knew he shouldn't bunk off but Ryan was his mate. He wanted to be as cool as Ryan but he knew he wasn't cut from the same cloth. He could smoke as much as Ryan, could shoplift as well as Ryan and would play the same video games and fancy the same girls as Ryan, but Ryan was going to be a career criminal, whereas

Michael wanted a career. Then again, this was £200 he was talking about, what could possibly go wrong...

Harlan sat at the table and waited for his breakfast to arrive. He had ordered himself a full English, with bread, fried bread and toast, each of which having a different use. The tea was in a pot but it was small, he knew he wouldn't get two full cups from it, rendering the little piece of white China useless. There were only two other tables taken, leaving three vacant. Either they were early risers, late risers or not there at all. The old man appeared, carrying two plates, one with his breakfast, the other was his assortment of bread. Both plates were shaking, it was either proving heavy for him or he had a health issue, early Parkinson's, maybe. Harlan stood up and made his way over to help him, taking the bigger plate but leaving the old man with the smaller one, so as not to embarrass him. Harlan knew old men still had their pride, even if their strength and resolve had long since left and he wanted to respect that.

'Thanks, although I didn't catch your name yesterday?' asked the old man.

That's because you didn't ask for it as you were too busy eyeing up the Queen's heads, Harlan thought, although he couldn't knock him for it, cash is still king, for now.

'Harlan,' he replied.

'That a first or a last name?' the old man asked.

'Does it matter?'

'Ha, hell no, I don't suppose it does,' and the old man started to laugh to himself.

The old man walked out of the dining room with Harlan watching him. He was slightly stooped and

Harlan knew it wouldn't be long before he would have a cane, or even that the old man did in fact have some sort of walking aid but would be too stubborn, which made him laugh, *Good on you, old man, be a rebel right to the end...*

The BowlRink got its name because it had both an indoor ten-pin bowling alley and an ice rink. It had an American themed decor to it and an American menu. There were racks of ribs, burgers with different named cheeses and toppings, and seasoned wedges instead of fries. The beer was sold in bottles, American brands such as Budweiser, Coors and a slushed iced machine with free refills for the youngsters. It didn't open until 4pm (11am on school holidays) and the building sat directly in-between Bounce-Back, an indoor trampolining activity centre and a McDonalds. Which was where Michael stood outside waiting for Ryan to arrive. He was ten minutes early but already it looked busy inside, the menu would be changing from breakfast to the burger options, or had that already happened? Michael could never remember. He had a fiver in his pocket so either way he would be getting something to eat.

Ryan walked into view, his hood up high over his cap and his jogging pants low down with his branded boxer-shorts on full view. He had his man-bag across his chest and he walked with an arrogant swag and a fag hanging from his mouth.

They fist bumped and walked into the restaurant, both of them ignoring the guy sitting begging to the left of the door. Michael ordered a cheeseburger and coke, Ryan, a Big Mac meal and Ryan asked for the orders not to be bagged together. They stood to the side and chatted whilst they waited and then their numbers were called to collect. They walked over to the condiment stand, grabbing a good handful of sauces and a couple of straws. Whilst there, Ryan took out his burger and fries and then unzipped his bag and pulled out the thick package. He then placed the package inside the bag, crumpled down the top and gripped it tightly in one hand and chowed down on the burger with the other.

'C'mon, bruv, let's go,' said Ryan, his mouth still full of food.

'What's the rush?'

'Shit to do and money to make, Mikey. Let me show you how easy this game is.'

Ryan took his drink and asked Michael to grab his fries. They walked back through the restaurant, past one of the staff sweeping debris from the floor into a dustpan and dressed in the grey uniform and cap. Past two women and four kids with four happy meal boxes and two coffees cups. Past the guy in the fluorescent vest and hard hat who had a box of nuggets in front him and his fries emptied out of the holder and onto the paper place mat.

Ryan pulled the door open and went through first, the sign of the man he would become, an alpha. Outside was the begging guy, sat cross-legged and with a thick jacket on. Ryan stopped and gave him the brown paper McDonalds bag and then carried on walking, as nonchalantly as he could. To anyone watching, it was just a random act of kindness from a young man. A teenager giving a free lunch to a homeless dude. Harmless. And sweet.

Ryan could feel Michael staring at him as they walked past the other buildings and businesses that propped up the trading estate.

'Just watch,' was all Ryan said on what had just transpired. They got to the final building, the arcades, and as soon as they stepped in, they were greeted with the sounds of copper coins falling down chutes and plastic guns making gunshot sounds at screens. It was already busy, older men were sitting in the over-18's section, pushing their pound coins into the slot machines and teenagers were playing the latest video games. Ryan walked around the floor, eating and dropping a few chips along the way whilst trying to locate the particular game booth he had been instructed to find. It was towards the far wall, the other side of the Jurassic Park booth. He slid inside and over to the far seat of the two inside, Michael went to sit on the other one but Ryan put his hand across it to stop him. 'No, come to this side, and watch.'

Michael gave a puzzled look but did as instructed, he walked around the back and stood against the side looking in and at the screen. He waited for Ryan to put some money in and fire up the game. But that didn't happen. What did happen was a guy in his early twenties slid into the spare seat, the one Ryan had stopped Michael sitting on, and pulled out a white envelope from inside his puffer jacket and placed it under his own ass. Michael watched as the guy gestured to Ryan to put in a pound and play, and then after a minute or so, the guy got out of the booth and walked back through the building and was gone from view. The game finished and Ryan put the plastic gun back into its holster, picked up the envelope the guy had left and then put that into his man-bag.

'C'mon, let's go,' said Ryan, and as quick as that, they were back outside the arcade and walking down past the various buildings and businesses, then past the McDonalds where they had met less than half hour ago, the beggar no longer there, and then past the BowlRink and out through the trading estate car park and over to the bus stop on the main road. Ryan still hadn't spoken about what had happened. Who the guy was he had given the concealed package to and what had happened inside the game booth? Ryan knew the suspense was killing his friend and he was smirking to himself, *knowledge is power,* he told himself. When the bus pulled up that would take them into town, Ryan paid for both tickets with a crisp ten-pound note from his fake Gucci wallet and they took the bench seat at the back of the bus and lounged across it, feet up on the fabric, like they owned the thing. Ryan unzipped his man-bag and pulled out the envelope. He made a scene of opening it slowly and when he did, he pulled out twenty-pound notes. Ten of them. Another £200. He could see Michael's eyes swell with a mixture of jealousy and lust. He knew now he had him, Michael was a fish hooked on the line, all he had to do now was gently reel him in.

The location of the pub matched the name, it was sat just behind a crossroad. It was a prominent building in a prominent location. Harlan waited at the lights, knowing it would take a few minutes. Four sets of lights, four streets. One axis point. He took that time to look over towards the pub, and more importantly, the car park. It was a vast piece of land that ran behind the pub and was easily twice the land-size of the pub itself. It was him who would have converted it into an actual pay and display car park for the average punter, allowing them to park their car there whilst they go for a beer, or a stroll, or walk the dog, or find a restaurant. He would make it 24/7 and stick a couple of old fellas in a tiny portacabin in there to take the dollar, and it would be a cash-only affair. He would pay them a decent cut, to top up their pensions and to give them some beer money. It would make just as much as the pub would. There, one piece of land, two businesses. Two revenue streams. Synergy, or something like that. The light he was waiting for turned green and he turned immediately left and down into the street where the pub was placed and then cut across the road and into the car park. Harlan drove to the far end, his thought process being why walk any further than you need to. Outside the front of the pub were eight wooden tables with two wooden benches each side. Sixteen benches. Four asses per bench, if each person spent a tenner an hour, for two hours. £1280. Not bad. Beer gardens work.

Harlan pulled the door open and stepped inside. The lights were off and it looked dark inside. The floor was a dark oak, and the fruit machines were turned off so there was no crude illumination and random noises coming from them. Harlan walked across the room and to the bar, and when he got there the guy who called in was just coming up from the cellar and Harlan's presence spooked him.

'Shit,' he said, sending one of the crates he was carrying crashing to the floor.

Harlan stood there, not speaking. He knew his appearance wasn't that of a folksy family guy. He was wearing scuffed biker boots, not boat shoes. Stained jeans not chinos, a tight tee not a cheesecloth shirt. Harlan didn't sport a short, back and sides or a set of clean, shaven chops. He was bearded and his hair stopped just short of his shoulders, and both showing flecks of grey.

Harlan waited for the guy to pick up the bottles and restack them and to compose himself.

'I like to be punctual,' Harlan said with a cold undertone. He had arrived on time, to the minute, and the fella he had come to meet wasn't ready. It wasn't a good start for him and Harlan needed him to know that.

'Erm, yeah... sorry about that, I was just trying to get the fridges stocked. You know how it is.'

'No, I don't. I don't stock fridges. I'm a bouncer, not a bar man. You know how it is...'

The guy was still on his knees hunting for the last of the escaped bottles that had rolled around behind the cleaning bucket and the yellow plastic *'caution – slippery floor'* cleaning signs, but what he was also looking for was a way to start the conversation again.

Harlan watched him as he stood up, resting an elbow on his thigh for a second before pulling his bulk up through the process of standing upright and then he walked over to the bar and offered out his hand.

'I'm Alan, but I'm known around here as Big Al, pleased to meet you.'

The nickname was befitting. Big Al was closing in on 17- 18 stone and his belt looked like it had been given extra notches on more than one occasion. Harlan took his hand and shook it.

'Harlan. So, Al, I take it the boarded-up windows were caused by our friends?'

Harlan was referring to the windows on the left-hand side of the entrance door when he walked in. The windows around the property were single glazed. The over-painted wooden frames had old-school brass levers that you opened out and placed onto a notch on the base plate, depending how far you wanted the window to open. The building was old, probably 1890s, and could well be listed, Harlan thought.

'You got it, it happened only last Wednesday.'

'Wednesday? Thought this was a weekend thing?'

Harlan wasn't clued up on football so Big Al had to explain to him that there were midweek matches, too.

'So, basically every time your team has a match, this shit happens?'

'Yes – this last one was pretty tame but that's only because the away team was at the other end of the country, and only the real diehard fans come down those sorts of distances.'

'Hence the Saturday punch-ups being the worst?'

'Yes. You haven't seen anything like it.'

'Oh, I have, trust me, you should see when my brothers have a booze up, claret everywhere.'

The joke was intended to let Big Al relax a bit, he had busted his chops for not being prepared but now wanted to see if they could work together, and in the face of adversity, must come some black humour. 'What's the worst it's been?' he asked.

'A month or so ago it looked like someone might die. The CID were here for a couple of days and I thought my licence was going to get pulled but luckily it had happened in the car park itself so the plod gave me a pass, saying it could be construed that the fight was not in direct correlation to my business.'

'Did the fella survive?'

'Yes.'

'Shame.'

. . .

The beggar wasn't really a beggar, it was just a ruse. He wasn't an affiliated member of the gang, but he was on the fringes and held a higher rank than the runners. A team leader, if you will. When Ryan handed him the package, he sat, still cross-legged, for a few moments, so if anyone saw the act of kindness from the teenager to the guy sitting begging, they would soon forget about it and carry on about their business. When the last person to see it had ventured into one of the buildings, he slipped the brown paper bag inside his jacket, stood up and started to walk away. He had his own bicycle hidden in the bushes around the back, where the various air conditioning units and dumpsters were stored. He pulled the bike back out and swung his leg over, it was getting on towards midday and he had a busy afternoon ahead. The package inside the brown paper bag contained well over a hundred 3"x 3" clear plastic sealable bags, that were full of white powder. He had a network that needed what he had, and he had what they needed. A classic supply and demand business right there inside his jacket.

The call came through to one of the burners. Straight away Jamal knew who it was. He had a system, different players got different numbers to call him on. He devised it and the others stuck to it; every team has a captain. Jamal was the brains not the brawn, but he was also the most ruthless, the others, they would hurt you, Jamal, well, he would kill you. He fell into the life of crime easily; England gave you anonymity, you could be invisible, the system didn't track you, and if you didn't claim anything from the system, then the system wouldn't claim you. Getting into the country was easy, staying in it was easy, and getting out was just as easy. You were a ghost if you wanted to be; you left no shadow.

'I've got it,' the voice said.

'Good. Now get it distributed this afternoon. All of it,' hissed Jamal.

'On it.'

'Call me when done. Then come meet me for your pay.'

The line went dead. Jamal had said all he had needed to say. He went back into the living room and swiped a controller from the hands of one of his guys, sat on the couch and took over playing Call of Duty. The curtains were still closed and one guy was hunched over the coffee table burning off little bits of the rock of weed he was holding in one hand, his zippo lighter in the other. It was smoke time. It was always smoke time.

The gang rarely left the house. They weren't in the country to sight see, they were here for the sight of cash, and to make as much of it as they could, as easily as they could, and as fast as they could. The plan was to then take their spoils to the Caribbean, or Brazil, anywhere where lots of green paper made you live like a king.

'Mikey, it is that easy. Pick up, drop off, and collect £200. It's like real-life monopoly, man.'

Michael was still looking at the wallet, which had now doubled in the number of notes stuffed inside, but he wasn't really listening to Ryan's sales pitch, he was too transfixed by the twenties he was seeing.

'Don't tell me you couldn't do with two hundred sheets?' Ryan could see he was winning.

'Of course,' replied Michael. He was all but salivating at the mouth.

'I can hook you up in one call, *one call...*'

Michael sat back. He was contemplating it, multiple thoughts running through his mind; his mum, the police, two-hundred pounds, a criminal record, respect. All of these things clashing against each other, the angel and the devil on top of young shoulders. Easy cash and respect won out.

'OK. I'm in.'

Ryan smiled and then held out a closed fist, Michael bumped it with his own. Michael had just found himself an income, Ryan had just found himself an employee.

4

Liam's burner rang during lunch break – it never rang during a lesson. He answered the call and put his hand over his left ear to try and cancel out the noise of some three hundred other school kids making the most of sixty-minutes of freedom. The instructions were simple. At 3.30, when school had finished, he was to cut down through to the school playing fields and there would be someone there to meet him. He would be in a camo-coloured coat and would have red sneakers on, impossible to miss. He was to hand him the package and would get his envelope in return. It ended, as it always did, with the words, *don't be late.* Liam hated these calls, they weren't nasty as such, but he knew the person at the end of the phone could be. He didn't know the person, had never met him, but he knew about him. This person knew his mum's name and the car she drove. He knew it was leverage, he had learnt about leverage at school, but that was to do with physics; this was a different kind of leverage, the kind that scared the shit out of you. The call had made him check his rucksack once again. He knew the package was in there, it had been the previous twelve times he had checked today, but the call made him reach in and feel around for it, his heartbeat slowing once he felt the rustle of padded paper between his fingers. He zipped his bag back up and went back over to his friends and carried on playing football where two school jumpers had been screwed up and placed on the floor to use as goalposts.

The afternoon was spent watching Ryan buy clothes. He spent over a hundred pounds on a new pair of Nike's and double that on a Stone Island jacket. Ryan didn't flinch at either purchase. Why would he, easy come easy go, plenty more where that came from, he told Michael. He treated Michael to some fried chicken and told him he would put a call in later to get him *in the firm.* But what he had omitted to say, was being *in the firm* meant that you were the property of a gang that distributed drugs across the town, who used teenagers as their mules. He also didn't tell Michael what would happen if you messed up, the punishments you would endure. What he sold him on was the easy money, the simplicity, the riding around town on your bicycle, something you would be doing normally, except you would be delivering parcels between postcodes for the people. You would be like a Deliveroo driver, except it wasn't pizzas in those packages. Michael was pulling the skin off the bone, his fingers sticky from the seasoning and his lips salty from the fries, and wishing it was him that had a Stone Island bag sat on the spare chair, but soon it would be. He would soon be sat flush with cash and treating his mate to dinner.

.   .   .

Liam had done as instructed. He left school with his buddies but made his excuse as to why he couldn't walk home with them, *'got to get my brace tightened'* was the reason he gave and they bought it. He cut down the grassy step back through the tranche of trees and onto the main school playing field, and then down the second grassy bank onto the more redundant one. He walked along and over to where the guy in the camo-coloured coat and red sneakers was standing. He took his rucksack off his back and put it on the floor and knelt down to unzip it. Liam reached inside and fumbled around for the package before pulling it out, standing back up and handing it over. The packages were never checked. The mules were trusted never to open them. The operation ran on fear. Teenage boys would frighten easily. They did frighten easily. Liam was handed an envelope, always the same colour, always the same weight and he pushed it into his trouser packet. The exchange was over. No fist bumps, no handshakes, just stony silence.

Liam walked home and when he got there, his mum was watching a gameshow, she had a coffee resting on the arm of the sofa and a cigarette burning in the ashtray. She called out to her son, but he was already up the stairs and heading for his room. He went in and into his wardrobe, he slid the other clothes that were on the rail out the way to find his bomber jacket. It was a black coat, not branded, cheap but looked cool and it had an inside pocket. He took the envelope out and tore it open. He counted out the twenty-pound notes. Ten of them. £200. He tucked the notes into the concealed pocket of his coat and then squashed all the clothes back up and closed the wardrobe door. He then went downstairs, took a Coke from the fridge and went and joined his mum on the sofa.

.   .   .

Harlan had decided to make Big Al's problem his own. The rules were simple and non-negotiable. The simple part was the fee; two grand a week, cash, and paid every Sunday up until the job was done. The non-negotiable part was the pub would be run his way. He called the shots, and if needed, he would make them, too. Harlan took the largest of the towels into the communal bathroom for a shower. He took off his jacket and shirt, he sniffed them, still plenty of life yet, although he would need to get some spares whilst he found a laundromat to wash those few items he had come with. The scar on his upper shoulder was the result of a pissed off drinker that wanted to make a name for himself. It was a battle the boozed-up brawler wanted, until it came to the point that he didn't. It was a battle that started with a broken bottle and ended with broken bones. It was one of the few times that Harlan had come to ending someone, permanently. Harlan won every battle he had ever had, with anyone or anything. Pain wasn't a feeling that he possessed. He was as strong as an ox and as impatient as one.

He was minus a comb so towel dried his hair and just ran his fingers through it. He smoothed down his beard until his right hand left his chin and continued going down through the last two inches of hair. He slipped on his t-shirt, his war-torn, tattooed torso now covered. He pulled up his jeans and did up his belt, the silver belt buckle proudly showing the club's logo. He went back to his room and put on his scruffy boots and took his leather cut from around the back of the chair. It was time for a beer and maybe a steak. He walked down the stairs and spoke with the white-haired old man who had told him the name of a few pubs within walking distance, although he hadn't been to a pub for quite some years so couldn't vouch for the calibre of the food, or the drinkers who frequented them. The walk was less than five minutes and the air had started to crisp. He walked past the first one, it looked too commercial, probably a chain and he hated both chain or themed pubs. He liked authenticity. He liked an atmosphere. He liked spit and sawdust boozers.

The next pub was quiet and had the vibe he liked. Mean and moody. Harlan stepped inside and took a quick headcount, 17. Eleven men; six women. There were a few seats taken but the majority were empty. He walked to the bar and was greeted by a young woman with a tattoo crawling up out from under her shirt and onto her neck. He wasn't sure if it was sexy or garish, but it was her neck, not his. He ordered a bottle of Budweiser, but then changed it to two, and he asked if they were serving food. She said yes and handed him a laminated menu. He found the meat section. He ordered a well-done sirloin (they never had any ribeye – he asked) with fries, no salad and asked for two fried eggs to go with it. He handed over the money and took a seat at a table that had a good view of the TV, a soccer match was on. Harlan wasn't a big football fan; he didn't see the attraction of a group of men chasing a bag of wind. Over the next hour, the pub started to fill up. An hour later it was close to full. It wasn't a particularly big pub. Maybe fifty people or so were in there. The game had finally finished and had been replaced by music, although Harlan couldn't seem to locate the DJ. The steak had been OK, it wasn't the worst he had chomped down on but it was the couple of eggs that had saved it. He had ordered another beer; it would be the last one before heading back to his digs. Stood at the bar were a group of men, dressed in designer clobber and baseball caps. Harlan had clocked them when he first walked in, they made up six of the eleven. They were rowdy and raucous with the laughter and language getting louder and coarser as the evening progressed, and they never left the bar. They didn't take a table, just stood there, in a huddle, which was where Harlan found them when he went up to order his final drink. He didn't make eye contact with the group; he didn't need to. He wasn't about to strike up conversation, he just wanted another beer and then bed.

One of the guys had caught sight of Harlan at the end of the bar and shouted to him, getting a laugh from his mates as a direct reward for his rudeness.

'Hey, you with the leather, you like the music, or would you prefer a bit of that ACDC shit?'

Harlan turned his head, gave a smile and then returned his gaze to the lady with the tattooed neck who was popping the lid off his bottle.

'Hey, Meatloaf, I was talking to you,' the same guy said, keen to keep the ribbing going.

Harlan declined to look this time.

'Oi, shithead, I'm talking to you, cat got your tongue or you as thick as shit, metalhead?'

The guys in the group all stood to face the biker now, they sensed their friend was getting agitated by the ignorance. They wanted to show solidarity. Harlan turned to face them; the smile now replaced with a stare. The one making the comments stepped through the group and walked over to him, stopping just two feet away from him.

'I said, I am talking to you. And what's with the leather and boots. Some sort of kink?'

Harlan sized him up. He wouldn't be a problem. Nor would the next two or three. If they all came at once it would be a bit more of a workout, but doable, but that wouldn't happen, the proximity too small for them all to join in. That would be reserved if the fight went outside, where space would work against him, but this fight wasn't going to get outside. Harlan knew that, and he felt sorry for the gobshite who didn't, not yet. Barroom brawling was his speciality. Harlan took a swig from his bottle and then rested it back on the bar. The guy giving the insults took this as a direct challenge and took another step forward and as he did, he met Harlan's crashing right hand. The guy wouldn't have known if it was the force, the power or the precision that closed off the communication to his legs, but whatever it was had him unconscious before he hit the floor. On instinct, the closest one in the group to Harlan shot forward in honour of his mate but was rewarded by an incoming headbutt. His nose broke instantly, but before he could even begin to shake the pain away, Harlan grabbed him by the hair and pulled him forward. Harlan had the side of the guy's head pressed down hard on the top of the bar, his face painfully angled in the direction of his friends.

'Anyone else feeling stupid?'

Silence.

'Now, you can either leave and get home without bleeding, or you can stay here and we can continue. It really doesn't matter a shit to me which option you pick.'

The guy was gargling under the weight of Harlan's hand pressed down on his cheek. His nose was busted and his neck felt like it was going to snap. Harlan pulled him up and then pushed hard back in the direction of the group. The guy on the floor was coming round, and one of the men helped him to his feet.

'Well. What's it going to be?' he said, taking two steps forward towards the lion's den.

The group stood down, no-one fancied taking on the bearded biker, they had already lost two from a start point of six, thirty three percent of their arsenal incapacitated. Not good odds. They left whatever was left in their pint glass and walked out, the one who had been knocked out was being held up by two of them.

The whole affair lasted less than a minute. Another challenge that Harlan hadn't backed away from. But he had been like that his whole life. He had taught himself to confront danger, to stare it out, and if that didn't work, to beat the shit out of it.

The barmaid stood looking at him, half scared by what had just happened, half excited by it. There was an out-of-town alpha male standing opposite her. He looked rugged, sexy and dangerous. Just how she liked them.

Harlan took his bottle back to the table, ignoring the stares and whispers he was getting and sat and finished his beer in peace. About twenty minutes later, when the last of the liquid bottle was gone, so was he. The lady with the tattooed neck saw him there one minute, hoping to maybe flirt with him the next time he came to the bar, but when she looked over at him again, his seat was empty. There was just a bottle standing on the table where he had been sitting. Like Elvis, her bearded biker had left the building.

He walked back to the B&B, and only looked over his shoulder once, he didn't expect them to be waiting for him. They were stupid, not suicidal. He walked up the concrete steps, took the green plastic fob from his jacket and pressed the silver key into the lock. He walked in through the reception area and up the flight of stairs to the 2nd floor and then used the brass key to enter his room. He took off his cut and hung it back around the chair at the desk, then flicked the switch on the cheap kettle ready for the last mug of tea before bed. Whilst he was waiting for it to boil, he touched the screen on the smartphone that he left on the bed charging. There was nothing showing. As always.

Michael had turned off his game console and was in bed when his phone rang. It was Ryan.

He reached down to the floor to grab his phone, pulling it free from the charging cable.

'You're in, Mikey.' His friend's voice sounded excited.

'Eh? What do you mean?' replied Michael, not expecting his friend to call so late.

'Mikey, you're in, they said yes. You're officially part of the firm now,' said Ryan, making it sound more grandiose than it actually was. 'Anyway, catch you later, gotta make some calls.'

The conversation ended. Michael thought the call could have waited, but Ryan was like that, impulsive, iras-cible, and impatient.

Michael looked up at the ceiling. *Part of the firm,* that sounded good, although what did it mean? He wasn't sure, but he would soon be spending serious dough on the designer brands, although he would have to hide them from his mum, she would get suspicious, he would worry about that later, he thought. He put his phone back on charge and went to sleep dreaming about the dollar he would soon be earning.

. . .

What Ryan also hadn't told his friend was that his employers hadn't actually recruited him. That he had done this off his own back. He had created the illusion he had gone to bat for him. That he had put his own neck on the block for Michael. The reality was somewhat different. All Ryan had actually done was cycle to the supermarket and buy a burner phone himself, and this would be what he handed to Michael after he finished school. £14.99 and for that, he got a free tenner top-up voucher. Not bad start-up costs, thought Ryan. He took it home, unwrapped it, put it on charge and dialled a number that allowed him to tap in the voucher code. All he needed now was work to come in and then he could cream his fifty-percent from the top. Child's play...

5

Jamal was a realist. Even though England had been easy so far, he knew you needed to grease the wheels, so to speak. *Keep your friends close and your enemies closer,* but Jamal had no friends. The other three thought they were his friend, but Jamal knew different. Thought different. If it came on top, he had a contingency plan, one which gave him a certain security should the Feds come knocking. The others, well they would rely on the guns and knives hidden around the flat, hoping to shoot themselves out of trouble if it came to it, but Jamal would rely on a tip-off, on yet another reserved burner phone.

'I'm going out. Keep an eye on the phones,' Jamal said, to no-one in particular, but to all of them.

'K,' came the response. He wasn't sure who responded, didn't care, either. He had delegated, they would deliver. That's how power worked.

He stepped out onto the pavement and looked both ways. Twice. He had people paid in the street to keep an eye, to report back if any vehicles looked suspiciously like unmarked cop cars, but that didn't mean he wasn't extra vigilant too. Jamal didn't venture out often, and when he did it was for a purpose. It wasn't to stroll in the park, or to go shopping. If he went out, it was for business.

Every time.

He pressed the fob and the Mercedes unlocked awaiting his arrival. It was a diamond white, C class coupe, flashy, but not over the top. It would get him pulled at night, he knew that, but that's why he didn't go out at night. Business was only done during the day.

Every time.

He got in, buckled up and set off. He had a pre-arranged rendezvous and couldn't be late. He wielded power over his underlings, the guy he was meeting wielded power over him.

He drove through town, passing kids on bikes, not quite knowing which of them, if any, worked for him. He kept it that way for a reason. If they never saw him, they could never identify him. It was a basic rule, and the basic rules worked. It was morning rush hour, so the roads were clogged but he had factored that in. He indicated off the roundabout, accelerated hard on the outside lane, then drove half a mile to join the dual carriageway where he could open her up and clear out the exhaust.

The meeting had been arranged down a back lane. It was past the retail park and then through a council estate. The backstreet had single car garages either side, but most had either the doors defaced or defective. They had met there before. They always met there.

Jamal saw the Porsche Cayenne come around the corner, it was a tight turn, but the driver made it in one.

The Porsche came towards him, at a pace no quicker than a crawl. Jamal stood to the side so the car could pull up alongside him. The driver's window buzzed down.

'Morning,' said Colin. He had an arrogant smile. He had Jamal in his pocket.

Jamal nodded his head. He didn't like being in his pocket, but needs must.

'You got something for me?'

Jamal gave another nod. Then reached through the open window of his Mercedes and pulled out a rucksack. Inside were bundles of notes, all tightly wrapped in coloured elastic bands. He passed the package through the window and onto the driver's lap. Colin felt the weight, felt good. But that's as far as the trust went. He was dealing with a fellow criminal, for Chrissake, hardly trustworthy people, whatever the myth said. Colin unzipped the rucksack and peered inside. He took out one of the bundles, and with the elastic bands still wrapped tightly around, flicked through the notes with his thumb. It was made up of tens, twenties and fifties. The notes would be untraceable. Colin gave another arrogant smile.

'Good work. This little arrangement suits us both, don't you think.'

It pained Jamal to hand over so much cash, but it was a case of needs must. A chain. Jamal had an end game, but he needed Colin to help get him there. He watched Colin buzz up the tinted window on his Porsche and he then slowly reversed back down the lane, made a sharp turn of the steering wheel, and watched his car go out of view. He got back into his Mercedes and did the exact same manoeuvre.

.   .   .

The first time the burner phone rang Harlan had been asleep. The second time, he was in the shower. The third time it rang he was stirring the spoon anticlockwise. Harlan knew the number. It was implanted in his brain. He pressed redial and it was answered almost immediately.

'H. Glad you called back.'

The voice on the other end was gruff. Like he had a throat full of gravel.

'Yeah, sorry I missed you. What's up?' Harlan asked.

'Nothing. Just checking in.'

'I'm good. You sure nothing's up?'

'Can't a brother check in on another brother?'

'You're not a brother, you're my Pres. Always was. Always will be.'

The president was a guy who according to his birth certificate was christened Jim Walsh, his moniker had changed when he joined the club, he was soon nicknamed Beam, after the whiskey, but now, there was no nickname, only a title: President.

Satan's Security had grown in both size and stature since Jim took over the role, but the standards didn't lower, in fact they only got higher. It was mandatory that a prospect needed to serve a minimum of 12 months before even being considered as being able to become a full-patch member, and that could only be achieved by getting the vote of everyone at the table. And this is where the president came into his own – he was notoriously hard to impress. If Jim felt you couldn't hold your own under pressure or follow orders to the letter of the law, you wouldn't get his vote. But what really mattered, something Jim prided himself on, and which had saved the club on more than one occasion, was if you could stand up to a police interrogation and not rat on your brothers. Then, and only then, would Jim assign his name to your credentials and let you become a member in his club. Harlan and Jim went back further than most, and Jim had only just received the title of Pres when Harlan was up for his vote. It had been unanimous; Harlan was well-respected and he was known as being *game*. Which was why, after only being in the club a full-patch for just a few months, Jim pulled him to one side during a club party and asked him to go outside for a smoke. It was a conversation that Harlan would never forget.

'You seem to be thriving here, lad.'

'Cheers, Pres, I appreciate that. This club means the world, you know.'

'Yes, I do know. Which is why we need to be tight, know what I'm saying?'

'Yeah, course. And we are tight, aren't we?'

Harlan watched as the president of the Satan's Security motorcycle club took a long drag on his rolled-up cigarette and contemplated what answer he was going to give.

'We are, lad, we are. But... we aren't tight enough.'

The look he gave Harlan was one of true command, Jim had asked a question and given an answer. And now he asked another question, the question was, did Harlan know what he was getting at.

'So, what do we have to do to change it?'

It was that reply, that singular sentence that told Jim everything he needed to know about his latest recruit into the fold. It told Jim the appointment he was about to make was already the right one.

'We need to change our line-up. Reposition some players, and retire others. The club is growing but it must grow from rules, and I need someone who can maintain my rules.'

Harlan couldn't see it himself, but his pupils had enlarged at being present at the new dawning of the club that he lived and breathed for.

'A club needs a leader, but it also needs leaders. Can you lead, lad?'

Another question asked. Another answer already known.

Jim had seen the respect Harlan held from his brothers. He knew the lad stood there in his smoke, and had a wise head on his young shoulders. That he was strategic, impulsive yet controlled and tough yet fair. He knew already where he needed him to be.

'Yes. I can lead. '

'I know you can, son, which is why you will be my new Sgt at Arms.'

Big Al was sitting on a bar stool, ignoring the creak that was coming from the wood that was doing its best to hold up his bulk. He was checking through the upcoming fixtures, seeing what teams were coming, and when. It used to be that he loved the away fans coming through his doors, but that was no longer the case, in fact, the stress had caused him a stomach ulcer. He couldn't afford the bearded biker, but he also couldn't afford not to have him. The biker had come highly recommended by one of his regulars. Dave was an ex-con, fraud and theft were his favourite pastimes and when it worked, Dave would be sat in Al's bar spending heavily, and quickly. When it hadn't gone so well, Dave would swap pints for prison wear and peanuts for porridge, with his wallet being sorely missed. Big Al had known Dave since they were nippers, and Dave had been in trouble with the boys in blue before he even mastered his times tables. It was after yet another fight, when the customers who had come in for a drink but witnessed a blood bath, had left scared and had caused yet another pool of lost punters. Dave had stayed behind and helped him pick up the stools and sweep up the glass and when he'd mentioned he was close to shutting up the doors for good, Dave had mentioned the biker as a solution. His *only* solution. Dave had told him that when he was doing his latest stint behind bars, there was a biker inside for an aggravated ABH charge. Dave said he had shared a cell with this biker and one night they were chatting about their lives, or rather, the crimes they had committed and the conversation had moved onto some of the hard-men they had come up against, be it out on the street or on the inside, and the biker had spoken about a member in his club who was, in the prisoner's words, *hard as fuck*. Dave then went on to explain that this fella was available to hire, that is if you knew how to get hold of him, which Dave did. He had made it very clear that the text could only say three words, and at first Alan had thought it was some sort of wind-up, until he saw the seriousness in his friend's face. Dave then backed up why this number was his only hope, and he scribbled his number down onto a scrap piece of paper, and once again repeated the code words he needed to include: I need you...

The Porsche was the only thing that made the house stand out, but not ostentatiously so, as now pretty much all makes and models could be attained with finance deals, even if you had to sell your deal to pay for it for the next twenty years. It was a straight-up semi; magnolia in colour and the occasional drip from the guttering. The décor inside showed a woman's touch, different shades of grey and glittery photo frames. The living room had two sofas, a three and a two-seater, identical in design but so very different. When it was family time, the husband and wife, alongside the two children, who were both biological to the mother, step, to the man of the house, would watch a movie together. These nights would involve a takeaway, crisps and some ridiculously overpriced ice cream. On date nights, the kids would go up to their rooms early and a romantic meaty meal would be carried in, alongside a few beers and everyone knew what came after steak night. It was when the football was on that everything changed. That was when the living room, with the fresh flowers and the family photos in their glittery frames, and with the 50" TV mounted on the wall above the liquid crystal fire, would be replaced with his friends, and cheap lager would be spilt over the expensive carpet.

Colin was upstairs, on the landing, and pulled down the loft ladder. With the locks in place, Colin put his left foot on the bottom rung, jabbing at it twice, checking it felt secure, then picked up the rucksack in his right hand and proceeded to climb the ten steps up into his attic. It was just like any other loft space; boxes of old toys and photo albums; the cardboard box that the TV had been packaged in and the Christmas tree, alongside a few plastic bags that contained the baubles and silver tinsel. There was also another set of boxes, the untouchable boxes, the boxes that only Colin could look through. These boxes were all the same in colour and dimensions, ordered online from some sort of company that specialised in removals. One box, with another on top. Four boxes. The top two, and the bottom left, housed all of his match-day programmes, dating back to when he was a boy when his dad used to take him to the games and right the way up to the present day. There were also the football sticker albums he used to collect. The first being Mexico 86, his prized sticker being that of a certain Argentinian who went by the name of Maradona, but that was when football was his passion. Now being a football hooligan was. The fourth box, the one on the right, that box was different – that box also had some programmes in it, but they were there as a smokescreen, as underneath them was cash. A lot of cash.

Colin lifted off the box that was on top and then opened the cardboard flaps on the bottom one. There was a reason he wanted the cash in tight, rolled up bundles each time he made a drop and the reason was there to see. The bundles were stood up, and then the programmes were laid flat over the top, to the untrained eye it would look like yet another box of neatly packed programmes, and not a collection of match-day souvenirs sat on top a bed of cash. He took a pile of programmes out from inside the cardboard box and placed them neatly on the floor before unzipping the rucksack and delving inside pulling out bundle after bundle of rolled-up notes and delicately stacking them into the box, one by one. When the rucksack was empty, Colin placed the programmes neatly back on top, folded back down the flaps and then placed the other box back on top. He walked back over to the open hatch, turned off the loft light by the pull-cord and then reversed himself back down the ladder until his feet were back on terra firma. He pushed the ladder back up into its aluminium guide and then with the help of the rod, he closed and locked the hatch. He started to walk downstairs just in time to help his wife who had just returned home from doing the weekly big-shop.

Big Al was still sitting at the bar, this time going through his books which he still preferred to enter manually with a pen into a red, A4 hardback notepad. Beside him were three empty packets of Beef and Onion crisps, and two-pint glasses. One empty, the other one soon to be. The numbers didn't make for impressive reading. They did, once. He had a profitable pub in a prominent position but that was before the infamous Cherry Pickers made the Crossways their new HQ. The violence had been gradual at first, but now it was just gory. The sound of a thunderous bike pulling across the road and into the car park let Big Al know that his help had arrived again. There was something about the man he had hired that made him feel nervous. Alan didn't know what it was, *exactly.* But there was something, and it was more than the bike and the beard, the leather cut and the solid frame. Then it came to him; it was the eyes. Eyes that told him the biker came with strong credentials, but zero conscience.

Less than a minute later the door opened and Harlan stepped in. His new employer was sitting at the bar. Al lifted his hand up as a hello, and Harlan nodded his head as he walked towards him.

'Drink?' the landlord asked.

'A cup of Rosie. Ta.'

Harlan watched to see if he got the slang, hoping he wouldn't have to spell it out. Alan got off the bar stool to make him a cup of tea. He appreciated it and knew the stool had appreciated it, too. Harlan looked through the notepad whilst he heard Alan out the back, in the kitchen, swilling clean a cup and filling the kettle. Harlan had a forensic brain where financials were concerned, not that he needed it, a layman with the I.Q of an eggplant could see the pub was in trouble, and when. The trade from Tuesday to Friday would ascend, each night would be better than the one before and Friday was the new Saturday. The reason for the decline was simple: football was played on a Saturday, but like the game itself, Saturday for the Crossroads pubs was a game of two halves. From midday to 3pm, the numbers were good. Real good. As much could be taken in those three as would be in the three nights, but the problem was after the final whistle had blown, when the Cherry Pickers had moved in. By 9pm the pub would belong to the local crew, the fight with an away team had already been done and now the pub would be full of drunken thugs with blood-stained clothing and degrading language. The regulars would be long gone, either back home and safe, or in another pub, and safe.

Harlan ran his finger across to the Sunday trade, already knowing the figures before he got there. The column was empty. The reason? The pub was closed. Not by choice, but because of the damage. Same for the Monday, it would open but would be empty, the fear still lingering in among the ale pumps. The problem also appeared at other intervals, and not every seven days, sometimes only four days after the previous slump. Harlan took out his phone and correlated these dates against the phone's in-built calendar. Wednesdays. Then it dawned on him. Big Al had told him that football was played midweek, too. Harlan didn't mind a pre-planned punch up; the club would often put on bare-knuckle events behind closed doors. It would be to settle a dispute between two brothers or just to let off some testosterone. He didn't much care for football, so two teams of thugs beating the shit out of each other wouldn't normally concern him, but now he'd been hired, it did concern him. And pretty damn soon it would concern them, too.

Big Al returned carrying two cups of tea and placed them down in front of Harlan, before shaking his hand due to the heat. 'Sugar?' asked Alan.

'Yeah. Two spoons or three sachets. And I take it you have biscuits.'

It was said as a statement, not a question, a direct comment to the size of his current employer. Big Al didn't pick up on the friendly dig, and went back out to the kitchen before returning with a handful of sugar sachets and a half-eaten packet of Rich Teas.

Harlan was right. 'So, pretty bleak, isn't it?' Alan said, referring to the opened notepad.

'I think you passed being bleak a few months ago. This place is close to closing.'

'Can you tell me something I don't know, please?' asked Alan.

'Yes – your tea making is shit.' Big Alan took the criticism personally.

'Can we turn it around?' Alan asked, an air of wishful thought to his tone.

'*Everything* can be turned around. So too, can *everyone*.'

And there it was, Big Al saw it again; those eyes. Turning from brown to black. Coal black.

Harlan dipped another biscuit into his tea and then gave out a loud curse when it broke off and dropped into his mug. This was why he hated certain types of biscuit; no backbone.

Jamal parked his car and returned to the flat. It had been an expensive morning. Ten thousand pounds had been paid out and they now needed to earn it back. Luckily though, the county had a large drug problem, one that Jamal was happy to provide a solution for.

'Any calls?', he asked as he walked through to the living room. There was a half-naked girl sitting on one of the brother's laps. A girl he hadn't seen before, which angered Jamal, he thought the team weren't as tight on security as they could be.

'You, leave,' he said, pointing a finger directly at her.

She looked at the guy she was sitting on, and his face confirmed the order. She stood up and picked up her top from the floor and skirted around the tall, skeletal-type figure who had just walked in and barked the order.

'Guys, buck up. You need to stay sharp. We need to vet anyone who comes here, that goes for your bitches, too.' Jamal was pissed. It was turning out to be a bad day.

'Anyone come back yet?' he asked.

'Yeah, you just missed Liam. It's in the safe. Want it bagged and tagged?' said the other brother.

'Yes. We need to get it out there. Any cash come in?'

'Yeah, a few bags. I've put them in the safe, too.'

That helped his mood. Counting cash was a hobby of his. Especially if it was profit.

Jamal knelt down and put the combination in, only those in the room knew it. It wasn't stored in any electronic device, anywhere, it was to be stored only to memory and Jamal had told them that if any of them ever revealed this code to anyone, he would personally cut their tongue out and post it back to their families. It wasn't an idle threat for two reasons. One, they had witnessed him cut someone's tongue out before, it was for a different reason, but he sliced it off with a bowie knife; and two, he had made them give him the names and addresses of their closest relatives, and to check they weren't lying, he had reached out to them on a false pretext. He was as cunning as he was callous.

The safe had taken a hit. Ten grand was a lot of money but it was just a game of retail, you bought at one price and then sold it at another. Or rather, bought as a multipack and sold out as singles. It worked on cans of coke, and it worked on pure coke, too. He pulled out the packages and delegated the tasks. One brother to get to work weighing out the powder into the plastic bags, the other guy to update the log – who had what, who owed what and where the mules were needed next. Jamal started on the cash.

Two hours later and the log was updated. The powder, weighed and bagged. The cash, counted. It was now back to the day job. Back to business. The mules were never tasked to fetch or carry past nine at night. That was a rule Jamal had put in place. This wasn't because he cared, it was because the parents did. Jamal recruited in the mid-teen range only, as under the age of sixteen you were very rarely stopped riding your bike in the evenings, proving of course the same police officers didn't see you still out on it come ten 'o'clock and gone, as from that point on, the police may look to show an interest. Jamal used 9pm as the cut-off. Ideally, he wanted all the runs done by eight, and the gang updated, but he was a realist too, sometimes things could go askew so he built in a one-hour buffer, 8pm – 9, but no muling after nine. Ever.

He made seven calls. To seven different people. Seven different locations and times. The eighth call was different. This person was told to come to the flat. Within the hour.

Ryan did as he was told. He felt as excited as he was scared, he had never met his real bosses before. He had met people higher up the food chain than him, the dealers and the henchmen, but *the firm,* they were always out of bounds. He checked himself out in the mirror in the bathroom. His new Nike's and his Stone Island jacket, his latest purchases looked cool. It was a warm evening, the jacket would probably make him sweat, but he knew he didn't just need to look cool, he had to be cool, and coolness is in a man's clothing, well that's what his older brother said. He had walked Tyson and had made his dinner. His mum was out of bed but still in her stained dressing gown and she had her pills and cigarettes beside her, an evening watching TV beckoned for her. Ryan made her a cheap-brand coffee in a chipped mug and carried it through to her. She smiled, showing her stained teeth through her lank and greasy hair. He never knew if she had depression or was depressed with her life, was there even a difference? He didn't know, but he knew his life would be different. He wasn't going to be sitting in a shitty house eating shitty food and watching shitty programmes on a shitty TV. He was going to have a massive flat, with a huge flatscreen and a king-sized bed, not like his current bed; a single mattress that sat upon a bed frame that had several broken slats on it. Everything in his flat would be big. And the flat would be big, too, the biggest in town in fact, as one day he would live in The Rise. The penthouse, to be exact. He left his mum to whatever she was watching, and whatever planet she was on, and on the way out the back door, he took the treat tin from on top of the fridge and pulled out a chew for Tyson, it was supposed to help keep his teeth clean. Tyson appreciated the gesture and wagged his tail before heading back over to his bed ready to eat it in peace. He wheeled his bike out through the back gate, being careful not to stand in any dog shit, and then hopped on and made an immediate left. It was going to be a forty-minute ride according to the GPS on his own phone. He felt as excited as he was scared.

6

The building was unassuming. He checked again on his phone's GPS that he had the right place. He did. He was expecting something as grand as The Rise. But then it dawned on him, privacy was paramount, being flash only got you the interest of the Feds, and he now felt stupid riding over in his two-hundred pound coat and one-hundred-pound trainers. He made a mental note to himself to dress down rather than up when on official business. The flat was on the ground floor. There were CCTV cameras above the main entrance door that watched him walk up to it, but Ryan was still too immature to always scan a situation for potential cameras. The entrance door was painted royal blue, and had been repainted royal blue for years. Painted blue every time it had been defaced with graffiti, and painted blue when it was time to use the Council's budget at the end of the financial year. He pressed his finger into the button on the intercom and the blue door released itself. He stepped inside and the stench of dog urine hit him. The lobby looked old and felt cold. It was nothing more than a barren space with a staircase taking you up through the building. The painted white walls had scuff marks from bags and buggies and had dirty hand prints at various heights, no doubt from residents using the wall as a keep-me-up as they tried to find their flat after a heavy night on the sauce. He looked at the number on the door of the first flat on his right side. It wasn't the one, but it did allow to instantly deduce which of the remaining three was the one he needed. He walked back across and then over to the far end of the lobby and knocked on the door. The door had two clunky and crude cameras above it, Ryan noticed these – they were too obtrusive not to. The door, like the entrance and every door on this floor, and no doubt the rest, was painted in royal blue. The door was open. Slightly. An invitation. He took it. He stepped inside and heard. 'Shut the door.'

There wasn't a face to accompany the voice yet. He did what he was told.

The hallway was small, tight and short. Within eight paces he had reached the end and it then turned 90° to the right. When he took the right turn, the first thing that hit him was the smell of weed, and the plumes of smoke hanging in the air, so thick it made him cough. Which wasn't cool. One of the brothers slumped in the armchair, with a bottle of beer in his hand, and wearing a thick curb gold bracelet, laughed at the cough. Ryan felt small and insignificant. And nervous.

'Come.' Another command, but from a different accent. This sounded African, or Caribbean, he wasn't sure. And it was coming from the far end of the room. A guy, with his back to him, was sitting at a table.

'Come over.'

Ryan did as he was told and walked through the central part of the room, apologising for getting in the way of the TV screen and arrived at the table. The guy giving the orders still hadn't looked up yet from what he was doing.

'Sit.' Another command. Ryan, again, did what he was told. He pulled out a chair, and lifted off the stack of porn magazines from it, placed them on the table and sat down.

'Tonight, I need you doing some multi's,' said Jamal, sucking hard on a spliff and then tilting his head slightly to puff the smoke slowly up towards the ceiling.

'Some multi's?' replied Ryan, unsure what he meant by it.

'Yes, multi's. Multi drops. A brother has gone down and I need you to fill the void. Do well, you could climb to the next level. If you're ready...,' Jamal had set the bait.

'I'm ready. Let me prove it.' Ryan was chomping at the bit, ready to climb to the next level.

'Good boy. Take out your phone, I'm going to text you where each bag is going.'

In front of Jamal sat small, transparent bags, each one looking like they were full of salt, except that it wasn't salt, as delivering salt doesn't with an intent to supply charge. Next to the clutch of bags was a small, electronic weighing scale and a packet of Stanley knife blades. The area was spotless, it looked like not one micron of white powder had been wasted. Jamal was wearing a pair of latex gloves and he kept them on whilst he sent a flurry of texts to Ryan's burner phone, his phone pinging with the receipt of each one received. Ryan could feel the excitement already. He had landed a bigger gig with the firm and he knew he could offset some of this workload to Michael tonight. What could possibly go wrong...

The packet of biscuits never stretched to the second cup of tea. Which was just as dire as the first, to the point where Harlan tried to see if he could actually stand his spoon up in it. He was hoping the landlord could pull a pint better than he could make a brew. In-between the first and second cup, Harlan stretched his legs, taking a walk around all four corners of the pub, including the cellar. It was a typical working-class boozer, in a working-class town, even if the town itself had some delusions of grandeur and thinking it was much more affluent than the statistics of joblessness seemed to show. Bournemouth had the same air of arrogance as London, and the same size drug problem, too. But Harlan wasn't here to take down a gang of dealers who had made this pub their home, he was here to sort out a bunch of boozed-up, off their tits, brawlers who thought it was fair game to turn Big Al's pub into some sort of Saturday night fight night. That was going to stop. When, was down to him; how, was down to them. If they wanted to have it, Harlan was more than willing to give it.

The pub was lacking a little love, or a little cash. It was tidy enough, the seats weren't ripped and the green baize was still green, rare for a pool table. It was only when Harlan stepped into the back office that he saw an assortment of snapped cues that had clearly been used in battle. The pub had been a goldmine, and Harlan had decided it was time to put it back as King Solomon's mine.

'When is the next game on?' Harlan asked.

The reply from Big Al spoke of clear rejection, 'Saturday.'

'Then it's about time I started taking a keen interest in this football lark I keep hearing about.'

Big Al wasn't sure what that meant, but he knew he liked the sound of it.

His new phone made a beep, and a buzz. Michael knew who it would be, as only one person had this number. The phone wasn't able to display the message on the home screen, it took him a moment to navigate the buttons to get into the display, to find the MESSAGE icon, which was in the shape of a closed envelope, and then open it up to read.

You're on! Meet me in the shed. 30 mins. Excited?

Michael didn't know what to answer, or how. He felt something in his stomach but didn't know if this was excitement, or fear. Or both. He composed a one-word reply. Two letters: **OK.**

His mum called him down for dinner, which was a problem. After dinner his chore was to clear the table and load the dishwasher, which meant allowing the time to eat his meal and clean up, a good twenty minutes would be lost. He knew to take his rucksack and put the phone in the front pocket of the bag and set it on silent. He put in a couple of jumpers over the top to bulk it out. His mum shouted up the stairs again. Irritation in her voice that the meal she cooked for him was going cold. He left his bedroom with his bag over his shoulder. He was leaving his bedroom as a fourteen-year-old who had posters of favourite rappers and girls on his wall, but by the time he would get back to it, he would be a criminal. It was a big leap. But he decided to take it.

Dinner was mashed potato, sausages, peas and gravy. Dad wasn't home from work so his plate was waiting for him in the microwave, with a plate over the top, ready for him to reheat when he returned home. He was told to slow down and '*Chew your food, don't swallow it*' but Michael was up against the clock. He asked his mum if he could do the chore later, but the request was denied. She let him know mum and dad play their part in buying and cooking the food, his part was to clean up. Fair's fair. The plates were rinsed and stacked and the program set. His mum was busy loading the washing machine when he called out to her.

'Back by 9 – no later.' Was the last thing he heard as he closed the door.

Ryan walked through the empty allotment; all horticulture was a daytime pursuit. Some of the patches were looking healthy, some barren. Ryan didn't know what made them grow, and it looked like some of the gardeners didn't either. The shed was amongst a clutter of other wooden erections, some painted, some varnished, some bare. Ryan looked both ways and then back behind him before he lifted the padlock out of the latch and carried it inside with him. He sat on one of the deckchairs, pulled out a pouch of tobacco and passed the time smoking and watching some YouTube.

Twenty minutes and Ryan was getting twitchy. He had smoked two roll-ups and watched everything he wanted to watch on his phone. Mikey was late, and in this game, punctuality was as important as the packages he was paid to carry. He had promised to make all the drops, but needed Michael to help. He couldn't cover the distance on his own. He had already sent him two texts and called him, but to no avail. He was thinking of setting off alone, pedalling as fast as he could around town to see if it was actually doable on his own, when he heard the sound of grass being flattened. He pushed the slatted door open just enough to peer through the gap. It was Michael.

'Why you so late? I told you not to be late. I have been calling you!'

Michael couldn't reply, he needed to get some air to his lungs and slow his heart rate. He was sweating and red-faced. Ryan decided to back off, his friend had obviously rushed to be here and now he was here, they could get out and get earning.

'Give me two minutes,' said Michael finally, still panting harshly and holding his chest with the palm of his right hand.

'OK. But be quick. We have lots to do,' replied Ryan, trying to hide his frustration and impatience. Michael opened his rucksack and pulled out a bottle of Coke, twisted the top off and drank it as fast he could until he needed to come up for air and belch. Ryan handed him his stack of small, transparent bags and told him to take out his phone. Ryan sent five texts, one after the other, each one an address and a quantity. He then asked Michael to count up the bags he had so it would be against the total number he needed. Michael counted and nodded.

'So, you are clear on what you're doing?' Ryan asked.

'Yep.'

'Sure? Follow the texts in order. Arrive, deliver, leave. Simple shit.'

'I got it. It's not rocket science.'

'Just don't mess up,' Ryan said, half in hope, half in fear.

Michael looked at Ryan having sensed the fear in his friend's voice but decided to brush it off. They stepped out and Ryan closed the door and slipped the padlock into the clasp but not pushing it fully home. Both their bikes were leaned up and far enough down the side of the shed to be out of the way of anyone who just happened to be there.

'Mikey. You sure you got this? Just do exactly what I said. Arrive, deliver, leave. Yeah?'

'Mate, is there something you're not telling me? I do know this isn't sugar in these bags.'

It's not what you're carrying, thought Ryan, *it's who you're carrying it for.*

'I'm just saying.'

'Yeah, I got it. Arrive, deliver, leave. Chill.'

They fist bumped, got on their bikes and Ryan rode pillion down between the various allotment patches and out onto the lane. Ryan then pulled away to the right, Michael to the left.

Liam was already at work. He had his address. He had his package. He had his orders.

Jamal could relax now. All the mules were delivering, the dealers, dealing and the security crew were on standby should anybody fall foul of the rules. The town, a sleepy part of the Dorset countryside, with its picturesque beaches and Premiership football team was completely unaware it had been corrupted by a gang of illegal immigrants operating through the county lines. A problem that had been labelled an epidemic by the Metropolitan police and one that had its tentacles into a swath of greedy, or gullible teenagers across the country. Jamal didn't care that his mules were young. On paper they were old enough to be tried as adults but he knew they would get a spell in juvie at best. And if they were old enough to take the cash, they were old enough to take the risk. The intercom buzzed. One of the brothers looked at the camera, then gave a large, seedy smile.

'Dinner is here.' He went to the door and turned down the latch. In stepped four women, all of them African American, all of them in tight dresses, high heels and maximised cleavages. They had been paid well to be here but were expected to perform. The door closed up behind them and tonight's dinner was about to be served. Jamal knew that just as night follows day, a certain type of girl would always be drawn to a gangster. Jamal felt good. It had been a good day at the office. He could now relax and enjoy the spoils of their success. The women had already been picked by the four and were already being pawed. It was going to be a fun night.

The sky had started to darken. Streetlights on standby, waiting for their cue to flicker into life. The first drop had been made. Michael had ridden into the street and it was half-way up on the left. It was a basic street, the cars parked on the road weren't new, but they weren't old, either. Most of them 5-7yrs old, and probably leased when new to company salesmen and now, financed to families when the time to trade it had arrived. He had been nervous when he arrived at the first address in the list; his mouth was dry and his knock at the door was weak. But the transaction went smoothly, the guy in the house was cool. He made him feel at ease and gave Michael a two-way slap with the tips of his fingers to finalise the end of their conversation. Michael rode away feeling confident, he wasn't sure if that had been a user or a dealer, but he was cool, this whole thing seemed cool, so far.

Ryan was at the opposite end of the town. He had chosen the rougher part, only because he knew his brother drank around here so if some trouble did start, he could name-drop him and hopefully that would stop him getting a kicking. The estate housed three of his six drops. It was an estate that had been overlooked with Council cash, *out of sight, out of mind* would be an apt description. The first house on the left was boarded up. The marine grade plywood that covered the downstairs had graffiti all over it, some words decipherable, some not. Some words were slang, some crude. Some were code, gang code, but Ryan didn't know the lingo so wasted little time in staring. He rode a little further into the estate and although he didn't know what deprivation meant, he definitely knew he was amongst it. The house he wanted was at the end of the first row. He rode up to it and seemed to get off his bike before it had even stopped. The door had a long, thin, vertical letterbox with a long, thin, vertical knocker. He pulled it back and let it slam home against the wood, twice. Three seemed a bit much for this kind of set-up. It opened up and there was a large lady standing in flip-flops, wearing patterned shorts and a black vest top, that had a large bleach stain just under her right breast. She had peroxide blonde hair and a thick neck that had a large mole hanging off the side, like someone had glued on a raisin. She looked intimidating enough. He knew already how many of the transparent bags she needed and he handed them over. She gave a grunt by means of acknowledgement and closed the door. He wanted to peer in through the kitchen window to see how she lived, but thought better of it. Then decided to do it, anyway. It was only a passing glance as he pulled the bike back off her wall but he could see a cluttered worktop with a couple of different cereal boxes and a 4-pint milk carton left out and with the top left off. There was an open case of strong lager on the kitchen table and at least a half-dozen scratch cards. It reminded him of his house, his mum, just a thinner, drawn-in version. Gaunt was how he heard her be described once.

The next house was slightly smarter looking but the guy who answered was even less desirable than she had been. He beckoned for Ryan to come in out of sight and he brought his bike in with him. He knew the estate and knew things didn't stay outside unattended for long. He handed the bag over and the guy took it, opened it carefully, wet his forefinger, pushed into the bag of powder and then rubbed it along the gum line above his four, front yellow teeth.

A few moments later he spoke with a low, gravelly voice.

'OK. Next bag.' Ryan handed it over and watched him do it again.

'You got to try before you buy, kid.' He said, and laughed to himself.

Ryan felt uneasy, and he knew exactly why. Up until now he had only delivered single packages, the contents concealed but he knew when it was either cash or drugs inside. But he had only made solo drops, and to people that you wouldn't think were in this game. They were all smarter, more, *upper-class*. But this guy, and the fat lady, were the type of people you associated with low-level living and narcotics.

'You can go now,' he said, and Ryan was only too happy to oblige.

Two visits, three bags done. Four bags left. He wondered how Mikey was getting on.

Michael had done his second and third drop. They were only a couple of miles apart and the mountain bike his parents had bought him last Christmas made climbing the hills easy. What his bike lacked in guile; it made up for in gears. The fourth house wasn't a house. It was a bungalow, and had a picket-type fence all around it. He lifted the latch and rode onto a sheet of tri-coloured pea-shingle, evenly distributed and freshly raked. The bungalow had a thatched roof and Michael couldn't imagine what someone like this needed with what he had in his pocket. It was a stable door and when he rang the bell, the top half opened inwards and there was a grey-haired gentleman standing there, he had a burgundy tank top over a check shirt. He looked like a headmaster and Michael had to stop himself from shaking his head in disbelief as he pulled out a bag of white powder and handed it over.

'Thank you, young man. Please be sure to shut the gate behind you, if you don't mind. Those pesky foxes get in if you don't and last week all my bins were gone through.'

'Yes. No problem. Have a nice evening.'

'And to you.'

The top section of the stable then closed and Michael could see a key being turned in the lock. He couldn't believe his conversation. It was as if he had just delivered him his evening newspaper. The movies depicted drug users as scumbags, people with tracked arms, lank hair, baggy clothes and dead eyes, but this man looked like somebody's granddad, probably played old people's games, like backgammon, or chess, not taking packets of white powder to sniff up his nose. He closed the gate as asked, and got back on his bike. He flicked on the light that sat dead-centre of the handlebars and checked the time. He still had forty-five minutes before his curfew and the last drop was on the way home. This had been a doddle so far.

By the time Harlan arrived at the B&B it was dark and he was hungry. He had yet to do a deal with the owner about getting some evening meals thrown in during his stay so was undecided if to head out after a shower to a restaurant or organise a takeaway. He was still deliberating which way to feed his belly when he walked in and heard the old man letting out a lingering swear word, making him laugh in respect to the ballsy owner. The living room door was slightly ajar, and Harlan pushed it open just a little bit more, just enough to get his head round and found the old man on his knees, some tools around him, and looking a little lost. The old man appeared to be building some sort of flat pack furniture, or rather, trying.

'Having fun?' Harlan asked, but not mocking him, rather, sympathising with him.

'This Taiwan piece of fu –, honestly, why give you

instructions you need a PHD to understand? And why so small, I have cataracts, for Chrissake.'

'May I?' asked Harlan.

'May you what, build it, be my guest. I fought for Queen and country, fending off the Germans with a bloody bayonet yet now a piece of pissing MDF beats me.'

Harlan laughed again, this time, out loud.

The instructions were for a bookcase, but what the old man appeared to be building was anything but. Harlan didn't think to take off his boots when he walked over to the pile of veneered wood that sat in the middle of the room, on a rug. The first thing Harlan did was push the pieces over onto the carpet, giving him a flat surface, the second thing he did was take apart what was already built and then lay out the pieces in order. Harlan had a mechanical, sequential brain, everything following a step-by-step process to achieve success, whether a Screaming Eagle engine or a Taiwan-made piece of furniture. Although it hadn't been made in Taiwan, but in Leicester. Harlan didn't have the heart to correct the old man, who seemed only too happy to blame the Taiwanese, Chinese, and anybody else who sprang to mind. 'Can I get you a drink?' asked the old man.

'A cup of tea would be sweet.'

'It would, if I was sweet, but I'm not, and by drink, I mean beer. I'll ask you again, do –'

'Ha, no need. A beer would be great.'

The old man left the room and Harlan continued with laying out the pieces and assorting the screws, pins and dowels. The old man stuck his head around the door, 'You eaten?'

'No, as it happens.'

'Fancy a sandwich?'

'Yes. Egg. Two rounds.'

'Nothing like being direct,' replied the old man.

'Nothing like free labour.'

Harlan heard the old man laugh all the way down the hallway.

Ten minutes later, he returned, carrying a tray, on it a plate of fried egg sandwiches and a can of Fosters. Thirty minutes later the tray was showing an empty plate and a crumpled-up beer can and the bookcase was built. 'Ta da,' Harlan said.

'Well, I'll be damned, it's straight and everything,'

The sarcastic banter had continued from the very first quick quip and Harlan liked him.

'I think that calls for another beer,' the old man added.

'I think... that you think well. And I also think you should be bringing in some crisps.'

Harlan heard the old man laugh again as he walked back down the hallway to the kitchen.

The bookcase was standing proud, centre-stage in the living room as Harlan and the old man sat in opposing chairs. Stan recalled his war stories, or rather war stories of others as Harlan had done the numbers; the old man would have needed to have fought the Germans as a foetus. As the evening wore on, and the beers had started to make the landlord start to slur just a little, Harlan decided to call it a night, before he did, he asked the old man a question.

'You ever heard of the Cherry Pickers?'

'You mean the local firm?'

Harlan sat up in his seat, surprised at Stan knowing about the Cherry Pickers, and also his terminology. 'Yeah – what do you know?'

'Not much. Not really. I know they have quite a rep, but I think they are scum, football is where dads take their nippers, handing down their love of the beautiful game to their offspring, so it spawns another generation. It used to be man and boy, in scarves, with a cup of Bovril, singing songs from the terraces.'

'How long they been going?' asked Harlan.

'Not sure. I mean we have never had it before, even when it was rife in the eighties, and then we spent years in the doldrums, I think they proper piped up the year we got promoted. It isn't about the football for them lot, it's about the fighting.'

'So, a couple of years?'

'Yeah. Three, four at the max, but I know now they are bang at it and the club itself is suffering.'

'You don't know anyone who knows anyone in the firm?'

The old man sat and pondered for a moment. He went to speak, then stopped, and pondered some more, before answering, 'Nope. No one.'

'Helpful,' replied Harlan.

'Nope. Or hopeful. Don't possess either of those traits.'

Harlan smirked and then stood up ready to leave for his room. 'I didn't catch your name.'

'Stan. Stanley Truman.'

Harlan was just about to leave the living room when the old man shouted back, 'I think one or two of those fellas work out at Charms Gym.'

'Cheers, Stan.'

'What do you want them for, you aren't thinking of joining them, are you?'

'What's that saying, *if you can't join them, beat them.*'

'Nope, it's the other way round.'

'Not in my book.'

Harlan left Stan trying to figure out what he meant and made his way up to his room.

7

It was hard for Colin to hide the excitement on his face. It was the fixture he had been waiting for. The last time they met, at their ground, it was pure anarchy and he loved every single second of it. The two minibuses, going up the motorway in transit, singing songs and counting down both the minutes and miles. Each of them high on drugs, and on life. Colin lived for fighting, the more gruesome the better and fighting without rules. Everything and anything went. He sat at the breakfast table, his wife out doing the school run. The glass table had a bowl of fresh fruit: apples, bananas and grapes, but that was for her and the kids, Colin had a bowl of Weetabix laced with several heaped spoons of sugar and his coffee. Black. One sugar. On the table was a notepad, on it a list of abbreviations or nicknames and in his hand was his burner phone. He was making calls and sending texts, ticking off or crossing the names on the pad as he went. In his mind he was planning a war, and with that, assembling his army. In a way, he was.

. . .

He picked up the smartphone, already knowing there would be nothing to see, but today felt different. This very second felt different. Without thinking he found himself unlocking the phone and starting to compile a text. The words were few, the message was clear.

I still think about you. I wish I didn't. But I do.

He added a kiss, but deleted it. That wasn't his place to do that anymore.

The message could have been for either of them. There were just two names in his contact list. Only two people in a land of billions, had his personal number. Only two people in a land of billions did he love. He added the name of the person he had written it for and after letting his thumb hover over the blue arrow, he dabbed on it and within a second it was showing as being delivered. In that same second he regretted it. But Harlan had a life full of regrets, what was one more?

The workout had been done, so too, the shower. His hair was damp to the touch and his neck hair needed cutting back but the grooming, if it could be called that, could be done next time. The smell of breakfast had hit his nostrils and then made its way down to his stomach, telling his brain he was hungry. He closed the door behind him and made his way down the worn carpet that covered the stairs and into the dining room. Stan was with a young woman taking her order, her young child beside her, sitting in a buggy and smiling contently at the pink cuddly rabbit she was holding. Harlan found himself looking, but only in a statistical way, he put the young woman's age as no more than twenty. The child, no more than three. He found himself wondering why they were in a backstreet B&B. Hoping it was as some sort of refugee, her one, or two-night stay, paid for by the local council whilst they tried to find her somewhere else, which he knew, if he was right on why she was here, would be a shitty women's hostel. But he could be wrong, she could be here through choice, not circumstance. But as nice as Stan was, this was never going to be anybody's first choice. The thinking was over. Not his problem. Not his concern. His mind went back to breakfast and what was on offer.

Stan hobbled over; Harlan noticed his limp had gotten worse. 'You ok there, Stan?'

'Yeah. Why?'

'The limp?'

'Just an old shrapnel wound. Gives me a bit of jip every now and then.'

Yes, Harlan thought to himself, acquired when just a figment of your fathers' eye.

'What can I get you?'

'The full English. Swap the fried mushrooms for an extra rasher.'

'You don't like fried mushrooms?' asked Stan.

'No, I don't. They look like old women's cut toenails. Hideous things.'

Harlan was waiting for some old war story about rations, but to his surprise he didn't get one, instead he watched Stan limp out of the room to the kitchen.

The list was complete. One or two unconfirmed but he had enough front-line soldiers written down to make Saturday's game doable. It was always Colin's fear, not being able to get enough numbers to have a right tear-up, but he needn't have worried, he had a loyal crew and he was a passionate leader. It also helped that he was the local drug kingpin, wholesale wise, that was. He had a contact at Southampton Docks and every fortnight he would get a kilo of uncut cocaine, three-quarters of which he would sell to the Somalians, the other quarter he would sell to his crew. He liked his entrepreneurship, splitting the brick into wholesale and retail prices, costs covered by the first, pure profit on the second, the best of both worlds. The added bonus was that on match days, he could, and would, ensure his crew were off their tits on a drug that only boosted your view of self-importance and invincibility. Colin couldn't see the smirk that came over his face, but the mirror caught it, and it returned an image of a smug, squat who suffered from small-man syndrome.

The breakfast ticked the boxes, even more so that Stan got confused on if it was an extra rasher or an extra sausage so had included both. Harlan took another mouthful of tea before the dregs in the bottom of the mug and got up and pushed his chair back up against the table. By the time he had eaten, the dining room was empty aside for himself and the young woman with the buggy, and as he walked past, he caught a glimpse of what he hoped hadn't happened, of why she was here. She had tried to hide it before Harlan was adjacent to her, but just as she went to cover the welt, the child dropped the toy pink rabbit and, in her quest to appease the little girl, the bruise became evident to see. It was a bruise that was pretty hard to miss. Harlan felt his stomach knot. He detested bullies as a rule, but those who hit women took a special place in his hatred. She looked at him as she got herself back upright in the faux-leather backed chair, she found herself giving off an embarrassed smile which only served to tighten the knot in his stomach. Why is it that the victims of domestic abuse feel a sense of embarrassed shame, whilst the preparators seem to show no shame at all? Harlan returned the smile, trying not to make it come across as a smile that spoke of pity, and walked out of the dining room. *Not his problem. Not his concern,* he told himself.

Michael woke up to a flurry of missed calls on his new phone. He hated to admit it to himself, but he found last night exhilarating, and he couldn't wait to get started today. Michael had purposely slept through his alarm telling him it was time to get up and head to the local shop to begin his early morning paper round. He also knew he would be bunking off school. Up until last night, Michael enjoyed school and had his sights set on becoming a mechanic and owning his own garage one day. But that was before last night, before Ryan gave him a burner phone and a load of addresses. That was before Michael became a schoolboy drug dealer.

The burner rang again. Michael answered it, hoping his mum had already left for work.

'You are alive then? Been belling you all morning,' said Ryan, before Michael even had the chance to say hello. 'So, did you enjoy last night? Yeah, you did, I know it.'

Ryan had asked and answered the question. The reason his friend knew the answer was that he had been Michael once, someone who had woken up one day as a student, and the following day woke up as a criminal.

'Why so many calls?' asked Michael.

'Because we have dollar to make.'

'Already?' said Michael, who pulled the phone from his ear to check the time on the screen, not yet understanding that the drug business was a 24/7 affair.

'Come on, G, time to get up. I have a load of addresses to ping over.'

Michael could hear the excitement in his friend's voice, and he had to admit, it was contagious. 'OK. Give me ten,' replied Michael, his legs already out from under the covers and both feet now on the carpet.

'Cool. I'll send the streets now. And remember, arrive, deliver, leave. Never forget that.'

'Yeah – I know.'

'Cool. Now get up and let's go make some proper dough.'

Michael heard his friend click off. He checked the time again. A couple of days ago, he was sitting in class. This morning he would be marked as absent again, presumed ill, not presumed to be delivering Charlie around the town.

The bruise was bothering him. It shouldn't, but it was. The young girl was now a mother, she had responsibilities, and from what Harlan could tell, she was living up to them. He didn't know how they had put their hand on her, and he hoped he wouldn't know. For their sake.

He had some prep work to do. Big Al had given him the overview, but for Harlan, the devil was in the detail. Rival football firms hadn't been a thing he had come across too often. Sure, he had evicted plenty of pissed-up England fans but they were generally removed without the need for violence, it was more a case of too much alcohol meeting too much passion. And football firms weren't criminal gangs, either. Yes, there would be some petty dealers in there, and maybe some armed robbers or backstreet debt-collectors, but in the main he imagined them to be straight up 9-5er's who lived for a weekend tear-up with an opposing crew. But even if he was right, and they weren't proper players, just plastic gangsters, they still needed to be stopped. And only because he was being paid to stop it. If this was happening in someone else's pub he wouldn't care. He would see it as a case of each to their own. But this wasn't the case, instead he was being paid good money to save Alan's business, and that was exactly what he was going to do. Harlan had some calls to make and he didn't trust the walls he was in not to listen, so he took his leather cut from around the back of the chair and headed back down the cheap carpeted stairs and made for the front door.

At the same time, as he walked through the narrow hallway, Stan appeared from the living room carrying a small plate with a mug on top. 'Off anywhere nice?' Stan asked.

'Just going for a ride. You know, get some fresh air in my lungs.'

'Nice. Wish I was coming with you. I was a bloody good rider in my day.'

Harlan could not only smell the bullshit, he could taste it too, but he wasn't about to call him up, or out, on it, or even to discuss it, but there was one thing he wanted to ask.

'Stan, quick word. In private?'

'Sure, pop in here,' replied Stan, stepping back into the living room and when Harlan followed him in, Stan shut the door behind him.

'What's the deal with the girl with the bruise?' Harlan asked.

'Oh, that poor girl. I'm not overly sure, except she arrived very late last night.'

'Did she say what happened?'

'No, not really. She was trying to cover her face, trying to make out that she hadn't been hit but she wasn't doing a good job. I could tell she had been crying, too.'

'How long is she staying?'

'Good question. I don't actually know. To be honest, she struggled to pay last night, she was a fiver short but I let her off that. I mean, I wish I could have let her off all of it but –'

'You don't have to explain yourself, Stan. You have a business to run and you already let her off what you could. Listen, take this,' and Harlan reached into his pocket and pulled out a handful of neatly folded notes. He peeled off two twenties and a ten. Fifty pounds in total. He knew Stan would go to a score a night if it was in cash but he had done right by the woman so Harlan wanted to pay for two nights for her, at full price.

'Take this but don't say anything. If she asks to stay tonight, then tell her you've covered it. Same for the next night. Let's give her time to sort out what shit she has going on without also having to worry about money.'

'You sure?'

'Yeah. But between you and I, OK? And maybe go and check on her in a bit and take the kid some crisps or something.'

'Yeah. OK.'

Harlan handed over the notes and then headed towards the door and before he got to the handle Stan shouted over at him. 'You aren't so bad, you know, for a scruffy biker, that is.'

Harlan could still hear Stan as the front door shut behind him.

The first few drops were as easy as last night. The addresses arriving on one phone and then located on another. All he needed for his enterprise to work he had: two mobile phones and one bicycle. He was kicking himself for holding off for so long before agreeing to join Ryan on his scam. Michael didn't even feel what he was doing was wrong, it just felt the same as delivering newspapers, except that he was getting much better wages for it.

After the last drop-off, he checked inside the old manbag Ryan had leant him. It wasn't leather, like Ryan's, it was fabric, and the zip was sticky, but he knew it soon would be leather, it would be the first treat to himself. Michael had stopped at the park, parked up at the far end, his bicycle resting up against the communal toilet block. The zip finally played ball, and he rummaged his fingers around inside, counting the little bags. There were three left. It was a key number. Three was when Michael had been told to contact Ryan to meet up for a reload. The worst thing you could do, said Ryan, was *to run out of gear*. Michael composed a text for his friend and then sent it:

I'm starving. Want to meet up for food? It was code that Ryan had told him to use. *Starving* meant he was down to the magic number, *meet for food* meant he needed to meet up and stock up. Michael waited for Ryan to reply, and passed the time by taking a piss up against the wall, even though the entrance to the gents was literally around the other side.

Ryan was just about to knock on the next door when he felt the phone vibrate inside his leather man-bag that was sitting just under his sternum. He would check it after the drop. Ryan knocked on the door and it was opened by a woman. She was strung out and the strap of her stained negligee was hanging down off her shoulder. Ryan was trying not to look at the hint of breast that was showing but he was fifteen, and hormones raged around his body faster than he could pedal his bike. She was no looker, but that didn't matter, it was flesh, and that thought he would hold onto until later, when he was back home and alone in his room. He slipped his hand into his bag and pulled out the little bag, dropping his hand down to his side with the bag propped up in his open palm, his thumb not only holding it in place, but also concealing it. The strung-out woman already had the money in her hand. Two rolled up twenty-pound notes. The exchange was fast, barely noticeable to the naked eye. Both dealer and taker knowing what was needed. Speed and stealth, key. The woman shut the door, too stoned to even smile, and even if she did Ryan knew her teeth would be far from white, and that helped, as he didn't want anything to put him off the image that he had stored safely away in his head later. As he walked back down to his bicycle, he was smiling to himself, he loved his job.

As he picked the bike up off the floor, he remembered that his phone had gone off. He reached inside the man-bag and pulled out the cheap burner. It was from Mikey.

I'm starving. Want to meet up for food?

Another smile came over his face. A reload meant Michael was doing well, which meant he in turn, was doing well. He was already becoming a big fan of pyramid selling.

He sent Michael a text. **Meet for food at mine in twenty.**

Ryan got on his bike and started the ride back to home. Today was going to be a good day.

8

Harlan had chosen the same pub and pulled open the doors and stepped in. It had only opened minutes before and his quick head-count came to a total of five, including himself and discounting the barmaid. It was a different barmaid to the other night; today's barmaid was older, nearing middle-aged, or right in the midst of it. Harlan knew the patrons already here would be the pub's stalwarts. Those spending every spare minute here and no doubt every spare penny of their benefits. Harlan arrived at the bar and waited to be served, having been beaten by an older fella who had a Jack Russell on a lead. After his Guinness had been poured, settled, and paid for it was Harlan's turn and he asked for a bottle of Budweiser and to see the food menu. The barmaid told him that there wouldn't be any food today as the chef hadn't turned in, so Harlan downgraded his appetite to a packet of Scampi Fries and handed over a tenner and collected his change. Harlan walked over to the far end of the pub, taking a table by a window but making sure he was sitting facing the door.

He was only one mouthful into his bottle when he spotted someone in his peripheral vision walking towards him. With every footstep the image was getting clearer in Harlan's side eye. Whoever it was had a thickset moustache and broad shoulders. Harlan still hadn't turned his head. The owner of the moustache appeared now in full view, standing opposite Harlan by the table, deeming it too rude to pull out a chair and sit down.

'Can I help you?' Harlan asked nonchalantly, before taking a small sip of his drink.

'Listen, mate, I'm the gaffer here and I heard about what happened here the other night. I really don't want any trouble here.'

'I don't start trouble, *mate*. I finish it.' The stare across and up at Mr Moustache said it all.

'OK, erm, well... as long as we, erm... understand each other?'

'I think what you mean is as long as *you* understand me.' Another stare.

The landlord found himself nodding, whoever it was that was sat there had an aura that said, *don't prod the bear.* Harlan watched him walk back to whatever rock the landlord had come out from and went back to his drink and crisps. He knew it would be only a matter of time, if it hadn't happened already, that this pub would have a bad reputation induced by bad punters, as the landlord clearly lacked the backbone to confront with conviction, and that only paved the way for bullies to move in and call a boozer their own. The landlord hadn't asked him for his view of events, showing a lack of respect to him, yet at the same time hadn't told him to leave, showing a lack of respect to himself.

Harlan moved on from thinking about the landlord

and went back to the reason he was here. He had already taken out both phones and they were on the table, side by side, separated only by size. He pressed down on the glass with his index finger on the smartphone, seeing if there had been a reply from earlier but there hadn't, which didn't surprise him, but did hurt him. He picked up his burner phone, the trusted Nokia, and thumbed down through his contacts until he came to M, for Mouse.

Mouse, shortened down over the years from Mighty Mouse, was the MC's go-to guy for intel. Satan's Security prided itself on having fingers in many pies, but also many chefs in many kitchens. From coppers on the payroll to snitches on the streets, the MC needed reliable data to be able to stay one step off ahead of the boys in blue.

Harlan hit the dial button and didn't have to wait too many rings before Mouse answered.

'H, how are you, brother?'

'I'm good. You?'

'Can't complain, although was a bit of a mad one last night so my head feels like a bucket of rusty bolts.'

'Lightweight. Anyway, what do you know about football firms?'

'Football teams, yeah a bit, I'm a city supporter when it –'

'Which is good to know, if I asked you about football teams, but I didn't.'

'You mean firms, as in?'

'Yes. As in.'

'Not too much if I'm honest. I know a few people who might, but they are old-school white supremacist type geezers. True St George believers. Not my type of dudes, but can ask.'

'Yeah, just put the feelers out. See if it is still as big and as underground as it used to be.'

'To be fair, I thought all that had stopped. The pre-arranged scraps, I mean.'

'Me too, but apparently not.'

'OK, give me a day or two.'

'Quicker if you can, Mouse.'

'On it.'

Harlan killed the call and went back over to the barmaid and asked for a bottle and a second packet of Scampi Fries.

The dog was glad to see Ryan, and was busy scrambling around his feet when he stepped inside the kitchen. Michael came in behind him and closed the door. Tyson's attention then moved to the stranger and started repeatedly jumping up in excitement resembling a yoyo on amphetamines. 'Tyson, down. DOWN, Tyson,' commanded Ryan to no avail. It wasn't until he reached to the top of the fridge and pulled down the treat tin did the dog focus its attention on what it would soon be eating. 'Go on through,' said Ryan, gesturing his friend towards the next room so he could distract his dog before throwing down the chew in the loose direction of Tyson's bed. Michal was heading in the direction of the living room.

'No, not there. Upstairs.' It left his mouth sounding more of a barked order than an instruction. The reason, Ryan didn't want to be embarrassed by the sight, and state, of his pilled-up mum. Michael walked up the stairs and Ryan followed, wanting to get him out of the house as soon as possible, telling himself it would be so they would be back earning, the real reason, like that regarding his mum, was the sight, and state, of his home. The bannister was festooned with a mixture of damp and dirty clothes. The landing had stains on the carpet and the chipboard wallpaper had chipped in places, and there were dark, damp patches up in the top corners. Ryan overtook his friend on the landing, getting to his bedroom door and opening it up and entering. Ryan's door had a fist-shaped hole buried deep in it, the height of the strike was in line with Ryan's head height, and caused by a punch thrown in frustration by his older brother in what was yet another sibling brawl.

'Shut the door, G,' barked Ryan, annoyed that his friend wasn't thinking. Michael did as he was told and then followed the new instruction of sitting down on the bed whilst Ryan buried himself inside the wardrobe before emerging with a trainer box. The next few minutes were spent hurriedly dividing the small bags between them, using the list of addresses and the coded quantities. Ryan then took the cash that Michael had already taken so far, before wrapping an elastic band around it and placing the bundle back inside the box. Michael waited as he put the box back inside the wardrobe before placing a few more boxes back on top, some full, some empty and then a couple of coats and hoodies. He didn't need to be quite as thorough; it wasn't as if his mum ever came in and cleaned up his room.

'C'mon, bruv, let's get out of here.' Ryan said, keen to get out and back to work.

Michael followed Ryan, which unbeknown to Mikey, was a visual metaphor now for their friendship. Luckily for Michael's trousers, Tyson's claws were still wrapped around the rawhide chew on his bed when they both walked through the kitchen. Ryan stopped at the doorless cupboard above the kettle and rummaged his hand around and came out with two KitKats, handing one to Mikey before getting back on their bicycles and getting back to work.

The pub had gotten busier, but only so far as the headcount had exactly doubled in numbers. Harlan wasn't impressed with the business; the landlord was as bland as the building itself, which was situated on a busy high street but looked no more appealing than the raft of charity shops that also took up residence there. Harlan knew the decline of the pub trade was blamed on the big chains serving food, with beer being a mere side show, but that wasn't the only reason. Harlan knew lazy landlords not moving with the times, not fending off competition, not sorting out the bad from the good, played a part in their demise. Pubs were different to clubs, sometimes acting as a precursor, sometimes acting alone. There was still a place for the British pub. The clientele was different; older, and that meant they would tend to stay in one place for the night. That, in turn, meant it was your till that benefitted, not someone else's. So, remove the riff raff and put back old school landlords and landladies; they could *make* a pub with their strength of character. Harlan worked both pubs and clubs, it didn't matter to him. Where there was trouble, trouble that other people couldn't stop, he would. For a fee. But he wished it wasn't that way. Yes, he was good at violence, one of the best around and had built a career and lifestyle from it, but he hated it. He truly hated it.

Liam really didn't feel like work today. Or ever again, for that matter. He knew he was too young to start having some sort of midlife conscience crisis. But what he did know was that he didn't want to cycle around town with little packets of powder hidden in his pockets making some cash for himself, but a whole lot more for others. The money was good, there weren't many lads his age making the dough he was making. But Liam was also a realist, knowing that at some point, his luck would run out and there would be a pull from the police and his pockets would be turned out. He wasn't sure of the repercussions of being found in possession of class A drugs, and he knew the police would know he was just acting like a mule and that they would probe him to give up his employers. And there lies the problem, for as scared as he was of the police, he was more scared of them. Liam decided to not text and quit, he knew he lacked the guts, so instead did what worked at home with his mum, which was to ignore the request to do as he was told. The plan worked up until it didn't, up until the messages became more violent and his stomach started turning.

The other three in the flat could see the steely look in Jamal's eyes. Each of them prided themselves on being gangsters, not afraid to give you a tool to settle a dispute, or to use young boys to peddle their drugs. But Jamal was different, he was the next level. He was not only dangerous, but emotionless. And it was those attributes, that made him a psychopath. Jamal was walking busily around the room, his crew having to move their heads from side-to-side to get around him blocking the TV. The room was thick with smoke and the curtains were still drawn, sunlight hadn't entered the room for days, if not weeks.

Jamal didn't suffer insubordination from anyone beneath him, especially that of a young, white boy. He had sent a text: **You want to be messaging me back.**

The text hadn't got a reply, which was why he was pacing across the carpet. Jamal was minus a top, his pigeon chest and wiry arms on full display, but Jamal didn't need a gym freaks body to be dangerous. Power, he knew, comes from presence, and also the ability to pull a trigger on a gun. Jamal had both those qualities. One of the brothers passed him a blunt; stuffed thick with weed and tapered down from the lit end to the roach.

Jamal's fingers were a blur and he sent two back-to-back texts.

Don't play me.

You have work to do. Go do it.

Jamal's jeans were low down around his backside, barely up from the top of his legs and only kept there against their will by a thick belt with a large H serving as the buckle. The bottom of his jeans gathered up, sitting on top of the high-top trainers he was wearing that were crisp white with the logo of jumping Jordan on the heel. The gang made good money, and spent it hard, whether on brasses or bling but Jamal was a saver, he entered into this game with a goal, *make as much as he could, before disappearing and living like a king.* To achieve that goal, he needed everyone around him, and especially those under him, to do as they were told, when they were told, especially young, white boys, those who were disposable. Literally.

Jamal put the phone down on the table that was cluttered with takeaway menus, rizla papers, stained mugs and empty beer bottles. 'Tidy this shit up,' he snapped, as he went through to the kitchen in need of a beer himself to try and settle his temper. By the time he returned, one of the crew, with a head full of cornrows, was at the table putting the trash into a carrier bag. Jamal picked up the phone, hoping for the mule's sake, that he had replied. He hadn't, and the beer hadn't done its job either. The next text said it all:

Don't make me come and find you. Or your family.

The last message sent a shiver through his whole body. The realisation hit him like a freight train. He wasn't delivering packets of powder for pocket money, albeit a lot of pocket money, he was a pawn in an adult's game of gangsterism and worse. And unbeknown to him when he first signed up, he had brought his family into the mix. He read the text again, and it was just as chilling the second time around: **Don't make me come and find you. Or your family.**

And then no sooner did he finish reading it, he ran to the bathroom and emptied the contents of his stomach down the toilet. A few minutes later, after he had scrubbed the bowl with the toilet brush, and wiped his mouth with the back of his hand, he dabbed the towel around his face to wipe dry the water in his eyes that had been caused by the retching. He brushed his teeth to try and remove the taste and then compiled and sent a text:

I'm really sorry, I was ill this morning. But I'm better now and just about to start.

Jamal had got the result he wanted.

Harlan knew the town was renowned for its beaches and decided it was time to see what all the fuss was about. He had carried the second empty bottle back over to the bar and had shoved the two empty crisp packets deep down inside. He had given the barmaid the very faint nod of his head, by means of appreciation and walked out into the summer sunshine back towards the B&B to get his bike. There was something about a Harley, when the sunlight hit the chrome and bounced back off it, creating a shadow on the concrete and giving the silhouette of such a magic, mystical machine. The Iron was a 1200cc, giving it both power and performance. It had the ability to open right up and force the fuel through the cylinders, igniting in a ball of fury. It would leave bystanders shocked at the sound of the thunder the tailpipes would emit. He enjoyed his rides alone. Cruising through the country lanes or ripping up the motorway, weaving at speed with the true feeling of being alive. And that's what an outlaw lived for. That feeling of freedom. But he also missed the club runs. When you would pull out of the clubhouse in a pack, your position was denoted by your status. Out front, the president, next to him, only a couple of feet back, would be the VP, then the Sgt at Arms and Treasurer, and so, all the way down to the latest prospects. At the back, the very back would be the hang-arounds, those on the very first run, if you called it a run, on their journey to become a Satan's Security member, a brother in arms.

Those runs now were a thing of the past, primarily due to his current location, as travelling the country and living out of a backpack made him rarely anywhere near the clubhouse. Being a nomad, a brother without a dedicated charter, worked for some, and it worked for Harlan, it kept him securely in the club, his home, but without the need to attend the weekly and monthly meetings, making votes and paying his dues. Harlan did pay towards the club, he had set up an arrangement with Jim, to pay into the club's running funds. It was done unconventionally by means of a Western Union money transfer to Jim's Old Lady, who would then give her husband the cash. There were a few behind the scenes deals between Harlan and his one-time Pres. The club knew that would happen, and sign-off on them, even if they didn't always know the finer details. That was the command Jim had in his charter, his judgement was never doubted, and never questioned. Harlan had been up and got his helmet, avoiding Stan, not out of rudeness but out of his need to not be caught up in small talk whilst being in the mood to go out and ride. The bike, as always, started on the button. The chugging sound left the exhaust from the two, powerful cylinders and he found himself, as he often did, sitting on the leather seat admiring the noise of his most beloved possession. To bike riders, a motorbike was their pride and joy, to an outlaw, a motorbike was their life.

The ride down to the seafront showed the different sides of the town, affluence in some areas, and poverty in places. No different to anywhere else he had been, but seaside towns just want to keep the slum areas more of a secret, so it doesn't hit the tourism trade.

He pulled down a steep hill and into a car park that

aggressively told its patrons they were being filmed by CCTV cameras and fines would be administered if people didn't pay, which only convinced him not to pay. And if anyone felt brave enough to pop out and put a wheel clamp on his Harley, they would be in need of a good dentist soon after.

Harlan put his bike up on its stand and waited at the kerbside, for the traffic to pass, before crossing the road and stopping off at an ice cream van that had stopped short of the beachside threshold to stop having to pay a costly annual council permit. Harlan liked whoever owned it already, just for their ingenuity and rebelliousness. He perused the menu, or rather, the stickers on the side of the window that had been bleached by the sun and opted for a classic 99. 'Any chance of two flakes, mate?'

'Course. Sauce?'

'Yeah, you've twisted my arm, chocolate. Ta.'

Harlan watched as the ice cream seller swirled the cone under the machine and then found his stare interrupted by two young lads who had dropped their bikes and run up behind him. 'Excuse me, mister, what's that logo? Looks wicked.'

Harlan turned and smiled. 'It's not a logo, kid, it's a lifestyle!'

'Whaddaya mean?'

The young lads were no more than ten, Harlan looked down at them, admiring their brashness, seeing himself in them. 'I mean when you wear the devil, you become one.'

He saw their eyes light up, like they were stepping into some sort of fantasy world, being narrated by a mystical sorcerer. 'What are the skeletons doing?' Asked the chubbier of the two. He had freckles and a bowl hair-cut. He wasn't as cool as his friend.

'The skeletons are bouncers, keeping out those who don't deserve their place in hell.'

'That's so cool, mister,' the other one said. He had a white t-shirt with a big adidas logo on the front and his hair was shaved and faded high up past his ears. He had swag.

'How do we get one?' he asked, wanting to be seen with such a sick image.

'You don't *get* one; you earn one. But what you can get is an ice-cream, what's your poison?' replied Harlan, waiting to see if any of them knew what he meant and was surprised when the one with the chubby cheeks replied. 'I'll have what you've got. And with 2 flakes.'

Harlan smiled to himself as the reminder never judge a book by its cover.

'2 flakes, what?'

'Please,' replied the one with the bowl cut hairstyle.

'Good. And you, sport?'

'Um, I'll....' and Harlan watched him peruse the window like he had minutes earlier.

'Do they sell vapes?'

Harlan went from smiling to laughing, he liked the chutzpah on the kid but needed to do his duty as a responsible adult, 'I don't know, but it's irrelevant. It's an ice cream, or nothing.'

'OK. I'll have a Calypso, orange.'

'Orange, what?'

'Please.'

Harlan repeated the order to the head that was hanging out of the open window and handed over a fiver. The owner went to give him back the change but Harlan told him to put in the charity pot that was on the counter top and attached to the window lever by means of a small chain. Harlan left the kids to their ice creams and headed over to the beach, feeling their eyes still staring at the back of his cut, with the devil staring right back at them.

9

Michael's first two drops since getting restocked went like clockwork. He was following Ryan's mantra of *arrive, deliver, leave*, and it was clear his friend knew what he was talking about. He was doing the numbers in his head as he was going, counting his wages. He wasn't sure if this is what it would be like every day, or how he would bunk off school each day, but for now, all he could do was picture himself getting a new pair of Nikes at the weekend. He was on his way to the next address. Whoever it was wanted three little bags, and for that they got a deal, twenty quid they would save, and as Michael rode his bike, he wondered why everyone didn't take up this offer, too young to understand that not everyone had a spare ton to spend on a party drug. The address was in one of the Charminster back streets, a place notorious for those who want a little chemistry to brighten up their day. The phone sat in the middle of Michael's handlebars and told him he would be there in four minutes and after this one he would get some lunch. A pizza, maybe, or some cheesy chips. He turned off the main road, by the laundrette and cycled the 300 yds to number 157.

Like most of the places he had been to, the house was nothing to look at, but also not shouting to the world that they were the consumers of cocaine. Michael propped his bicycle against the bricked half-wall and walked up to the UPVC door that had a cat flap, although the plastic part was missing, so it was basically just a hole. He went to knock on the door but the person on the other side of the door was already there and the door was opened just before Michael's knuckles got there. Being less than 24hrs to the game, Michael didn't know what to look out for, or who. So far, everybody had been nice; pleasantries, alongside the cash and product, had been exchanged which was why he didn't expect to be pulled inside the open doorway by the collar of his hoodie and then, with the door slammed shut, held up against the wall by his throat.

'Give me all of it. NOW.'

Michael felt the traces of spit land on his cheeks. The person shouting had dilated eyes, and he had said it through gritted teeth and a screwed-up face. He felt the fingers push deeper into his throat, the tips of the fingers like pressure pads.

'I...I..., it's...I...'

'Stop fucking babbling, give me of it, cash an all.'

More spit. More pressure. More fear.

Michael tried to reach his hands into his man-bag but the man who was holding him, both by his throat and against his will, didn't trust him and Michael felt his head come forward before being slammed hard back up against the wall. The speed and force made him bite down on his lip and he felt the stickiness of blood appear almost instantly.

'If you want more, then keep pissing me around.'

'I'm not... I'm not trying to –'

'NOW. For fucks sake.'

Michael went to try again to put his hand into his bag, but slower, and spoke, just.

'It's... it's in here. I'll get it.'

'Damn right, you will.'

Michael couldn't control the shake of his hand that went into the bag, which was why when his hand reemerged, two little packets fell onto the floor. He went to bend down to get them.

'Leave them,' he heard, and followed again by the wall hitting the back of his head.

'Cash. I want the fucking cash.'

Michael's hand went back into the back and came up with a fist full of scrunched up notes, a mixture of colours, and amounts. Probably close to four-hundred quid. He watched as the man, who had a teardrop tattoo under his left eye, frogmarched to the door before opening it up and pushing him out hard by his back. He ran back over to his bike, and was a good two hundred yards or so up the road before the tears started to fall.

Ryan was at the KFC in town. His meal had arrived and he was into the last piece of chicken, a drumstick, his favourite and which he had saved until last. His mouth was full when his mobile rang, and he decided to ignore it. It was his lunch break, after all. The second bite of the chicken drumstick coincided with the second call, making whoever it was, important. Ryan put the chicken down onto the paper and wiped both his hands onto his trousers.

'Shit,' Ryan said, answering the call at the same time as noticing the grease stain he had just induced onto his new, and expensive, grey joggers. 'Mikey, what's up, I'm busy.'

Ryan waited for his friend to speak, and when no words were added, he spoke again, still angered at the stain that he was making worse using the lemon scented wipe that came with the meal. 'Mikey, G, what is it, man? Speak, bruv.'

And that was the problem, his friend couldn't speak, he was still too shaken up.

'Fuck's sake, Mikey, what is it?' and then the penny dropped; there was a problem.

The beach was getting busy, the rising temperature bringing out the sun worshippers. Harlan looked across at the beach front bars and restaurants, trying to work out their rough figures then deducting the extortionate rates the council would charge for such a prime location. He then took what was left, which would have been a tidy profit, but then divided that by twelve-months, as summer trade was just that, whereas overheads are an annual affair. Harlan wasn't sure where he would one day end up, and what he would be doing. He knew he couldn't bust heads for a living, age would one day put pay to that. And that was the thing, no matter how tough you were, time beats everyone, someday, and it is that someday, when you stop being a something, and instead, became just a someone. The truth was, he didn't expect to even live this long. A decade of fast living in his twenties, where late nights and fistfights were the norm, followed by another decade of barroom brawling meant he was still lucky to be alive, plus, he knew being an outlaw didn't come with a pension plan. Harlan knew that someday he would need an *out*. Someday.

The sun was making him sweat, being dressed head to toe in black wasn't always a good idea, and the last of his ice-cream had melted and ran down his forearm before he could stop it with his tongue. He had taken a seat on one of the benches and looked at the sea, when he wasn't stamping his feet to shoo away the seagulls which were testing his shoestring patience. He felt his phone ring in his pocket, taking his attention away from both the scenic view and the damned seagulls. It was Mouse. He was known for coming back quickly, but this was quick, even for him.

'H, you good to talk?'

'Yeah, course. What you got?'

'In a nutshell. Not a lot.'

'Great call.'

Harlan was about to end the conversation, but Mouse beat him to the red button.

'I mean, it's not a big thing now, my contacts say it still goes on, but no real *faces* anymore, and even the skin-heads are out.'

'Meaning no real firms, just some chancers loving a tear-up?'

'Pretty much. I know the London teams still have a presence, but the big players are out.'

'OK, seeing as this phone call was about as much use as wiping my arse with a flip flop, I have one more thing I need you to check, but it may not lead anywhere.'

'Shoot.'

'Cherry Pickers, and no, I don't mean the hired machines that lift you up high, I mean a football firm called The Cherry Pickers.'

'You're down Bournemouth way, then?'

'Yeah, for now.'

'OK, I'll ask around but don't expect much, I think you'll need to ask around locally.'

'Yeah, I thought as much, but forewarned is forearmed, as we like to say.'

It was a saying the MC held dear, which was why members like Mouse were so crucial to the club; it was just as much about what you knew, as who.

'Leave it with me, brother.'

'Cheers, Mouse. I appreciate it.'

Harlan ended the call and went back to the view.

Ryan immediately lost his appetite. The drumstick now unfinished, the last few chips gone cold and the thick, gloopy gravy had started to congeal. He felt stuck to the shiny, slippery seat. His friend, now his employee, had just been roughed up and the gear and cash taken. It now fell on Ryan to sort, as he wasn't allowed to bring other lads into the fold without thorough vetting from his bosses. The realisation then hit him hard, he would need to put right the loss personally. He had told his friend to meet him at his house but Michael refused. He was too scared and wanted to go home. He called Michael back and on the third call his friend answered.

'Mikey, man, you just can't ignore me, bruv.'

'Sor... I... I just don't want –'

'I know. I know. But we got to put this right. He has my gear.'

'Please, Ryan, just leave it. It's not worth it.'

'I can't, bruv. I can't leave it.'

If Michael knew him well enough, that's when he would have been able to decipher the fear in his voice from the bravado. Ryan knew he was in a dark place, and there was no light ahead. He couldn't go back to his bosses, informing them he had inadvertently lost their drugs, and worse, their cash. Which left only one option, trying to get it back himself.

Ryan left the restaurant, shaky on his feet and over to his bike that was leaning against the lamppost. He pulled out a pouch of tobacco and tried to roll a fag before getting on his bike but his fingers weren't working, they were too busy showing signs of worry. The town centre was busy, people all around him, mums holding the hands of their children, and Ryan felt a pave of jealousy and envy come over him. He wanted a coherent mum, but more so, right now he wanted to be an innocent child. His burner beeped again; and for the first time he didn't want to see who it was who had messaged. He pulled it from his man-bag slowly, fearing the worst; but it was just another address; another punter.

The task of getting their drugs and cash would have to wait, for now, but unfortunately, it wouldn't wait forever.

Harlan was back on his bike, riding along the beachfront, still savouring both the scenery and the smell. Fresh, salty air entered his lungs and he liked what the town had to offer, so far. His mind went back to Big Al, and his little problem. It was unusual to take on a pub or club that didn't have a criminal problem, or a criminal element. Harlan had no issue with criminals, or how they made their money. The problem only came if it caused him a problem regarding the venue he was being paid to protect, and even then, if there was a criminal face behind it, it was never personal, only ever business. But Alan's problem was different. There weren't drugs being dealt or girls being pimped. It hadn't been taken over and fronted by a *face,* or profits being taken by a gang of chancers. This was different; a football firm had arranged vicious fights on Alan's property and then taken over his bar and called it their own every match day, scaring his customers and drinking his beer in the process. Which made the firm nothing more than bullies. And Harlan hated bullies.

He saw an empty stretch of road on the other side of the red light and as he waited; two cars back from the front, he sat there flicking the throttle. Short bursts of fury leaving the pipes. The light never had a chance to get to green before Harlan opened up the throttle, overtaking the two bland cars and was soon roaring past the beachside apartments leaving nothing behind him except the sound of an angry Harley being ridden by an angry outlaw.

'Chrissake, Beth, where's my away shirt?'

Colin was checking the wardrobe, angrily flicking through the neatly pressed clothes that were on hangers having been ironed by a dutiful wife. 'For fucks sake, Beth.'

It was darts night at Colin's local and he wanted the town's away shirt, and so far, he couldn't find it. His wife of six years, Beth, knew when her husband was losing his temper. She also knew it always involved football. 'It's in there,' she shouted back up the stairs.

'It fucking isn't,' came the reply, from inside their bedroom. 'Beth, fucks sake.'

He heard his wife come up the stairs and she entered the bedroom, wearing her open-toed slippers that had cost him the best part of fifty-quid at Christmas. He didn't mind spoiling the family, but in return, he wanted an easy life, regular sex and his football shirts there when he wanted. Colin watched as his wife, who was just a little over five-foot, stood up on her tiptoes and sifted through the hangers trying to prove him wrong. Beth came away from the wardrobe empty handed with her confidence now crestfallen.

'Fuck's sake, you know I have darts,' Colin said, in a way that made her feel like shit.

'Funny how the kids' shit is always washed and ironed,' Colin added.

'God's sake, Colin, it's not like that at all. That's so unfair.'

Colin grabbed her by her arm, his fingers clasping tightly the bare flesh of her bicep.

'Don't mouth me off, Beth.' Colin's voice had gone from shouting to being sinister.

He held her arm for a few seconds, so his message could sink in before releasing his grip.

His wife rubbed her arm and left the bedroom, to find his beloved away shirt and to dry her eyes. Colin checked his watch, a £5k piece that he treated himself to, and it wasn't helping his mood. He should have left by now and instead he was waiting for his wife to find him his shirt. Finally, Beth arrived, his shirt draped over her forearm apologising profusely as he slipped it over his naked torso, covering the tattoo of a British Bulldog proudly sitting in front of a St George's flag. Colin walked past Beth, who was standing up against the beech-coloured wooden door, stopping to give her a kiss, like nothing had happened.

Colin didn't notice his wife wipe her mouth with the back of her hand as he walked down the stairs, which was just as well.

Ryan's burner had been quiet for forty minutes. It was as if the universe was talking to him, telling it was now or never. Time to avenge his friend and get back their drugs. Ryan had resisted the temptation to call his older brother, Rob, who had a reputation of liking a good row. It wasn't Rob's beef, therefore not his problem. Ryan had kept his drug running away from his brother, instead telling him his cash was coming from stealing from shops and selling his wares to his friends. Ryan didn't think Rob would like him mixed up with drugs, and as much as they had sibling rivalry, he wanted his older brother to respect him and he wasn't sure that would be the case if he knew he was a drug runner. That loyalty to his brother left him with nowhere to go except to go alone. It was his problem. Ryan was already in Charminster, at the opposite end of the high street, having made a £40 drop. It was time to grab himself by his balls and get some respect for himself. He lifted his hood up over his head and pulled up his snood and set off in the direction of Sycamore Road, destination, 157.

Ryan pulled across the traffic, getting an angry honk of the horn from the DPD driver he cut in front of, then rode past the laundrette into Sycamore Road, passing barking dogs roaming around gated gardens and boarded up windows. His phone told him 157 was just up on the right. He turned his handlebars and mounted the kerb, riding the last few yards on the pavement. He pulled up outside the house, his nerves being hidden by his teenage temper, and he was here to right a wrong, and maybe make a name for himself, sending a message that you don't fuck with the double R, a crew name he had made up on the ride over, bringing together the initials of him and his brother.

Ryan dropped his stolen bike on the street, blocking off the pavement to anyone who may be walking by. Normally his instincts would tell him to look both ways before stepping onto a property but he wasn't relying on instincts now, instead he was operating on gut feel. It was ignoring his street acquired instinct that made him miss the twitch of the filthy, and torn, net curtain that alerted the occupant to his arrival. As he approached, Ryan wished that he was carrying, a strap, preferably, or even a blade, but he had nothing upon him aside from swagger, and that was diminishing on each step he was taking to the door that had some sort of hole at the bottom. Ryan furled his fingers into a fist and knocked at the door, whilst trying to settle his breathing. He heard the sound of a chain, and of a lock being turned and then focused his eyes on the door handle that would turn next.

'I've already got my gear, man.'

The voice was polite. Disarming. And it caught Ryan on the backfoot.

'Um... listen, my pal came –', and Ryan knew by saying the word pal he had made himself sound, just as he looked, a young kid trying to play a tough guy. He tried to correct himself.

'A member of my crew came here earlier, with your blow.'

'Oh, your crew? Well excuse me, Mr Peaky Blinder.'

Ryan saw a row of yellow teeth smirk, and the teardrop tattoo appeared to mock him, too.

He tried to hide his faltering voice, 'And you bumped him, G. That's not on, bruv.'

'Yeah, mate. I get it. I'm sorry. Look, come inside and I'll get your dough.'

Ryan went to step inside but stopped, unsure if he was being played.

'Quick, man. I have nosey neighbours; I don't want them seeing our business.'

Ryan knew in the game of doing drugs, secrecy was big so Ryan took the invite. The man with the teardrop tattoo stood to the side of the door and Ryan squeezed past him, out of sight, and out of mind. Ryan heard the front door shut behind him, and that was the last thing he heard.

10

Harlan played the odds, which was why he had bought two portions of fish and chips. Stan was sitting in his armchair, watching his favourite early evening gameshow, when he walked in and put his head around the door. 'Stan, you eaten?'

'No, not yet. Why?'

'I've got you cod and chips. Where's the plates at?'

'Have you? Then the least I can do is dish up.'

'You mean the least you can do is make the tea.'

'You and your bloody tea. Sugar?'

'Three. Ta.'

'Three, what, don't you like your teeth or something.'

'Just get your crinkly old ass out there and make the tea. And don't be doing that limping shit, either.' Harlan could hear Stan laughing down the hallway and into the kitchen.

Ten minutes later and Harlan had finished and he was eyeing up Stan's plate that was resting on the arm of his chair, with a quarter of the battered fish left waiting, plus some mushed up, mushy peas. 'Are you going to finish that?' he asked, directing Stan's eyes to his unfinished plate.

'I'm done. Why, want it?'

'I will feel bad for the Third World if I don't,' replied Harlan, a grin coming over his face.

'Take it. And then after, you can take the plates,' Stan said, his own grin becoming a hearty laugh. Harlan stood up and walked over to the plate, picking it up and taking a bite straight out of the fish before he even got back to his seat. 'You sure do like your food, big boy.'

Harlan went to reply, but his mum always told him it was rude to talk with your mouth full.

He finished off the last of Stan's dinner and sat and watched the end of the quiz show. When it finished Stan started to flick through the channels with the remote, which had a piece of parcel tape holding it together, before settling in on a programme about cash in people's attics. Harlan couldn't contain his boredom and decided doing the dishes was better than the drivel his eyes were being subjected to, so he left the room with a plate in each hand. The kitchen was small, and cluttered. Pots and pans were hanging from hooks on a fake beam and there were two microwaves sat side-by-side on the worktop. They were different heights, widths and colours, which played havoc with Harlan's OCD. The kitchen, although compact, was tidy. Stan ran a tight ship but even so, Harlan knew he could do with some help around the place. He pulled down the front of the cheap model dishwasher and loaded in the two plates, at the bottom, leaving a space between them believing they would wash better. He flicked the kettle and pulled a mug from the stand, checking it for cleanliness and then instantly feeling bad for doing so before putting it down on the side and tossing in a teabag. His burner phone rang and he lifted it from his pocket. It was Mouse, again.

'H, I have a bit more intel. I mean it's not much, but it's something.'

'What you got, brother?'

'I went back to it, what's that saying, curiosity called the cat, something like that, anyways.'

'It killed the cat, but whatever.'

'Yeah. Whatever. Anyway, this football fighting is now arranged on the dark web, on some punk ass forums. www.wannabeaganster type shit, lol.'

Harlan laughed at Mouse's turn of phrase, and appreciated his brother sticking with it.

'What do these forums say?' he asked.

'Basically, it's where they arrange the meets. Back of factory car parks, industrial estates, shit like that. It still goes on, just more underground, like my fellas said.'

'What about the Cherry Pickers, do they get mentioned?'

'That's what I'm calling for, someone was online just a minute ago, setting up a meet.'

'Did you get the name?'

'Yeah. Well, their username at least. Some geezer by the name of 'BigDogCol', and you are going to love the next bit.'

'Go on?'

'Big, Dog, Col, is anything but. I mean for a start he ain't no dog, and two, he ain't big.'

'Meaning he's small time?'

'No, I mean he is small. Like Papa Smurf, small.'

Harlan gave another laugh, this time at the smurf analogy. 'So, what do we know?'

'Not too much, yet. His socials are pretty shut down

but I am getting the vibe he doesn't get a payslip with how he makes his bread. Making him one of us.'

'No, Mouse. Not one of us. We may fall foul of the law, but we don't fall foul of our code.'

'You know what I meant.'

'No, do you know what I *mean?*'

'Yeah, totally. Anything else you need, brother?'

'Give me an hour.'

'Sweet. Hit me up soon.'

'Later,' Harlan said, meaning he was out, the conversation was done.

Colin licked the tip on both his forefinger and thumb before placing his foot up against the wooden up-stand that was slotted into the holes in the thick carpet. It was four apiece, the outcome resting on this last game, and Colin was up next, throwing for the match. He picked out the first dart of the three from his open palm then steadied his left hand before zeroing his eye on his intended double. Just as he was about to throw the dart, he heard a noise, a celebratory sound, and it was coming over by the fruit machine.

'Oi, dickhead.' All the players turned to face whoever it was Colin had released his fury on.

The fruit machine player was no more than nineteen, wearing the same brand jacket and cap. There was a little strip of tartan on both. His face had gone from smiling at having pocketed twenty quid to nervousness at a raft of pissed-off stares from having put off a player on their throw. What the young lad didn't know, was that the player he had crudely interrupted, happened to be Colin, the leader of the Cherry Pickers. 'I'm sorry, mate. I was miles away.'

'You'll wish you were miles away, you annoying little prick.'

'Hey, mate, I said I'm sorry.' The reply sounded more antagonistic than it was meant to.

Colin pushed his way through the crowd of players, commanding a leadership position, a position he felt at home in. '*Mate?* We aren't mates. I've had better shits than you.'

'It's okay, I'm leaving,' said the young lad with the branded apparel.

'Yeah, good idea, shit head, whilst you can still walk.'

Colin watched the asshole fall out of the young lad which brought a smile across his clean-shaven face, a face that came with a full neck and the start of a double chin. The lad went to scoop out the pound coins from the tray inside the machine.

'Nah, leave that there. Call it a rudeness tax.'

The sentence was clear. So too, the intent.

The young lad pulled his hand clear of the coins, and shoved it into his jean pocket, doing the same with his other hand. He gave a fleeting glance over in the direction of the dart team, but avoided direct eye contact before dropping his head down and heading for the door. The last thing the young lad heard as he pulled open the heavy door was the sound of sneering laughter coming from the direction of the peppered dartboard.

Colin took a breath, steadied his hand, then hit the winning double.

.   .   .

Harlan read the message back: **I still think about you. I wish I didn't. But I do.**

He wasn't sure if the feeling of regret was for sending the text, or for everything that had gone before it. He hadn't moved on, and now, he no longer tried. The memories weren't as frequent, but were still as vivid and for that he was glad. He dragged his thumb across the screen, bringing the message with him. It revealed a dustbin sat on top of a red background. He dabbed the screen and confirmed the request and watched the message turn to dust.

He put the phone back down. It didn't need charging; it very rarely did. He felt tight, his muscles knotted, and knew this was caused by stress, self-induced stress, stress caused by making not bad decisions, but the wrong ones. He had trained himself to put his body through pain when he felt like this, to push himself up and down until his biceps burned, to lean forwards and backwards until his stomach felt like it was going to split. Harlan took off his t-shirt and tossed it into the corner of his room, covering yesterday's underwear as it hit the wall and slid down onto the pile. He twisted his upper body from right to left, then rolled his arms and shoulders both forward and backwards. The pre-workout was done, it was now time to destress.

Ryan didn't hear his phone ring. Owing to the fact that he was unconscious.

The set of press-ups were done. The final few had caused his forearms to shake, almost uncontrollably, his fists were buried deep and his fingers had started to whiten. Harlan had pulled his hair into a short ponytail, just to stop it falling into his grimacing face as he lifted his body weight up and down. The burner phone rang again, giving Harlan a brief respite, and if he was honest with himself, he was glad of the break. For the third time today, it was Mouse. 'H, I've come up trumps.'

'What you got?'

'A way in. A way to reach out to the Cherry Pickers. Well, Colin big boy, to be exact.'

'Mouse, if you weren't an outlaw, St Peter would welcome you with open arms.'

'I am going to hell, brother, as my patch keeps telling me.'

'Good. I'll meet you there.'

'Ha. Brothers forever, forever brothers, right?'

'Until the last ride, brother. Until the last ride,' replied Harlan.

'It's an encrypted number.'

'Do I need a smart phone to call it?' Harlan asked.

'Nah, straightforward burner should do it.'

'Ok. Hit me.'

Mouse reeled off the eleven digits which Harlan wrote down on the small pad that was on the bedside cabinet.

'Anything else, you need?'

'I'm good for now. I'll let you know if it changes. Do me a favour, buy a round for the boys.'

'Yeah, will do.'

'I'll square you when I see you next. '

'No sweat H – I know you're good for it.'

And Harlan was, he paid his way and cleared his debts. That was another code he lived by.

. . .

Jamal had slammed the phone down so hard on the table the battery cover flew off, landing on the floor. Jamal watched it fly through the air and then when it settled, he went to kick it but missed, which then made him stomp down hard on the tiny piece of plastic and splinter it out of shape. The kids weren't supposed to say no, ignore, or go AWOL, that wasn't how fear worked, meaning they clearly weren't that afraid of him. Which meant lessons needed to be learned, and repercussions needed to be felt. Jamal wasn't about to let anyone derail his plan; the plan to get in, get rich, and get gone.

'Yo. Pass me another phone,' Jamal ordered, to no-one in particular.

The one closest was slouched down deep in the sofa and had a full ashtray balancing on his left thigh. He reached into his jean pocket and pulled out a phone and held out his arm, the thick gold, curbed bracelet dangling down off his wrist.

Jamal swiped the phone, read the number from the backless phone and entered it into the one he had just been passed. He rang it again and again, and heard it ring through to voicemail.

'Shit,' Jamal shouted, at the wall, and a slither of saliva dropped from his mouth and landed on his whimsical, wispy beard.

'We may need to go out. Some of dem boys aren't picking up. Punters aren't getting their food. Fucks sake.'

The Somalian gangster sat in the single seat; cream, cracked leather, stood up and pulled the handgun from his waistband, then imitated pulling the trigger at the imaginary young kid who was begging for forgiveness by his feet.

'Nah, no guns. Not until I say so.'

The darts had finished, and Colin had used a small cluster of the coins the young lad had left to buy himself another pint. As he took a large gulp, the glint of his gold tooth that sat at the back of his mouth. To his teammates, he was brash, boisterous but funny. To certain teammates, he was the leader of the crew; The Cherry Pickers, determined to fight their way to infamy, and put their town on the map. Colin had started to feel bad for how he had spoken to Beth, and knew he needed to apologise, because he needed to get his leg over.

He knew he was over the limit. But the limit didn't matter. What mattered was the name he was making for himself. The name that propelled his position, and inflated his ego.

Not so small, now, eh, he said to himself, in his head. The statement was intended to be heard by someone, the someone who made his life hell when he was a kid. When he was picked on for his size. His dinner money taken and on one occasion, his head flushed down the toilet. But that was then, this was most definitely now. *Not so small now, eh.*

The off-licence wasn't far away, and he could have walked, but then why have a bike. He had been mindful of Stan's customers and neighbours, keeping the sound of the powerful engine down to a minimum. The shop was empty when he got there, and the young girl behind the counter barely looked up from her phone when he walked in. She had ginger hair and freckles, wearing a pink hoodie over a black t-shirt sporting a large motif of something he had never heard of. Harlan walked down through the two aisles, past the packaged food and the toiletries. The far wall was full of cheap wines and over-priced spirits. He still couldn't see what he was after. He walked back to the counter, opposite the ginger-haired girl with the pink hoodie on her phone, separated only by a selection of sweets and chocolate. 'Can I help you?' she asked, sounding less than interested and annoyed at being disturbed.

'Sorry to be a customer, my bad. But as I'm here, and you're being paid to be, shall we focus on customer service, you never know, you could be good at it. I doubt it, though.'

The look on her face went from sour, to apologetic, to that of a smile, when she took in his full features. The weathered face, with a faint tan. Long, shaggy hair. A beard, a blend of sculpted and bushy. It was his broad shoulders and the leather vest that further garnered her desire, and created the smile. Harlan was less than interested, you had a few seconds to impress him, and she hadn't. Harlan liked to show respect until he needed to rescind it, he got to that stage with the ginger-haired girl behind the counter in the first seconds of entering, and then confirmed with her first four words.

'I'm after a mobile phone. Preferably one with some charge in it.'

'I'll have a look,' she replied, the smile still there; the smile still ignored.

He watched her take a step back before bending down looking under the counter, coming up with two boxes. One box said Nokia, the other being a brand he hadn't heard of.

Harlan was a creature of habit, which was why he pointed to the one in her right hand; the Nokia. 'How much?' he asked. His hand was already in his pocket to pull out the cash.

She turned the box around, hunting for the little white label, her boss still using ticket guns to price his products. '£19.99.'

Harlan peeled off a twenty, and handed it over. He waited as her pink, false nails clacked into the till and then it opened, a tray full of change coming into view. She went into one of the smaller compartments, her finger trying to slide out the single copper change.

'No, it's fine. I'll take it, it comes with a sim?'

She read the back of the box, scanning for an answer to his question, wanting to be helpful.

'Yeah. Says here that it does.'

'Good. I need a top-up voucher. A tenner will do.'

She went through the carousel of top-up vouchers, and pulled free the one for his handset. Harlan took a tenner from the folded-up pile of notes that was still in his hand and went to hand it over. 'No, it's on me.'

'No. It's not.' And he put the ten-pound note down on the counter and walked out carrying the phone. The rucksack was hanging from the handlebars, and he unzipped it, put the box inside and then zipped it back up, then put his arms through it, one by one, and fired up his bike for the ride back to his room.

The Porsche pulled up on the drive and Colin rummaged around in the centre console, looking for some mints, or some gum. He found neither. Still, it was an attempt to freshen his breath before he kissed her, and it's the thought that counts. He got out and walked towards the front door, and felt steady enough on his feet. He pressed down on the key fob and as the front door opened, the headlights on his beloved car switched themselves off. The lights downstairs were off. His wife had gone up for the night and he knew he shouldn't wake her but winning at darts always made him horny. He walked through to the kitchen and pulled open the door on the American style fridge-freezer. He was hungry but the thought of making a sandwich seemed like too much hassle, so he opted for one of the kids' microwavable burgers. Colin hadn't registered the first ding on his mobile, instead believing it to be the sound of the microwave, telling him his cheeseburger was ready. It was only when the pinging sound went again, did he connect the dots to his mobile. There was a new notification. An unknown number. He thumbed in his passcode with his thumb, his other hand occupied by the burger and dabbed onto the message icon and read it:

I hear you think you boys are tasty. Let's see. Get your crew together on match day.

Colin couldn't hide the smile coming across his face. He took another large mouthful of the imitation meat and then, just using his thumb, typed a reply. **Game on.**

The second smile was bigger and lasted longer than the first. He didn't fancy anymore of the burger; it was time to wake his wife up for sex.

Harlan smiled. The text had worked. People were so predictable. Whoever Colin was, he didn't know the art of war, which was to first learn your enemy. He looked across at the three phones. Two burners and one smartphone. Tonight's phone was bought purely for a purpose. To connect with BigDogCol; or Colin to his friends. Harlan knew Colin wanted a reputation, it was the same for many that he had come up against, but reputations, like respect, were earned, and it was time for Colin to find out all about his reputation, and to learn some respect. The reply had come pretty much instantly, **Game on.** Which Harlan knew was Colin's mistake. This wasn't a game for Harlan, for him, fighting was his profession.

Harlan looked out the window, out to yet another landscape, another town with no name. It would be another night in another strange bed. Another night alone. The workout hadn't helped. Normally it did, but tonight felt different. There wasn't a reason, not really. It wasn't a special date, but he supposed that's what made it worse. It didn't take long to make a lifetime worth of memories and missed moments. Harlan stepped away from the window, and let the curtain fall. Reminiscing, like guilt; which were often one and same thing, served no purpose. He was there; she was somewhere else, maybe, with someone else. That was the problem with this life that he chose; too many somethings. He flicked the kettle and made himself the last cup of tea of the day.

11

Rob thumped on his younger brother's door. 'Get up you lazy shit. Tyson needs to go out.'

There was no reply, which only fuelled his fire. Tyson had been bought for the pair of them, by their mum, a belated Christmas present purchased with a bingo win. Tyson wasn't a pedigree; he came as a six-month old puppy with a crooked tail and fleas. Rob was twelve when the dog arrived, and his younger brother was just a nipper. It became a common bond between them, with Rob teaching Tyson some party tricks and Ryan wanting him in his room at bedtime. As Rob got older, and smoking weed and getting off with girls became his new favourite pastime, the walks started getting less and less and Tyson started getting fat, and then started to get obese. When Rob started earning a wage, labouring on a building site and getting a ton a week in wages, his solution was to pay his younger brother to walk the dog, starting off at a couple of quid, but now, with Ryan wanting more for less, it was a tenner a week deal to walk the dog. He checked his phone; just enough time for a quick coffee and a bowl of corn flakes, providing of course they weren't stale, or gone. Rob put his head around the door of the living room, she was there, in yesterday's clothes, and snoring.

Rob was used to seeing his mum asleep on the couch, sometimes with her medication, sometimes with empty cans of cider, but all too often, both. The snoring confirmed his mum wouldn't need a coffee, as all too often he had taken in a cup, be it the living room or in her room, to find the cup still there several hours later, full, and with a film of skin around the inside of the mug. Tyson was wagging his tail when Rob entered the kitchen, unsure if he wanted breakfast, or a wee.

Rob tilted the box for all it was worth, determined to get a full bowl of cereal. He searched amongst the cutlery on the draining board for a clean spoon, or cleanish. He opened the door and then stood up against the sink, spooning cereal into his mouth. He watched Tyson run around the garden looking for a place to cock his leg. He checked his phone again; his lift would be arriving any minute. He tipped the bowl up to his mouth and slurped up the last of the milk and then took a large mouthful of coffee before tipping what was left down the side of the bowl in the sink, which was full of plates, all stained with various colourful sauces.

Tyson ran in and sat by his bowl, hinting that he was hungry. 'Chrissake, dog.'

Rob checked his phone again, surprised his lift wasn't angrily honking his horn outside. He took a tin from the cupboard. The label read "chicken". Rob very much doubted that to be true as he pulled the ring pull and watched the gelatine slop fall into the red, plastic, chewed bowl. Rob ran back upstairs and stormed across the landing towards the door with the fist-sized hole in it. His fist. He slammed his open palm onto his younger brother's door and bellowed, 'Get up, NOW. Lazy prick.'

Nothing.

'I mean it Ry, get up before I come in there and drag you out. You're pissing me off now.'

Nothing.

Rob put his hand on the handle, about to barge in and forcibly remove his brother from his pit, but just as the handle went down, Rob heard the angry honk from the transit van that was now outside waiting for him. He took his hand off the handle, cursing out loud as he ran down the stairs, stopping to grab his fluorescent vest from around the bannister and slammed the door behind him. If he would have opened Ryan's bedroom door, he would have seen he wasn't there.

Harlan had sent a text to Alan, telling him to meet him at the pub for a coffee, in his case, a tea. The plan was already devised in his head. He wasn't meeting Alan for his agreement; he was merely just going to enlighten him on what was about to happen. The dining room was quiet. Only two tables were taken. One, a couple, middle-aged, or very close to it. They had natural yoghurt pots in front of them, and a bowl of fruit. There were two glasses of orange juice, one fuller than the other. It was the other table that he was more interested in. They seemed happier. The child was on her lap, and she was bouncing her left leg up and down, the child smiling on each bounce. Harlan could see the makeup was working, the welt being better concealed, it was just a shame it was there in the first place. But at least she was here, both safe and sound. He didn't know what the future held for her, but for now, the future could wait. He decided to forgo breakfast, he had told Stan to keep his act of hospitality a secret, but he wasn't sure if he had, and he didn't want any awkward moments, or worse, an awkward conversation. It was a random act of kindness, and he wanted it kept that way.

He knew also, that maybe his act of altruism could cause her some concern, thinking there would be some sort of ulterior motive. There wasn't, but rather than explain it, his non-interest in her would confirm it.

Harlan had misjudged the morning traffic and was getting frustrated with the constant snarl-ups, added to that, the constant wave of roadworks and temporary traffic lights. By the time he got to the pub he had made a mental note not to live in a seaside town with a city-sized traffic problem. Harlan wasn't a fan of either congestion, or road traffic planning officers, believing the latter caused the former. He leaned the bike over on its stand and walked over to the pub, still cussing to himself on why a three-mile journey should take the best part of twenty minutes.

'Morning,' said Alan, oblivious to Harlan's bad mood.

'Why does anyone here own a car, it would be quicker to walk. Backwards!'

'Get caught up in it, did you?'

'Caught up in it, my bike is going to need a fresh MOT the time that took. Ridiculous.'

Big Al nodded his head, not quite knowing what to add so instead played it safe, 'Tea?'

Harlan nodded in return, a cup of tea would help, that was, if it was drinkable.

'And can you make it without the need to have to steam clean my teeth after.'

Big Al wasn't sure how to take him yet, unsure on his sense of humour, or if he had one. Harlan watched as he went out the back and used the time to check his latest burner. There was a message: **I'll let you know the time and location today.** It didn't take an Oxford Scholar to figure out who the message was from, as only BigDogCol had this number. He was still looking at the screen when Big Al returned with a mug in one hand, and a fresh packet of bourbons in the other, having stopped off at the shop purposely.

Big Al placed the piping mug down, and then blew on his fingers to cool them down.

'Okay, why we here so early?' asked Alan.

'Because,' Harlan replied, before biting into a dunked biscuit, then continued, 'I said so.'

Alan recoiled, the curtness was cutting, just the way it was intended. He continued.

'I'm going to go through one last time. You, unfortunately, have found yourself in my world. And my world isn't nice. In my world, tough times call for even tougher decisions, and in my world, violence only ends when someone steps in who is more violent.'

Harlan let the words sink in for a few seconds before carrying on. 'You are dealing with some boneheads who believe this pub, your business, is their own HQ. And I'm about to tell them, in my own special way, that it isn't.'

'Is this shit going to get worse?' Alan asked.

'It isn't going to get any better,' Harlan replied, and he

watched Al's face drop. 'Until it gets better. And that's why I'm here. To make shit right.'

Alan picked up his stooped head and for the first time since they met, Harlan saw a real look of fire in his eyes. Big Al was back in the game, Harlan knew, even if his tea was shit.

Harlan dunked the last part of the biscuit and waited until his mouth was empty before speaking. 'I have set a little something up.'

'What sort of something?' Big Al asked.

'Let's just say you might want to sell burgers on the day.'

'Mate, I've heard you're good. The best. But there are loads of them and only one of you.'

Harlan smiled. Then dunked another biscuit.

'Yo. Get me more kids,' hissed Jamal. The complaints from the no-shows last night had worsened his mood. The safe door was open, stacks of cash looking out at him but that didn't put a smile on his skeletal face. He wanted more, and he wanted subordinates.

'Still no word, Jam?' asked one of the brothers.

'No. And jam is what you put on bread. It's Jamal. What is it...?'

The brother wasn't sure if he was joking, and he found himself pulling a half-smile.

'I said. What's. My. Name?'

All eyes fell on the brother, the half-smile turning into one of nerves. 'Jamal.'

'Correct. Keep it that way. Now go and find some kids. And vet them. Thoroughly.'

Jamal watched as his crew got up off the chairs and

made their way single file out of the living room. The thick fog refused to follow, instead stayed firm and intact, hanging just below the ceiling, patiently for the crew to return and resume smoking. The room didn't know what time it was, the curtains never letting in natural light. If the tables had wraps of tin foil and needles, it would be called a crack den, as it was, only cannabis was consumed here, and instead of a den, it was base camp one. And Jamal was the General.

He looked at what was left. Half of the half, gone. He knew he would need to reach out to the one person that he needed, and Jamal hated needing anyone.

The gang had stopped for a brew, meaning Rob could have a break from shovelling sand into the mixer. It was back breaking work. And dirty. By the end of the day his rigger boots would have a sticky clump of cement stuck to his soles and his t-shirt equally stained from rubbing his hands across his midriff. The constant shovelling had created calluses on his hands. The constant fighting had caused scuffs on his knuckles. Being both the newbie and the non-skilled, meant when the gang stopped, it was down for him to make the tea. He hated being a labourer, being the bitch, but that's what bunking off school had resulted in. He knew, already, he would regret that decision, opting to play truant, so to play the arcades, rather than revise. It was that reason why he was shovelling in the sand, rather than laying down the bricks. 'Robbie. What's the crack, I'm fucking gasping.'

Rob had added the teabags and was topping up the mugs, not bothering to wash them. Builders seemed to prefer their tea with bits of the site floating in it. Perhaps that's why they called it builders tea, Robbie thought, as he gave each mug a stir.

He sat on an upturned beer crate, which had become his go-to chair, so much so, it went in the back of the van every night. It was during tea break that he checked his phone. And it was because he was checking his phone that he saw the text: **Game on.** A coded text.

The gang didn't see the smile that came across his face. He had a tear-up to look forward to.

The sausage and egg sandwich Beth had made him had hit the spot. The expensive coffee, made from the expensive machine, had washed it down well. His wife had left him to his phone, knowing not to ask questions when he was calling his friends discussing meeting up to watch the football. What she didn't know was watching the match came second to the real reason he was ringing around his mates. Colin knew he had a staunch firm, and a strong customer base. On fight days he would make a tidy packet on his tiny packets. He made it clear that no-one else could sell coke in the firm, that was his gig, and his alone. The garden wasn't sprawling, it was a new-build house so it was compact, but laid with plastic grass and a raised decking area that housed his new BBQ. There was the small goal post, for when he fancied a kick about with his stepson, keen to get him into football, and maybe, one day, fighting. Colin was a man's man, and was keen for his boy to turn out the same way. Beth had wanted a puppy, but Colin had made it clear, it was to be a British Bulldog or nothing, so Beth's hopes for a Cockapoo were on hold for now, or until he had mellowed, but there was no chance of that happening anytime soon. His phone pinged; a reply: **Game on.**

Colin smiled; and added Rob's name to the list on his notepad.

The new burner, bought with a sole purpose, was laying on the bar top, looking up at him, just waiting for an instruction. Harlan had already hooked Colin, and it had been easy. If it was the other way around, Harlan would have done some due diligence. He would have asked some loose questions, intended to reveal the size of the firm reaching out. To see if they were worth confronting, was there anything to gain in this meet. He knew the old school firms would do that; they wanted scalps, literally and figuratively speaking. They would want to be known as the *Top Firm,* the ones other cities would want to be, but now, as Mouse had confirmed, the romanticism, if there was any, had gone. It had gone underground, and under the radar, but it was also unnoticed, career criminals didn't want to be involved in mindless violence, meaning the Cherry Pickers were chancers, not gangsters.

It was time for a reply; to control the narrative. Big Al was putting the hoover around, and had stopped asking questions. Which was good, as Harlan had made it clear he wasn't there to answer them. He had a job to do, and he would do it well. But as for explanations, there weren't to be any, plus it wasn't what people did that put people in prison, it was what people said, so for Harlan, the less these people knew, the better. He picked up the burner and entered the message area. He thought for a second about his reply before typing:

I'm not hanging around. You up for this, or what?
He read it back and then sent it.

The message was designed to be impatient and inviting. *Let's see what you're made of, Colin.*

Harlan beckoned Alan over, there was business to discuss, time to talk profits. Alan stepped on the button on top of Henry the hoover's head, and walked over, panting and having already untucked his cheesecloth shirt from inside his jeans. 'What's up?' he asked.

'Take the weight off your feet, let's talk recovery plans.'

'In what sense?' Alan asked, unsure where the conversation was going.

'You are taking a hit. You are losing at least a day and a half of sales, and weekend sales, we need this problem gone, but after, I think you need a new reputation. Agree?'

'Right now, I would agree to anything. I mean, I have sunk pretty much all of what I have to pay the bills. I'm literally all in.'

'Yeah, I imagine. I've seen the numbers.'

'And I've not got your bill, yet. I mean, no pressure, but you're my last chance saloon.'

'Good job that I have spurs on my boots then.'

Alan smiled. Harlan had been hard on the overweight publican, but that was to set the scene, it was now time to show his softer side, for Alan to know he was here to not only take care of his problem, but to help him. 'We need a few things to change.'

'I was thinking my profession, oh, and my waistband.'

Harlan laughed. He liked quick wit and male banter. If you had either, he liked you, if you had both, he would spend time with you. There was a big difference between the two.

'So, what you thinking?' Alan asked, his brow still glistening with sweat.

'Two things. The first one, you'll do.'

'What's that?'

'You are sat on a prime piece of land here. We need to earn from that.'

'You mean the car park?'

'You should be CID. Yes, the car park. It's twice the square footage of the pub, if not twice again. You don't open until midday every day and currently, shut on Sundays, we need that land to earn you dollar.'

'But don't I need a permit, or some sort of zoning licence?'

'Yes, if you do it legit, which is why you won't. Well, not for now at least. We will open it up as a cheap, cash only car park. We will turn the outside cameras to face it, so offering security but also knowing if you don't pay, we will take it away. If we get it set up and running, when the council, with its clipboard kid, rocks up, and closes it for a bit we can then launch an appeal that it was a proven need within the community and assisting businesses in the local community thrive. That should get us your licence.'

'But if that doesn't work?'

'Then we just open it back up, different 'company' running it, fuck all to do with you. We will create a huge paper trail on who owns and runs the company, and then as and when they trawl through the paperwork to close to down, hey presto, we just open it back up again.'

'Will that work?'

'The beauty is, they cannot block the entrance to the

car park legally, as the entrance is needed for the pub. Which is why the car park will be run, on paper, by anyone but you.'

'If we apply for a licence, though, I'll need a solicitor for that. I can't afford one of those.'

'That's okay, I have a solicitor that owes me a favour....'

I'm not hanging around. You up for this, or what?

The text sounded keen. Colin liked keenness. He knew those eager for a fight lacked the preparation to be any good at it. He was a voracious reader of war generals, seeing himself as the modern-day embodiment of Sir Winston Churchill and Sun Tzu, combined. Bournemouth was his patch to protect; his beach to fight on. Over the last two years he had demoted, promoted, retired and replaced his crew. He once read a book by a fella called Jack Welch, some sort of US business titan, who preached on dismissing the bottom ten-percent of his company each year, thus always increasing the bar. It was a proven strategy, and Colin used this for the Cherry Pickers. Those who got knocked out, got thrown out. His firm. His rules.

He took a bottle from the fridge and twisted off the cap, leaving it on the worktop for his wife to find and dispose of later. He was the king of his castle, and kings didn't clean. He slid open the patio door, and wearing his tan-coloured moccasin slippers, walked out over the plastic grass and sat himself down in his wife's egg chair. He looked again at the text:

I'm not hanging around. You up for this, or what?

The notepad said he had sixteen confirmed, and he

knew he could get that to twenty. He hoped whoever it was that reached out could match his numbers, if not, more fool them.

He fancied a cigar, to gloat. Another lamb had reached out to the slaughter, which always made him feel good and what better way to feel good than chomping down on a big Cuban. But that would mean getting up, or out, off the swivelling chair, and performing that task outweighed the pull of rolled up tobacco leaves. The cigar could wait, the reply, couldn't.

3pm. Crossways pub. All in but no tools.

The text was all true. Except for the last sentence. Colin was many things; a fair fighter wasn't one of them. If someone set foot on his patch, they entered his world.

The reply was instant: **Flights booked.**

Colin found himself staring down at the screen. It was time for that cigar after all.

Harlan had stopped before revealing the second part of his recovery plan to send a text.

Flights booked.

He knew to code the reply, and it was a code the MC used often, to announce a club run or confirm something criminal. The MC knew their phones were often tapped, their emails screened, and bank accounts checked. That was the way it was if you operated off the grid and outside of the law, but this was where the police fell down, by not understanding, or worse, respecting the cunning of the career criminal. The reply was only two words, **Flights booked.** But it said so much.

'What's the second part?' Alan asked, when Harlan

put down the small handset, with the screen facing the wooden table.

'Let's just say, we need people to know they are in safe hands from now on.'

'What the *hell* does that mean?'

'Exactly that. That hell is coming...'

12

They had taken Jamal's car. After all, it was his errand they were running. The music was loud, and with a low bass. The lyrics, misogynistic and brutal. Each of the three occupants were smoking, and tobacco wasn't the only ingredient. It wasn't the first time they had some of their kids go quiet, or quit. But those who did, knew *never* to speak. It was also a risk, getting teenagers to run the streets, but the rewards were equally as high. The kids carried the drugs, stashed the cash and felt like kings. The reality was they were nothing more than minions. Paupers to the princes. When recruited, the job spec was sold on the ability to earn easy cash. What wasn't told at first, instead, drip fed, was that it was also your family that was signed up, meaning, if *you* spoke, *they* would suffer.

The town was busy. Traffic, as always, heavy. The pavements were awash with young teenagers on scooters, some manual, some electric and bicycles. The art now was knowing which of these kids were working for them. The way to confirm or deny came in the shape of the burner phones they were holding. Each kid they drove past, numbers would be rung, if someone stopped and answered, then they would be told to pull into the next side street and wait for a white Mercedes C-class to pull up.

It had been a productive hour. Three times the phones had been right, and the roadmen were busy working. They had enough product and they were earning, both for themselves and the gang. Next up was Liam. The first two calls went unanswered, and they all knew the kid was lucky it was them calling, and not Jamal.

'Try him again. Man is starving here,' said through a plume of smoke coming from the passenger seat. The man sat in the back, the odd-wheel, as he wasn't related to the two in the front but not being blood didn't matter. It was dollar that brought them together, not DNA. He dialled the number again, the small, black handset pressed tight to his ear. Nothing.

Harlan walked out into the car park. It was time to make a call.

The gym was busy and the music was blaring. A mixture of genres, but each one picked to match the testosterone in the room. It was a long building. Rectangular, not square, situated on a busy street and parking was a bitch. It was privately owned, so minus the sales pitches and sterile environment, instead, it was a steroid environment; it was the place to go to get juiced up. Colin was halfway through his set. It was chest day. His friend was spotting him and offering words of encouragement. 'Push it out, Col.'

Colin's forearms were shaking. It had become personal. 'C'mon, Col. C'mon.'

Colin took a sharp intake of breath, the bar just inches up from his chest and bowing.

'Do it,' his friend shouted, urging Colin to complete his set.

Colin exhaled, trying his best to release the pent-up, trapped air out of his lungs, trying to control his burning chest, his shaking arms and his exhausted ego.

By the time his forearms were outstretched, every vein was vexed and his teeth were together, and gritted. His friend helped him drop the bar into recess, the sound of steel-on-steel coming together. Colin started to pant heavy but there was a sleazy smile on his face, knowing he had completed his set and lifted more, and for longer, than his friend who was standing over him, congratulating him on his workout.

Colin swung his torso forward, until sitting upright, his legs either side of the padded-out bench, revealing a large, oval circle of wet sweat in his wake. The friend passed Colin his sports battle. The gym was fairly busy; big-biceped men curling dumbbells and thick legs protruding out of shorts lunging forward with a heavy bar resting across the back of their necks. Colin wasn't a natural gym goer, lacking the natural size and stature to become big, but this gym was where he felt his ego needed to be. Gangsters and backstreet gyms went hand-in-hand. Colin lifted up the spout on his bottle when he heard his phone ping inside his grey hoodie that was balled up on the floor down by his feet.

'Pass my phone, Paul,' Colin asked.

Paul reached into the hoodie, fumbling around for a large, rectangular piece of plastic. His hand emerged, holding the phone. Knowing not to look at the screen, he handed it over. Colin tapped on the screen and another sleazy smile appeared on his face: **Bring your best players for the match.**

Colin liked the football analogy within the coded message. The code served a purpose; that if the law got hold of it, to the untrained eye, the jury's eyes, it reads as it is. Two mobile phones discussing a football match. The reality was different; it's two mobile phones discussing meeting up to fight. Colin not only smelt blood; he could taste it.

The pub was situated on a 4-way crossroad. There was a lone man walking around the pub car park, sometimes kicking away loose stones and chippings from the worn concrete, talking into a mobile phone. The only possible thing that stood out, if you happened to glance out of your window at the same time as his back was towards you, was the chilling image that sprawled out across his leather sleeveless vest. Cars were going by too fast for their passengers to get more than a passing glance, but the devil was staring right back at them.

Harlan was on a call to the man he admired most in the world, the man who had polished his rough edges, and taught him the value of playing the long game. The conversation was held outside, in the top end of the car park, with the sound of passing traffic, for a reason. Walls have ears, and it was much better to act secretively in plain sight. Harlan had sent the text when sat inside the pub, but had made the call when outside.

The text had been sent from the same phone as before, to the same number as before. **Bring your best players for the match.** Harlan had sent it to play with him, to massage Colin's inflated ego. The message was easy to decode, *show me how good your firm is.* What the subliminal message was, and he knew Colin never had the CV to get, was, *because anything less than your best won't be good enough, and even your best isn't good enough.* Colin had chosen to take another man's business, to make his property his own, but that had all changed when Harlan decided to take the problem on, and make it his own.

'Cheers, Jim. Later.'

Harlan had signed off the call to his president, in his own signature way, *later.* The call had been made on a different phone. It looked identical to the one he had sent the message on, but that was where the similarity ended. The phone that had sent the text had only one purpose. And only one number. The phone he had made the call on, had a much bigger purpose; his life. And it had many numbers. Many, many numbers.

Harlan put the phone into the opposite pocket of the one with the identical phone and walked back towards the pub. It was time for a cup of tea.

'You aren't too easy to get hold of, young 'un,' said the voice from the back seat.

Liam hadn't intended to ignore the calls, but he would admit, if only to himself, it had been easier. 'Yeah. Sorry, just been busy.'

'Yeah, man. Sweet. Anyway, we need to see you. Where you at?'

Liam looked around, trying to find a street name but there wasn't one nearby, so he got back on his bike, and with his phone still pressed to his ear, rode one handed until he found a street sign and read it off to his bosses.

'Wait there wideboy. We be at you soon.'

Liam wasn't sure what they wanted, but he didn't think it sounded good. The thought was confirmed by the cold feeling that shot up his back even though the sun was shining.

The brother that wasn't driving, sat in the passenger seat, stopped skinning up the next joint and typed in the street name into the German car's in-built satnav. His brother turned off the hazard lights by the button on the dash and, without signalling, pulled out into the traffic, ignoring the aggrieved Transit van driver who had to brake suddenly to let him out.

The driver turned up the music via the steering wheel. 'Tune,' he said, banging his palm on the steering wheel in line with the bass.

It didn't take long to pull into the street and Liam was just up ahead on the left, on the pavement. The C-class pulled up and the passenger window wound down and Liam was gestured towards the car. As he approached, he was told, 'Get in.' The teenager didn't hear the instruction, or if he did, tried to make out he hadn't. The order was repeated. 'Get in.'

The cold feeling that had ran up his spine a few minutes earlier returned, and in earnest. Liam had ignored the gang yesterday and was now regretting that decision, bitterly.

'What about my bike?' Liam asked, hoping it would get him off getting in the car.

'It's fine. Leave it. No-one will touch it,' the passenger

said, gloating in his belief that he was a feared gangster, ignoring the fact he spent most of his time holed up in a seedy flat getting stoned. Liam put his hand on the handle, even though every fibre in his body told him not to. The teenager opened the door and got inside, and no sooner had his backside touched down on the soft leather, than the driver flicked the powerful car into gear and roared up the street, with the tyres screeching and the turbo whistling. Above the sound of the loud exhaust, came the sound of three Somalian men laughing, which was more than could be said for the teenager sat alongside them, and whose already pale face was getting whiter by the second.

The driver pressed down on a small button on the leather steering wheel with its white stitching, and took the music even louder, the thumping bassline now making the car shake. If it was designed to scare the teenager, it was working. The driver was racing up and down back streets, accelerating hard and braking heavily. Finally, the white Mercedes came to a hard stop, sending the frightened Liam shooting forward causing him to put his hands on the rear of the headrest to save himself a broken nose. The car had pulled into a small car park belonging to a block of council flats, far away from prying eyes out of peering net curtains; close enough to not be seen as suspicious. The driver held the volume button down, bringing the bass to the music to the dead stop as the car itself seconds before. Both the two front passengers turned to face him with their dead-eyed stares. Liam turned his head to face the man sitting next to him and he too was staring right at him.

The frightened young teen put his hand on the handle, hoping it would open. It didn't. He also knew it wouldn't. Not until whatever they had in store for him, happened.

'Calm down, young un', here, take a drag on this,' the passenger said, passing his arm through the gap of the centre console offering out the spliff. He watched as Liam looked down at the lit joint, at its length. 'Go on, young un', take a puff. It's real Rasta shit.'

The driver laughed at his brother's comment; an arrogant, low-level laugh. The passenger watched, his pupils darting from the teen, to the spliff, and back again. He was manipulating the young lad, and it was working. Liam coughed, the air was dense from all the accumulated smoke, both past and present. Liam wasn't a smoker himself and had suffered with asthma as a child, and now, kidnapped, and scared, he was starting to hyperventilate.

'Young un', what's da problem lately? Why is man not returning calls?'

The passenger had retracted his offer of a smoke, and after he posed the question, leant forward and blew his smoke directly into the face of the scared teen. 'Well?'

Liam was quiet. His mouth, dry. His fear, palpable. He waved away the smoke but another waft came right back at him. 'I take it your deaf? As man can't hear no answers.'

It didn't seem fun anymore, for the young teen. He had gotten used to cycling around, covering his own little patch. The cash was good, and the job was easy. As easy as it could be delivering drugs. It wasn't so easy now. Liam was locked in a car, with three men who looked both high, and dangerous. The passenger was still pressing for his answer.

'I..., I, it..., I mean, I –'

The next sound came a nano-second after the action. The teenager didn't seem it coming, only felt it. The person sat next to him had punched him in the side of his face. It was a jabbing shot, a jolt, designed to startle the young lad, to scare him. Liam found himself putting his hand straight to his cheek, covering and rubbing it, checking for damage. His eyes welled and it was taking every ounce of courage not to cry.

'Man up, young un'. Man up.'

Liam removed his hand from his cheek, revealing a red swelling on his cheek bone. The punch had been harder than intended. Liam went to speak but stopped. The man sitting next to him started to move which caused him to flinch. He started to speak. The words came out slowly. One at a time. Monosyllabic. 'I. Got. Scared.'

'Scared of what? Have we not been good to you? Man is thinking yes,' the passenger asked.

He watched, and waited, for a reply. It wasn't forthcoming. The second smack to the side of Liam's head soon sorted that. 'I'll ask you again, young un'.'

'Yes. You have.'

'That's better. There, that wasn't so hard, was it.' It was a rhetorical question.

Liam, for the second time in a matter of minutes, put his right palm over his right cheek. And for the second time in the same matter of minutes, tried his best not to cry.

'Now, the best way to say sorry, is to stop PISSING US OFF!'

The sudden burst of shouted anger shocked the frightened young man. His vision had become blurry. He tried the door handle again but it was the same as before; locked. The passenger leaned forward again, and a little further than before. The words he said next were given with a deadly sense of realism. And malevolence.

'It's a nice house you live in. And your mum, she seems nice. Be a shame to ruin her pretty face, young un', a real shame. But, that's on you. The size of her smile is on you.'

The young lad, with the swollen face, couldn't hold his tears back any longer.

Colin had given his friend a tenner, telling him to get the beers in. He took a seat and dropped his gym bag on the floor, down by his leg. By the time his friend arrived at the table, carrying a pint in each hand and with a bag of crisps hanging between his teeth, Colin was busy on his phone, his fingers a blur.

'Who's that?' asked Pete, Colin's gym buddy and best friend – when it suited.

'A gobby bastard who is going to be chewing on glass soon.'

The laugh that followed was one that Pete had heard before, a laugh that had told him his best friend had slowly, but surely, turned into some sort of psychopath.

'Those crisps for me, Pete?'

'Nope.'

'But came out of my change, I imagine.'

'Yep.'

Colin laughed again, a different type of laugh. And that was what scared his friend: how quickly he could switch. 'Do you want a bag?' Pete asked.

'No. I'm good. But after this I fancy a maccys.'

'Good shout,' Pete said, spitting off a slither of cheese and onion crisps as he did.

Colin went back to his phone. And back to being a gangster.

Pete sat and finished his crisps in silence, and then moved onto the nearby fruit machine, leaving Colin to his *bit of business*. Colin's concentration was interrupted by the electronic chants coming out of the machine, and the sound of falling coins.

'Next round on you then, Petey boy, and mine's a Salt and Vinegar.'

Pete put his hands inside the tray, his fingers moving around like spiders' legs to ensure he had scooped every last pound coin. He hadn't won the jackpot, which was two-hundred quid, but a score helped, even though a tenner of it would go on the next round.

Colin's glass was down to the dregs but before Pete went to walk over to the bar, Colin beckoned him back to the table.

'We may need to be tooled up for this one, Pete. Dusters and coshes.'

'Really? It's going down, then?' Pete asked.

'Yeah. I don't know the size of their firm. It's not the main players. Probably some sort of splinter gang, wanting to make a name for themselves.'

'No idea who they are?'

'Nah. Probably just lads, to be fair, but wanting to mix up with the big boys. Trust me, though, after we have fucked them up, they will have wished they watched the football instead.' The original had returned; the laugh of a psychopath.

Pete went to the bar to get the drinks, and to let Colin's lust for violence subside. Pete didn't mind a scrap, but when his friend started to talk about getting tooled up, he knew people were going to hurt. And badly. He could still remember the last time...

Eight people. Eight men. Harlan did his headcount. Out of the eight, only half were of fighting age. Half of that again looked like they could row. All of that number looked like they couldn't have a row with him. He didn't like the way he had to categorise people, on having to take them at even less than face-value, but it was this approach that kept him whole. It was the same barmaid as the first night, the lady with the tattooed neck.

'Has your chef been found yet?' He asked.

The barmaid smiled but her poker face was poor; Harlan could see the smile was one of lust, not from his quip about the absent chef. 'He sure is. Want to see the menu?'

Harlan nodded then his eyes followed her as she went to the far end of the bar, returning with a laminated menu. Still smiling.

He perused what was on offer, drawn to two options. 'How many sausages with the mash?'

'Two. I think? Or 3. Not sure,' she replied, trying to conceal the fact she was checking him out but Harlan had noticed, although he didn't let it show. 'Okay, sausage and mash. Ta.'

He watched her ring in the amount and hand over the card machine. He declined and handed over two five-pound notes. And after she handed him his change, he watched her tight little ass walk back down the bar and disappear out of view to give the chef his order. By the time she had re-emerged, Harlan was sitting down at the same table as before. He placed two out of his three phones on the table. It was the phone that wasn't on display, the one still in his pocket that pinged. Typical.

He took it out and read the text: **I like the seaside.**

Harlan smirked, at both the code and the sarcasm, But more importantly, the sentiment.

He took a swig from the bottle, and as the glass was pursed to his lips, he touched the screen on the smartphone with his index finger; and aside for the battery icon, which was now on red, there was nothing to show. Nothing except the woman who was on the screen starting back at him. Which was not nothing. Not nothing at all.

The view outside the window was just that of another busy road, cars and buses passing by. People on foot were walking past the windows. Carrier bags in their hands, spending what they had for what they needed, or what they hadn't on what they didn't.

The people watching came to an end when the barmaid appeared, carrying a white plate with steam emitting from it. She placed it down, maybe bending more than she needed to, and looking at him on the way back up to see if he liked what was on offer. But his face was stoic, showing no sign of liking her cleavage, which only made her want him more.

He turned his attention towards the plate. There were four sausages. For the first time since he had met her, he smiled. And for the second time since he met her, he watched her tight little ass walk away.

13

He knew the patch didn't define him, but it did make him. When he first stepped inside the clubhouse, all those years ago, he was a piece of hardened stone, tough, and durable, but by no means the finished product. It was the club, its members, that acted as a sculptor, putting in the hours to polish him into the man he was today. It was what people didn't know about him and his brothers. That really pissed him off. He knew the people who would be behind him; in their cars, shaking their heads at the patch that adorned his back. They would pass their judgements to whoever would be sat next to them, telling often preposterous tales, which would have started life off in the media and then morph into something much bigger, and much less true. The tales, or lies, would label each and every member, as being nothing more than mindless thugs who were behind every single crime the country had ever suffered. What they didn't know, or what they chose to ignore, was the many good deeds the MC had done. The club often held charity nights; the difference being the proceeds would go directly to the families themselves, rather than being lost in red tape and protocol of a charity where for every pound put in, half of that would get lost. Satan's Security dealt with that problem by delivering bags of clothes, food or Christmas presents, to the houses where these items would be in short supply. The MC would also pay for the upkeep of youth clubs and playgrounds, and due to the fear of reprisal, this also ensured that anyone who felt like defacing these places with a can of spray paint would think again. The MC may not be to everyone's taste, and the rumours that there was criminal activity inside its ranks being true, didn't detract from the fact the MC would clip the wings of those that needed clipping, and in turn, made the streets around their clubhouse a safer place. Harlan had done his research since he had been here, and there wasn't a local MC, and he knew the town, from what he had seen so far, was all the worse for it. He was, as he often did when new in town, riding across the town. But he wasn't sightseeing, instead he was looking around at the part of the town the council would rather forget. Harlan had been around the block enough times to know regardless of how shiny a city looked, behind the scenes would be some rust. The rust, being that of drugs, gangs and guns. What made Harlan different was that he accepted these things. He knew you would never rid a community of crime, but what he knew more, some cities needed it. That crime bosses, if they had a moral code that matched their criminal one, could keep a check on the crime levels and ensure it had some standards to it. From what he could tell, this town needed a gang to step in and claim its crime. And he knew just who could do it.

Harlan had seen enough for today, and with a quick

turn of his wrist, accelerated hard through the quiet streets on route to Stan's B&B.

'Where have you been?' asked Stan. He was exasperated and his limp seemingly more pronounced now, as he walked down the hallway to see him. Harlan hadn't even had a chance to turn around from closing the door when Stan was upon him, stressed and although he wouldn't admit it, shaking.

'Calm down, Stan, you're gonna have a coronary.'

'Bollocks to that, you need to hear what happened.'

'What are you banging on about?'

'Come in here, quick,' Stan said, and opened the door to his living room.

Harlan followed Stan inside, and everything looked the same as yesterday, everything that is except the seat he had been sat in, was now occupied by the woman with the welt, except this time she had a black eye to go with it. Harlan could feel the fire in his belly start to ignite and the muscles underneath the tattoos in his chest and arms had started to tense.

He deliberately didn't linger his look on the woman, wanting to try and keep a lid on the rage that was forming and in need of an immediate outlet, notably on the head of whoever it was that hurt the woman sitting in the armchair. Her daughter on her lap.

'Okay, tell me everything. And I mean, everything.'

Stan went to tell the story stood up, but his leg was aching, so sat down, and letting his body fall the last few inches. He got himself comfortable, pushing and rubbing his back into the chair before he started to tell Harlan what had happened.

'I was putting the hoover around, in here actually, although looking at it now, it seems I forgot to turn it on. Anyhow, I heard the front door go and by the time I turned the ruddy thing off the reception bell had rung.'

Harlan looked down at Stan trying to be patient but wanting him to get to the point. Not easy.

'I walked out and then walked up and around him, to get myself around the desk to serve him. I thought he was a punter at first, a contractor or something like that, here for work, or what have you.'

'And then?' Harlan asked, still trying to be patient. Still not easy.

'Well, he didn't want a room. He asked me if Danielle was here.'

'Danielle?'

'Yes, Danielle,' replied Stan, then held out his arm in the direction of the woman sitting opposite him with the fresh new bruise to accompany the previous one. Harlan turned his head to face her, feeling bad he hadn't as of yet, acknowledged her, being too interested in what had happened instead of how she was feeling.

'Mrs, stupid question I know, but are you okay?'

Danielle looked up at him, her eyes telling a story, one of confusion and shame.

'Danielle, isn't it?'

Danielle nodded and then broke his stare, preferring to stare down into her abyss.

'Danielle, this won't happen again – I promise.'

She didn't look up and then it hit him, she would have heard this line before – a thousand times. A thousand false promises from a man who couldn't keep to his word, or his fists in his pockets. The rage in Harlan had returned, he wanted revenge for her. He wanted blood.

'Then what happened?' his eyes now reverting back to Stan.

'I asked him who he was. Why he wanted to see her. I mean, I'm not a total wooden top'

'What was his answer?'

'Well, he said he was her brother. The lying little shit.'

'But, judging from the state of her face, you went and got her?'

Harlan saw Stan's face drop. He had shamed him. He hadn't intended to, but he also knew he was in no mood to now repair Stan's battered ego. 'Stan, what happened?'

Stan took a second to compose himself, trying to stop the feeling he had washing over him of letting her down. 'Yes. Yes, I got her. Trust me, H, you can't make me feel any worse. I –'

'Stan, I'm not here to make you feel bad but, for the love of God, just spit it out.'

For the first time, since Stan had started speaking, Harlan looked down over at Danielle and felt bad for talking about her like she wasn't there. 'Stan, let's do this outside.'

He watched as Stan lifted himself up out of the chair, with all the grace of an elephant stuck in a cat flap, and Harlan waited for Stan to walk past him, over towards the door, for him to follow, as a mark of respect for whose house it was. Harlan pulled the living room door shut behind so they could talk in private, as best they could. 'So, what happened next?'

'This next part is my fault. Regarding what room she was in, I mean.'

'Stan, can we jimmy this along a bit.'

'Okay, yes. Sorry. So, after you paid for her second night, I moved her to the only room that's on this floor, because she had a buggy so I wanted it to be easier for her.'

'Yeah, I noticed. That was nice. But, anyway...'

'You got to understand, he came across as being concerned for her, like a brother would. So I went down to her room, and knocked on her door to get her, but what I didn't realise, at least at first, was that he had followed me. I gave it a knock, and I could hear the telly was on, some sort of kid's programme. What's the pig one called, Pep –'

'STAN!'

'Okay. Sorry. Well, she didn't answer at first, so I knocked again, a little harder. Eventually she answered and I told her that her brother was here to see her. That's when it happened.'

'When *what* happened?'

'When he hit her.'

'Tell me,' Harlan asked, his tone turning flat. Cold. Emotionless.

'She tried telling me she didn't have a brother, when he barged past me and lunged for her. She tried to get back inside but he managed to grab her just before that and pulled her out. That's how she got her shiner, she hit her face on the edge of the door when he pulled her forward.'

'Did he manage to get her out?'

'No. Thank God. I started wrestling with him, and I would have kicked his arse if he didn't leave when he did.'

Harlan was now downwind in Stan's bullshit, but he also knew Stan would have tried to help her as he was a stand-up guy, and nobody's fool. 'So he just left?'

'Yes. After we scuffled. Danielle was screaming and her poor kid was crying.'

'Did the kid see?'

'No, and again, thank God, she was still inside and from what I could see, out of sight. Bless her heart. One of the residents from upstairs came out and down the stairs, and that's when he left. Piece of shit.'

'Did you call the police?' Harlan asked.

'No. I don't do police, if I can help it.'

That was the answer Harlan wanted. Now he could administer his own version of the law.

A few minutes later Harlan and Stan returned to the living room with Stan carrying two cups of coffee; Harlan himself had a mug of tea and a carton of juice for the child. Stan passed the cup to Danielle, who cupped her hands around it, until the heat got the better of her and she placed it down on the floor beside her, which wasn't easy with her child still on her lap. Stan got himself back in his chair, just as awkwardly as before and then Harlan took a step closer to Danielle but being careful not to startle, or scare her. 'Danielle, this can't continue.'

She looked down toward the floor, hoping a hole would appear and swallow her. But there wasn't, all there was, was the truth. Harlan spoke again, softly. 'What's all this about?'

He had passed the young child the carton, forgetting she wasn't old enough to pierce it herself. Danielle took the carton from her daughter, and through her still shaking hands, pierced the carton with the short straw before handing it back to her.

'I need you to tell me,' Harlan asked, with heartfelt compassion in his voice. He could feel her pain, and pretty soon, whoever did this, would feel their own.

'It's my fella. He... he just, he...'

'Just take your time, no rush,'

'He used to be so nice. So sweet. But now, when he gets on his gear, he just... he just...'

'When he gets on it, he does this? Is that what you mean?'

Danielle bowed her head again, and for longer. Harlan knew what was happening. She gone from being beaten up, to beating herself up. Believing it was her own fault.

'Hey, stop that,' he said. A little more forthright than intended.

Danielle looked up, startled by Harlan's command, but the look of kindness on his face told her it had come from the right place. 'This isn't on you. Ever. Remember that.'

She looked back up at him and Harlan could see she had soulful eyes, a wisdom beyond her young years, and he hoped what was happening to her wouldn't make her grow old before her time. He also knew the quickest way to release a side of him that was better left caged, was to be a bully. What would make your retribution worse, was if you bullied women or children. He knew it was time.

'Dani, where is he now?'

He had seen that look before. It said she was scared of what would happen, not now, but next. That if she went against him, then how far would he go in return. Harlan knew that was how fear worked, it worked on the inside. Where it was at its scariest. Harlan knew he needed to stop her going down that torturous road.

'This needs to stop. You can't live like this. You need a role model for your daughter, someone she will one day look up to. Not a man that beats her mummy. She can't have that. You can't have that. I won't have that...'

Harlan's words lingered. Each of them taking their own version of the last few words. All except the young child who was busy giggling at the juice shooting out of the carton when she squeezed it.

'I need a name and address.'

'What will you do?'

'We are going to have a chat. A chat whereby it will only be me doing the talking.'

Danielle knew it was time. Time to do the right thing by her young baby girl.

The Mercedes pulled back into the street and like he was told, Liam's bike was still there. They had picked him up to scare him. It had worked. Liam had only just got his trailing leg out of the back of the car before it sped off, and above the sound of the stainless-steel exhaust and thumping baseline, he was sure he could still hear them laughing at him. Liam walked over to his bike which had slid down the wall and was now laying on its side, but it was still there, which was something. He reached down and picked it up by one of the handle bar grips and was about to get on when his burner pinged. The next punter, no doubt. Liam took out his small handset and read the text.: **Be nice to your mum.** Liam read it, and then emptied the contents of his stomach onto the street. This wasn't fun, after all.

It took Liam a few minutes before he felt able to ride, and a few minutes more to comprehend the position he was in. What had gone from doing a few errands for some pocket money, had turned into having a mobile and a patch, had ended up with his family being threatened. Liam didn't realise he had been groomed, until it was too late. Now, he was an active member in a county lines gang, and he was in it too deep to turn back. The snare was too discreet for him to spot, until it was too late. He was now at their mercy, and as he rode off in the direction of the next person wanting their drugs, the weight of his family's safety rested heavily on his shoulders.

Danielle had told him where he would most likely be found. It was a pub in a rundown area of the town, befitting he thought, when she explained the type of customers that pub catered for. There was just enough charge on his smartphone to give him the directions across town and fifteen minutes after leaving Danielle in Stan's living room, he grabbed the brass handle on the door and stepped inside to yet another strange pub, in yet another strange part of the country. What wasn't strange, was that he wasn't here to be social. Danielle had shown Harlan a picture of him, from her phone. It had been taken in happier times; she was dressed in a floral dress and his hand was around her waist with the sunlight behind them. It looked like a holiday photo, which made Harlan smirk, as the next photo he would be in would be taken from a hospital bed.

17 people. Sixteen of which were male. One female, stood next to someone of comparable age, husband and wife, Harlan presumed. That left fifteen people. Fifteen men. He was here for only one. The tasty bastard who thought it was fair game to hit a girl. Harlan was here to change his way of thinking. Within the first sixty seconds, every pair of eyes had looked his way, which was thirty

seconds after he had seen them. And that was the difference, speed of thought, and more importantly, speed of decision. Harlan walked over to the table. It was at the far end of the pub and adjacent to the pool table. Two guys were playing, one bending down at the baize, eyes focused on the prize with his opponent stood at the opposite end, hoping he would miss. It wasn't either of these Harlan wanted, instead his prize was sat down at the table, waiting to play next. Which he wouldn't be able to.

The player waiting to play was the first to spot him walking towards them but had no idea he was bringing hate and fury with him.

'You need to get up.' It wasn't said as a request.

The man looked up, at first unsure if it was directed at him. It was only then that he saw the coal-coloured eyes burning into him. 'Steady on, mate. You sure you're in the right place?'

Harlan knew two things were wrong in that sentence, and proceeded to point it out.

'Believe me, we aren't mates and unluckily for you, I'm in the right place.'

Harlan could see one of the two players at the table shuffle forward towards him. He wasn't sure of his intentions, so made his own very clear.

'Stay where you are fella, or you'll be picking out splinters from your mouth for months.' The threat was there for him to hear, and Harlan hoped, for his sake, he would take it. He turned his attention back to who it was he had come for.

'You will be standing up. You can choose to do it yourself, like a man. Or I'll lift you out that fucking seat, like a bitch. Your decision. But, a word of advice, be quick, as I'm in need of a cup of tea and you're making me wait.'

The man now had four sets of eyes looking at him. His three friends, and a stranger, dressed head to toe in black. It took him a few seconds to unsaddle the stool and stand fully up, but when he did, he wasn't upright for long. Three seconds to be exact. The first second, to take the step forward to be close enough to strike. The second, to size up and strike his jaw, and the third for him to fall to the floor. Harlan deliberately pulled his punch, sure, it was enough to knock him to the ground, but not enough to knock him out. As like he told Danielle, he was here to have a word.

Harlan knelt down and gripped him by the collar of his designer polo shirt, and hauled him back to his feet before ramming him up against the wall. It was now talk time.

'Listen, you worthless piece of shit, you need to think before you start laying hands on a woman, you need to think about who they might know. And what they might do.'

The wife-beater was groggy but the words were still sinking in. He went to speak.

'Don't. There is nothing you can say that I want to hear. This time I'll leave your jaw intact, but if I have to find you again, I'll smash it so bad you'll only ever suck soup. Got it?'

The nod of the head, and the look of fear in his eyes told Harlan he got it. Harlan still had hold of him by his collar, and decided to leave him with another piece of advice.

'And get off the gear – you have a daughter, that should be your drug. Fucking sort it.'

He let him go, and watched as he tried to flatten his shirt and find his arsehole. Harlan saw him for what he was, a coward until his chest was puffed out by cocaine. A blown-up bully. He turned to face the other three; two stood by the table, the other one still on his stool. He knew he had made a mistake, that he had turned his back on three potential assailants, and there were weapons to hand, namely pool cues and bottles, but that was what bullying did to him, it made him at times, vulnerable.

He had gotten away with it, this time. But he made a mental note. He faced the man who was still sitting down. 'You need to close that mouth, fella, otherwise it might get confused with one of them pockets.' And then, as if by magic, the man closed his mouth and tried to look anywhere but up at the bearded man, dressed head to toe in black. Harlan then turned to face the two pool players. 'I take it we won't be mentioning it to those with the pointy hats?'

They both took the hint. No police.

'Good lads,' Harlan said as he walked past and headed back towards the pub door.

It was time for that cup of tea.

14

The café wasn't particularly pretty, or clean. The owner's once white apron was now covered in a mixture of grease, sweat and stains. The linoleum was sticky and the countertop cluttered. The fly catcher crackled as he gave his order, bringing another life to an end. But Harlan wasn't here to admire the décor, mime to the music or count dead flies. He was here to decompress. To slowly release the adrenaline that was still within him, brought on by yet another asshole believing they could go about their business without repercussion. He knew the guy would now be seeing life differently, his jaw aching and his ego bruised. But for every bully he dealt with, there would be more. Bullies breed like bacteria, there are millions of them. The numbers were stacked against him, but his morals, well they were firmly onside and as long as he could throw a punch at these cretins, he would do. Harlan chose a Belgian bun, hoping it would still be in date, but if it wasn't, it had found the perfect place to be. The owner rang up his bill but Harlan didn't bother to hear it, he had already placed a fiver on the counter and was off to find a seat. He took one against one of the walls, unable to sit at the back of the building due to the layout, or rather, the chest freezer that for some reason was placed front of house, rather than out the back. He could still see the door, but he was side-on, rather than his preferred position of directly facing it. But, so far, he hadn't had to bust any heads, so there wasn't a real need to be on point. However, it wouldn't be long until some heads would be bust and blood would be spilt. The tea was piping hot, nothing wrong with the urn, Harlan thought, as he blew and slurped at the same time. The adrenaline, although not at fever-pitch, was still there, and he knew why.

It was a long time ago, back when he was too young to be the man of the house, even though his dad had told him that's what he was now. Which was why it hurt so bad the night his mum had come home, in the back of a police car. It was the first time she had been out since the divorce, which was nearly a year before. Since the spilt, she had dedicated her life to her son, trying to do the best that living on benefits would allow. Harlan was already becoming an unruly teen, knowing already he wanted to live outside of the law, sick of how his mum had to struggle living on a pittance, even though she also had a job washing dishes at a trucker's cafe. They were always one bill away from losing the house, one bill away from ruin. It didn't come to him until later why she had gotten so thin. There wasn't enough food for them both to eat. She would tell him, when she sat down at the second-hand dining room table, with its mixture of mismatched chairs, with only a cup of tea whilst he had a plate of fish fingers and oven chips, that she had *eaten earlier*. It was a lie; she hadn't eaten earlier that day. Or at all. Looking back now he could see just how much she had sacrificed for him, even if he was too young to know or worse, respect. But he could forgive that, at least, just a bit, but what he couldn't forgive was not being there that night. The night she came home battered, bleeding and bruised. She had asked Harlan to be home for 7, and to stay home, please. He had begrudgingly agreed, even though he wanted to be out with his friends, smoking stolen fags and drinking cans of cheap lager.

She was going out with her friend, Sharon, who had been like a surrogate mum to him, babysitting when he was younger, back when his mum had her job at the factory, before being laid off when the interest rates rocketed and cutbacks needed to be made. The taxi was booked for seven-thirty and she said she would be back by eleven; twelve at the very latest – and she would bring him a burger. It was nearly 4am when she finally arrived home. Harlan was already pacing the house, and with mobile phones not being a thing back then, he had no way to get hold of her. What had started as teenage petulance at half-twelve, when there was no burger to show for staying in, had now turned into concern – the gut feel when you know something is wrong. He was at his bedroom window waiting for a taxi to arrive, bringing his mum back home to him, when he saw the police car turn into the small cul-de-sac. He knew even before it drove down the hill and stopped right outside the house, it was regarding his mum. By the time the officer had opened the door of his patrol car Harlan had raced down the stairs and opened the front door and was walking, in his socks, over towards them. It was then he saw her. The bruises. The blood. It felt like his heart had stopped when he saw her. He felt his whole body turn cold. Why?

Who? Where? The questions in his mind soon topped; it was the tears in his eyes that didn't. The female officer helped her out of the car and walked with her into the house, gently setting her down on the frayed sofa before fetching her a glass of water. Harlan wanted to ask what happened but knew to wait, to let the officers settle her. They had asked her again if she wanted to press charges, but from her swollen lip, she had said no. They stayed with her for a bit, and would have stayed longer if the crackling radio that was on the male officer's shoulder hadn't told them there was a report of a suspected burglary at a warehouse in town. Harlan had never forgotten the compassion the two officers had shown, which was why, even to this day, and even though he is the type of person the police are duty-bound to try and catch, that until proven otherwise, he will treat an arresting officer with the same level of respect that had once been shown to his mother. She had left the pub, as promised, with enough time, and enough money left over, to treat him to a cheeseburger and chips, as even though she hadn't been out for over a year, hadn't done anything except raise her son and run a home, she still felt guilty of spending what little money she had only on herself, which was why not only did she keep some back for his burger, she had also kept enough to add some chips. It was when walking down to the kebab shop, that it happened. Her best friend was still at the pub, after catching the eye of the mechanic of the local garage and now having a last drink before the inevitable *inviting home for a coffee* that was sure to follow. It was this decision to not stay with his mum that caused Harlan to never speak to Sharon again, even though his mum had told him countless times it was her that had said to stay and have a drink. The kebab shop was at the bottom of the hill, and there was an unlit alley way just before it, which was where it happened. The first thing she felt was the hand coming around her neck and going up over her mouth. She then remembered being dragged backwards, the heels of her plastic shoes scraping across the concrete and his grip around her neck getting tighter. She was struggling for breath and fearing she would be raped if she didn't do as he said, she stayed quiet. The last thing she remembered was the punch. It had come after the hard slap, after he had demanded her purse. She didn't resist, handing it over from her shaking hands. The slap had come from the derisory amount she had in there. The second slap had come after he had said she was lying. The punch came from realizing she wasn't. When she woke up, she was lying on her side, with her vision impaired and the taste of blood in her mouth. She had tried to stand up but when she did, she felt faint and slid back down the wall until she came to a stop on the hard, cold, wet floor. She was in this position, and quietly sobbing when she was found. The police had been called and soon she was sat in the back of the car but refusing to go to the hospital, or to give a statement. She just wanted to go home, to her son.

It didn't matter that he was still barely in his teens. It didn't matter he was too young to be out with her in the pub that night. It didn't matter that actually, if he hadn't asked for a burger, she wouldn't have had to walk past the alley way. What mattered, was that he hadn't kept his mum safe. He was the man of the house now, and he had failed. He wouldn't fail again – he may no longer be able to keep his mum safe, but woe betide anyone else who put their hand on a woman when he was around.

His tea had gotten cold.

'Mum, you seen Ryan? The little shit isn't walking Tyson.'

It was clear, by his pacing, that the dog hadn't been out for his walk. It had been a long day and his back was aching. He needed a bath, if there was any hot water, to wash off the gritty sand and the sludgy cement that had accumulated on his bare flesh. Rob hadn't seen his younger brother for a day or so, which wasn't unusual. Rob wasn't in the house long, the lure of cheap lager down at his local pub, The Three-Legged Fox. Weekends were the same, he would be up and out early, a pre-fight fry-up, before the pre-arranged fight at either the meeting ground, The Crossways, or he would be sat in a minibus, on the way to an away game, for an away day fight. Week-days were a few pints, a few quid on the fruit machine and a hook-up with his on/off girlfriend, Cherie. The weekends were different; they were filled with lines of coke, shots of Jägermeister and dancing shirtless in Big Al's boozer. Rob was hungry and went back to the kitchen, hoping for a microwave meal or some frozen nuggets. He was in luck. The chicken nugget bag had just enough to make a wrap. He would add the chips to it, later, when the pub had closed and he walked past the late-night chippie. The bag said 18-20 mins from frozen, which was enough time for a quick bath, or enough time to run Tyson around the block. The dog won the conun-drum, with Rob searching around the messy kitchen trying to find the chained lead ready to connect himself to his dog. He opened the back door and before he had a chance to steady himself, Tyson pulled forward, eager to begin a long-awaited walk which resulted in Rob pulling him back, hard and added a choice word by means of reprimand. Rob had forgotten what an arduous task it was to walk Tyson, which was why he had subcontracted it out to Ryan.

Where are you; you little prick Rob muttered, as he walked down the path hoping Tyson had already emptied his bowels in the garden somewhere. He reached in for his mobile to call his younger brother, Tyson was pulling like a banshee, and Ryan was going to get the wrath of his vicious tongue, which was better for Ryan than it sounded, as if he were here, he would be getting a smack in the mouth. Tyson was pulling so hard that he was starting to pant and Rob was regretting the decision to choose the dog over his dinner. He scrolled down his contact list. He skipped past, B, for brother, then R, for Ryan, ending up at S, for shithead.

He went to dial but Tyson saw a cat and lunged, and the moment was missed.

'Get back here – stupid mutt,' he hissed, then regretted it. It was Ryan's fault, not the dogs, and definitely not his. He pulled Tyson back to him, deciding to dial out whilst stationary, to save both his arm socket and his phone. He tried again but just as he did, he had an incoming call. It was from Colin.

'Alright mucker, how's it going?' It was Colin's standard opening gambit.

'Yeah. Sound. You?' Rob replied.

'I'm good, be better day after tomorrow. You excited?'

Colin was referring to the rendezvous. Where he took his own team of men to a match, except it wasn't a ball they'd be kicking. It would be each other.

'You excited?' Colin asked, wanting to hear the excitement in his understudy's voice.

'Defo. Tooled up, right?' Rob replied, wanting to be sure he knew his instructions.

'Yeah. But concealed. They think it's just a simple straightener, ha.'

The laugh was sinister. Rob hated to admit, but there were times when Colin scared him.

'Know much about them?' Rob asked, wanting to know more about the opposition.

'Nah, I couldn't be bothered to do any research. It's not their main firm so they will just be chancing it.'

'Nothing to worry about then?'

'Is there ever?' Colin replied, adding his signature sinister laugh.

'We got enough?' Rob asked, keen to know they had enough men up for the fight.

'You leave the army to me – your job is to turn up and do some real damage.'

'Yeah, OK. Got it.'

'Good – I'll text you tomorrow.' Colin ended the call.

For Rob, what had started as a laugh, a way to release some anger with some mates had turned into something far more serious. He was one of Colin's front line soldiers, and with no way of standing down, or stepping out. Rob had been recruited, but retiring wasn't an option. He liked a pint, and a fight, but now it seemed the fun was being replaced with brutality. Colin wanted blood, lots of it. Black eyes weren't enough, he wanted broken bones and battered bodies. Rob looked down at his dog, with his tail wagging, and envied how happy he was. Tyson loved life, and didn't want to hurt anyone, and if he did attack, it would be done out of fear, not mindless aggression. For a second, he wished he was back to being a nipper, back when he too, loved life. Back when Tyson first arrived home, back when Rob and Ryan had a common bond, and a happy home. But he wasn't a nipper, he was a man. And he was one of Colin's bitches. 'Come on, boy.'

Ryan felt sick. His head hurt and his face was tender to the touch. He felt disoriented and with the curtains drawn, he didn't know what time it was. Or what day. He tried to shake his headache away but it had the reverse effect, only making it worse. The room he was locked away in was empty except for the single bed he found himself on. The mattress was dirty, and Ryan counted at least three rusty springs protruding through the foam. The carpet curled up in the far corner and the wallpaper had lifted off the wall in places due to the black mould that was underneath. The room smelt as it looked, damp and dirty and there was an empty glass bong in the centre of the carpet and a spoon. It was apparent to Ryan where he had woken up; a crack house. He wanted to cry but he couldn't. Or wouldn't. The feeling he had of being a junior gangster was now a fading memory, as he wasn't sure now, if it had all been worth it.

He had tried to get out. Twice. But the door, although moving an inch, wouldn't go any further than that no matter how hard he pulled on the handle. The reason was simple, and crude. The man with the tear-drop tattoo had tied a rope between the handle on the outside of the door to the one of the railings on the bannister. Ryan was literally pulling against an immovable object. He wondered if Rob would be worried about him. Probably not. They were like ships passing in the night now, each up to their own thing and barely a grunt would pass between them if they were in the same house at the same time. He knew his mum would be too strung out to notice his absence. She had been a good mum, once, he thought. Or hoped. But now the cans of unbranded lager and cider washed down with both prescribed and some, not so prescribed, pills would render her helpless. He knew he was on his own. And for the first time in a very long time, he was afraid.

It seemed like an eternity before he heard footsteps, and getting louder. It wasn't the first time he had heard them, but it had been a while. A few minutes later he heard the flush go, and then he heard the footsteps again, this time getting quieter. Whoever it was, was back downstairs. A minute or so later he heard some coughing, and then the sound of the television being turned on. He knew he had been here for hours. If not days. What he didn't know was when he was getting out. Or if...

By the time Harlan got back to the B&B it was late. He heard Stan, behind the closed door, chuckling to whatever it was he was watching. He was in two minds to check in on Danielle, but decided against it. He had done his bit, he had, *had a word,* with the scumbag who liked to put his hands on her. But it was now on her to do what was right – to bin him off. Harlan knew that she had a window of opportunity to make some changes to her life. The scumbag wouldn't be getting tasty with his fists anytime soon, but there was the problem, as *soon* he would be gone. And fear, like milk, doesn't last forever, so she needed to get him out of her life and start afresh. He had laid the foundations, she now needed to build her own house.

He put the key into the lock, turned it and stepped into his room. That's all it was now; a room. Long gone was the house. Long gone, the dream. The British mentality of making, 2.4 children and a financed car on a block-paved driveway. Harlan had opted out of that, and the government pension scheme that went with it. His money was made using his wits; and his fists. His cash was put into assets; designer watches – watches that would rise in value, even if his social standing wouldn't. He had been an outlaw too long now to be anything else, and for too long now to *want* to be anything else. He didn't pride himself on much, but he was proud to be a brother of the Satan's Security MC. He took off his t-shirt and tossed it into the corner, there was no more life left in it, and he made a mental note to ask Stan if he could use his washing machine in the morning. Harlan grabbed his leather wash bag and went to the bathroom. He wanted a hot shower and a wet shave, in that order. The shower was electric which would have been good, but the split in the hose had lessened its power and what should have been a hail of hot water, was barely more than a drip. Stan had told him he was going to replace it today, which was what he had also said for the last three days. Harlan laughed to himself at Stan's frugalness, or forgetfulness, as he stripped off and stepped into the cubicle. The shampoo read that it was infused with certain plants and oils, but all he cared about was whether it would clean his hair. He was about to find out.

He stepped out of the shower ten minutes later; his hair smelling like a hanging basket.

He took the lid off the shaving gel, and squirted a large dollop into the palm of his right hand and then lathered up his cheeks and neck. Harlan looked at himself in the mirror, trying to remember the last time he was clean shaven. He couldn't and then set about tidying up the perimeter of his facial hair. He swished his razor around in the foamy water, freeing up the follicles that had gathered at each edge of the blade. He put his hand in the lukewarm water and pulled the plug, watching as it glugged itself away and then he put the tap to cold, and washed away the scum line that ran around the oval sink. Harlan gave his armpits a burst of deodorant and then walked back to his room, a towel bound tightly around him and his hair still dripping. Both the burners were on charge, the one he ran his life by, and the one recently purchased, to set up the demise of BigDogCol. The smartphone could wait its turn to charge, it wasn't as if it was busy; in fact, it was nothing more than a GPS, giving him needed directions when entering into a new town. He sat down on the edge of the bed whilst the kettle boiled, and thought back on the day. It had been eventful, drama filled, which was nothing new. Harlan wasn't sure anymore if he went courting for trouble, or if it just followed him around like a bad smell. But it hadn't been a bad day; he had a plan in play for Al's problem and had stopped, for now, Danielle's. And there was Jim. He had called his president for a reason, which was what it mainly was now between them. *Business.* But that was only because they had moved in different directions. Harlan had left the charter after deciding to go it alone – deciding to be a self-employed enforcer rather than that of the club's. Jim had given him his blessing, and up until recently, Harlan was the only nomad in the Satan's Security brotherhood. Jim was still at the helm of both his charter, and the club as whole. His word was gospel and his time for anything, limited. The club was a seven-day a week affair, and aside from taking his wife out once a week for a slap-up meal, every other minute of the day was spent on club business. But, even being at some times, at the opposite ends of the country, Jim had a lot of time for his protégé, and still hoped one day he would return to the fold and take over if not the club itself, then the charter. And for Harlan, he still idolised his president. It's what made them tight. It was why Harlan had called him. The kettle clicked off, little puffs of steam leaving the spout. The mug was already prepped, the teabag and three sachets of sugar sat waiting. He lifted the kettle from its baseplate and topped the mug up to the top before stirring it anticlockwise, hoping to scoop the sugar up from the seabed and into the murky water. Harlan did, as he normally did, before getting into bed with his last tea of the day, he checked the phones. His own burner was quiet. The other one showed an envelope; a message. He thumbed his way from the menu and to the text section. He knew before he read it who had sent the message. It didn't take Sherlock to figure it out as only one person had the number. The message read:

See you soon, for a kickabout.

Harlan smirked to himself, liking the arrogance of BigDogCol, but also as Colin had no idea just what he had got himself into. He didn't reply. Colin wasn't worth letting his tea go cold for.

15

J amal was up before his crew. He had two rashers
sizzling in the pan and had just added a splash of
rum to his black coffee. It had been a good night
judging by the drops. His crew had been out and
done the collections last night and he was looking
forward to counting the takings and updating his log.
The others thought it mad, writing it all down, believing
it was a sure-fire way to incriminate themselves on the
good thing they had going on. But Jamal was as clever as
he was chilling, the logs were all coded, and in a mixture
of Somalian slang and italics. He had devised it all
himself, with no-one else in the crew knowing it all. It
cemented his importance to the crew and maintained
his position. He knew that knowledge was power. The
bacon had fried to a crisp, just how he liked it and he
lifted each rasher out by his fingertips and dropped it
into the two buttered slices of bread. He added some
spicy sauce and put the two pieces of bread together, and
took a bite, before rubbing his greasy hand into his
jeans, which were in danger of falling down. Jamal was

barely much more than a skeleton, with the bacon having more fat on it than his body. It was the lack of mass that rather weirdly made him look more frightening, with his chiselled jaw line and prominent cheekbones adding to the devilish stare he could give, perfected by gritting his gloss white teeth which he hissed through when wanting to turn on the scare tactics.

He walked through to the living room, eager to count the envelopes in turn, knowing by a mark, in pencil, at the top of the envelope, which of his roadmen it had come from. He sat at the table and made some space for himself amongst the boxes of trainers, dirty dishes, boxes of bottled beer and knock-off fags. Jamal placed the envelopes in front of him in a line, and evenly spaced, his OCD taking over. He put the last piece of his breakfast into his mouth and when there was just enough room, he added a sip of spiced coffee in there to swill it down with.

He heard footsteps upstairs, someone was awake. The noise got louder; he heard footsteps walking down the stairs. He swung his head around to see who it was; it was a brass. She was dark-skinned and wearing a PVC miniskirt, or leather, he was too far back to tell. She met his stare, and wished she didn't. Jamal stood up, his jeans barely above his balls, and clinging on for dear life by the belt with the encrusted buckle. He didn't speak, which only made her more afraid, and Jamal started to walk towards her, slowly. Licking his lips, purposely. By the time he got to the hallway all he heard was the door shutting and the sound of her high heels scrambling across the lobby. He laughed to himself, but wished he had stayed sat down, so he could have watched her fat ass on the camera running out of the building. Jamal was security conscious, you had to be, when you had a safe full of cocaine and cash.

He walked over to the safe and entered the code, retrieving his log and rechecking the stock, even though he had already done it last night, and nobody had been in there since. It had become a force of habit. The stock was low, he would need a top up over the weekend, half a brick didn't last long but he would rather carry that than a whole one. There was a logic to it, though – the half brick would be turned into baggies and out on the streets quickly, meaning if they were ever to get raided, which was unlikely, the safe would only ever have enough in there to be classed as nothing more than simple possession. The guns, that was a different issue, they were hidden well, but loaded. Jamal took the log over to the table and got to work. Each envelope was counted, then recounted. Then the amount was cross referenced against the stock the kids had been given, meaning he knew how much each one would have left. He would randomly arrange a stock-check, sending one of his firm out to see what the kid had on him, armed with the figures Jamal had sent them with and if the numbers didn't tally, the slap across the face would be hard, but the threat about their family, whispered in their ear, was what made sure the next time they showed up, the books would be balanced.

It took close to an hour to count the cash, work out the takings and update the log but it was time well spent. Jamal prided himself on knowing his business inside out and was able to maximise his margins and move product around with the data he received, data that increased his sales. The other three were upstairs, probably still asleep and definitely still stoned, which is why he knew that he was not only the boss, but he would be the one person for whom crime did pay. His end game had never wavered and he was as ruthless about achieving it as he was the day job that would be paying for it. Jamal put the log and the cash back into the safe, locked it and went back to the kitchen and put another two rashers in the frying pan.

His workout was done. His muscles felt tight; pumped. It was another ritual; another habit. Living a nomadic life-style, rituals and habits helped. Working out wasn't the same as riding fifty-deep on a club run, or at a patch party, when a prospect has been deemed worthy of being a brother. Harlan remembers the day he got his patch like it was yesterday. As an outlaw, to be handed your top rocker, is up there with the birth of your child, and meaning more than six numbers on a lottery. The rocker connected you to a band of loyalty like no other, where the man standing beside you would die for you, as you would for him. Things had changed when he left to be a nomad, the silence had gotten louder over the years. Was he lonely? Sometimes. Was he alone? Always.

His mobile said it was breakfast time, and after a quick shower, and with his shoulder length hair still wet, with fresh droplets of water landing on the shoulders of his t-shirt, he walked downstairs and into the dining room. It was busy, with only two tables free. One in the centre of the room, and one over at the far wall. Neither table suited him, but the one at the wall did give a slightly better view of the room. Another ritual; another habit. Stan appeared with a jug of fresh orange juice and carried it over to the table by the window. Harlan looked at the occupants, two adults, two teenagers. Both teenagers were girls. In the two-second glance he saw they were the same age, more or less, and, as not identical looking, or even close, he deduced one was the daughter, the other, the best friend. The parents looked working class but with aspirations to get to the next level. Harlan knew his powers of observation, his ability to spot a problem before it actually became one, was what had kept him whole, so far. Stan approached the table, his little notepad in his hand.

'Morning, mate. Sleep well?' Stan asked, when he was close enough to do so.

'Yeah, ta. Looks busy here today. New punters?'

'Yes. Had a few check in yesterday afternoon. Didn't pay cash though!'

Harlan smiled. He liked Stan's spirit, and pictured him as a bit of a rogue back in the day. He made a note to push him on it and he knew Stan would have a few tales to tell, even if some of them were as made up as the Easter bunny. 'Still, all helps, right?' Harlan replied.

'Sure does. Keeps the government in taxes. Robbing shits.'

Harlan could see this conversation going on a while and he was hungry so cut it dead and got back to his belly. 'You got a fry-up still going on?'

'Course. Full works?'

'No. Sack off the black pudding and replace with an extra sausage, or a bacon. And same for the toe nails, replace them with an extra egg.'

'Got it – unless you want to change the whole bloody menu for a beef casserole and dumplings?'

Harlan laughed again. He liked that Stan was a mixture of curmudgeon and wit and knew he would be a cool Granddad. 'No, that's all the changes. Shouldn't you be closer to the kitchen?'

'Prick,' replied Stan, with a devilish smile.

He watched Stan limp his way out of his dining room and Harlan went back to scanning the room before relaxing and thinking about what he needed to do today.

The fear had turned to anger, then to frustration. From there it went back to anger and ended up at acceptance. He wasn't getting out of here by his own accord, and maybe, he wasn't getting out of here at all. He had heard the footsteps coming back up the stairs but it seemed like hours ago. Since then, the place had been quiet. Yes, there was noise outside. Noisy neighbours, barking dogs, loud cars. But that was on the outside, inside these four walls it was silent. And scary. He hoped by now someone would be missing him. Even if it was just his bosses. Telling them what had happened could wait until after, after that was, they had saved him. But he knew they wouldn't save him; how could they? They didn't know where he was and he knew that instead of being concerned for his well-being, they would be infuriated by his absence and believing he had ripped them off. Actually, it may be better for his legs that he was locked away in here, after all. His next thought went to Michael, with the thought quickly turning to guilt. He had bullied his friend into working for him, giving him only the plus points, namely that of money, but had hidden the fact Mikey could find himself in spots of bother, until it was too late. For the first time he hated what he had become, a teenage drug peddler, literally. His stolen bicycle was no longer used for doing wheelies and jumps, instead he was riding around the town carrying class A drugs and other people's profits. It was stupid; *he* had been stupid. He told himself he was going to change. That was, if he ever got out of there.

The gym was busy. It was the type of gym where it could be busy at half-ten in the morning, where the men lifting weights weren't constrained by the 9-5 life. It was a gym where anyone who was anyone, worked out there. Fraudsters, fencers, dealers and debt collectors. Colin felt in his element, he felt at home with these people, and if he was being honest, he got off on it. From the bullied kid at school, he was now a prince among thieves, with aspirations of being one of the kings. Colin wasn't alone, he never went anywhere alone if he could help it. His friend lifted another steel circular disc onto the bar, and span up the knurled nut onto the threaded bar.

'You up for tomorrow, Tone?' Colin asked, as he lowered his back down onto the bench, and put his hands up onto the bar, and fumbled around to set up a grip he felt comfortable with.

'Yeah, course mate. Always.'

'Good lad. All in, remember. Give this melt and his mates a good hiding.'

Colin looked up at his friend, from down on the bench, wanting to see a glint in Tony's eye. He had got what he wanted; his mate had given him a smile, but what he didn't know was that for Tony, it was to appease his friend, not because he wanted to turn up, tooled up, and inflict serious damage on some strangers. What had started off as a bit of Saturday fun, taking on other firms for a spontaneous punch-up, had now resulted in his friend wanting to do real damage, and that could end up in serious prison time. That wasn't what Tony had signed up for, but he was in it now, and Colin was becoming increasingly difficult to say no to.

'Remember to bring the dusters, yeah?' Colin asked, the barbell resting on his chest, ready for the next push.

'Yeah. Anything else?'

'You've still got your gloves I gave you?' Colin was referring to a pair of leather gloves. To the outside world they looked like the gloves you would see on a Granddad driving his Jaguar, but to the underworld, they were a Godsend. The gloves had been adapted so ball bearings were stitched into the knuckles, cleverly concealed by the leather, and when a punch was thrown, the results were devastating. It would take a head made of concrete to withstand being hit from a fist laced with steel.

'Yeah – wouldn't leave the house without them, ha.'

Colin laughed at his friend's remark. It was the same sinister sounding laugh that turned his friend's stomach.

The pub had a handful of customers when Harlan arrived, and Big Al was serving behind the bar, alone. Harlan liked that he had cut his costs, recognising that whilst you find ways to expand, you at first, retreat. Seven men. No females. They would come tonight. A few drinks after work but more likely they would come later, after the shower, gloss and floss. But for now, just seven men. None looked like they would, or could cause any trouble. Harlan approached the bar and waited for Alan to become free. One of the seven was chewing his ear about the cost of living and Harlan could tell Alan was nodding in the all the right places, the sign of a good landlord.

Finally, he broke free from the diatribe, and made his way down the bar. 'Alright Harlan. What you having?' he asked.

'I'll take a coke. Not a bad start?'

'Mostly my midday regulars. I can count on them being here at least 3-4 times a week.'

'Better spending their giro here than somewhere else.'

'Exactly. Ice and a slice?'

'Just ice. Ta.'

Alan filled the glass up to the top, waited for the fizz to settle, then added a squirt full more from the dispenser. It wasn't real coke, but it made a healthy margin and Harlan was happy to play his part in helping Alan pay his bills. He took a sip from the glass, before picking it up, to avoid spilling it as he manoeuvred it from hand to mouth.

'I need a word. Come and find me outside when you have a minute.'

Alan nodded his head, unsure what the *word* would be, but hoping whatever it was, that it would be related to returning his pub back to him, as he had met up with his accountant prior to opening and it hadn't left him with a spring in his step, more an ulcer in his stomach. Harlan took his drink outside and sat on one of the tables. The beer garden was empty which was a plus, and the road outside was busy, another plus. There were a lot of people who put their trust in encrypted apps, or phones that could switch between numbers but Harlan preferred the old school method of talking into someone's ear, perfectly timed to when a car comes past. *What the eye can't see, and what the eye can't read, can't get you nicked.* Another ritual; another habit. Harlan was halfway through his coke when Alan walked out, carrying two packets of crisps and a fresh coke. He watched as Big Al sat down opposite, trying to get his bulk between the seat and table, which wasn't easy when they were one item screwed together. Finally, he was in and Alan offered a bag of crisps to Harlan. 'I'm fine, thanks,' he replied, knowing that would be the answer Alan was hoping for.

'You wanted a word?' Alan said, through a mouthful of Cheese and Onion crisps.

Harlan wasn't impressed with the lack of table manners and gave Alan a look that said as much. Big Al took the hint, and Harlan waited as he hurriedly munched his way through his bulging mouthful before finally returning up for air. 'You wanted a word?' he repeated.

Harlan waited for some cars to turn into the road, to time his reply.

'Tomorrow will be quite a day here. You need to be prepared for it to go off.'

'Go off?' Alan asked.

Another car turned into the road. Another reply. 'Yes. Go *off*.'

The penny dropped for Alan by the annunciation, and then his face changed.

'How heavy is all this going to get?'

'Like a two-ton weight dropped from Hell. It's show-time. My advice, sell tickets.'

Harlan looked directly into Alan's eyes, hoping he was up for this. He had called him, asking for his help and now he was here, about to deliver. It was time for Alan to know a war was coming. Harlan knew it wasn't easy. Confrontations aren't easy, even less so when they are planned, your mind works against you, your body shows signs of stress. He knew it wasn't easy, but Alan had found himself in his world and in that world, violence was common, but luckily for Alan, so too was victory.

'Tomorrow will be the change. This pub will be yours by the end of the day. But there are a few things I need you to do for me.'

Alan had lost his appetite, the second packet of crisps was unopened, he wasn't a fighter and the look on his face told Harlan as much.

'Get yourself together. You chose this trade over flower arranging, and there are times you need to stand up and do what's asked. This is one of those times.'

Harlan then pulled a piece of paper from his pocket and slid it across the table towards Alan. He watched as Alan opened it up and watched as Al's eyebrows narrowed. He knew next that Alan would look at him and he did. 'I need that sorted. Got it?'

Big Al nodded, a confused look coming over his face.

'Good. Now you best get back in there and serve your punters.'

His wife had made a Caesar salad. Colin had eaten everything but the salad, which was the chicken, and pushed his plate away to the centre of the table. One of the kids had tried to copy but Colin had told them to eat it. *Do as I say, not as I do.* Colin had become bored in the marriage, sure enough, she was a good-looking woman, and once upon a time he may have been punching above his weight, but not now. Now he had a reputation, he was a man to be reckoned with. His aim of being a gangster was already in play and his dream of being the 'guvnor' of one of the biggest football fighting firms was well under-way. Another victory tomorrow would only further his reputation and when he then boasted about it on the underground forums, he knew other firms would want a go, and so it would continue, until one day he would be sat on his throne, looking down at his rivals. *Made it, ma! Top of the world.*

His wife asked him what had just made him laugh but he couldn't explain it. He knew she wouldn't get it. She had come from good stock. Her parents had raised her well and although not overly academic, she wasn't a doughnut; but her main play was her looks. She had a tight body and her ass looked good in jeans, which was what got her bought drinks but also what got her knocked up with her first kid at a young age. Colin knew he wasn't as lucky. He was short on height and stature and his school years weren't fun, but that day he first fought back, when he gave his nemesis a hiding so bad in the youth club, that's when it all changed. What had started off as a row over who was playing next, with Colin knowing it was his turn, that he had put his pound coin down first to play the winner, that he was in the right. The lad was bigger, older and a bully. He had made Colin's life hell for a couple of years, tripping him up whenever he used to walk past him at school and then the ultimate embarrassment, his head being shoved down the toilet. Colin felt the anger swell around him and when the bigger lad pushed him, he snapped. Colin swiped the pool cue from out of the hand of one of the two boys that were playing and swung it viciously into the body of his long-term bully. From there Colin unleashed a lifetime's worth of fury, pummelling his fists into the older lad's head until one of the volunteers heard the commotion and came running. Colin never forgot that night. It was like he had been reborn. He had turned from the bullied into the bully. It felt good. Right. The world was here for the taking.

His wife cleared the table and Colin took himself, and his bottle of beer into the front room, slumped down into the expensive sofa, put his feet up on the pouffe and started to scroll through his phone. He had made it clear lately he was the man of the house, and as such, menial tasks such as cooking and cleaning were down to her, plus, if she wanted, she could delegate some down to the kids, he had told her. Colin was going through his army. Making sure everyone was down for tomorrow. As always, he would supply the pre-fight liveners, the cocaine, which would make him a few extra quid. If he got home early enough tomorrow, he would treat them all to a Chinese. But he already knew he wouldn't be home early. Or sober.

Harlan pulled back into the car park just as it was turning dark. There were nine cars in it. A mixture of blacks, blue and whites. Some quite new, some not. Mostly not. He knew some of these would be driven home, and some of them would stay there as their drivers would be over the limit. Not his problem. As long as they were inside, spending, the rest was just apples. He walked through the beer garden, getting a mixture of looks. Some were admiring, some were envious, some were non-committal. Every face told a story, and in that regard, Harlan was well read. He stepped inside the pub and looked from left to right. Thirty-six. Including the fourteen that were outside. Some of which were sitting down, a couple were stood up, vaping. Thirty-six heads. Twenty-four of which were male. The youngest looked barely legal, the oldest looked more of a war veteran, rather than a Friday night power drinker. The music was good, maybe a bit too loud, Harlan thought, but it seemed decent enough, and modern. There was a blackboard affixed to one of the pillars advertising live music for the following weekend. He knew he wouldn't be there to see the band, but he hoped they would be good. For Alan's sake. He had already clocked the leggy blonde looking him up and down, and also the tattooed lump stood next to her, who had seen her looking. He made a mental note of the fella's position to him, and the distance, purposely putting himself adjacent to his right, and four strides away. Past knockouts had told him four strides ended up being the perfect starting point when he needed to take a running start. He hoped he wouldn't need to, that this fella's ego would quickly get in check, as his t-shirt looked too new, too white, to get covered in claret. The bar itself was busy. There were two barmaids working, neither of which Harlan had seen before. Big Al was also there, and he was pouring a pint of Guinness to the old war boy who was at the far end of the bar, alone. Harlan wondered if Alan knew him; he hoped he did.

'What can I get you?' She was mid-twenties. Curvaceous, and attractive.

'A bottle of Becks, cheers,' he replied. He noticed her micro expression. A lustful smile. She returned with the bottle, the top off and as she handed it over, he felt her fingers deliberately run across his hand. She had tried to make it subtle; she failed. He knew anyone stood behind him would be looking at his patch, each one having an opinion, each one surmising on the man who was inside. There were those who loved the look of an outlaw, the 70's ride free/party hard still loomed large for those who could remember it. For others, those who knew the bikers only since the 90's, they would see them as powerful gangsters, up to their necks in criminal activities and who would bite the heads off pigeons for fun. It always made him smirk when he got people dissecting the patch into their own warped interpretation of what an outlaw biker was, and all too often, it would be wrong. Some of his closest friends were criminals, that he couldn't, or wouldn't deny, others in the club were nothing more than law-abiding citizens who just happened to love Harleys and wanted to be part of something that they never had. Harlan waited at the bar for Alan to become free and he used the time to add the extra people to his headcount. It was at an even number now; forty, but that was what was inside the four walls, not sure if the extra four were actually part of the original fourteen outside. The music stopped for a second. But then started again, this time with a voice attached to it. The DJ had arrived. His microphone was giving feedback and Harlan knew he had about thirty seconds to get it sorted before he would start hearing shitty voices from his audience. Alan finally got free from having his ear bent and came out from behind the bar to join Harlan, who was still standing there. Still four paces away from Mr Tight-white t-shirt. Alan was holding a pint in his hand, which was about a large mouthful down from being full. 'I've done what you've asked,' Alan said.

'Any problems?'

'Nope. All went to plan.'

'Good. And you've got this, yeah?'

'Yeah. I mean, erm... well, I –'

'Al, it was a simple question. Have you got this?'

'Yeah, mate. Yeah, I've got it.'

Harlan didn't like being called mate. He wasn't his mate. Alan was his problem, not his friend. Big difference.

'Are you staying for a bit?' Alan asked, trying to make small talk to hide his blushes.

'No. I'm having this and heading off. You don't need me tonight. Tomorrow is when the fun and games start.'

He said it to see how it sat with Al, to see if he was still missing his bollocks.

He was. Which was fine. Alan was a straight-goer, and that wasn't a bad thing. The underworld wasn't as glamorous as people on the outside thought it was, the truth was if you didn't have a tight crew, or even if you did, a criminal without a code wouldn't think twice about throwing you under a bus. Literally. Which was why Harlan knew he was one of the luckier ones, he was a member of Satan's Security, and proud of it. The MC didn't just have a code, they wore it. And with pride. He also knew the reason they had been so successful over the years was down to Jim, the club's president. His vetting process was lengthy, but it made all the difference. It was why they hadn't ever had a rat. Yes, some had left, but they had left with good standing, they hadn't been put *out on bad,* which was a place no brother wants to find himself. It was Jim's diligence that made the club what it was, and what kept his members whole.

He emptied the rest of his bottle into his mouth. 'Right, I'm off.'

'Don't want to stay? It looks like it's shaping up to be a good night, plenty of birds in, too.'

'I've seen enough birds down by the seaside, and most of them shit in my ice-cream.'

'Fair play, mate. Fair play.'

'Right, I'm off. I'll be here tomorrow, at 2. Remember, this place needs to be closed.'

Harlan knew Alan would be thinking of the lost trade. Just before the game he always did well. But it was after, when the game kicked off, that it went to shit in a bucket. Which was why he was here – to change the result. In more ways than one.

16

Harlan was up and out before the day broke. He needed a ride. Needing to be alone. Just him and his Harley. He could feel the salty air land on his face as he roared past the beach, his exhaust pipe growling like an angry dog protecting its bone. The roads were quiet, the day was yet to start but Harlan needed this time. He pulled up outside a beach fronted coffee shop. The owner was outside, winding up the awning ready to let the daylight enter his dwelling, hoping the view from the inside would bring them in from the outside. Harlan normally avoided the multinationals, not wanting to make the fat cats fatter. But this was independently owned and every fiver would be appreciated, which was why he got off his bike and walked in. 'Morning mate,' the owner said, trying to tie his apron around his back before adding, 'What can I get you?'

'Just a tea, ta. Any chance of a bacon sarnie?'

'Sure. Just give me a few minutes to set up the grill. Milk and sugar?'

'Yes, and three.'

'Three? Mouthful of fillings?'

'Not one.'

The owner's glib comment irked him, but Harlan put it down to it being early, so he let it pass. He walked over to the window, looking out at the sea. There was a big day ahead, not for him, but for Big Al; the reason he was here. If it all went to plan, and it would, then he would be checking out tomorrow. At the minute there was no next job, no new town. He would take that time to go back to his brothers. Back to the clubhouse. Back home. A few minutes later the owner shouted from the back of the building. His tea and sandwich were ready. Harlan turned and made his way to the counter and picked up his breakfast, deciding he wasn't worthy of saying goodbye and resenting for once, not choosing a multinational.

The sea wasn't still, but it wasn't in danger of being surfed, either. It was breaking a long way out, the white froth gently making its way up to the shoreline, which was just a few inches away from the edge of his boots. The bacon was overdone. Edible, but overdone. The tea was weak, and when he lifted off the polystyrene lid, lifeless. If he had to describe its colour for TripAdvisor, he would choose beige, like the owner himself. The beach was starting to get some visitors. Three. Which was three too many; it was time to go. Harlan walked back to his bike, stopping to dump his cup and sandwich wrapper in the bin, which had some graveyard shift seagulls waiting for scraps. His phone told him it was nearing seven, the only question now being did he want one of Stan's fry-ups to wash down his bacon sarnie? The answer was yes, which was why he pressed the starter button on the

Harley and rode back to the B&B, his early morning well-being mission was over.

Ryan heard the footsteps again. They were getting louder, meaning whoever it was on the outside of the door was walking upstairs, not down. It felt like days since he had last eaten, or drank anything. He was dehydrated and weak. He needed this to end, one way or another. This was torture, and he was afraid it was slowly killing him. Ryan's dark thoughts were interrupted by a hard knock at the door, and a less than welcoming wake-up call.

'Oi, get up, shithead. You're getting paroled.'

Ryan went to speak, but couldn't. It was over. His stint in solitary confinement had come to an end. 'Th... thank... thank you.'

'Shut up, kid,' came the reply from outside the door.

It hit home. He was a kid. A stupid kid trying to be an adult. He wasn't a gangster; he was a teenager. He was astute enough to know this was his crossroads moment and he knew which road he was going to take. The tears he had tried so hard to stop, he now couldn't.

He heard some cussing outside and then watched as the door handle started to turn. The self-reflection stopped, immediately, replaced with a swell of fear. Was it just a ruse? Was he about to get a second kicking. Or worse.

The door opened, it didn't fly back in a fit of rage, nor did it open slowly, and eerily. It just opened, like locking someone in a room for a few days was a natural thing to do. And maybe it was, if you were a coked-up psychopath with no grasp on what was right or wrong.

'Well, you clearly aren't wanted. How does that feel?'

Ryan knew what he was referring to. It was true, no-one had come to his rescue. They either didn't know, or didn't care. Or both. That realisation hurt more than the beating.

'Anyways, I'm sick of you being here. Get your shit and get out.'

Ryan had no shit to get, it was just a saying but it was the cue he was waiting for. Ryan walked over to the door, but to get out, he had to get past the man with the teardrop tattoo. Was this the bear trap? Was the invite to exit just a ploy? Ryan didn't know, and didn't know what to do. His head told him to make a run for it, to just bolt past and make for the stairs and then the front door. Then to run away, run like Forest, and never, ever come back here. Or anywhere close. But would he get past him, or get away? The risk was higher than the reward. Each footstep he took got slower. And shorter. His heart was racing and his mouth was dry. But his brain said keep going. To keep moving forward. He found himself in touching distance, not of the door, but of the man with the teardrop tattoo. The prize of freedom was just a few feet away. He took another step forward, his route starting to deviate, to no longer walk in a straight line from his starting position to the open door, instead, he was starting to arc, to walk around his prison warden. He was nearly there when, BANG. Before he knew it, he was up against the wall, the collar of his t-shirt gripped and twisted, he was struggling to breathe.

'Now listen here, you were kept here to see if whoever it is you work for, was going to come and get you. But they didn't, which tells me you aren't worth shit to them.'

Ryan was looking directly into his eyes. They were dilated.

'But just to be clear, if you do go telling tales like a little bitch, and I get a tug for the feds, or your old man, or your punk-ass pimp, then next time you won't be getting out of here. Well, not alive, anyways.'

Ryan didn't want to try to speak. Because he couldn't. He just nodded. Nodded and prayed this was the end of it.

'Now, piss off.'

It was the end.

Ryan didn't stop to straighten his ruffled collar, he just wanted out of there. He scooted around the man with the teardrop tattoo and out onto the landing. Resting on the floor was what had kept him captive, a rope, with one end still tied to the rail on the bannister. Ryan ran down the stairs and in his rush to leave, he ran straight past his bicycle which was propped up against the wall of the hallway, in front of the radiator. He turned around to get it, and wheeled it out the hallway, pushed it up and over the threshold and then as soon as he could, he got on and started to peddle as fast as his legs would let him. So fast, in fact, that twice his feet slipped off, with the pedals coming back around and hitting him on his heels.

The energy drinks in the refrigerator were his. The kids had been told not to touch them. Same for his protein bars. Same for a lot of things. The once family home had now become his very own fiefdom, and it was fast being run by an iron fist. His wife had told him the steroids were fuelling his rage, but he didn't care. He had set himself a goal and nobody, not even his wife and kids, were going to derail it. He had been awake early. He was too excited to sleep any longer. Fight days always felt like

Christmas. Colin had everybody in place; fifteen of his trusted allies. His soldiers. All ready to defend their club. And not just the football club, but also *his* club; the mighty Cherry Pickers.

As was usual on every Saturday, Colin had Sky Sports on in the background. He was an ardent fan, both national and international, and had travelled up and down the country following his team, and across Europe, supporting his country. He had used the last of the Weet-abix for his breakfast, and covered the bowl to the top with milk before splashing two heaped spoons of sugar over the top. That was alongside his cup of coffee, sugared, and his can of Monster. The sugar, then topped up with some of Columbia's finest, meant he would be absolutely buzzing by the afternoon, or as his mates would say, *off his nut*. He heard stirring from upstairs, it would be either his wife or one of his step kids. He did enjoy the family side of life, but only on his terms, which was getting less and less. He was becoming a busy man, a *known man*. His dreams were starting to come true. He checked the time on his watch; still hours to go. It was the waiting that he hated. 2pm couldn't come quick enough. He imagined it would all be over in half an hour, and then it was party time, curtesy of that fat fuck at the pub. A smile came across his face; a punch-up and then loads of pints in a pub he now called his own to part. Life felt good. He checked his watch again.

Harlan had decided to opt for fried eggs on toast instead of a fry-up. It wasn't as if he was counting his cholesterol level, it was just he felt like eggs on toast.

'Did you shit the bed?' Stan asked.

'No – your bitch ass snoring woke me up. You part hippo?'

The banter was becoming habitual now between them, and Harlan loved Stan's spirit. He could have made a good outlaw back in the day.

'How do you want them eggs?'

'Soon,' replied Harlan, trying his best to keep a straight face as he said it but cracking under the pressure. Stan called him a swear word under his breath but it was too faint to hear, although Harlan had a pretty good guess what it was. With Stan now busy in the kitchen and the dining room pretty much empty, he took out his burner and sent a text.

Pretty much straight away he got a reply. It was one word: **Left.**

The reply had made his eggs taste that much better; it was as if that one word was all the seasoning they needed. The yolk was nice and runny. Just how he liked it. For a cantankerous old git, Stan was handy in the kitchen. With that thought in his mind, Stan appeared, carrying two mugs, and limped his way over to his table.

'Mind if I join you?'

'And if I said no?' Harlan said.

'Then I would sit down anyway as it's my pissing table.'

Harlan nearly choked on the piece of fried egg and toast that he had in his mouth at Stan's comeback. 'Sure, take a pew.'

Stan pulled out the chair and slowly, but surely sat down. 'Here, I made you a tea.'

'Ta.'

'I saw Danielle this morning. Bless her, she is a sweet thing really.'

'How is she?'

'I think she is getting there. Definitely looks like a weight's been lifted.'

'That's good – how long is she staying for?'

'Not sure. She is due to check out today, unless she wants to stay for some more R&R.'

Harlan went to reach for his pocket but Stan stopped him.

'No, don't. If she wants to stay for a couple more days, at least over the weekend, then it's on me.'

'You sure?' Harlan asked.'

'100% - listen, I can still help a damsel in distress, even if my best fighting days are behind me.'

'You're a top fella, Stan. I mean it.' Harlan was touched by the gesture Stan had made.

'I know, right. Never did get that bloody OBE though.'

They both laughed at the comment, and Harlan had a feeling he would be keeping in contact with Stan after he had finished up his bit of business here.

'So, what you got planned today then, fella?' Stan asked, before slurping on his tea.

'Oh, nothing much, I'll just be kicking about.'

Stan noticed the twinkle in his eye. Knowing there was some truth to the comment.

Harlan thought about taking a shower. Then decided against it. Logic told him it would be better to have one after. When he would be washing off Colin's teeth from his fists. It was the thought of exploding enamel that made him look inside his rucksack. He put his hand right down to the bottom, then over to the corner, and brought out a towel. It was small. Hand sized. He couldn't remember which B&B he accidentally took it from. And that was the problem; there had been so many over the years. He unwrapped the towel and inside were a pair of brass knuckles. He slipped them over his fingers, then turned his hands into fists. The knuckle-dusters were a gift from the club, more specifically, Jim. Over the years, when the 1-on-1 turned into 5, 6, 7 onto one, the crude bits of metal had proven invaluable, and victorious. There was another benefit to using blunt metal instead of sharp, or bits of metal that go bang. Prison time. They were classed as offensive weapons, same as anything else that could hurt, but he knew the time behind bars would only be a couple of years, not five plus. Harlan knew he had been lucky, so far. He was yet to stay at Her Majesty's Travelodge, but he had been close. Too close. He was also a realist; and in his line of work you couldn't make an omelette without breaking a few eggs. Or teeth. He slipped the knuckles back over his fingers, and then, for some unknown reason, buffed them clean with the towel, before putting them in his pockets. The smartphone was charging and from the corner of his eye, the screen sprang to life. He walked over to it with a slight knot in his stomach. It couldn't be, could it? By the time he got to the phone the illuminated screen had gone back to black, requiring a wake-up call from his fingertip. He felt himself pause before he touched it, then shook his head at how silly he was being, and as an act of manliness to whatever soft side of his psyche had appeared, dabbed his finger hard down on the screen. There wasn't a reply; it was nothing more than his phone telling him an update was due. He ignored the message, same as the last three messages telling him to do the same. He went back to focusing on business. Back to focusing on BigDogCol, and his soon-to-be demise.

He gave his wife a kiss on the cheek, his mouth still chewing on the sausage sandwich he had asked her to make him. The kids were outside, playing on the trampoline housed inside a safety net, which was the only way that his wife would let them have one. It grated on him how safety-conscious she was. Elbow and knee pads when on their bikes. Goggles when in the pool. High-factor sun cream and seatbelts. It was different when she was out, when Colin was on babysitting duty. The expensive ice-cream would come out, 15-rated movies and swearing. He was determined to take off the cotton wool they were tightly wrapped in. He grabbed his keys to the Porsche and picked up his holdall that was now down by the front door.

'What time will you be back?' his wife asked.

'When I'm back.'

'Which is when?'

'Which is when you see me. You have two kids. Not fucking three.'

Colin picked up his holdall and walked out the door, and slammed it shut to show his displeasure at being interrogated. He buzzed the fob to unlock the door and reached over to put the bag down into the passenger footwell. He got in and fired up the powerful engine. Someone had told him he only bought the car to make up for having a small dick. The ensuing bottle that cracked over his head seconds after made him never want to say it again. Colin had arranged to pick up Tony, and Rob. The rest of his crew would meet them at the disused industrial estate, where the weapon inventory would be allocated, so too, the cocaine. He flicked the car into reverse and pulled off the driveway, onto the road and left the leafy, suburban street deliberately faster than his neighbours would have liked.

Rob was in the bathroom. He tried a few times to have a designer beard. Even letting the Turkish barbers have a go at making it work, but it was no use, his facial hair was too wispy, which his mum had told him had come from *his dad's side of the family.* This was why he was in the bathroom, his face full of foam and a disposable razor in his hand. Tyson was barking downstairs, hoping someone would get infuriated enough to take him for a walk. The first part of the dog's game plan was working. It was pissing Rob off, but he knew the dog had shit out on the second, as Colin was on his way and his lazy-ass brother was still nowhere to be found. It was starting to concern him, not a lot, but just enough to have sent him a text last night: **Shithead, where you at?**

Rob checked the time on his phone, which was propped up against the can of shaving foam on the shelf just above the sink and was playing some heavy drum and bass music. He needed to get a wiggle on, so he started shaving with a little more speed and a little less precision. Two minutes later he was slapping cold water onto his cheeks and checking his chops for near misses. It was good enough, he would do. He pulled the plug and took a towel with him to his bedroom to dry his face, leaving the sink with a rim of soapy water and his unwanted hairs. His mum had been awake, and coherent enough, to have done a wash and amongst the clean clothes in the washing basket, which Tyson had chewed more than once, was his favourite t-shirt. It was his favourite as it had become his lucky mascot. Every time he wore it for a rumble he was yet to lose, and beside the broken nose, was yet to get properly hurt. He took it from the pile and hung it up in front of him, with his arms outstretched. It was in need of an iron (his mum hadn't gotten that far) but it was clean, and when he put it up under his nose, it smelt pretty decent, too. He took it with him to the bedroom and emerged a few minutes later, dressed, wearing aftershave and his Timberland boots. He walked across the landing and stopped at his mum's bedroom door. It was ajar, just. He pushed it open, gently, knowing she would be asleep. He stepped inside and walked over to her dresser, which was full of medication and painkillers. His mum was on a cocktail of drugs, prescribed at will to try and help her with her many ailments; depression, insomnia, fibromyalgia and chronic fatigue syndrome. Rob was no longer sure how many of these were real, or just in her head, and yes, the last few years she had been a shit mum but he loved her, nonetheless. He took out his wallet and counted out his keep, and left it on the side, next to the fresh packet of paracetamol. He put an extra twenty on top, for her fags. She wouldn't know he had paid extra, but he did, and that was all that mattered. She was dead to the world. She wasn't snoring but her mouth was open. He pulled the duvet up under her chin, and despite the pain she was in, most of it mental, she looked peaceful. He hoped one day she would get better, that her demons would one day leave her be. For her sake. He crept back across the room and closed the door and as he walked down the stairs; he

heard the sound of a car horn. Colin was outside, ready
and waiting.

Harlan turned his Harley into the road. Big Al's pub was a
few hundred yards up on the right. He rode past, slowly,
but not too slowly. He drove down the road and found a
space and walked his bike back into it, killed the engine
and put it on its stand. He didn't want his bike in the car
park when they showed up. He wanted the pub looking
as desolate as possible. It was time to turn the tables, and
change the result. Alan was a nice man, and a liked landlord, and he didn't deserve to have his business turned
into a battleground every time twenty-two men kicked a
bag of wind around a grassy field. Harlan didn't care they
punched seven bells of shit out of each other, that was
their prerogative. He also wasn't here to pour scorn on
football hooligans. What he did have a problem with, was
they had involved the *straights*. Their passion for
inflicting pain on their rivals was impacting another
man's livelihood – and that shit wasn't on. Harlan had
grown to have a moral code. You don't hurt women or
children and you don't bring the *straights* into your world.
Colin had messed up; he had gone against Harlan's code
and for that there would be repercussions. He knew
Colin's moniker was BigDogCol, it was now time to show
him just who was the biggest dog in the pack. The empty
car park had become his bear trap, and in a couple of
hours he would have snared them all.

17

Outside of the natural light coming in through the net curtains, the pub was in darkness. The rich, deep mahogany muted, with the only colour on display was that of the brass rail that ran around the foot of the bar. Sat in the far corner, almost out of sight, was Alan. He had a cup of coffee next to him. It had gone cold. Harlan walked over to him. He knew, for Alan, it had just gotten real. Alan had gotten used to losing his pub, and his customers, every time the local football team were playing at home. He was now used to the fighting and the fear. He had gotten used to the damage. Familiarity doesn't always breed content; it just breeds familiarity. And now he was here to change that. Harlan pulled out a chair, and sat down, opposite Big Al. 'I don't know why the long face but snap out of it. Sharpish.'

Harlan knew what he was going through, beating himself up, but it was tough love time.

'You have,' Harlan looked down at his phone, 'exactly thirty seconds to decide if you want to do this.'

It wasn't a ploy. Harlan knew that when things were about to get heavy, some people couldn't deal with it, couldn't deal with the responsibility, even if it was in their own interests. Harlan knew that most people couldn't make the tough decisions, even if it was for the right reasons. It was time for Alan to decide. Did he want what was easy, or, what was right?

Alan looked down at his cup, his eyes without sparkle. But then, like Harlan knew he would, Alan reconnected. Alan lifted up his head and there was now resolve, not rejection, in his eyes. There is a point when decent folk fight back, when they've had enough, and this was that moment. The fire was back in Alan's belly. 'Let's do it.'

That was all Harlan needed to hear.

The entire crew were sitting in the minibus. Colin had a mate in the local scrapyard and for a grand, it had been repaired, serviced and was now the proud owner of a bent MOT. It was stored in a local lock-up and used only on match days. Benny was entrusted with the keys and, as such, was the designated driver. Colin had known him for a few years. Benny had been a doorman at one of the clubs in town, and Colin used to slip him a quick ton to do a bit of dealing inside. Benny was a brawler; a street fighter, but he wasn't a strategist. That was Colin's role. The weapons had been distributed. Brass knuckles. Coshes. Broken pool cues and an iron bar. All chosen for being easily concealed and easily used. Colin wanted his crew to have a reputation of being utterly ruthless. That if you came to his manor for a row, you wouldn't come twice. For Colin this had become more than just a bunch of blokes having a roll-around, he wanted a name. He wanted notoriety. Everyone in the van was picked for their ability to have a row and could stand up and be counted. Inside, Colin was giving a pep talk to a group of men who were scaring local supporters and who had turned a local pub into a caged arena. Colin was getting off on his battle cry speech.

'Right, lads. Listen up. Big day today. I don't know who this chump is but he wanted it, so he is gonna get it, right?'

'Right' replied a few from the fourteen.

'That was weak as piss. I said, RIGHT?'

'RIGHT.'

'That's fucking better. So, we stash our weapons down our trollies, and we only use them at the end. When they've already lost. Just a few whacks with the coshes and dusters, just to send these mugs on their way. Got it?'

There were nods and agreements. Not as loud as Colin would have liked but he got their agreement. His orders were understood. He looked over at Rob, sensing unrest.

'What's up with you, big man? You left your bottle back home, eh?'

'Nah mate. Course not.'

'What's the wet face for then?'

Colin said it so everybody else would look at Rob. It was deliberate. Shame him to rile him, that was the plan. He knew the best leaders ran their army on belittling and contempt, he had read it in a book somewhere.

'Come on, spit it out. If you want to bitch out, do it now.' The mocking continued.

'Nah, Col, it's sweet. Honest. It's just my brother.'

'What about your brother?' Colin asked, minus any concern.

'I just can't get hold of the little shit.'

'Why's that my problem?'

'It isn't,' Rob replied.

'I know it fucking well isn't. Now get your head in the game, will ya?'

'Course. Sorry. Yeah, let's fucking do this.'

Colin stared at him, just enough to make it uncomfortable before moving on with the sermon. 'I can hear the result now. Cherry Pickers one. The other team didn't.'

The van erupted in laughter. How much of it false, Colin couldn't tell.

He knew though it was time to inject some spice into his speech and so he leant forward and unzipped his holdall that was on the floor between his legs, putting his hands inside before bringing them back out clutching little transparent packets of white powder.

'Look lads, my mate Charlie has turned up.'

The laughter was immediate, so too was the flurry of notes being handed to him, each one trying to get a line quicker than the others. Each one wanting the white powder up their nose and in their system. Pretty soon the minibus was awash with fourteen fellas snorting coke from the back of their hand. Colin looked on. He was £500 richer and his army was ready. It was time. It was fucking time.

'Home James,' he shouted across to Benny, who started up the van and put it into gear.

. . .

The cameras were turned off and Alan had put up signs in the window. They were torn from an A4 notepad and the words were in capital letters, written in a black marker pen:

CLOSED UNTIL 5PM – SORRY FOR ANY INCONVENIENCE.

Big Al stuck them to the window with a little blob of blue-tack in each corner. He turned to face Harlan who had made himself a cup of tea. 'We will be open later, right?'

Harlan looked down across the bar at him, declining to answer. Alan may have found his resolve but he was still showing doubts, which was understandable, it was his business, his livelihood, Harlan knew, but it was starting to grate.

'I'm sorry. It's just, I'm... It's the unknown.'

'For you it's unknown. For me, this is as routine as you changing a barrel. You just need to do as that list says. Do that, and everything will work out like I said.'

Alan nodded his head in full agreement, it was a nod that said all his eggs were in Harlan's basket. Harlan checked his phone. 2.50pm. Ten minutes until kick off. Time to get ready.

He could feel Alan's eyes on his back as he turned and headed for the back door, to the car park. It was a sunny day with just a hint of breeze. The car park was expansive, and there were plenty of loose chippings on the floor which told him if he ended up grappling on the floor, it would scuff his cut, and that would be sacrilege, which is why he would take it off. But not yet.

.   .   .

The minibus was full of football chants being sung, and feet stomping. Colin had whipped his crew up to a frenzy and the pub was little more than a mile away. The traffic was busy with supporters making their way from all corners of the town trying to find places to park that didn't cost the earth or didn't get them tickets. Benny had put on some dance tunes, which added nicely to the pumped up feeling from inside the van. Colin was a little less high than the rest of his mob, he knew a good General keeps his eye on the ball during battle, but lets his hair down better than the rest in victory. And he would be victorious, he had no doubt about it. He had gone from the bullied to the bully, the hunted to the hunter. *How dare this prick message up and ask for a rumble, didn't he know who he was?* – he was about to find out, the prick. Colin hated being offered out online. It was well known the bigger firms do the offering, touting about on the forum to see who wants it. It was manipulative. Designed to show, by getting no comments on their arrogant post, that none of the other firms fancied their chances. That was Colin's target, to be one of the top firms that everyone else feared. There was a personal, selfish reason behind it – to be asked to join the national team of hooligans, England's Finest. This was a highly, selective, highly secretive group, made up of all the top boys in all the major firms. Chelsea, Millwall, West Ham, all the top London geezers, then the northerners, the scousers and Manchester mob. Colin knew this was a proper naughty crew and you didn't choose to join; you were chosen. If he got his crew known well enough, feared enough, the invite would surely come. He could taste it.

The van pulled up to the traffic lights. The other side,

down on the left was the pub, The Crossways. Their battleground. Colin checked his watch. 2.55pm. *Bang on, Benny.*

Harlan felt his phone vibrate against his thigh. He took it and read it. Smiled and put it back.

He was standing in the centre of the car park, looking out towards the street. Behind him, a wall of trees. To the sides, some narrow wasteland, on the other side of a chest-height slabbed wall that ran the perimeter of the car park. One way in; same way out. It couldn't have worked out better. All he needed now was Colin to show up, and then the fireworks could begin. He didn't have to wait long; the minibus had already caught his eye, and he watched it with interest as it made its way through the lights and indicated into the same road he was on. He watched as it drove toward the pub, before turning into the car park and making its way up the very slight incline before pulling up. He watched as the passenger door opened and somebody, tall, but slight, got out and walked to the back of the van and pulled open the sliding door, revealing a van load of men, or as he saw it, bodies.

The contents of the van spewed out. Harlan saw someone emerge from the pack, and start to take centre stage as they walked up to meet him. He was small, stocky and obviously the mouthpiece of this team of degenerates who had no idea what they had gotten themselves into. The swag in his walk told Harlan he fancied his chances, or himself. Or both. The crew got within ten feet of him and then stopped. Forming a line. Harlan counted Maid Marian's men. Including their obvious leader, there were fifteen. Fifteen fellas, ranging between

5-8 to 6-4, at a guess. Some looked tasty, others like they should be at parents' evening. The text had said no tools, but Harlan had been in the game long enough to spot the tell-tale signs of when someone was carrying.

'On time, I see,' he said, smiling.

'Fuck the time. You pissing me about?'

'Quite the conversationalist, I see. Go on, explain.'

It was part of the mind games that Harlan excelled at. He knew that nine out of ten times, fights are won before a punch is thrown. He was goading Colin; and Colin knew it.

'You reached out for a straightener, but is this all you fucking got? This a wind up?'

'Oh no, short stuff, this ain't no wind up.'

'You what? Listen mate, there are fifteen of us, all here for a proper row, but you, you melt, are standing here on your own. You wired up wrong or summit?'

'There are a couple of things wrong in that oh-so-elegant assembly of words there.'

'Yeah? And what's that?'

'I'll break down each mistake, one at a time. One, trust me, stumpy, we ain't fucking mates. And two, now this is the important one, I'm not here on my own, not by a long stretch.'

'Really? I can't see no cavalry about.'

'You don't need to see; you just need to listen.'

The sound was so loud that at first all fifteen of them looked up, expecting to see a fleet of fighter planes overhead but the sky was empty. What wasn't empty was the road. It took a few seconds for the fifteen to re-plot their coordinates and go from looking up to looking out to their right, but what they saw took their breath away. The formation was what stood out first. The road they had just driven down, the road which was now so familiar to the gang, was being taken up by bikes; two abreast and ever-so slightly staggered riding behind the leader out in front. Next was the thunderous roar coming from little blips of the throttles creating loud bangs of fury from the exhausts. The bikes were a mixture of black gloss and chrome; some standard builds, some chopped. American made. Then there were the men themselves, some were wearing bandanas, some weren't, but each man was without a helmet. Stoic and serious looking. It wasn't a sight; it was a spectacle. A true show of strength in numbers. Net curtains were twitching and windows were being closed. The fifteen men, all stood in line watching as the bikers entered the car park and slowly rode up the slight incline before stopping when the ground levelled out. The bikes matched the crew, parked up in a line and it was then Colin knew what they were doing, they had blocked the gang in. The gang were now trapped.

· Colin knew that things had just gotten very, very real.

'Remind me what you said about cavalry again?'

This was a dick measuring contest that Harlan excelled at. It was one thing fighting for a bit of fun, it was a different ball game when you did it for a living.

Colin and his crew were trapped. There was no way around, which only left through, but stopping was a row of bikers, all of which had gotten off their bikes and stood, in an arc, with brooding intimidation. Harlan watched as Jim, his president, stepped forward and spoke to him, through the crowd as if they weren't there.

'H, this that little cluster of wannabes you were talking about?'

'Yep – this is them. Don't amount to much, do they?'

'No. No they don't.'

Harlan could see Colin turn a funny shade of crimson. The berating was getting to him, making him look smaller than he already was. 'Anyway, I'm getting hungry. You?'

'Starving. Which is why we need to get this show on the road, then we can get some scran.'

It was clever. Two men talking to each other deliberately ignoring what was in front of them, which happened to be Colin's Cherry Pickers, the self-proclaimed hardest firm in the town. 'I agree,' and he turned to face Colin, 'so, half pint, we doing this or not?'

Harlan watched Colin form fists. It was time to dance.

'We're fucking doing this,' Colin replied, and stomped forward towards Harlan, his face contorted, his intent, clear. Harlan was ready and as Colin got close enough to throw a hook, Harlan blocked it with the outside of his left forearm and threw a hook off his own. It didn't miss, but he had pulled it too early, losing impetus; losing the power to knock him clean out. Those two punches were all that was needed to start the melee. Colin's crew were already stood facing the bikers; nine of the toughest bikers inside the inner workings of Satan's Security. Nine men who had been around the block. There were a few seconds of standoff and then it all became a blur, two teams of opposing men running towards each other with fists flailing. Within seconds men were falling, either by being pushed or pulled, and those on the floor found themselves being kicked by an opponent who happened to spot them there. Colin was still throwing wild, over-reaching punches and Harlan either blocked, ducked or slipped each one. He had two opportunities so far to end it, but Harlan had resisted, instead he wanted to see just how much fuel Colin had in his tank. Harlan had his guard up, and although his hands were clenched, his fingers were loose, not balled tightly. Harlan was starting to pant; his ploy was working. He knew most hotheads were just that, hot air. He then watched as Colin stopped and sunk his hands in his pockets, believing he had one up on him when he brought his hands back out, this time with a knuckle duster on each hand. What he hadn't counted on, Harlan knew, was that he could do the same. Harlan replicated the move, but slower, sinking his hands inside the pockets of his black jeans. He watched Colin's eyes follow his arms into his pockets and out again, this time with a set of knuckle dusters of his own. It was no longer man versus man, it was metal versus metal, each of them knowing that one punch, if accurate, if unblocked, would win this fight and break whatever bone it hit in the process.

One of the bikers' eyes had split. Rob had caught him with an uppercut and he felt the biker's eyebrow split on impact. He expected claret to fall, and it did, but what he didn't expect was when the biker wiped his eye with the back of his hand, looked at the blood, licked his hand clean and then smiled, like he was some sort of real-life vampire. The eerie smile was made further sinister by his two front teeth, which were gold. It was a situation Rob hadn't been in before, and he was scared, although too scared to admit it. The bikers were outnumbered, and not tooled up, but they kept coming, seeming impervious to pain. Rob threw another punch and instead of blocking, or ducking, the biker just took it, and then smiled again. Rob threw another one, hoping this one would be enough to maybe knock him down, or at least stop him walking forward. He threw a straight this time, aiming for the bridge of the biker's nose but the second he threw it, he wished he hadn't, and he also wished he hadn't come up against a brawling biker who knew *exactly* what he was doing. It was as if Rob watched in slow motion, as if he was watching it from outside of himself, as the second his arm travelled in the direction of the bikers' nose, when it was on route and only centimetres away, the biker dropped his head forward, for two reasons. The first, to protect his nose, but second, and more importantly, so his aggressor's hand hit solid mass. Rob's hand broke on impact, the flat of his fist no match for the biker's skull. He let out a cry of pain but he never had time to wallow in it. The smiling biker dropped him to his knees with a one, two combination that went first to Rob's exposed ribcage before the hook went crashing into his chin. Rob was out before he hit the concrete. Jim had Benny in a choke hold and the part-time bouncer was struggling to hold on to consciousness. His eyes were starting to bulge and his face was starting to redden and swell from the trapped blood. One of the Cherry Pickers had seen Benny's plight and pulled the piece of iron pipe he had picked from the treasure trove of tools from down inside the left leg of his jeans and headed over to help his mate. He was stopped dead in his tracks. 'You take another step and I won't just put him to sleep, I'll put him in the morgue.'

The man with the iron bar was in a situation with no way out. If he takes a step forward the man holding him may do as he said, and kill him. If he stays where he is, he may kill him anyway. Jim made the decision easy for him. 'Drop that fucking pipe, dickhead, before you become the reason your friends check out of here, for good.'

The next sound that came was the clink of the iron bar as it hit the concrete. Colin's crew were in a mess. The bikers may have been outnumbered, but the Cherry Pickers were outclassed. The men that Jim had picked were rougher, tougher and more ruthless than any firm they had faced before and the beatings they were receiving were brutal. It was made worse by the fact that the ten men in leathers and dirty jeans weren't even breaking a sweat.

Harlan glanced over Colin's shoulder, just to check on progress. He knew Jim would have brought warriors with him, men who didn't surrender, irrespective of the odds. There were a few faces he didn't know amongst the members, but most he knew, and he could vouch for every one of them. Those he didn't know, Jim could, and that was enough for him. Colin saw Harlan's focus drop off for a split second. He sprang forward, throwing a right cross at the same time, hoping speed plus power would cause some pain. Harlan saw it before it was too late, and brushed it aside, moving around in a semi-circle as he did so, resulting in them now having swapped places.

They both danced around each other for a few seconds, like two pugilists in a prize-fight, except they weren't fighting for a belt, or the big payday, or for Colin to save face, they were fighting for the sole aim of hurting the man in front of them before they got hurt themselves. The brass knuckles had upped the ante and Harlan knew no matter how hard he was, brass was harder and he wanted to end the game now. It was time. He took a step forward, pulling his shoulder as if to throw a jab, or to feign a right, Colin took the bait and tried to slip it, but the jab didn't come. What did come was the sweeping kick to the base of Colin's calf, and although it didn't quite take him off his feet, it did make his guard drop as he tried to steady himself. That was all Harlan needed to throw a pulverising punch into Colin's solar plexus. The air left Colin immediately and he was doubled up in pain, leaving him wide open and at Harlan's mercy. Harlan took pity on him and gave him a few seconds to recover. It was during those few seconds that Harlan decided to take off his brass knuckles and put them back in his pocket; he wanted to beat Colin without an aid, just on power and precision alone. Colin recovered, maybe not fully, but enough to raise his guard and growl, telling Harlan he was a dead man. Harlan knew that wasn't going to happen and it was boring to hear. Colin threw two quick jabs. Harlan blocked both and returned one of his own. It was lightning quick and landed high on Colin's left cheek, the red welt coming all but instantly. Colin threw another jab, again blocked, and a swinging right, coming in high and hard. Harlan ducked it and as he came back up, he ploughed a hook of his own into Colin's ribcage. The sound that left Colin's mouth told Harlan he had broken one, if not two, of this bastard's ribs. It was over. Colin lowered his left arm to defend his shattered ribs and that left just enough room for Harlan to mark the axis on Colin's chin, and then strike. It was delivered with maximum speed and precision but at only 80% of his power. He sent Colin crashing to the floor, leaving him lying there, limp and at the mercy of Harlan's scuffed boots. Harlan wanted him awake for the talk that was to follow. He bent down and grabbed Colin by the scruff of his neck and delivered his speech in a chilling tone. 'Listen, you worthless piece of shit, you've had a good run here, terrorising this place and its punters, but it stops. Now.'

Colin was groggy, but coherent, which all that mattered. Harlan continued.

'You sent your top boys here today to see me, but you didn't do your homework, which is why your arrogance proved to be your downfall. We could have beaten you so bad even your mothers wouldn't recognise you. And we still can, whenever the fuck we feel like it. Remember that. Remember that you may have a crew but I have a fucking army.'

Colin was starting to drift in and out of consciousness. Harlan slapped him hard across the face. 'This is the last time you ever come here, got it? You even think of coming here again and I'll end you. You crossed the line, bringing your fight to someone's place of business. My line. And that's a line you don't *ever* want to cross. Now get up, take your crew, and piss off.'

18

As individuals, they were fearless. As a club; they were fearsome. The band of brothers stood, as a group, and watched the Cherry Pickers stumble back to the minibus. The beatdown was as severe as it needed to be and Harlan knew that whilst they were waiting for a triage nurse to assess their injuries, they would be thinking through some serious life changes, the first one being, to avoid Big Al's pub. The Satan's Security club members watched the van reverse back and then the wheels turn as the driver arced the vehicle around. The minibus slowly made its way down the slight decline and after waiting for a taxi to whizz past, pulled out onto the road and disappeared from sight. If the windows of the van had been open, the battered and bruised occupants would have heard the cackle of laughter from the men with the devil on their backs. Jim threw his arm around Harlan and pulled him in towards him. 'There we go, kiddo. All done. I think that calls for a beer, which, by the way, is on you.'

Harlan turned his head to face his president, the smile across his face said it all. Respect.

The near-on headlock from Jim turned into a hug, their hands slapping against the leather on each other's backs. The hug lasted until it got uncomfortable, until masculinity kicked in.

'There are a couple of new patches I want you to meet,' Jim said, and took a small step forward placing himself between Harlan and the members, who had formed into a small, semicircle. 'Brian. Oaktree. And Dogging Dave; don't ask.'

Harlan laughed and then went to speak but Jim interjected. 'Yes, *Dogging* Dave!'

Enough said, and everybody laughed, including Dogging Dave.

Harlan gripped each of the brothers' hands, pulling them into him for a back slapping hug, like he had just done with Jim, minus the lingering emotion.

'Did someone say beer?' Simon 'Double' Nott said, in his raspy voice. Simon was the chosen successor to Harlan as the new Sgt at Arms, voted in by the officers of the club. Harlan had even sent his vote via a text, even though he was no longer allowed to officially vote, being a nomad. Simon had prospected at more or less the same time as Harlan, although Harlan couldn't remember who arrived at the clubhouse first. Simon had proved to be a thinker, and not just a mountain of muscles. It was as if Harlan had left the club a mini-me. Simon was a fine fit for the role as the club's enforcer.

'I heard beer was mentioned, and I believe it's H's round?' Mouse said, his grin spanning from ear to ear. Harlan was glad Mouse was there, he had come to rely on him for a lot of intel over the last few years and he had always come up with the goods.

'Okay, okay, the beers are on me. For a bit!' Harlan replied, knowing just how much his brothers could drink. It felt good to be back around the club, he missed them. They were misfits, and men that society thought it could do without, until it couldn't. Harlan led the way down the car park and avoided taking them through the back door, it would be disrespectful to Alan, it would have made him no better than Colin in giving the impression he owned the place. Which was why he was taking them in through the beer garden and then into the pub through the double doors. Alan was standing behind the bar when the door opened and still in awe from their grand entrance into his establishment on their big, loud, bikes twenty minutes earlier. But now his jaw had dropped even lower to the point he was at risk of tripping over it. The sight before him was nothing short of mesmerising, a band of men dressed in their tribal clothing - leather cuts and sewn-on titles, and he now knew why these clubs had stood the test of time; loyalty. Alan felt privileged just to be in their company and when Harlan stepped forward and reeled off his order, Alan, for the first time in a long, long time, had a smile that came from a truly happy place. Simon and Dogging Dave had made their way over to the pool table and Alan turned away from the pump for a second to flick on the light. Some of the other members had gone over to the tables and got comfortable for the long session ahead. Harlan was left alone at the bar and Alan was busy adding pint after pint to the top of the bar until the order was complete. Harlan had already done the maths. He had two twenty-pound notes in his hand and was about to hand them over, telling Alan to keep the change, when Big Al beckoned him down the end of the bar, out of earshot of his brothers.

'Please tell me that's it. That it's all over,' Alan asked. There was an air of apprehension in his voice.

'It's over. They won't be coming back.'

'Really?'

'Really – rowing with us once is a mistake, twice, well that's a death wish.'

'I... I just, I mean... it was something out of a movie.'

'No, it wasn't, movies aren't real. That was. Real life hurts. Ask Colin.'

Big Al smiled, the second smile in minutes, another smile that said finally, the clouds over him had parted and finally there was some sunlight shining through.

'I don't believe it. It's finally over.'

'Yes, it is – for good. It's back to being your boozer. Enjoy it.'

'I intend to!'

Harlan could see the relief on Alan's face, believing this day was never to come, but it had, and he now had his business back. Harlan was sure if he looked closely, he could see a tear in Alan's eye but he was too respectful to keep the conversation going, so he changed tact.

'Forty quid cover it?' he asked.

'Are you joking me? These beers are on me. You guys are, and always will be, honorary guests!'

Harlan turned to face his brothers and shouted 'Free beer!!!'

The pub was empty except for the handpicked members of Satan's Security, but the whoops and cheers from the announcement of free beer made the pub rival that of a rock concert. If the club is shown respect, then it's returned tenfold. It's only when it isn't shown respect that there is a problem. Harlan knew what to do next. Another plan had entered his head. He shouted for Mouse to come and help him carry the pints across to the various tables and then winked for Jim to slip out from behind his table and join him outside for a smoke.

The beer garden was neatly kept. There weren't any dog-ends knocking about on the ground and the tables looked like they were regularly treated. It was clear that Alan had pride in his business and wanted to offer a safe, friendly place to drink and that's what his pub was, until Colin and his crew took over once or twice a month. Harlan had done his job but he wanted to do more. He had already set Alan a task, but that was for him to do. Harlan wanted to do something himself, to help put the place back on the map. Jim was rolling himself a fag and Harlan waited for him to put it to his lips and light it before he revealed his plan.

'Thanks for this, Jim.'

'No worries, brother. Reckon that's it all done now?'

'Would you come back here after that kicking?'

'Hell no.'

'Then I think you've answered your own question.'

'You always were a smart arse.'

'I had a good teacher.'

'That you did, son.'

And there it was. That word. Son. Jim had started referring to Harlan as son a long time ago. Not straight away, the endearment came later; much later. They were tight from the beginning with Jim already seeing the man that Harlan would later become. Harlan was always by Jim's side when it mattered, knowing instinctively what loyalty meant. His promotion to a senior officer within

the club came early in his career. But it was after, when
Jim needed more than an enforcer, when he needed a
confidante, that Jim's respect for his protégé deepened. It
was this respect, and love, that had allowed Harlan to
step away from the club when he had needed to, when
the pressure had become too much. It had all come to an
end one wintery Saturday night, after a night of soul
searching. Harlan had put in his request to become a
nomad and Jim, who had stayed with him during those
dark hours, had granted his request. It had never been
spoken about since. Jim may well call him son, but to
Harlan, Jim would always be his president. Always.

'Landlord a good fella?' Jim asked, before taking
another drag on his rolled-up cigarette. Jim held it at the
very end, pinched between his thumb and forefinger. Jim
suffered a health scare a few years back, believing it to be
a heart attack and had stopped for a while. Tests proved it
wasn't, and that was all he'd needed to get back on the
smokes.

'He's alright. Just keeps his head down and wants a
happy boozer.'

'Nowt wrong with that.'

'Agreed. Which is why I want us to open party here
today.'

'Yeah? *Open party?* This fella deserves it?

'Open Party' was a term Jim had coined for when he'd
started to open the doors of the clubhouse to the public.
It wasn't a regular thing, but when the time was right, the
word would be out and from midday people from far and
wide could come in and share a beer with the club. Jim
would lay on a free BBQ, and would personally fund it
himself so as not to lighten his brothers' pockets. These
nights were to show those who normally would never get

to see inside an MC's clubhouse that, actually, outlaw bikers weren't in there drinking blood and plotting anarchy. Jim didn't change anything on these nights, members could party as hard as they would any other night. This wasn't the Lord Mayor's show, with the walls freshly painted and silver cutlery. The only thing Jim banned was drugs. Nothing else but weed was allowed. As these open parties got bigger, with the word spreading around that *these bikers are alright* Jim had started to put on live music in the car park and a free raffle with bottles of spirits or duty-free fags given as the prizes. Anybody was welcome and all you needed to be was respectful. Jim had opened his doors, it was up to you if you left at the end of the night through those doors, or through a window. Harlan was keen to give Alan an open party.

'Yeah, he is. His pub has been derailed for months, and he has lost a few quid. That crew arranged their punch-ups here and then spent the rest of the night trashing the gaff. Every home game, this place was empty except for those muppets as the punters were scared off. Then by the time they left, the pub was trashed so Sundays were also a write-off. He could do with a good night here, to bring his punters back.'

'Then, son, an open party it is!' Jim grabbed him, giving him another hug. It was time to celebrate. Jim pulled open the doors to the pub and shouted at the top of his voice.

'IT'S AN OPEN FUCKING PARTY.'

Every brother found something near them to start repeatedly banging their hand against, building up to a crescendo. Harlan looked over to Big Al who was getting a PHD in biker life, and Harlan could tell, from the Cheshire cat grin on his face, he was absolutely loving it.

Harlan stood and watched him for a few seconds, smiling to himself. Alan deserved this. He would see him tomorrow for his wages, but for the rest of today, Alan could just enjoy being a landlord again, a landlord free from worry. Harlan went over to the table and picked up his pint, and then strolled over to the bar, to tell Alan what an open party meant. He gestured his head for Alan to come down to where he was standing.

'Another pint?' Alan asked, believing that was the reason for the beckon.

'Not yet.

'Tea?'

'Ha. No. Listen, we are going to party here today and what –'

'Of course. Please, tell them to stay as long as they want.'

'Let me finish. What I'm saying –'

'Sorry.'

'AL! pause your jaws a second, will ya.'

Alan went to speak again but Harlan tilted his head slightly, as if to scorn him.

'We are going to stay here all day. So, tell everybody you know to come in and have a beer with us, tell your pals, and their pals, that Satan's Security is here. We will be buying beers, there will be a pool competition, loud music on the jukie, basically one big fuck-off party. Get it on your social media and your twitter thingy. It's time people knew the king is dead, long live the king.'

'Really? I'm going to have a biker party here, in my bar?'

'Yes. Really. But, like Elvis, for one night only.'

The third smile came across Alan's face. He was happy before, but now he was fit to burst.

19

The first stop was the hospital, where three of the fifteen got off the minibus and went into Accident & Emergency. As soon as they left the bus, Colin immediately black balled them out of his crew. The minibus was silent. All the swag was left back on the Crossways car park, on the concrete floor, alongside a lot of their skin. It was more than a beating, it was a lesson, and it had been as humiliating as it had been painful. But what it had done, now the swelling had started to subside, was tell him that he needed better fighters. Men who could not just throw a punch, but who could also take one in return. He looked around. The silence was deafening. He needed to change his crew. He was on a mission to join England's Finest, and the van was shouting at him that his band of battlers weren't good enough when it mattered. What Colin didn't want to think about, what he wanted to ignore, was that his lack of research had cost him the victory. What he didn't want to think about, and what he *couldn't* ignore, was that his self-assembled crew were no match for the ten bikers who had shown up from nowhere. Colin put his fingers up to his eye, it was puffy, and sore. Too sore to touch. He was pretty sure his cheek bone was broken. And his ribs. Breathing wasn't easy, so in a way he was happy the van was silent. He was self-medicating on coke and parac-etamol but everything still hurt. Colin knew he would take a couple of weeks to properly heal but he also knew his missus would take care of him. And his ego, like his battered body may be bruised but he still had his busi-ness. Jamal would need another reload soon.

Rob's house was the second to last stop for the minibus. He wished he had gone into the hospital with the others but the scornful look from Colin had told him to sit still. His hand had swollen to twice its normal size and he couldn't move his fingers. It was definitely broken, which would mean he would be off work for a bit, which meant he wouldn't be able to pay his keep to his mum, and she desperately needed that. It was then when he realised this was utter nonsense. What had been a couple of scraps when drunk, or high, had resulted in Colin sweet talking him into joining the Cherry Pickers. From then on, Saturdays weren't his anymore. He had gone from going to watch the football to now fighting whilst it was on. He was no longer a fan of the club; he was just one of the crew. And for what? To end with a busted hand and no dough for his mum. His respect for Colin was left back at the carpark, and now, all he wanted to do was get home and get patched up. He kept moving his lower jaw from left to right, like he was gurning, trying to free it up, trying to stretch away the pain. The shot to the ribs had left his chin open and the biker who hit him had caught him with a beauty of a hook that sent him to sleep standing up. Rob could still see him licking his own blood and smiling. He hoped he wouldn't see it in his sleep, as in the flesh was enough. He glanced over at Colin, and felt his stomach churn. He wasn't a friend; he was a bully. And a control freak. Even down to not letting anyone bring their own gear, even if it was better, or cheaper, than the coke he sold everyone before the fights. He couldn't get out of the van quick enough. He was going to have a sleep, if he could, then take Tyson for a walk, if Ryan wasn't home.

The van pulled into his street and when his house was approaching, Benny pulled the minibus onto the pavement. Rob reached out for the lever and slid the door open to get out when he heard Colin speak. 'I'll give you a bell later.'

'Nah, don't bother.'

For the first time since he'd met him, Rob wasn't interested in what Colin had to say.

Rob stepped down onto the street and didn't even look back. They weren't his friends, they were just like him, lost souls who had been manipulated by a megalomaniac. The minibus engine was still running when Rob walked the few, painful steps down to his house and into the back garden when he heard Benny slip the van into gear and slowly pull away. As he walked down the garden, he could hear Tyson scratching at the door. Rob awkwardly turned down on the handle with his unbroken hand, even though the door was designed to take a right-handed opening and the stretch sent a shooting pain through his body. He was barely a foot inside before Tyson was jumping up at him, his tail wagging and his tongue out.

'Down, boy,' but Tyson was too excited to listen. Judging by how high the dog was jumping, Rob knew he hadn't gone out for a walk today, but Rob was in too much pain to be annoyed. He would deal with him, later, when he stopped hurting.

Alan had been busy. He had posted to the pubs social media and added a photo that Harlan had taken, of Alan in the middle of two bikers, in their colours. Harlan had told him to tell everyone he knew that there was a biker party being held in the pub and that was exactly what he had done. It had gotten so busy that Alan had texted Shanice asking if she could come in and do a shift. He had added the picture of him between the bikers for added manipulation and the text he got back was instant: **Try stopping me! Lol** ☺

Shanice used to work all weekend, Friday through to Sunday but lately the pub was usually smashed up by nine on a Saturday night and then closed on Sunday and he knew the thugs had cost her a pretty penny in lost wages, but she had stayed loyal. And for that he was grateful. The pool table had a raft of pound coins stacked up with people wanting to take on Simon 'Double' Nott who was yet to be defeated. There were so many people down that end of the bar, standing drinking, chanting and taking selfies that Alan had to push tables together to house all the glasses and bottles that were being consumed. He hadn't seen his pub this busy for months, maybe ever. He checked his watch; it was coming up to seven pm, and normally by now the floor would be awash with broken glass and most of his customers would have quietly slipped out so as to escape the constant football chanting and debauchery. What hurt his bottom line the most was when the women would leave. Respectable women won't drink in a dangerous pub, and rightly so, but when he looked out from across the bar all he could was a sea of women talking to the bikers, with skirts maybe slightly shorter than normal and lipsticks a more vibrant shade of red. Alan could now see the allure of being a biker, you had birds, booze and your brothers, which was why he wished he was a couple of dress sizes smaller and two decades younger. He kept looking over at Harlan, who seemed to have an intuitive sense of when he was looking, and the biker would nod his head of approval at him. The man who he had hired to help had an air of refined confidence about him that he could only envy, it wasn't brash, quite the opposite, it was subtle, and silent, but that's what made Harlan even more the enigma. He knew he could never repay Harlan for what he had done for him, even the money seemed derisory, as in less than a couple of hours he had turned his pub from being known as a battleground into a biker bar, and even though he knew the bikers were here for one night only, he sensed the legacy would linger for quite a while to come. By now, Alan had a good understanding of who was who in the MC, including their nicknames: Double Nott was over there, playing pool. Mighty Mouse and Dogging Dave were happy taking selfies with anyone who asked. Don 'Gentle' Mann was vaping inside, but Alan sure wasn't going to stop him. Don had on a bowler hat, and looked like the coolest uncle any kid could have. And there was Jim, who he heard everyone refer to as 'Pres', and Alan could see the respect he was shown from his men wasn't just down to his title, but for the man that he was. It was also clear there was something different between Jim and Harlan, something that he knew he would never know, nor did he want to as that was their business, but he found himself envying a friendship that went that deep. His thoughts were interrupted when, again, another large round of drinks had been ordered by one of the men in leather, and again, another fifty-pound was left on the bar to cover it.

He had just finished pouring, as had Tasha, who was being run-ragged by the constant stream of people wanting drinks and also by Mouse, who had made it his mission to get her number. Jim was standing at the far end of the bar, where it was quieter, and he was checking something on his phone. Alan decided to take two tumblers from under the bar and put them to the optics, squirting two shots of brandy into each glass, his favourite tipple. He waited for Jim to finish on his phone before walking down and handing him one of the glasses.

'What's that for?' asked Jim.

'Just to say thank you. We really needed this,' Alan replied, holding up his glass.

'No worries, man. But really, it's Harlan you need to thank as this was his idea.'

'You mean the party?'

'No, all of it. He called the other day to give me the lowdown on what was happening here. H is one of the gamest men you'll *ever* meet. He will take on the world if he thinks there is an injustice being done.'

'There was definitely that,' Alan said, which was an understatement to say the least.

'Nah, mate, you aren't getting it. See, H gets offers of work every day but he won't take on just anyone. And that's the thing, he doesn't do it for the dough, he does it for the person. I bet he made you sell your story to him?'

Jim took his mind back to that first meeting he had with him. 'Yeah, yeah he did.'

'Exactly – if he feels you don't want it enough, or if you aren't a man with morals, he won't help you. But once he agrees, he is all in. He makes your problem his, and will do *whatever* it takes to turn it around.'

'You can say that again. He is quite a man.'

'He is more than that. He is a man every man *wants* to be. *Should* be. You're very lucky, Al.'

Jim was right; he was. He raised his glass for the second time, and for the first time, Jim chimed it with his.

Rob was in luck. There was one bag of budget peas in the freezer. He took it and placed it over his broken hand. Right now, there wasn't anything he wouldn't do to try and stop the throbbing. He scoured around for painkillers, hoping his mum hadn't taken them all. He pulled open the one drawer where the front was still attached. Until it wasn't. It came off in his hand and most of the contents fell to the floor. He moved quicker than he wanted to, or could do, to kick the single double A battery under the cooker before Tyson could get his already salivating lips on it. The drawer contained everything but painkillers; old mobile phone chargers, unchecked lottery tickets, a half-empty box of ear buds, some of which had wax on. Everything but a paracetamol or an ibuprofen. His jaw was getting stiffer by the minute and he needed to try and sleep away the pain. He took a treat out from the tin and hurled in the direction of Tyson's bed, hoping to escape the kitchen unnoticed but feeling bad that once again, he hadn't been walked. The living room curtains were open, which told him his mum had at least got up today, but with the ashtray still resting on the arm of the sofa; and still full, he knew she hadn't done anything *motherly*. He checked the time and then it dawned on him; she would be at the Bingo.

His mum had never been much of a domestic Goddess but the last eighteen-months she had pretty much given up completely. For a while, Rob had started to put the hoover round on a Sunday afternoon, and would bleach the bath and toilet, but soon it became too much like hard work so he stopped. He felt hungry but his jaw told him anything more than a tomato soup would be out of the question so he decided to revert back to his original plan of trying to get his head down in the hope of feeling slightly better tomorrow. He knew Tyson would soon be whining again and Ryan's refusal to do what he was paid to do was now really starting to piss him off, so much so he was mumbling out loud about him as he gingerly made his way up the stairs. *Lazy sonofabitch.* He had to stop halfway to catch his breath, which proved to be a double-edged sword as breathing out hurt just as much as breathing in. Rob continued the climb, with it feeling on par with a trek up the side of Everest. He had to stop again when he got to the landing as he started to feel faint from the pain. After waiting a minute for the feeling to pass, he went to step inside his bedroom when he thought he heard a sob coming from Ryan's room. Rob dismissed it at first but then it came again, and a little louder. His brother was crying. Rob ignored the pleasantries of knocking and waiting, and instead just flung the door open ready to hurl a few days of abuse at him for ignoring the dog.

'Where the f –,' the sight of his little brother beaten, and crying stopped him dead in his tracks. 'Bro, what's happened?' The concern was genuine. Sibling rivalry had turned to concern. Ryan was sat on his bed, his knees up under his chin and Rob watched as he looked up at him, before dropping his face down to his knees, out of sight. 'Bro, tell me?'

The tears came harder and Rob hadn't the emotional capabilities to offer much more than to ask what had happened. This was his mum's job, to be his little brother's pillar of strength, but nowadays she was either stoned, or asleep. He took a step forward. And then another. Then another. He was in touching distance now of his sobbing *shit of a brother* but he might as well have been in no man's land as he was unsure what he was able to offer in terms of support if he got any closer. Ryan still hadn't looked up, his face still resting on his crossed arms that were sat on top of his raised knees. It was the go-to position of someone wanting to be an adult but still a child, that middle part of life called adolescence. Rob took the final steps to be able to reach out and touch his brother and without thinking, he finally stood next to Ryan, rubbing his back. It wasn't much, but it was real; it was meant. His brother was hurting and needed him. The room fell silent for what seemed like an eternity, but eventually Ryan's sobs slowed and he finally lifted his head up. His face was red from having it huddled down into the fabric of his hoodie, and his head had started to sweat. Both his eyes were puffy but one was black. Rob asked him again, 'Ryan, you need to tell me, bro.'

Ryan turned his head and Rob was able to see into his brother's eyes, and into his soul. He wasn't just beaten; he was broken. Again, without thinking, Rob sat down on his bed and then cradled his arms around his brother. His hand was broken, and his ribs busted, but right there, right then, he wasn't in pain; his brother was.

Rob wanted answers, wanted to know who had set upon his brother but knew he needed to be patient which was rewarded when Ryan finally spoke, 'I'm sorry. I'm really sorry.'

The tears were back in his brother's eyes but Rob wanted him to fight through it, to tell him what had happened, and by who. 'Sorry for what? Tell me, bruv.'

'I've really messed up. Like, proper.'

'How? You're not making sense?' Rob's patience was starting to thin and he was struggling not to show it.

'I've done something stupid. Really fucking stupid.'

'C'mon, it can't be that bad. It's not like you're dealing drugs.' Ryan was about to laugh his comment away when he saw his brother's eyes change. The penny dropped.

'What the fuck? You're dealing? Nah, no way. This is bullshit.'

He waited for Ryan to answer; wanting him to answer. His brother was a tearaway, there was no denying it, but drug dealing. He wasn't buying it.

'Ryan, come on, stop shitting me.'

Rob sat and listened to his little brother, the one who used to follow him around everywhere when he was a baby. The one, who when he was just a nipper, would ask him to come in and kiss him goodnight when he got home from work. The one who used to try and copy the walk he walked, and talk he talked, when he started wanting to be cool. Now he was listening to how he had met someone in the park one day who asked him if he wouldn't mind dropping some money off to a house just down the street. Rob knew as soon as he heard that, that it had been a test. If the money had got there; all of it, then the young kid could be considered trustworthy. Of course, Rob knew the young lad, his brother would have been tailed and if his brother had decided to make a detour then he would have been followed and *accidentally* knocked off his bike at best, or worse, been given a beatdown.

He listened to Ryan tell him that after that, he had been given a mobile phone and was told he would be given *one or two jobs a week* and each time he delivered the envelope he would be told to wait whilst its contents were counted. Rob knew this was to build credibility with their new employee, whoever *they* may be. Rob also knew what was coming, the point when his brother was accepted into the fold and soon the envelopes would be replaced with little bags of powder. And that was how quickly, and succinctly, his younger brother had become a drug dealer.

'So, how did you get the beating?' Rob asked, with his brother's revelation being up to date, or up until he came home with a black eye.

'Mikey got mugged so I went to sort it, and got this.'

'Mikey? Don't tell me you got him involved? What the fuck, bro?'

It was the first time Rob had shown anything less than compassion. He understood how his brother had been used, and groomed, that was on them. But getting Mikey involved, that was on him.

'What happened then, when you went to sort it?'

He listened as Ryan told him how he had been invited in, before wincing when Ryan then told him about being thrown up against a wall, and punched. He sat and imagined the fear his little brother must have been feeling when Ryan told him about being locked in a disgusting bedroom with nothing to eat or drink. Rob felt anger run through his whole body, his unbroken hand forming a fist. He wanted to tear this man with the teardrop tattoo, limb from limb, but he was in no fit state. He knew the junkie with the teardrop tattoo, was a bully, but what about if he was connected to a proper firm? Rob felt a mixture of emotions come over him; anger, hurt, denial, disappointment. All the feelings a father would have after hearing all this, and that was what he had inadvertently become to him over the years. But there was a feeling that was new. Fear.

His brother's face was not as red as it was, his core body temperature had lowered, but so too, had his confidence. Out of the two, it was Ryan who had that twinkle in his eye, that certain *something,* and Rob believed his little brother was set for big things. But that was before real life became *real.* When the wrong postcode cut off the right choices. When being raised on benefits lowered your aspirations. Rob had become a product of his environment and a victim of circumstance. He didn't want that for Ryan, and maybe if he had been a better big brother, Ryan wouldn't have taken the same bad decisions. But he hadn't, which was why, alongside the feeling of fear that he was experiencing for the first time, he was also feeling guilt.

'Please, Rob, don't tell mum.'

It wasn't a request; it was a plea. It wasn't said for the fear of repercussions, as there wouldn't be any, it was said out of love. She may no longer be the matriarch, she may no longer cook a Sunday Roast or have movie nights sharing a burnt pizza and cheap popcorn, but she was still their mum. And they never wanted to let her down.

'Please, Rob.'

Rob agreed, using nothing more than a nod. He wouldn't grass him up, but their mum was the least of his worries. His little brother, the one who would run into his room and nick a splash of his favourite aftershave or would be an *annoying little twat when* he had a bird over, was now nothing more than a puppet to a gang who peddled their drugs using kids peddling their bikes. He knew that once you were in the clutches of a gang like this, it was nearly impossible to get out. It was a sorry sight; two brothers both in a dingy little bedroom, both battered and bruised, after both making bad choices. But he needed to get his brother safe.

'What are we going to do, Rob? They will come after me as I've lost their drugs.'

Rob looked at him and went to speak but Ryan hadn't finished.

'And my best friend.'

'I really don't know how to sort this, bruv,' but then a thought entered his head. It was a long shot. 'But I may know someone who can.'

20

Benny dropped him back to his Porsche pulling up behind its rear bumper. Colin got out without bothering to say goodbye to his friend; soon to be former friend, as Colin was about to relegate those who he felt had let him down back at the pub. He needed warriors; and winners. Men who could take a leathering and not go down, or, if they did, could get back up and beat the shit out of someone. He thought Benny was that, he was wrong. He wouldn't be wrong again. He would go out and get better. Once he stopped aching. Getting into his car was proving painful. So painful that he couldn't do it and instead rang for a taxi. Whilst he waited, he took to his holdall hoping to find more coke. He was in luck, there was one small bag left. He emptied it out onto the back of his right hand and used his forefinger on his left hand to manipulate as best he could into little straight lines. He brought his cocaine laden hand up to his nose and then pushed one side of nostrils down onto the powder, pushing the same forefinger hard into the side, closing it off. He inhaled hard, taking a deep hit. For the briefest of seconds, the pain. His wallet was bulging from the five-hundred or so quid he made flogging his product to his crew, so there was that. The taxi arrived and wound down his window to check he had the right fare. Colin nodded. He could tell the driver was the cheery, chatty type so he put himself in the back seat and directly behind him, so as to obscure himself from the rear-view mirror. He was in no mood to talk. The car looked freshly valeted and there was a nice scent to it. It wasn't a Porsche, of course, but then again, the driver wasn't a drug dealer. It took just over fifteen minutes to get home and Colin was in need of more painkillers, and more coke, both of which he had at home. The first being in the medicine cabinet, which was one of those wall mounted cupboards which, on the second shelf of three inside, had a green plastic box that contained plasters, gauze and pain pills. Next to the green box were the family medicines. Different coloured gooey liquids that were for colds and coughs. Medicines that over-promised and under delivered. It grated Colin that everything needed to be *child safe* or *out of reach*. But there would be painkillers, as despite her incessant need to wrap up the kids in cotton wool, she was a good mum and there was always something for every eventuality. He had done well; he knew that. But so had she.

The taxi pulled up outside and the driver totted up the fare. '£14.60, guv.'

Colin went to his wallet and pulled two notes. A ten and a five and handed it through the gap in the seats and then held out his hand for his change. He knew you didn't get rich giving your money away and forty pence was forty pence. The driver hesitated for a second before handing over the change, seeing if it was a wind-up. It wasn't. Colin got out and with a bit of a struggle, slid his holdall across the seat before picking it up and shutting the door. His ribs were killing him and his breathing was now laboured. He needed to get in and get on the sofa with his feet up. He would tell the kids to go up to their room as he really didn't want any noise, or any conversation. It hurt to talk and sometimes that's all they did.

He walked slowly to the front door, trying not to put any pressure on his left foot, which would have sent more pain up his left side. He turned the key and got inside, pushing his butt into the door to close it. The house was quiet. Too quiet. Colin walked down the hallway, past the photos of the kids in their school uniforms. A new year; a new photo. The hallway was like a shrine to the kids which was something else that pissed him off. The kitchen was light and airy and he expected to see the kids out in the garden, on the trampoline and his wife sat on one of the expensive grey wicker chairs she had moaned at him to buy. But they weren't there. What was there was an envelope with his name on it, propped up against the fresh flowers that were in a tall, fluted vase. He pulled out a chair ready to sit down to open it but as he went to sit down his body convulsed with his rib telling him it didn't like what he was doing. Deterred, Colin took the envelope with him to the medicine cabinet. He opened the cupboard door and luckily the medicine box was on the middle shelf. He lifted it down, slid the locks outwards and opened the lid. There was, as he knew there would be, a packet of paracetamol and a packet of ibuprofen. He didn't know which would be best for how bad he was feeling, so decided to take two of each and after popping them free from the foiled packaging he then hobbled over to the fridge to get a beer to wash them down with.

The fourth tablet got stuck at the back of his throat, so he took a longer swig, and another, until the tablet was gone and replaced with a loud belch. Colin then set about opening the envelope, half expecting a love note, as she used to do that for him, although he hadn't had one for a while, or a shopping list, which was more likely. He pulled the note free from its paper house and opened it up.

'You must be fucking kidding me,' he said out loud. To anyone who was home.

There wasn't. The house was empty, and according to the letter, it would be for quite some time. The note wasn't long. No more than a few sentences.

Colin,

I can't do this anymore. The man I fell in love with has turned into a vile human being and being around him is like trying to navigate a landmine. The kids can't even speak to you anymore, in fact, they are actually scared of you. I want you to be happy, but until you stop trying to be someone you aren't, or weren't, then I don't think you will be. You have become nasty, aggressive and a bully and I am done with it. Please don't try and contact me.

'Bitch.'

Colin screwed up the note and threw it across the room, regretting it immediately as it only served to make him clutch his broken rib in agony. How could she leave him, he thought. Hadn't he given her everything. She lived in a beautiful home, got driven around in a beautiful car. Her nails and lashes were paid for. Her kids were dressed in designer clobber and her tan came from a few foreign holidays a year, not out of a bottle.

He downed the rest of the beer, instantly grabbing another, the lid twisted off and flicked across the worktop where it would stay. Colin looked out to the garden, with its plastic grass and decking. It was a family garden. Designed how she wanted it. The fake grass; her idea. The decking; her idea. The safety net around the trampoline; her idea. Flowers and hanging basket; her idea. And now what, she ups sticks and pisses off? *'Bitch.'*

Rob wanted his bed. Actually, he wanted a hospital bed. It felt like every inch of his body was hurting. He thought he could handle himself; he couldn't. The beating from the biker let him know he was no match for someone who seemed to like pain. But he couldn't go to bed, nor could he walk the dog. He had something to do. Somewhere to be. He closed the door on Ryan, letting him be alone with his thoughts. He didn't know if that was a good thing or not. Rob didn't think about his father much, but he was thinking about him now – hating him even more for not being here now. Not being here for his son. He had called a taxi and had been told it would be twenty minutes, which only made his anxiety worse. He had no idea if the guy would even talk to him, let alone help. The bite into the hardened biscuit reminded him how sore he was, like he had somehow forgotten. He had only taken one because he felt shaky, believing his blood sugar was as low as his morale.

Rob decided to wait outside as Tyson's incessant jumping was proving too much for both his frail body and fraught mind. He had told Ryan to stay in until he got back, although he didn't believe Ryan wanted to go out today, or any other day for that matter. If he was feeling any better later, he would come home with supper for them both.

The street was starting to wind down for the night. There was a stray football lodged under one of the cars, and another car had a flat front tyre and had been like that for weeks. The cars, like the houses, like the residents, were down on their luck. The shine had gone and signs of wear and tear, apparent. The perfect metaphor for this postcode. Rob had lived in two houses in his lifetime, both council houses. He had nothing against that, his issue was the stigma people from a council estate came with. Believing it to be unfair. But now, standing there, waiting for a taxi, realising he was nothing more than a football thug and his brother was a drug dealer, maybe the preconception fitted perfectly.

The taxi arrived and Rob manoeuvred himself awkwardly onto the passenger seat. He purposely left off the seat belt so not to press on his broken rib but the beeping from the alarm and the look from the driver told him he had no choice but to wear it. The pain from his hand was getting close to unbearable but he had to do this, he had to see if this person would help. The driver indicated and pulled out, and the ride started off smooth until he went over the speed bump a little faster than Rob could handle. He looked out of the window, up towards the sky and quietly regretted every bad decision he had ever made.

Alan's pub was close to bursting. It had gone past its allocated capacity, according to the licence that sat inside a frame on the wall, but nobody cared. And it wasn't as if there was any trouble, not with a bunch of outlaw bikers in there. Harlan had taken himself outside to make the call, and to get a brief respite from the noise. He knew Alan would be doing cartwheels inside his own head when he looked at the takings in the morning. With the arrival of Shanice, there were now three people behind the bar serving, including Alan, and they still weren't keeping up.

The number Harlan rang was taking an eternity to answer, and he knew why, for the curmudgeonly old git kept the phone high up on the French dresser. Finally, Stan came to the phone.

'Hello?'

'Stan, it's Harlan. You busy?'

'I was born busy. Why?'

'You got any room free?'

'Free? I don't do free, son. I leave the charity work to Geldof.'

'No, you buffoon, free - as in available.'

'Then say available, instead of free. As the word free brings me out in shingles.'

'Putting an extra spoonful of sugar in my tea brings you out in shingles.'

'Well, as nice as this chat is, I'm getting bored, and I was watching Strictly, so that's saying something.'

'Look, dickhead – have you any rooms available?'

'Dickhead? I take it you're bored too, of having front teeth.'

Harlan laughed out loud at this. He had only known Stan for a few days but it felt like a lifetime. A good life-time. 'I need some rooms.'

'And I need a Bentley and a blow –'

'STAN!'

'Ok, yes, I have some rooms. Why?'

'I need them. All of them.'

'I'll repeat my last word seeing as you're clearly hard of hearing, why?'

'For my mates. They are in town. But as you clearly don't want the cash-only business, I'll send them to the Hilt – '

'Slow down there a minute, cowboy. I didn't say that.'

'So, fancy some punters paying in readies?'

'Does the Pope wear a funny hat?'

'Good. Set them all up. Oh, and check you have enough grub in for breakfast.'

'I have three rooms. How many are staying.

'Nine.'

'Nine? Didn't you hear me when I said I only have three rooms. They won't all –'

'They will.'

Harlan ended the call knowing that him having the last word would royally piss him off. He put the phone back into his pocket, chuckling, and walked back inside the pub.

If Harlan would have let Stan speak, or if he had made the call a few minutes later, he would have seen the taxi pull up outside. He would have seen him get out the car, and with his good hand, close the car door. As it was, Harlan was now back inside and with a Jack and coke in his hand. He looked around the building; there were people in all four corners. Men and women of all ages. All smiling. All drinking. This is what Harlan left you with after his work was done. Profits and people. He charged for his time, for what he would have to do to make whatever problem you had, go away. But when he *did* leave, he always left a legacy, for what he put in place was as firm as the foundations itself. He was good at what he did. The best.

Mouse had come to join him; he had a bottle in each hand and Tasha's number in his pocket. They were deep in conversation when out of the corner of his eye, Harlan spotted someone coming in looking worse for wear, and his razor-sharp ability to *never* forget a face told him he was one of Colin's crew from earlier. Mouse spotted him a few seconds after.

'Fuck me, that fella looks like he had a fight with a lorry, and lost.'

'He did; and he did. That's one of those melts from earlier.'

Mouse squinted his eyes, 'Oh yeah. What is he doing here? This is the last place I'd want to be!'

'Not sure.'

'Want me to go and find out?'

'No. Let's watch him for a second. See what he wants.'

It didn't take long to find out. The man with the busted hand was scanning the pub from where he stood, being careful not to let anyone bump into him and cause any more pain; like he needed that. He was holding his swollen hand high up his chest, by the wrist, with his other hand. Harlan's eyes were already focused on him when Rob spotted him.

Mouse looked at Harlan and then over to the man with the busted hand. 'Let me go and see him. If he has nothing worth hearing, I'll bust his chops for a bit and then toss him out.'

'No, I'll go,' Harlan said, already passing Mouse his glass and heading over.

It took a few seconds to get to him, the parquet floor, which usually had enough room for women to dance around their handbags, now full of people of all ages and sizes. He was sure he felt his ass get groped as he walked over and on a different night he may have turned to see who'd done it, and offer a cheeky smile or a smack in the face, depending on the sex of the groper.

'What you doing here?' Harlan's voice was aggressive. Designed to set the scene of who was in charge here, both in the conversation and in life.

'I'm not here to cause trouble.'

'Too right. As, a) judging by the state of you, you couldn't, and b) you wouldn't get a chance. Which makes me ask you again. Why you here?'

'Can... can I have a word?'

'Marzipan.'

Harlan watched the man with the busted hand process his reply. The length of time it took for him to get it told Harlan he wasn't dealing with the shiniest spanner in the toolbox but the penny did finally drop. But if busted hand man didn't get to the point soon it would be him that would be dropping. To the floor.

'A word about what? Let's have it right, you have a cheek coming here and if it wasn't already swollen, I'd bust your jaw, just for coming here.'

'I know. I'm sorry. It's just... I'm... I'm desperate.'

'For what?' Harlan asked.

He waited for the fella to speak. Whatever it was he wanted to say, it was taking courage. Finally, it came. And it was meant. 'Help.'

'Outside,' said Harlan. His ability to read people told

him the fella stood in front of him wasn't a threat. And that he was scared. He wanted to know more.

The beer garden was busy with people talking and smoking. Which was why Harlan walked out through the picket gate and headed up to the car park so as to be far enough away from unwanted ears. He turned around to face the man who had come to find him, only to see him a few metres behind, walking slowly, and painfully. Harlan smirked, knowing it would be quite some time before this fella laced up his gloves again. He finally got up close enough to speak but Harlan wasn't in the mood for small talk, there was a perfectly good party going on back inside and right now he was missing it.

'Speak!' It was a command. Cold. Emotionless.

'I don't know where to start?'

'The beginning. As the word suggests.'

Harlan was giving him short thrift. As far as he was concerned, he was no better than anyone in the little firm that terrorised this venue and his curtness only served to hammer home that point.

'It's... it's my little bro.'

'Brother. You mean brother.'

'Yes. Sorry. Brother.

'What about your little brother?'

'He is in trouble.'

'There's a number for that. A few nines, I think.'

Harlan looked at him; deep into him. He was mocking, bating, goading, wanting to see if this fella was genuine. If he was as scared as he made out. Was he real? If not, the conversation would be coming to an end. And quickly. And painfully.

'I can't call the feds – that would only make it worse.'

'Right, you have sixty-seconds to tell me everything. Go...'

Harlan listened as the man with the broken hand and busted rib told him about how his brother had been groomed by a drug dealing gang, and how he ended up being held in some squalid little crack den and beaten.

The story had taken longer than sixty-seconds but Harlan had stopped counting. There wasn't much that he hated more than a bully, except for someone who bullied kids.

'Do you know who this gang is?'

'I don't. But Ryan does.'

'Ryan?'

'Ryan. My brother.'

'Find out what you can.'

'Will you help me?'

'I'll help your brother.'

'Thanks' and before he could finish his sentence, the man with the busted hand started to cry. An evening of pent-up emotion finally burst out of him and his battered body started to vibrate. Harlan's view of him changed, going from a mindless thug to a concerned brother. The young man in front of him was lost. And not just in the situation his family had found themselves in; but in life. He could see, like he had been all those years ago, that he had been at a crossroads, but unlike Harlan, he had taken the wrong turning and ended up at the dead-end of life. Harlan took a step forward, to close the gap, to put his arms around him. But he stopped. It felt too foreign. Physical embrace was reserved only for his brothers. And for the two people in his life that he would give anything for to hug again.

'C'mon, chin up now.'

He waited and finally his request was fulfilled.

'You will definitely help us?'

'Yes, I'll help you.' Harlan changed his answer. It was subtle. But the change was huge.

'Thank you.'

'Give me your number. And then stay by your phone as I only ring once. Miss it and you've missed your chance.'

Harlan added each digit in turn. 'What's your name?'

'Rob. It's Rob.'

'Yours?'

'Harlan.'

'That your first or last name?'

Harlan didn't answer. He was already on his way back to join the party.

21

Stan's lowly dining room was as Alan's pub had been. Every table was taken, mostly by burly men in leather cuts and Stan had now added sweating to his ever-growing list of ailments. Harlan sat on a table of four, with Simon to his right and Jim and Don opposite. Harlan knew Stan had no idea, and probably no care, for rank, which was why their table was the last to get served. Harlan looked around the room, smiling to himself. It felt good to be around his brothers again. The men sat around him, with sore heads and soon-to-be full stomachs, had been there for him in a heartbeat. And it was down to Jim. His Pres. He had made one call for backup and the calvary had arrived. He knew he would do the same for Jim, in the same heartbeat.

Stan finally arrived carrying two plates with his tea towel over his shoulder. Harlan caught the smirk on Stan's face as he purposely made sure neither of these plates were for him. Simon, the brother who had replaced him as the club's enforcer, took a piece of toast, folded it in half and split the fried egg, sending the gooey yolk all over his meal like Mount Vesuvius. Simon had asked Stan for the biggest breakfast he could offer but judging by his size, it wouldn't be enough. Nor would a second. Stan finally arrived carrying the last of the plates; his and Jim's. When he arrived and placed the plates in front of them, he couldn't resist some banter.

'Now will that be all, sir, as I really need to go and polish your ego, I mean your bike.'

Harlan took it; and raised him.

'Yes, that will be all. Now what have I told you about being seen in society?'

'Twat,' Stan replied, but only in earshot of the table.

Jim laughed out loud, so too did Simon, dropping a piece of bacon from his mouth as he did.

Halfway through their meal Harlan saw Danielle come in. Their eyes locked for a split-second and she offered a shy smile. He hadn't checked in on her for a couple of days but hoped things had gotten easier. There wasn't a spare table for her and her daughter. Harlan stood up, pulled out his chair and asked her to take his, saying he would take his breakfast out the back, with Stan. Jim looked up at her, sensing her nerves which was why he then ordered Mouse and Oaktree to give up their two-seater table and come join theirs. Danielle went to offer her thanks but Jim brushed it away, saying that's what decent men were supposed to do, offer their seats to women and children. She blushed, which told Jim that she hadn't met too many of them in her life. Mouse helped her manoeuvre her buggy into position and held the chair out for her, prompting a second shy smile, and he took his breakfast with him over to Jim's table knowing he would be finishing the rest of his breakfast standing up. Harlan had already given up his seat to

Oaktree, who was one of the recent prospects to make his patch, and was making his way out to see Stan.

When he arrived in the kitchen, Stan was busy scraping bits of bacon rind and leftover beans from the pile of dirty plates into the bin. 'Need a hand?' he asked.

'Can start to pile up the dishwasher if you wouldn't mind.'

'No worries – and cheers for the rooms.'

'Cheers for the extra business.'

'Everybody squared you away.'

'Yeah. And all in used notes. My fav.'

'What you doing tomorrow?' Harlan asked.

'Judging by how much you lot eat, still doing the bloody pots. Why?'

Harlan told him what he had in mind and then went back to loading the dishwasher.

Jamal was happy. Sundays were his favourite. The reason was simple; Saturday nights. It was when the clubbers went out and when the out-of-towners arrived. Jamal knew a decent Saturday night would be worth more than Monday to Friday combined which was why he had extra soldiers on Saturdays. It was a well run enterprise; with the young boys picking up a handful of little bags and dropping off the cash to the bigger dealers. These dealers would then take what was theirs and then reach out to one of the burners in the flat and then whoever was on duty from Jamal's crew would then go and collect. And so it would continue, all the way into the dawn of Sunday. Jamal found himself surrounded by piles of cash, which was the reason for the beaming smile that had come across his gaunt face.

It had been a late night, or an early start, Jamal wasn't sure which but the piles of fives, tens and twenties made it worthwhile. The safe door, like his ashtray, was full. It was time to order some more work off Colin, which pained him, as he didn't like the arrogance of the little white rude boy who thought he was Al Capone. Back home, he knew, Colin would be taken somewhere and chopped up, but here, on this island he had to play the game, before he could go back to *his* island, and be a king. He was still angry about Ryan, angry to the point of retribution, which would be severe, as according to his log, Ryan had robbed him of close to a thousand pounds. That needed dealing with, and his only question now was what finger would Ryan lose to learn his lesson. This is what made Jamal feared; his lust for torture. He knew his three gang members didn't like him, which was fine, but they did fear him, which was perfect. Jamal had imposed himself as the leader earlier on, back when they first moved to the UK, when they lived in Brighton. Back then it was a five-man crew, but one had put his fingers in the till, and when Jamal found out, he made sure there were no fingers available to do that again. From then it stayed as a four-man gang, and Jamal ran a tight ship with an iron fist. He didn't mind that his firm smoked all day, every day, or that whores were brought in, as long as they picked up the cash and ran the soldiers on the streets. Everyone knew their place and everyone knew Jamal's position. He was taking a long drag on his spliff when one of the brothers walked in. He was shirtless, sockless and hungover. He walked over to the table and took some rizla papers that were next to the full ashtray and then walked over to one of the chairs and slumped himself down and began to roll his first joint since being awake.

'Any word on Ryan?' Jamal asked, his head, as always, on business.

'Nah, brudda. Nuttin.'

'We need him found. Today. Young un' has done us for a quid.'

Jamal turned his head to face him, wanting to see some sense of urgency.

Nothing.

'I said, he has done us for a quid. You listening?'

'Yeah, man. Chill, I heard you.'

'Then if you heard me then you would have heard me say young un' has stolen a quid. Meaning you need to go and find it. And him.' Jamal's eyes were burning into him.

'Okay. Okay. Let me smoke this and get some breakfast and I'll go sort it.'

'You best sort it. Your role. Your soldier. Your problem.'

The guy slumped on the sofa, barefoot and topless, puffed a plume of smoke up towards the ceiling and sensed today was going to be a bad day.

Harlan and Jim were in Stan's back garden, it was nothing more than a small slabbed area and a couple of window boxes that had dead plants inside. Moss had grown where there would have been concrete grout and most of the slabs had cracked. Jim had gone outside for a smoke and Harlan had joined him. He had something else to run past his president, something that would have made the journey down to the coast worth it.

'Want one?' Jim asked, as Harlan walked over and stood next to him, their backs facing the building. Harlan shook his head. He had quit a few years back although a good party would always leave him tempted for a bit of tobacco, and sometimes with a bit of extra *seasoning.*

'That Stan fella seems a good crack?' said Jim.

'Yeah, to be fair, he is. Full of shit but fucking funny with it.'

'Captain bollocks of the first battalion, then?'

'You know!'

'Anyway, how you keeping? And don't go all Stan on me,' Jim asked.

'I'm okay. Just doing what I do. Know what I mean.'

'Yeah, I do. But, H, when you want to stop doing your thing, you come back home, right?'

'Right.' They looked at each other. A thousand words were said right there without any words being spoken.

Harlan pulled the conversation away from sentiment and into business. 'Fancy some fun?'

'I was built for fun. What is it?'

'Did you see that fella come in last night to find me.'

'Yeah, of course. I had one of the lads keep a look when you went outside.'

Harlan knew he had. He sensed it on the way out and purposely pretended not to see one of the new patches when he walked back in. Harlan was good at spotting danger, but Jim was better. And Harlan knew there was no way he was going to let his protégé out of sight when he was around. Harlan kept everybody safe. Jim kept Harlan safe.

'Well, he is in a bit of bother.'

'So? Fuck him.'

'Yeah, which was my first instinct, but the thing is, it's not really him, it's more his brother.'

'Go on?'

'His brother has got himself involved with county lines.'

'You're shitting me? Groomed I take it?'

Harlan nodded his head. Jim had kids which he idolised. Two girls. They were his princesses and he felt lucky his kids were now grown up, young women, out of the catchment area of these *modern-day pimps* as Jim would to call them. Like Harlan, Jim detested this new wave of scumbag who were hiding behind young kids. Making all the money but taking none of the risks. To Jim, the people behind this new craze of using children to push their Class A's weren't gangsters, but cowards. In Jim's world view, an outlaw lived and died by the sword. Straights were more or less a no-go, but children, they were *always* off-limits. Always.

'I take it, you have a plan?'

Jim knew Harlan was more than just brawn, he had a brain, too. A strategist. A thinker. Someone with a forensic eye for detail and a strong sense of what was right. Put together, Harlan was a force of nature and Jim knew he was lucky to have had him as a brother and not as an enemy. Nobody wanted Harlan as an enemy.

'You up for paying these melts a little visit?' Harlan asked.

'Does a bear take a crap in the bushes?'

Harlan smiled.

'What intel do we have?' Jim asked, taking out his pouch of tobacco and starting to roll his second smoke.

'That's the thing, I am going to get that this morning. I'm going over to see the kid.'

'And when you say *I,* you of course, mean *we.*'

'You wanna come and see him too?'

'What did I say about bears and bushes?'

Harlan smiled, again.

'Just you and me for the intel. We can come for the guys after,' Jim said, in-between two long sucks of his smoke.

'Ready?'

'Born ready, son. Born ready.'

Jim threw the butt of his fag onto the floor, and stubbed it out and down into one of the cracks on Stan's patio slabs.

Rob hadn't slept. For two reasons. The first was his hand hadn't stopped throbbing all night. The tablets hadn't touched it, even his mum's prescribed painkillers, which could genuinely put a horse to sleep. He had stayed still all night, on his back, his broken hand resting on his chest, gripped by the wrist by his other hand. Like he was in a coffin. He had seen every hour of the night and that hadn't been helped by the second reason; Ryan. Rob had arrived back home with a couple of cheeseburgers and had sat on the edge of his brother's bed but neither of them were in the mood to eat. Or talk. Both were nursing wounds that were so much deeper than the superficial broken bones and busted heads. Rob had left his brother's room a little after midnight, and the last time he had pulled the covers up to his brother's chin he was barely walking, but tonight it felt right. Ryan needed him and he was going to be there. That's what big brothers did.

It was still dark outside when Rob decided to get up and make a coffee. He could hear his mum snoring as he walked past her room, and by the time he got to the foot of the stairs he could hear Tyson was up and awake. Rob entered the kitchen, praying Tyson would keep all his four paws on the floor as he was pretty sure he couldn't take another knock to his swollen, throbbing hand. Rob opened the back door for his dog to do his business, kicking the door shut behind, glad to not have to use his hand. He picked up the kettle, carrying it over to the tap to fill it up before realising the task would require two hands. *Fucks sake.* The curse wasn't aimed at either the kettle, or the tap. Or the situation. But, at one person. Colin. He was blaming his hand on the fact he had gotten a hammering last night but the reality was he was to blame; for being gullible. By the time the kettle had boiled Tyson was scratching at the door, wanting to come in. And wanting breakfast. Rob looked at the tins of dog food on the side. It was the cheap brand; no ring pull. Meaning a tin-opener, meaning the dog would need to wait. Rob added the water to his mug and took the milk from the fridge, smelling it before pouring some in. It wasn't great but it would have to do. He sat on the sofa and before he knew it, had started to do some soul-searching again. An hour had past and Rob went back to the kitchen to make a second cup when he heard foot-steps above him. Experience had told him it was too early for his mum to be awake and probably by a few hours, which meant it was Ryan. He added a second cup and then filled them both. Both with three sugars. Both with enough milk to make the coffee look more like tea. *Fucks sake.* Another realisation that carrying both mugs upstairs was a two-handed affair. He decided to leave Ryan's where it was; *sod it.* He would be there for him but he wasn't going to be his personal butler. Rob knocked before entering, but entered anyway. Ryan was sat upright, his back against the wall and his legs out straight, the duvet resting on his midriff. Rob could tell that like him; his brother hadn't slept much. And like him, because he was hurting, both inside and out.

'Alright bruv, how you feeling?' Rob asked. He knew it was a stupid question when he said but that's what people seemed to say in these situations.

Ryan shrugged his shoulders. Rob could tell that he really didn't know.

He took a seat on the bed. He had promised his brother he would sort it and he was here to deliver on that promise. Rob went to speak but found himself drowned out by the sound of two big-bore exhausts that seemed to make the whole house shake. Rob stood up, went to the window and looked down at two bikes pulling up outside. He watched as the two men seemed to get off their bikes in unison, each swinging their trailing leg up over the leather seat and onto the floor before putting the bikes on their stands. Yesterday afternoon the men wearing the devil on their backs were enemies, today they came as his heroes. They walked down the path and then they were out of view because of the stone, square plinth that hung above the front door. Rob never understood why every council house had one of these plinths when all they seemed to do was collect bird shit. The knock at the door was loud. Three, single knocks. Bang. Bang. Bang.

'Who is it? Please, Rob, don't answer it.'

Rob turned to face his brother, noticing he had pulled up the duvet higher up his body, as if ready to hide.

'It's okay,' Rob replied.

'No, please, Rob. Don't.'

'Bruv, it's fine. Trust me.'

'Who is it?' Ryan asked, his fear evident.

'Help. It's our help.'

22

It wasn't a sight that Rob ever expected to see in his life; two outlaw bikers stood on his doorstep, arms crossed, with their Harleys behind them. They weren't here to collect a debt; or to settle a score. They were here to help. Rob gestured them in, as the neighbours opposite were already looking out their window to see why two men in leather cuts were standing at his door. Harlan stepped in first; Jim followed. Rob had forgotten to close the kitchen door and Tyson came bounding up the hallway in search of affection from the strangers.

'You guys want tea or coffee?' Rob asked, trying his best to downplay his nerves.

'I'll take a tea. Milk, 3 sugars. Jim?'

'Coffee. Black. One sugar,' Jim said, stroking Tyson.

With Rob away in the kitchen Harlan looked around the living room. It was small and the paintwork had started to stain a nicotine yellow. There was a TV guide magazine resting on the arm of the sofa, that had signs of chew marks. Caused by the dog Jim was stroking, no doubt. The carpet was threadbare in places and the dust on the dado rail hadn't just appeared today. The TV was flat, but not a brand Harlan knew, and there was still a video player underneath, on the walnut stand that was in-keeping with the room's décor, which was a mixture of tired wallpaper and poorly applied paint. The love for this room had left a long time ago, and Harlan only hoped that the love for each other, hadn't. He had seen it before, and more than once, when hard times cause the laughter, and the love to stop. When a family becomes nothing more than a group of strangers sharing an address. But Harlan wasn't here to judge, or put pay to the squalor, he was here to help Rob's brother, and was keen to get on with it.

Rob arrived with a mug in his unbroken hand, it was Jim, who nodded in the direction of the shelf on the wall as he was still busy with the dog. Rob went back out to fetch the second mug and returned and passed it to Harlan. The tea looked a decent colour, and he took a sip. It didn't taste too bad. There may be hope for this kid, Harlan thought.

'Where's your brother?' he asked.

'Upstairs. In his room,' Rob replied.

'I need to go and have a word.'

'I'll take you up.'

'No, you won't.' Harlan didn't need a chaperone, or a minder. What he needed was to be left alone. He had a way of getting the information he needed and he could read a room better than most. Harlan put his cup down on the walnut TV stand and squeezed past Jim and the tail-wagging dog. The house reminded him of when he was a boy, although it seemed like the mother, or the father, who was left raising the kids had given up. There may well be a reason for it, Harlan knew, but the crux of the matter was, no matter what shit you had going on, you still needed to raise your family right. He got to the top of the stairs and set about finding Ryan's room. The first room on his right had its door shut, and behind it he could hear the low drumming sound of someone asleep. The reverberations echoed of an adult so Harlan discounted this as the one. The next door along was open, and Harlan put his head around it and saw nothing much more than a set of weights on the floor, a cabinet with bottles of aftershave and deodorants and a TV mounted rather crookedly on the wall. There were a few posters of scantily clad women and a pair of expensive trainers in a box down by the bed. What wasn't there, was Ryan. Which left him the door with the hole in it, he should have seen that first, and if he did, he would have instinctively known it belonged to Ryan, as younger brothers seldom have the balls to punch a big brother's door in. Harlan got to the door and knocked, it was a gentle, non-threatening knock, designed to befriend. He waited for the reply. It came. Faint, but it came. That was all he needed. When Harlan walked in, he saw a bedroom that took him back to his own childhood. It was small and had an air of damp about it. The TV was smaller than his older brother's, as was the bed. Ryan was sitting upright, in his single bed and his hands were clasped. He looked nervous, the bruise on his face told him he had every right to be. Harlan stepped towards him and he could see Ryan edge his back deeper, and further up the wall.

'Hey, its okay. Relax,' Harlan said, trying to come across as congenial as a man could dressed all in black, with a beard, shoulder-length hair and a concrete stare.

Harlan's appearance left you in no doubt he wasn't a community support worker. Ryan wasn't relaxing; far from it.

'Listen, I am here to help. But to do that, you need to talk to me. OK?'

The look Ryan gave him told him there was still work to do establishing trust.

'Your brother reached out to me. Told me you were in a spot of bother. Judging by your boat race it seems he was right.'

The tilt of Ryan's head told him the rhyming slang was lost on the teenager.

'Face. I mean your face.'

Ryan got it; and for a split-second there was a smile on his face. Harlan was making progress. 'So, work with me kid. Who is behind this beating?'

Ryan's mouth opened but no words came out. Harlan wasn't sure if it was because he didn't want to grass, or knew not to, which Harlan appreciated, but he was here to help, not offer therapy. He had used up all his charm tactics and if the kid didn't want to help himself, there was nothing more to do. Harlan got up and headed for the door.

'Wait,' Harlan heard. His plan on getting the kid to talk had worked.

'I'll stay if you speak. If you don't, we're off. My advice, speak.'

Ryan cleared his throat and then spoke. It was getting him to stop that was the next problem.

His mum knew something was wrong. He was off his food and had become withdrawn. His teacher had called to say his work had started to slip and he was behind on his homework and she wondered if *everything was alright at home.* His mum had tried to talk to him but Liam had flounced off to his room, slamming the bedroom door behind him. He knew she was only trying to help. But how could she, her son was dealing drugs for an OG. There was no one who could help him. He was trapped and he knew it. Sundays were the only day he now liked, and only because it was quieter. The burner phone didn't ring as much so he had more time to be anything but someone's mule. His face had started to flare up again, which was the indicator his mum needed to tell her son was stressed. He had suffered from psoriasis as a child and it would get worse when he was worried about something, like when he was about to start senior school. If the truth be told, his flaky skin condition was the reason he started doing what he was doing. The first few months at big school had been awful. It was hard enough being the tadpoles in the pond but when your skin was red, angry and scaly, you were cannon fodder for the bullies. The change in medication and the new calming techniques prescribed by the doctors had worked wonders but the damage was done; he was labelled and it stuck. For the first three years. But that all changed when two simultaneous things happened; he turned fifteen and ran into a Somalian. From then, once his feet were under the table, so to speak, there was new found confidence in him and he went from being bullied, to doing the bullying. Then came the girls. For the first three years of senior school, they wouldn't touch him; literally. But when he started wearing the latest treads and had an air of swag, and money, about him, they were soon like flies around shit. Life was good on the merry-go-round he found himself on. Until he wanted to get off. Which was the problem; he couldn't. Liam looked at himself in the mirror. It was like his skin had gone back three years. If only he could.

'This is the address. You sure?' Harlan asked. There was a reason he checked, and then double-checked, as there was an occasion that he put through someone's door to collect a debt for the club but only to find it was the *wrong fucking door.*

Ryan nodded his head but that wasn't enough.

'I need more than a nod. Is this the place?'

'Yes,' Ryan said. Eventually.

Harlan knew Ryan was caught between a rock and hard place. Unsure whether to trust the biker that was standing in his room but really wanting to. On the other hand, what if he couldn't? What if that only made it worse? Harlan needed to quell his fears.

'Ryan, listen to me, what you got involved in was stupid, and your own fault.'

He let his words linger for a second, letting Ryan know he had to assume the responsibility for the situation he had put his family in. And then he backed off.

'But ultimately, you were groomed. These parasites sucked on you and took your blood, and by blood I mean your soul. You're what nobody in the crime world wants to be.'

'What's that?' asked Ryan.

'Disposable, son. Disposable.'

Ryan's face sank. The realisation hit him hard, he wasn't a junior gangster working his way on to the big league. He was a puppet on a string until they wanted to

cut his strings. Or him. He was, what the biker told him…
disposable.

'Let me ask you a question,' Harlan said. His eyes staring directly into Ryan's.

'Why do you want to be a gangster?'

Ryan shrugged his shoulders. He didn't know. He thought he did, once. But not now.

'I'll tell you why. Because of shit TV. Because you see the flash motors, fit birds and the bling. You see plenty of readies and respect. Am I right so far?'

Ryan nodded and then with a heavy heart mumbled, 'Yeah.'

'And then sometimes you see someone offed or banged up. Yeah?'

Another nod.

'OK. Well, let me enlighten you on a few facts. One, when you get shot, that shit stings. Or worse, it kills ya. And do you know how long dead lasts? For fucking ever. Two, you get banged up. Now trust me when I tell you it isn't all video games and gym time. Prison is an ugly, scary place and if you aren't a face, you're a bitch. Simple as. You know the worst time in prison?'

He shook his head and spoke.

'It's when your family leave you after a visit. When they leave and you can't. Or Christmas, when everyone is at home, celebrating whilst your banged up in your cell, with a cold turkey dinner and a fuck load of fuck all to open. And the cash, that's gone. You heard of the Proceeds of Crime act?'

Another shake of the head. Again, no words were leaving his mouth.

'If you can't prove where the cash came from that

bought your car, your bike, your watch then the feds take it. No paper trail; no paper. Sounding good so far?'

Another shake of the head.

'And then there's the girls. Trust me, they don't stick around when you're banged up. No, they're away copping off with the next wrong un' that will buy the drinks and dress them up in the designers. You want to be a gangster now?'

Ryan shook his head. And for the first time since the sermon began, spoke. 'No.'

'No. I didn't think so.'

Ryan took a moment to let it all sink in. He had been lucky. Yes, he had some bruises but maybe he had missed the bullet.

Harlan went to leave but as he put his hand on the door the teenager called out to him.

'Why did you become a gangster then?' It was a genuine question.

Harlan smiled before delivering his answer, 'I'm not. I'm an outlaw.'

Rob watched as they got on their bikes and fired up the powerful engines. The blip from the throttle made the little girl who was skipping further down the street start to cry.

'Oops,' Harlan said.

Rob waved at them as they walked their bikes back just enough to be able to flick into gear and roar off. He wasn't sure what had been said. He wasn't sure what they were going to do. All he knew was he had asked them for help and they had turned up. If he could make his brother's problem go away, then he would fulfil his promise.

And right now, that's all that mattered. He stepped back inside but not without looking up and down the street. Ryan's kidnap and subsequent revelation had spooked him. And if he was honest with himself, it had scared him, too. Which was why he found himself locking the door and sliding the chain across, something he hadn't done since he stopped *acting* like the man and started to become it. Rob carried the mugs back into the kitchen one at a time and put them in the washing up bowl with the rest of the dirty dishes. He would get Ryan to wash up; that was the least he could do. Tyson was scratching at the door again so he let him out and hunted around for some food. There wasn't much in. Nothing high in cholesterol and taste anyway. There was some bacon in the fridge and two crusts of bread. It would do. He promised himself he would go to the hospital in a bit as the swelling seemed to be getting worse. The kettle was close to boiling and he had some music playing on his phone from his Spotify app which was why he didn't hear his mum enter the kitchen. She looked dreadful; a cross between looking like she hadn't slept for a hundred years but also that she had. Her hair was lank now. It never used to be; it was always shiny and had a natural autumnal colour. Now it just looked lifeless and greasy. She was still pretty, but now you just had to look deeper to see it.

'Who were those men?'

'Just friends of mine, ma,' he replied. Wishing.

By the time Harlan and Jim got back, the dining room had been reset and the kitchen was clean. Jim went straight out the back to have a fag and Harlan knocked on the living room door. 'Come in,' Stan shouted, over the sound of the television whose volume was so loud it made the plates in his French dresser shake.

'Well?' Harlan asked.

'Yes, it's a whole in the ground. Jack and Jill hung around one for a bit.'

'No, you tit. Did you speak to her?'

'Yeah – course I did.'

'Well?'

'Didn't I just answer that?'

'STAN!'

'Okay. Okay. Yes, it's sorted. I didn't have you lot down for that sort of thing?'

'Which is why you should never judge a book by its cover.'

Harlan shut the door before Stan had time to come back with another quip. He walked down the narrow hallway, past the dining room and out through the kitchen and over to see Jim, who was on his phone calling the members who by now were back in their rooms hoping for a bit of shut eye.

It took a few minutes for them all to come down. Harlan had put the kettle on and was busy dropping tea bags into the ten clean cups. He didn't care who was a coffee drinker; they were getting tea. His round; his choice. A few of the members declined a seat, preferring to stand and stretch themselves out from a night on Stan's cheap mattresses.

When everyone had finished sugaring and stirring their tea, Jim began.

'Right, listen up. There is a little bit more we have to do here today. Up for it?'

Jim looked around the room at his brothers. He knew

the answer before he even asked the question. In his club, the motto was simple: *One in. All in.*

'Good. I thought as much. Harlan has the SP. I'll let him explain.'

Harlan was one of the few who were standing up. Not because of Stan's mattress, but out of respect. Jim was addressing his members and Harlan wasn't a direct charter anymore. He was a nomad, which was why he waited in the wings for Jim to invite him to chair the meeting. He took one of the spare chairs and turned it around, sitting with his legs spread-eagled and his chest pressed up against the back. The plan was simple. Two teams of five. One active. One acting as a decoy. One team wearing their colours. The other, without. Jim assigned who would be on which team. He tried to make it out that it wasn't decided on fighting ability on who would be put where. But it was. Jim needed three more ruthless men to ride along with him and Harlan, which was saying something. Harlan was a natural born fighter, but Jim was a born leader. It was what made them a formidable pair back in the day. His troops for today's mission were chosen and it was time to go and get busy. The Somalians were here. But Satan's Security was coming.

23

R yan hadn't said much, only an address and the headcount as he saw it. Four men. Whoever they were, they had scared him. But Ryan was a fourteen-year-old kid. It was easy to scare a teenager. Not quite so easy scaring someone that couldn't be scared. Even less when he had nine mates who also couldn't be scared. There was a lot to do. Justice needed to be served. Kids needed to be set free. And the fella who thought it was fine to hold someone against their will needed a refresher course on childcare. The plan was concise and the reason to split into two splinter cells was to keep them out of the big house. It was thinking about the *after* that protected the *now,* a skill that both Harlan and Jim excelled at. The lights turned green and the ten-man show of strength moved on in search of their first stop.

Alan was in the cellar so didn't hear the two seven-seater taxis pull up. But what he did hear was the sound of bikes being started and engines being revved. The boys were coming to get their bikes, he knew. It had been a late night and by the end, nobody was really fit to walk, let alone ride. Alan went back to the arduous task of changing dead barrels for new when he was interrupted once again, this time by the sound of the pub's door being thumped.

'I'm coming,' he shouted up through the open hatch on the floor but knew he was too far away to be heard, which was confirmed to him by more thumping.

'Okay, okay, I'm coming for Chrissake,' as he hauled his bulk up onto the ladder and out through the hatch, stopping for a split-second to catch his breath before moving on in the direction of the door. Alan set about sliding across the top and bottom latch and then put his key in the lock and turned it. He hardly had time to pull open the door before it was done for him and in stepped five bikers from last night.

'You lads are early!' Alan said, a bit taken aback.

'And thirsty. You got a new barrel on yet, mucker,' Dogging Dave answered.

'Just doing it now,' replied Alan.

'Good. Chop chop.'

'You lads want a beer now?'

'We haven't come here for tea and cake,' Mouse answered with a mischievous grin all over his face.

'How did you get on with Tash?' Alan asked.

'Nah, no good. I think she must be a lesbo.'

'Or the fact she likes her men over five-foot and not named after a fucking rodent.'

The quick quip from Brian brought a hail of laughter and even Mouse had to admit it was good.

'Where is everybody else?' Alan asked.

'Bit of business across town,' Don replied. Don 'Gentle' Mann had been the VP for coming up to five years and he was considered a man of few words. But when those words were delivered; people listened. Alan said no more, knowing when to speak and when to keep schtum where the bikers were concerned and went behind the bar and pulled five pints before going back down to the cellar to finish flushing through the lines. The five members stood and chatted amongst themselves until finally Alan re-emerged, with a forehead full of sweat and his cheeks blowing.

'That must be like trying to fit a whale in a wetsuit getting your fat ass down that hole?' said Terry, who had a foam of lager around his top lip. His comment brought another burst of laughter. In a biker's world, everybody in their small circle was fair game where mickey taking was concerned, but at the same time, everybody in their chosen circle was also shown absolute loyalty. It was a fair trade-off. And it worked.

After the pints were finished, it was time to get to work. And more importantly, to be seen. The CCTV cameras were turned back on and Jim had made it clear that their cuts were to be kept on at all times today and he didn't care how hot it was.

Mouse and Alan went through the list that Harlan had left the landlord, checking off what was coming, and when. It had finally dawned on Alan what Harlan was doing. He also couldn't fail to notice that for the first time in months that his pub wasn't smashed up. That he didn't have to put some chipboard up in the windows whilst replacements were being made. That he didn't have to make an emergency dash to the cash-and-carry to get replacement glasses and that he didn't have to spend all morning trying to get the stench of weed and stale urine out of the air. For the first time in months, he had a boozer that could open on a Sunday. Alan wasn't a religious man but right then, he felt like putting his hands together and thanking what God it was that he believed in for sending Harlan to him.

The app on Harlan's phone told him that they were less than two minutes away from 157 Sycamore Road. Ryan had described him well enough for Harlan to despise him; which was something no man wanted. He found it hard to stop his hand forming a fist as he rode his Harley. The club's vice-president, Don 'Gentle' Mann, was back at the pub, keeping an eye on business there with the rest of the members who were chosen to stay behind. This led to a change of formation, with Jim out in front and Simon 'Double' Nott to his right, just a few inches behind with Harlan off to Simon's left, third in position in the pack. Behind him were two more members. Five men. Five bikes. One aim. Harlan couldn't get there quick enough as there was vengeance to serve and it was a dish best served in the heat of the moment. He saw Jim indicate, telling his crew to turn right into the chosen road. Like dominos, the Harleys all turned in, one at a time, until the formation was resumed and the spectacle was now within touching distance of the man with the teardrop tattoo. Jim signalled for the four bikes to pull over and nestle behind him. Harlan knew why Jim had deliberately pulled a few houses down and far enough away that the bikers couldn't be seen from the bedroom window. It was simple. To not give the person behind the door a clue the rumbling noise was anything to do with him.

'How do you want to do this, H?' Jim asked.

'Simple, Pres. I will go in the front. Two go around the back. Two wait out here in case he decides to go all SAS and jump out a fucking window.'

'Good plan – apart from the fact you aren't going in there alone. You and I will take the front door, Simon and Beaver will take the back and Hippy will man the escape. Deal?'

'Deal.'

Harlan waited for Jim to quickly brief the others and then waited some more until Jim got a prank on his burner that the back was covered. 'Right, son. Avon calling.'

Harlan smirked, liking the Avon house call reference and then set off in the direction of 157's door, complete with its busted cat flap. Harlan checked his pocket for his brass dusters, just in case. They were there; like he knew they would be. The knock Harlan gave to the door was subtle; non-threatening. Inquisitive. Inquiring. It was when he heard the chain slide that it all changed. The force of Harlan's shoulder barge sent it crashing open and the man behind it, crashing to the floor.

'Get up. NOW. Whilst you still can.'

Harlan waited for him to scramble up to his feet, and as he did, Harlan swept his leg away sending him back down to where he came from. 'Didn't I just say get up?'

Harlan was in the mood to mock; to belittle. To frighten.

He waited for him to get up again before giving him a hard shot to his stomach, not hard enough to break anything, yet, but hard enough to leave him gasping for air.

Harlan grabbed hold of him by his shirt and threw him up against the wall.

'Word on the street is you like holding the young dealer's captive for a while, huh? Well, trust me, by the time I finished with you that teardrop you have will be fucking real.'

Harlan's hand that was around his throat made it difficult to speak. Or plead.

'I'm thinking we take him up to that room he kept the kid in and have a little fun. Sound good?' said Jim, already salivating at the thought of what was to come for him.

'Yeah. Agreed. What better way to spend a Sunday than pulling someone's teeth out. You got the pliers?'

Jim reached into his trouser pocket and pulled out the pliers. The look that came across the man with the teardrop tattoo said it all. He was bricking it.

'Not so much fun when you're on the receiving end, is it?'

Harlan pulled his hand away from his throat to let him speak, and as he did, Harlan proceeded to smash his fist into his jaw. He was out cold and slithering down the wall to the floor. Jim was smiling. 'You still got it, kiddo.'

Harlan laughed.

'Let's get the sack of scrawny piss upstairs and Hippy can babysit him for a bit. I'll leave him the pliers.'

This time they both laughed.

Five had become four. But the four left were formidable. Jim. Harlan. Simon. And Nigel. On their own they had been in hundreds of fights, and losing less than a handful. Together they hadn't lost one. The reason being;

loyalty. They would die for each other if it came to it. It's what you wore the patch for; to be there for your brother. Harlan added the address into Jim's phone, which was positioned in the centre of his handlebars, on a cradle. Jim wasn't big on technology and had hands *like cow's tits* as he often said, his fingers never getting to grips with finer points of a touchscreen keypad. They fired up their engines and rode quietly down the road, hiding the fact back at 157 they were holding someone hostage. The next address was a short ride across town but carried the biggest risk. The intel from Ryan was sparse, at best, but it wasn't as if they hadn't ridden into the unknown before. The maths was four-against-four; one apiece. Highly favourable odds and once successful, highly financially rewarding. But one thing Harlan knew was that people do like to hold onto what they have. Meaning the persuasion needed would be far from gentle. He couldn't wait.

Every part of Colin was hurting. The man who inflicted his pain hadn't thrown many punches, but what he had, landed. And what landed, hurt. Colin had never been given such a masterclass before but that was then, and this was now. Jamal had called him in need of more product, which meant more money, which was the best medicine money could buy.

The house had never been as quiet. But he was too arrogant to say he missed them. *Her loss* he had told himself last night; when sat drinking alone. And this morning, when eating breakfast alone. The trip to the loft had told him his money was safe. The bottom box on the right with the layer of football programs was still in place. That's all that mattered. Money. Women could come and go, so too children. It was cold-hard cash that counted. And he had it; but he wanted more. Which was where Jamal came in. He would need to see his own dealer on the way, but that was no more than horses for courses. Basic business; he had found himself the wholesaler, buying directly from the manufacturer. Or as directly as his status would let him as he was no Escobar, or Mafioso, but he had his place in the chain and Jamal was his customer and it was he who would flood the streets of this town. Colin smiled, until it hurt him, on the little niche he had carved out for himself. He checked his watch and began hunting around for his car keys, having given up trying to start the washing machine, its array of settings and buttons proving too much for him. With his car keys found he headed out the door and off to make some more bread. It was only when he got in the Porsche and pulled down the glovebox in the hunt for a little livener, that a lipstick fell out and made him realise just what he had lost. She was good for him. Good to him. Yes, he paid the bills, paid for the holidays, and, when her looks failed, he would have paid for her surgery. But what he got in return he knew he couldn't put a price on. It was true, he had given her a house; but she had given him a home. She had given him a family. And she had given him love; she had *actually* loved him. And he had fucked it. He picked up the lipstick and took off the lid, then turned the base to bring up the waxy colour, finding himself reminiscing of the many kisses they had shared with her lips in this pastel shade of pink. *Selfish bitch.*

One thing Ryan didn't say, because he didn't know, was that they had a white Mercedes. And that it wasn't there.

The four bikes pulled up and killed the engines, removing the thunder and restoring the peace. Until the peace would be broken; like their bones. The four Satan's Security members stood in a huddle talking through the next plan.

'What do we know, H?' asked Nigel 'Eager' Beaver.

'There's four of them that I know of.'

'Tooled up?'

'Probably. It's not a trap house, it's their actual HQ.'

'Foreign, aren't they?' Jim said.

'Yeah. The kid said they looked like African pirates,' Harlan replied.

'Good – so they will be off the grid. Meaning no harm, no foul.'

The smile that came across Simon's face said it all; this would be fun.

'There are cameras, though. They will see us coming to the door.'

'What's the plan then?'

'Anybody here smell smoke?' Jim said, opening his hand to reveal the lighter.

Of the four, Nigel was the least conspicuous. He wasn't covered in facial hair; he didn't wear a bandana or have a wrist full of leather bracelets with skulls on. He wasn't covered in ink nor was he a body full of protein and steroids. Which was why he was the perfect choice to walk in the building like he was someone's next door neighbour. Harlan, Jim and Simon split up and kicked around outside, either on their phone or just enjoying a smoke in the Sunday sun. Which was another reason they weren't wearing their cuts. As far as the world was concerned; Satan's Security MC were in town, but they were milling around at the Crossways pub helping the landlord set up shop. Nigel had clocked the camera that was above the main entrance door and made sure his face was obscured as he waited outside for a few seconds deciding which way to play it. He opted to hit the trades-man's button that was at the bottom of the keypad, under the rows of round pressable buttons belonging to the flats that were inside. Experience told him that someone would buzz him in. He was right. Once in, and after his nostrils started to ignore the stench of stale urine, he started to climb the first set of stairs, ignoring the four blue doors on the entrance floor. His peripheral vision had clocked which of the four flats belonged to the pirate gang; it was the one laced with surveillance cameras outside. Nigel pulled the heavy door open to the 1st floor in search of a fire alarm. He found one, and with the help of the thick sovereign ring on his right hand, smashed the glass sending a shrieking, wailing sound around all four corners of the building. It took a couple of seconds for the residents of the building to cotton on there just may well be a fire before their blue doors started to open and people started leaving their flats. Nigel waited back before blending in with the crowd on his way out, and as he reached the ground floor, he saw the blue door with the cameras above it and three dark-skinned men leave; looking just as the young teen had described. Everybody from the block of flats stood outside the building expecting to see roaring flames or black smoke. When none arrived, the excitement dwindled and normal service resumed and everyone started to make their way back in. The look of Jamal's face told his neighbours he was less than impressed with being disturbed and he angrily barged through the crowd to get back to his flat; back to counting his money. The last of the trio stepped in and shut the door and as he walked down the small, tight, short hallway and turned the 90 ˚ at the end, he found himself back in the sun-starved living room back with his crew.

And a room full of bikers.

'What the f –'

The non-brother of Jamal's gang never had a chance to finish the sentence before the biker that was standing behind the door put the piece of rope he had in his pocket around his neck and pulled it tight. With Simon being a good foot taller than the gang member, he was held up on his tip toes and his hands were desperately trying to pull the rope that was now slicing into his throat and cutting off his air supply.

Harlan had Jamal on the floor, with his arm up high behind his back, at the point of snapping. The last of Jamal's gang was face down on the table, his head awkwardly twisted to the right so as to see his leader trying his best not to scream in pain with the pressure Harlan was applying to it.

'Hey, Jim, these fellas don't seem all that, do they?' Harlan had started the mocking.

'Maybe that's why they use kids, as they haven't the cahoonas to do shit themselves.'

Harlan looked down at the man whose arm was close to breaking at the seam.

'That right? You lack the balls to do the dirty work?'

Jamal didn't answer. Harlan twisted his arm some more.

'I'm asking you a question. Your arm is saying you should answer it.'

Jamal went to answer but as he did, Harlan twisted it some more.

'Argghhh.'

'Nah, save it. Instead, what I'm thinking now is seeing as you don't have, and as my president so elegantly put it, the cahoonas to do it, that we will do it instead.'

Jamal went to speak again, sensing his empire was about to get taken over.

'You little fu –'

The crack was deafening. Harlan twisted and turned at the same time, breaking both his arm and wrist at the same time.

'H, there seems to be a safe shaped object over there. I'm thinking…' said Jim, having to raise his voice over the screaming Jamal.

'And I like what you're thinking.'

'Simon, I think your fella looks tired, I reckon he needs to go to sleep,' Jim said, giving his Sgt at Arms the green light. Simon let the rope fall from his hands, replacing it with his powerful arms, putting one under his chin and the palm from his other on top of his head. It didn't take long for the man in the choke hold to lose consciousness and say goodnight to the world, leaving Simon free to let him drop to the floor and head over to the safe.

It was locked. Of course it was. Simon tried brute force to open it but for all his strength, steel was stronger. They weren't just here to administer punishment for grooming young kids to push their drugs, they were here to take over. Harlan had told Jim about the amount of drops Ryan was doing, and that Ryan said there were at least five others on the payroll that he knew of and Jim had run the numbers in his head. It made good reading, which was why he decided to help Harlan put pay to this gang of deadbeats and remodel their little enterprise as their own. The club had been involved in dealing narcotics for years, albeit at a distance. The difference was the MC's dealers were adults. Grown men making grown up decisions. Grown men who knew the score and were accountable for their own actions. They weren't young kids getting paid a few quid a week for the risk of a few years in juvie.

Outlaws had been in the drug business since the 70's, but it was done with as much of a moral code as it could be. Jim had it all worked out in his head, which was more than taking the contents of the safe and whatever product was in there, instead he wanted their pipeline. And by that, he meant their phones. A drug business is only as good as its customer base, all of which are stored on burner phones. Drug users don't care who is running the show; just as long as *someone* is. Satan's Security would take the phones, and as such the business. Jim already had a source for the product, so it had been agreed by the officers of the club, when sat around Stan's dining room, that they would set up a team here in town to deliver the drugs to the customers of the man lying on the floor with his arm in bits.

'Number for the code. NOW,' Harlan demanded.

Despite the pain he was in, Jamal remained staunch, not prepared to give up his gains.

Harlan decided maybe one broken arm wasn't enough, and kicked Jamal over to his other side and picked up his other arm and began the process of bending it back until Jamal's face told him it was close to snapping. 'I repeat, give me the fucking code.'

Nothing.

Snap.

Even Jim winced when he heard the bone crack, rendering the fella with not one, but two broken arms.

Harlan knelt down and spoke, with a hiss, into Jamal's face.

'You will run out of bones before I run out of patience. Next will be your legs. The last will be your neck. Your call, the code or I'll put you in so much pain you'll wish you were still in the womb.'

Harlan put his ear close to Jamal's mouth, and heard, from a low gargle and with little bubbles leaving his mouth as he spoke, the digits to the safe.

'Good man. I thought you would see sense.' And with that, Harlan stood up, turned his back, and took a couple of steps away from Jamal before turning around and with as much venom as he could, sent a kick so hard into Jamal's face that he was out cold before his head had a chance to snap back.

Harlan shouted over the digits to Simon, who pressed the numbers into the keypad and opened the door. The safe wasn't as full as they would have liked. It wasn't a bad payday, but it wasn't the riches they had in mind, nor was there any product, aside from a few ounces that had been turned into grams. The finished product.

The money was on its way elsewhere.

'Grab every phone and charger,' Jim said. It was time to get out of here. It was a shame the safe wasn't flush with cash, but they had done what they had come to do.

Simon cleared away everything that was available, stuffing it all into a bag for life that Nigel had found on the cluttered table.

Jim spoke to one member who was awake, 'Now I am pretty sure you don't want to see us again, which is the same for us, because, if I do see you again, you guys will end up skinny dipping with concrete armbands on. Get me?'

The one with his face still pressed down hard on the table was let up by Nigel so he could speak.

'Yeah, man I get –'

Jim twisted hard from his hips, which brought the right hook around with maximum force and then there were three people fast asleep on the stained carpet.

Harlan's burner rang. He took it out and answered. It was a very short call. Seconds.

He ended it and shoved it back in his pocket.

'We need to leave; now.'

24

Rob had been told enough to tell from the bedroom window that the person who had knocked hard on the door and who was now sitting in the white Merc, was one of them.

Ryan hadn't seen him; Rob had made sure of that. His mum was still out; somewhere. Which left one scared teenager, an excitable dog and his one-handed self. Ryan had told him that they were tooled up, and the knock at the door was less than nice. Rob did the maths. Which was why he had called Harlan and had barely any time to answer.

'They are here,' he said. The panic was evident.

'Who is?' Harlan asked.

'Them. They are here.'

'No. They are here.'

'I'm telling you. One of them is here.'

In Harlan's quest to serve his own form of punishment he had miscounted. There were only three unconscious men on the floor. Not four.

'Stay there. And DON'T open the door.'

The last thing Rob heard was Harlan say *we need to leave; now* before his mobile clicked off.

Twice, Rob peered through the once white, but now grey, net curtains and was lucky each time not to be seen. The second time was a close call, so much so that Rob banged the back of his hand against the wall as he shot back behind the curtain in his need not to be seen. The car stood out like a pimple on a pensioner. It was new, sleek and shiny and it wasn't trying to be discreet. The driver had hip-hop blaring through the powerful music system, the window was down and his arm was hanging out of it, a large, thick gold bracelet resting at the base of his wrist. Rob had been told to stay in, and to not open the door, which was advice he didn't need; there was no worry of him leaving and definitely no chance of him opening the door. It wasn't as if Tyson could help. He had been named after the youngest heavyweight champion of the world, who was known for his fearless aggression, but Tyson shared all of the name and none of the attributes. Rob was pretty sure the dude with the gold bracelet and whatever tool he was carrying, wouldn't be put off by a slobbering, tail-wagging dog. Rob checked the phone; which he had done less than thirty seconds before. And which he would check thirty seconds from now. And which he would continue to do until Harlan arrived. Rob knew it was risky going back to the pub and pleading for help, after first pleading for forgiveness. With no dad to turn to, it felt eerily right to turn to the biker. Bikers. The beating they gave was next level, a masterclass, but that was then. And Ryan came after. And this was now.

.   .   .

Harlan, Jim, Simon and Nigel left the flat before first tearing apart the CCTV system. With three men in various degrees of unconsciousness, two arms broken, an empty safe and a stern warning, their job there was done. Back at the bikes, it was decided Nigel would ride back with the bag to the pub where he would put on his cut and would be seen outside with the rest of the MC. With the engines fired up, Nigel set off one way and the other three bikes roared down the street, turning right at the end and then heading off in search of Rob and the white Mercedes. The formation was now linear; Jim, Harlan and then Simon. There wasn't the time or the need to ride in rank. The roads were Sunday midday busy; cars heading out or heading home. Sunday drivers at Sunday speed which was being loudly intercepted and rudely overtaken by three black Harleys. Harlan was focused to the point of pain. He was already imagining what he would do when he got there; if Ryan had been hurt. Again. The lights at the intersection were red. This brought to a standstill the row of cars that were approaching it, but didn't stop Jim, Harlan and Simon who just dropped down a gear and sped right through the red light like it was normal; and legal.

It wasn't a long ride to Rob's, but it was even quicker if you had no regard for the speed limit. Flashing cameras weren't a concern for the club as a rule. Most of the driving licences were moody, and the hire purchase agreements for the bikes equally as fraudulent. The downside was the lack of insurance but the motto was *if you crashed your bike, you didn't deserve one in the first place.* Being an outlaw meant being at one with your bike; and your brothers.

· · ·

Rob watched as he got out of the car and walked up to the door. He clearly wasn't taking no for an answer, believing that despite no-one answering, there was in fact someone behind the door. He checked his phone again. It had been nine minutes since he had called. And fifteen minutes since the white Mercedes had first pulled up. If he was prepared to wait for fifteen, would he be prepared to wait all day and night? The banging on the door was fiercer than the previous visit. Either his patience was running out or his temper was rising. Or both.

Tyson barked again, hoping whoever was on the outside would be pleased to see him, but Rob knew that wouldn't be the case. The knock came again, only seconds after the first release of rage on the door, which was the only thing separating Rob from the man with the gold bracelet and white Mercedes. Rob felt his chest rise and fall in tandem with the heavy breaths he was taking. This was fast becoming the worst weekend of his life. A spot formerly reserved for the day his dad walked out on his family. But then it went silent. The knocking stopped for a few seconds and was then replaced by some talking. Rob couldn't hear what was being said and he was too scared, and not too stupid, to open the window to eavesdrop. He counted to twenty before coming back up from under the window sill and peering through the net curtain. But the man with the gold bracelet was no longer outside the door, or on the path. He was now at his car. And seconds later he was in it. And seconds after that he was driving away. And seconds after that; three Harleys rode into view.

. . .

Harlan was the first of the three off his bike and paced hard up the path to the door. His hand was formed into a loose fist ready to knock on the door but Rob opened it, meaning Harlan knocked into fresh air, followed by falling forward half a step in doing so.

'Where is he?' Harlan snarled, ready to commit another felony.

'He has just left. Literally just a second ago. Coloured chap. White Mercedes.'

'Ryan OK?' Harlan asked, looking over Rob's shoulder for the young teen.

'Yeah. Thank God.'

'Right, stay here. And bolt this fucking door. I mean it.'

'I will. I promise.'

'Don't make me promises. Do what you're supposed to do and keep your brother safe.'

Harlan knew Rob was about to say thank you, but he didn't want to hear it; or have *time* to hear it. He turned his back on Rob and walked back to his bike at the same pace as he'd arrived.

'White Merc. Coloured fella. Missed him by seconds,' he told Jim.

Then he will only be seconds away. Let's go,' Jim replied. The intent was clear, so too was the instruction. All the bikes fired back up and their feet were barely off the floor as the three Satan's Security members screamed down the road in hot pursuit of the white C-Class.

Colin had made his collection; and now it was time for it to be collected. He could set his watch on how regular Jamal could flip his product. Sometimes he regretted buying the Porsche, as it was hardly lowkey. And what he needed when carrying a kilo of cocaine was something lowkey. But so far, he had gotten away with it. He was yet to be pulled, so maybe it was being *loud* that kept him quiet. He had told Jamal; through the encrypted app, that he would be at the usual place. With the usual amount. And at the usual price. The cocaine was wrapped tightly in parcel tape. Which was ironic; as it *was* a parcel, just not one the Royal Mail could deliver, legally. The parcel of coke was sitting inside a rucksack; which was behind the passenger seat of his Porsche. Colin had been waiting for ten minutes. But only because he was ten minutes early. The routine was clear, a different one of the four every fortnight, meaning he would only see the same face once every eight weeks. Familiarity breeds complacency, and Colin knew that in his line of work, complacency could mean some serious time behind bars. To pass the minutes Colin was plotting the rebirth of the Cherry Pickers and once his rib had healed, he was going to go hard on a recruitment mission. This time, picking the meanest men out there. Those who didn't just love to fight but those who were good at it. It was thinking of who to recruit; and how, that made him not hear at first, the sound of the split-pipe exhaust coming out of the back of the white Mercedes. Jamal's Mercedes. It was a tight corner but the location was perfect. Past the retail park, through the council estate and down a back lane with its defaced single garages either side. The Mercedes stopped just in front of Colin's bumper. The two expensive German cars just inches apart. The transaction would be swift; ill-gotten gains for ill-gotten goods. Two rucksacks exchanged. Cash for drugs. Colin made the signal, telling Jamal's henchmen to leave the car and bring the bag while doing his best to hide the excitement of doing another deal. The door of the Mercedes opened and the curbed bracelet glinted in the sunlight. The next thing that glinted, was the chrome work of three loud, powerful bikes that came around the corner. The guy with the cash got back into the car, scrambling to press the round starter button on the dash before it dawned on him, he was blocked in. At the end of his bonnet was a Porsche, in the rear-view mirror were three bikes. But minus the riders, as they were already off their bikes and now the two cars were surrounded.

'Fuck me, we meet again,' Harlan said, as he rapped the driver's window of Colin's car.

Colin's face had gone from a sleazy smile to one of shock, which was then replaced with a mixture of remembrance and fear. The first causing the second.

'Wind the window down,' Harlan ordered. He knew Colin had no intention of doing that which was why, after the second time of demanding, Simon moved Harlan out the way and hurled a half-broken brick through it.

'Oops,' Harlan said, as Colin's face came to the realisation of what had just happened to his beloved car.

'Now, didn't I tell you that I didn't want to see your ugly mug around here again?'

Colin went to speak. He just didn't get to finish.

In the rush to try and start the car, the man with the gold bracelet had forgotten to lock the doors, which was why Jim was now sitting next to him on the passenger seat.

'Now, I may not be an Oxford scholar, but it seems to me you've found yourself in a spot of bother here, my old China,' Jim said, with his customary scary smile that was reserved for situations like this. Jim watched as he started padding around his blue body-warmer, looking for anything that could be used as a weapon.

'I think that unless you pull something out of there that goes bang, and that can go bang quicker than I can put what is in my pocket through your skull, I would put your hands back on the steering wheel.'

Jim watched as he slowly did as he was told. The reason for his compliance was evident. Out in front was a windowless Porsche, an unconscious Colin and two thickset men. One big; one bigger. Both looked like they could invade a country by themselves and next to him was a guy who was bordering on the psychotic.

'What do you want, G?' the Somalian asked.

'G? No, J. But we can cover the alphabet another day. What I want. No, what I am going to take is that little black bag of yours.'

'No way man. Fuck you.'

'Oh, dearie me. You haven't got the memo have you! We have already visited your pokey flat, and E, F and G were left on the floor, one of which, the skinny ugly looking one, has two broken arms and one empty safe. So, shall we try this again?'

The penny dropped. So too did the resistance. Jim reached across to the back seat and picked up the rucksack.

'Hey, it's not all bad, sugar tits, at least you get to keep your bracelet.'

Jim got out of the car and stood next to Harlan and Simon, who also happened to be holding a bag. First came the smiles; then the laughs. They were in a back lane and in a strange town, but for Harlan, he was home. The back slaps between them said it all; the job was done. The gang had been disbanded, the man with the teardrop tattoo was currently being held against his will and now they had a bag of cash, a bag of coke and a bag of burner phones. Not a bad morning's work. Harlan put one of the rucksacks on his back with Simon doing the same with the other, and they followed Jim as he led the way out of the lane, with the defaced garages either side, through the council estate and out past the retail park. No patches meant no prying eyes, especially from those with the flashing blue lights and talking lapels. Which was just as well, as what was now on Simon's back came with a ten year sentence. Which was why the red lights were now being obeyed. So too, the speed limits. They were outlaws. That didn't mean they were outlandish.

This time, his jaw was broken. It had dropped significantly on the right-hand side. The side Harlan's fist had connected with; and smashed. He came around to a headache from hell. No man should be able to punch *that* hard. For a few seconds, he sat there, stunned and with his head spinning. It wasn't his peripheral vision that told him there was a brick-sized hole in his window, it was the wind coming in through it. There was shattered glass around his feet and he had already come to the conclusion that the cost of repairs from the main dealer would leave him a grand out of pocket. It was when his mind was on the money that he twisted hard to his left to check the bag was there. It wasn't. And all the twisting had done was reaffirm his ribs were broken. The pain that followed had told him that his ribs didn't go much on such a sudden movement. The white Mercedes that was parked in front of him was no longer there, meaning either the driver had driven off with his cash. Or they had.

His body slumped down into the leather seat taking his ego with him. In less than 24hrs he had lost a fight, his wife, his drugs and his money. He had spent so long creating a costume; trying to mask the fact he was a loser by trying so hard to be a winner. The desire to be a *someone* had cost him *everyone*. The realisation hit him harder than Harlan had. He wasn't a gangster; he was a broken man, sitting in a broken car after breaking up his family. The tears that followed didn't fall because of the pain.

25

Alan took a step back and looked around his car park. Which was now more than just a waste piece of gravelled land with a few weeds dotted about and loose stones getting embedded in tyres. Much more. The list Harlan had given him a few days ago, the list written on a piece of paper torn from his notepad which first confused him, but now, amazed him. He took the biro that was wedged behind his ear and ticked off each of the tasks his hired help had set him.

Bouncy castle – tick

BBQ – tick.

Sumo suits - tick

Children's face painting stand – tick

Children's hair braiding and henna stand – tick

Toffee apple/candy floss stand – tick

Alan had to admit; it looked good. He now had a family fun day set up inside his car park and it felt good. Really good. There was a new feeling appearing in his oversized stomach and for a second he didn't know what it was, until it hit him. Pride. He felt proud. He realised he could be more than just another landlord trying to serve enough pints to scrape by, he could be a pillar of the community. He could be 'the fun-fair pub'. Alan thought he understood the trade, knowing what customers wanted, but Harlan had shown him just what could be achieved if you thought outside the box and created a brand. He was due to pay the biker today but he knew it wasn't enough. Nowhere near enough.

The previous night had been phenomenal. Everybody loved having a beer with a biker. Alan had got up early to count the takings and by the time he ran the card machine report and counted the cash in the two tills, he was flabbergasted. He knew it had been good, *but this good?!* His calculator had told him he turned over close to seven-grand. He had run the numbers twice. Then twice more, just to be sure. But it was there, *seven grand.* He was so impressed that he made a promise to himself that on Monday he would start his diet.

After the takings were counted, he had been busy on his socials. He set about shouting out to anyone who had a pulse what was on offer at the Crossways pub today and his smartphone was keen to show him it was being well received. Hearts, shares, comments, tags – it was gaining traction fast. He could see the magical number of ten-thousand being hit by the time he locked up tonight. If he did it; he would *definitely* start his diet tomorrow…

'Al, get some beers pulled, the boys are back,' Don shouted through the back door that was being propped open by a beer crate.

Harlan followed in behind Jim and Simon, with respect to ranks back in place. He was now a nomad, a decision he had taken for a personal reason and it was right to follow in last. They parked their bikes just inside the car park, in front of the chest height wall and parallel to the beer garden. By the time they had lifted their trailing legs up and over the leather seats and set them on the stands, there were nine Harley's parked in a row. Each unique. Each the same. It was a photo just in itself. Harlan handed his rucksack over to Simon, who went off in search of Don, who would look to store it somewhere out of sight, and out of mind. Jim followed Simon, needing a word with his VP regarding what had happened, and what needed to happen. The club worked, because respect and loyalty worked. Jim ran the show, but it was a democracy. Every officer had a vote and only if it was at a tie, would Jim cast the decider. Harlan walked around the carpark admiring Alan's achievements. The bouncy castle was big, and bouncy. The BBQ was a 45-gallon drum that had been crudely cut in two, by a blunt saw by the look of it. There was a fella whose face Harlan remembered from last night busy adding firelighters to get his own party started. The kid's stalls were impressive and there were cuddly toys to hand out. Harlan hugged each of his brothers that were outside either blowing up balloons or drinking beer from a bottle. Some were doing both. Actually, it was only Mouse that was doing both. Harlan walked inside and saw a pint on the bar waiting for him. He tipped his head in acknowledgment towards Big Al, and then took a well-deserved mouthful of lager. Don 'Gentle' Mann brought over their cuts, and Jim, Harlan and Simon slipped their arms through the holes, shuffling their backs until the cuts fell where they were supposed to and nestled neatly on their broad shoulders. Nine men, with no family ties to each other, stood there loud, and proud, as nine brothers.

Alan checked his watch. It was time to open the doors to his public. When he unlocked his double doors, and pulled them open by the curved, brass handles, he was faced with close to thirty waiting people, each wanting to grab a table and enjoy the day. Alan welcomed them in, like a suited Savoy porter.

Shanice was behind the bar, and happy to serve, thankful she was able to work on a Sunday again. Tash was there, too, and Mouse's antenna was already tuned in ready to try again with her. The little kids who had come in with the adults were looking up, and already in awe at these men dressed in black, some with tattooed faces and with various degrees of facial hair and with the devil on their back. Satan's Security were still in town.

The door kept opening; more and more people came in to enjoy the fun fair, spending their Sundays as they were supposed to; as a family. Alan was now behind the bar serving and Simon and Dogging Dave were back at that pool table with yet another competition in play.

By the early afternoon the bouncy castle was awash with young kids who were smiling on the way up, and giggling on the way down. The BBQ was doing great business and everywhere Harlan looked someone was taking a bite out of a burger or adding mustard to a hot dog. The club were mingling with Alan's customers, taking off where they had left off last night or starting a conversation with someone new. Harlan had chatted to the latest patch members, getting to know them and it was clear why they made the cut, ready to wear *the cut.* He had shared a beer with Don inside the pub, catching up on things back home and listening to the wise old man's view on the world, said with succinct words that were carefully chosen before spoken. Harlan was then outside, in the beer garden and talking to Brian which was why he missed the silver SUV pull up. It was only when he heard a bit of a commotion that he turned his head, as he knew now only too well whose voice it was that was getting narky.

'For Chrissake, mate, do you really think this taxi malarky is for you?'

Harlan smiled to no-one in particular. He had come to love Stan and his sharp tongue.

The to-ing and fro-ing of the buggy in the back of the SUV was coming close to Stan bursting a blood vessel and he took a second to look around the periphery for the man who had invited him here. Harlan watched Stan's eyes scan around until they landed on him and then waited the few seconds for the inevitable.

'Don't just sit there like a bloody plant pot, come here and help and this fella is as much use as someone trying to blow out a bushfire. Ow, that's my fucking toe.'

Harlan really wanted to stay where he was and just watch Stan get madder and madder but behind the buggy, and in danger of getting dizzy, was Danielle, who he thought didn't want to spend her Sunday afternoon stuck in the back of a taxi. Harlan stood up and walked over to help and after repositioning the buggy and straightening up the wheels, the buggy was finally out, so too was Danielle.

'I suppose you want paying next, although God knows why,' Stan said to the driver, rooting around in his pocket for some cash. Harlan told Stan it was fine, he handed over fifteen quid and told the driver to keep the change. Stan looked at him, shaking his head.

'Keep the change, he should have kept his previous career,' not caring that the driver was standing right beside him. Harlan laughed and then gestured for Danielle to lead the way; forever the gentleman. When they arrived at the gate, Harlan stepped in front, opened it and then bent down slightly to lift the front of the buggy over the kerbed threshold and down onto the grass. 'What would you like to drink?' he asked her.

'Let me get these, please,' Danielle replied.

'Not a chance. Women don't pay on my watch.'

'Are you sure?' she asked.

'Yes – he is sure, now choose something expensive. I hear Champagne is good,' Stan interjected, a big mischievous grin on his face.

'You give my ass a headache,' Harlan said, trying to hide his own smile. But Danielle couldn't, her face had broken out into a big, bright, beautiful smile which was why Harlan had invited her; so she could be young and free again.

Danielle asked for wine and Stan, a real ale, Harlan headed back inside. There was a slight lull at the bar when Harlan got there and Alan asked him to step out into the back. Harlan lifted the hatch and walked through the gap and then down past the girls who were serving. He stepped through the back room where Alan was counting out a stack of notes and putting them in piles on the worktop. After a couple of minutes Alan had stopped counting and took a step back, his body language gesturing for Harlan to step forward and count it himself.

'Check it, please. It's all there, though.'

'I don't doubt it,' Harlan replied, declining the offer to

count it and instead putting the cash into the white envelope that Alan had there ready. He slipped the envelope, that was now close to splitting, into the inside pocket of his cut.

Harlan held out his hand, 'It's been a pleasure doing business with you.'

Alan went to shake his hand, but instead had a rush of blood to his head and stepped forwards and threw his arms around him, pulling Harlan in hard for a hug. Harlan took the embrace for as long as could, which was six seconds before pulling away and re-stabilising the relationship between them. 'You have a real chance here now,' he said.

'I know. I... I just can't believe they are gone,' said Alan.

'They are. And they won't be coming back.'

Alan shook his head in disbelief – he just couldn't believe how effective the man standing opposite him was.

'But I have got one thing wrong,' Harlan said.

'Not from where I'm standing.'

'No, I did. Regarding the car park. Don't sell space. Sell fun.'

Harlan was referring to outside, where if they listened, they could hear the sound of happy kids playing and their parents soaking up the sun whilst drinking Alan's beer.

Harlan was a man of morals, not one of arrogance. When he got it wrong, he said so.

Alan nodded. He nodded in full agreement and went to give him another hug but Harlan shot his hand out for him to shake before he got close enough. One bear hug from a man the actual size of a bear was enough.

. . .

Harlan returned with the drinks on a round tray. A white wine. A real ale. A coke. And a cartoon of juice. He handed out the drinks, starting of course, with Danielle, and ending, of course, with Stan.

'Twat,' he heard him mumble under his breath.

Harlan waited for Danielle to set up the carton of apple juice for her daughter and then for her to take a delicate mouthful of her wine before he spoke.

'Danielle, you can do so much better than him. I am not here to pry, but I am here to advise, remove him from your life.'

He let his words hang in the air for a few seconds before continuing.

'I don't know his relationship with your daughter, and you might say he is a good dad. But I'm here to tell you he isn't. Not really. A good dad; a good man, doesn't lay his hands on their child's mum. Dads provide; they don't punch. A good dad will treat his daughter as his princess, but he should treat their mum as a queen. Have a look around you, what do you see?'

Danielle put down her glass and looked, but unsure what she was supposed to be actually looking at.

'You can't see it, can you?'

Danielle wasn't sure if it was a trick question or not. She looked again to see if she had missed the obvious. She had; she just didn't know it.

'What do you see?' he asked again. His voice, gentle.

Danielle looked again but then gave up.

'I don't know.'

'Exactly. You don't see it. What you don't see is happiness. Families here together; mums, dads and their kids having fun as a unit. As a family. If you don't have that feeling with him, then you don't need my speech. You just need to do the right thing.'

He watched as her eyes glassed over. But not from pain. Or shame. But because someone had been nice to her. Someone who had just told her it would be alright.

'Thank you.'

It was so quiet Stan didn't even hear it. But Harlan had. He smiled. Enough said. The moment of sweet silence, when two people don't need words, was broken by Stan.

'Christ, even I was welling up then.'

'No you weren't, you're far too tight for tears,' Harlan replied.

'True.'

Harlan left Stan and Danielle to their drinks as Hippy had just ridden in. By the time he walked his bike back to join the others, Don was standing there holding Hippy's cut.

'Here, brother,' he said, handing him the thing Hippy treasured most in the world.

There were now ten bikes in a row. Ten bikes. 10 brothers. The band was reunited.

'How did you leave him?' Jim asked.'

'Crying for his momma,' Hippy said, sounding like a true sadist.

'Lesson learned?'

'Yep – we even did some homework.'

Jim, Harlan, Don and Hippy fell about laughing.

'C'mon brother, let me buy you a beer,' Jim said, putting his arm around Hippy and leading him towards the direction of Alan's beer pumps.

The pub was busy in all four corners and all the seats in the beer garden were taken. Harlan was doing the numbers and they were adding up nicely. He was back surrounded by his brothers; the pub was full and his job was done. Everyone was happy. He just wished he was.

The sumo suits were proving to be a big success and everywhere he looked, young kids were having candy floss peeled from their faces by their parents. Harlan joined the queue for a burger as his stomach was telling him it felt like his throat had been cut. He added a dollop of red sauce onto the cheese slice, squashed the two halves of the brioche bun together and took as big a mouthful as he could. He was facing down the car park and out towards the road when he spotted the dog. Tyson was being walked on an extendable lead, which was why he had appeared first, and for a good few seconds before the person on the end appeared in sight. Harlan was surprised to see who was walking him. It wasn't Ryan. Or Rob. It was a woman. Their mum. Her sons then came into view and they walked up the car park lacking any sort of confidence. Harlan noticed Rob's hand was now being cradled in a sling. He walked down through the crowd to meet them sensing they felt out of place.

'Rob. Ryan,' Harlan said, with a very faint nod of his head.

'And you must be?' he asked.

'Sharon.'

Her voice was frail. She looked like a person that life had shrunk over the years. She was stick thin and her skin had greyed. 'Pleased to meet you. Come, let's get you guys a burger. Or two,' and Harlan took command of the family knowing that any looks they might have otherwise got now wouldn't happen with him leading the pack.

Ryan and Rob had taken both a burger and a hotdog, each splashed with fried onions, the yellow and red sauces spewing out the sides. Harlan had to coax their mum to get something but finally she caved and got herself a burger, complete with a processed cheese slice. Harlan waited for them before he asked Ryan to help him get the drinks. Once out of sight of their mum, Harlan pulled the young teen to one side to have a quiet word with him. Jim noticed and walked over towards them.

'You ok, H?' Jim asked.

'Yeah. Just need a word with Ryan.'

'I'll do that.'

Harlan looked at him, quizzically, but the hint was clear.

'OK?' replied Harlan and he left them to it, but looking back twice unsure to why Jim wanted to speak to him.

'Ryan, isn't it?' Jim asked. It was a direct question. Forceful.

Ryan nodded his head. His trust in people hadn't yet returned.

'Look, lad, you fucked up. Proper. But you know that. But I also know why you did it. You want to be a big man. A somebody. Right?'

Ryan shrugged his shoulders. Not out of disrespect but because he was out of answers.

'Let me tell you something. Don't base your idols on those driving around in a flash car and blinged up. Those with a hip full of dollar and a wanky walk. Do you know who you should base your idol on?'

Another shrug. But this one was different. This time Ryan wanted the answer.

'The fella who saved you. That's who. The one that walked into your life today and saved it.'

Their eyes met. Jim knew he now had the kid's attention.

'I have known that man since he was not much bigger than you. He was young and full of rage. Full of hate for the hand life had dealt so far. The kid could fight. And I mean *fight*. He was afraid of nobody and would take on, and beat, the biggest men you've ever seen. But that wasn't his biggest strength, do you know what was?'

Ryan spoke. It was only one word but it was enough. 'No?'

'It was his ability to channel that aggression, that rage, that desire to be someone, into the right place. He knew it wasn't how much cash you had that made you a man, but how much morals you had. He came to me as a piece of rock, a solid piece of stone, but because he wanted to change, to learn, to grow, I chipped away until I found the man that stepped in and saved you. And I don't mean he saved you from that gang. I mean he saved you, from you.'

Ryan couldn't remember his father; it was too long ago. But it still hurt. Except for now. Now it didn't hurt. There was a guy he didn't know giving the advice he didn't know he needed. Ryan nodded his head. He would change. Today.

Jim held out his open hand for Ryan to grip. He did.

Harlan stood back at the BBQ and he smiled. That was why he was the president. And always would be.

.   .   .

The sun was starting to leave the party and the young kids who were still there were being told to put their coats or cardigans on. The BBQ had finished and the owners of the bouncy castle were starting to deflate it. Alan was out from behind the bar, meeting and greeting his customers and thanking them for sticking by him and promising the good times were here to stay. Harlan kept looking over at Ryan, checking to see he was ok. He didn't know who the friend was that arrived but whoever it was, they seemed close, and seemed to share a few secrets. Harlan knew that feeling well. It was when looking at Ryan that he found himself directing his stare over towards Sharon. She was holding a glass of wine but it was barely touched. She looked tired. She saw him looking at her and smiled. It was a half-smile; it was a half-life. Rob had explained to him that she was struggling. He had sympathy for her, just not a lot. He went to the sweet stand and then walked across the car park to where she was standing, with a toffee apple in each hand.

'Here,' he said, holding out the larger of the two, but secretly hoping she would pick the other one. She didn't.

'You ok?' he asked, watching her as she struggled to remove the cellophane from around the scarlet red apple.

'Yeah. I guess. I don't really know what has gone on, but I know you helped.'

Harlan nodded his head about a quarter inch, in acknowledgement.

'Can I ask you what happened?'

'Nope.'

The look he gave told her not to push it. Whatever the problem was, he had dealt with it. That was all she needed to know.

They stood in silence for a moment, licking their

toffee apples. Harlan knew she wanted to say something and was counting down the seconds until she said it. And then she did.

'They really need a dad,' Sharon said, as if to pass the buck.

'No. They need you to stand up and do your job.'

Her mouth dropped, wide enough, Harlan thought, to fit the toffee apple in whole. He knew most people would feel bad, dealing out some tough love. But he didn't. Which was why he was good at it. Harlan went back over to the other side of the car park and rested his back up against the wall and continued to people-watch. The live band had turned up and were busy murdering someone else's song. But it was keeping the pub busy and the gate to the beer garden was seeming more like a turnstile. He liked his job; of turning places around. Of removing someone's problem and replacing it with profit. He pulled the burner he had bought for the job out of his pocket and removed the sim card, and then snapped it in two and dropped it in the bin beside him. He went back to people-watching, until Jim arrived. There was a fag hanging from his mouth and a bottle in his hand.

'Take a walk with me, son,' Jim said, and then turned his back and started walking down towards the road knowing his protégé would follow. It wasn't until they were out on the pavement, and out of earshot and both facing the houses opposite.

'Nice thing you did today.'

'Thanks.'

Harlan watched as Jim turned to face him.

'I'm worried about you.'

'Really? Why?'

'Because you can't keep taking on everybody else's problems.'

Harlan didn't speak. It was a profound statement and it threw him.

'And you can't keep running.'

'I'm not?'

Jim looked at him. Into him. Harlan knew that since adulthood, no-one knew him better than Jim did.

'H, you are. And you have been since that night. At some point you need to stop. Because whilst you're running, you're not living.'

'It's not that bad.'

'Yes, son. Yes, it is.'

Harlan went back to looking out in front of him. The houses were a visual block, but his mind was way past the other side and out into the distance. Or was it the future? He didn't know.

'But I can't tell you what to do. You're your own man. But I will be here when you run out of breath.'

Both men looked at each other. There wasn't a need for any more words. The hug said it all.

'Right, you filthy lot, it's time to go.'

Jim looked around at his men. They were a rabble. Misfits. Dropouts. They were societies unwanted. But not to Jim. He wanted every goddamn one of them. The patch on their back couldn't be bought; only earned and every one of them had passed the test and proved their mettle. And right now, as he looked around the room, he couldn't be prouder. They had arrived to help their brother; had turned around a pub, saved a kid and taken over a business in the process. Outlaws, yes. Outstanding. *Definitely.* It was time to go.

The sight was impressive. Ten bikes pulling out into the road in a razor-sharp formation. Ten devils on ten backs. Ten Harleys. Ten Men. One club. The gates of hell protected by those deemed worthy of such a task. Jim was out in front, his VP just a few staggered inches behind. They were followed by Simon and Nigel. Next came the members. Three of which were newly patched. At the back was Harlan. Although one day, Jim knew, he would be leading from the front. Big Al was in the car park watching them leave, marvelling at the spectacle. Sharon stood in the middle of her two boys, her arms around them both. Next to Ryan was his best friend. Michael. *Mikey.* Danielle was kneeling down and had her hands over her daughter's ears to try and cover the noise. A few seconds later they were out of sight. A minute later they were out of earshot. Satan's Security had left the building.

Even Stan had been impressed.

Liam was down by the river. Waiting for no-one to be around. Waiting for it to be quiet. Which was why the sound of the burner phone hitting the water sounded so loud. And seemed so poignant.

The End.

ACKNOWLEDGMENTS

Once again, a huge thank you to Wendie Michie for making this book what it is, and better than what it was. I may have had the idea for Harlan, but it is Wendie who gave him his heartbeat. Your dedication knows no bounds and your talent knows no limits.

To Kev Woolls for inviting me into his clubhouse and for his time and patience in answering my questions. You have not only greatly helped this book, but have provided insights that will benefit many more books to come. Thank you.

To Elizabeth Young, Emily Godwin and Joe Long for reading the book in advance; thank you for all your helpful suggestions and edits.

And to Tim Lazarchuk and Patrik Dahlborg Lau, thanks again for your help with the cover art. Much appreciated.

WHAT DID YOU THINK?

I hope you enjoyed Child's Play. I would love to hear your thoughts on the story. If you are happy to leave a review you can do that in the following places:

On the platform where you purchased the book

On our website: www.harlan.store/reviews

On Goodreads: https://tinyurl.com/msfpapzr

Cheers, H.

AUTHOR Q&A

Why Child's Play?

First and foremost, it was a play on words. But it went deeper than that. We all know that criminality exists. It's a fact of life. And although society doesn't want to agree, it exists for a reason so there is no point trying to sweep criminality under the carpet. However, what we don't want, and I feel I can say this on behalf of the masses, is for kids to be used to bolster an adult's criminal gain nor do we want it affecting the lives of those who didn't sign up for it. We need to be real with what poverty, society, or status can breed, which is often survival, risk or greed. Child's Play was written to highlight the sad fact of young teenagers being used as drug mules and to show the grime behind the glory for those teens involved.

Is there a theme to the Harlan novels in terms of highlighting criminal issues?

Yes, but only in the sense of criminal enterprise. Some crimes are too heinous to highlight, at least in a way where you can tackle them by means of an antihero novel. Harlan is involved in crime, judge that as you will. It means he is perfectly placed to showcase the seedier side of Britain (and who knows, maybe other countries should Harlan decide to travel...) so the reader will get to hear about activities that they might not get to otherwise, and with as much realism as I can inject. As we have learned so far, Harlan accepts criminality by others just so long as it doesn't affect those that it shouldn't. Harlan stands up for those who can't stand up for themselves, and even those who can't speak!

On that note, the next book tackles dog fighting I believe?

Again, another side of criminality that society has no place for. If two men want to bare-knuckle fight in a desolate car park, or in a barn, then fine. We have had pugilism since time began. Prize fighting as a whole, is far becoming a bigger sport with the booming bare-knuckle splinter cell emerging, just in the same way cage fighting did when it first appeared. But two men fighting through choice, for monetary gain, is one thing. Two dogs fighting for their very survival is quite the opposite. The third book in the Harlan Action Thriller Series covers a gang involved in that and, of course, Harlan won't stand for something that sits directly outside of what he believes is right.

Is writing a series difficult?

I think the beauty of series writing is that it allows you to create suspense that can run not only alongside a novel's plot line, but also before it arrives and after it leaves. I think the skill in series writing, as perfected by the masters of this genre, is to write a novel that acts as a standalone thriller but also one you must read so as not to lose the life story of the main character(s). Some authors say not to write a story with a series in mind but I always knew Harlan was a series, and primarily because I knew Satan's Security MC had an abundance of stories to be told.

Satan's Security features prominently in Child's Play.

I wanted, and will always want, Harlan to be as real as a fictional character can be. In his first novel, I Need You, Harlan could go and attack the antagonists as a lone wolf (with the help of the local (fictional) Pirates MC). In Child's Play though, it couldn't be done, there were simply too many of them and too little of him. That was, until his brothers turned up. I think it is easy to get absorbed with your lead character's immortality in this genre, whereby bullets bounce off the hero and death-defying feats are achieved but Harlan is a regular guy, with a past, that can have a fight and knows *some people.* Also, although Harlan is the central character at the minute, and where the arc of the stories is derived from, at some point in the not-too-distant future, the MC itself will become central and with it, all the weird and wonderful characters that will spawn.

So, there is more to come from Satan's Security in future books, then?

There will always be a continual reference in the Harlan novels, and a thread running through them, just because the club is so integral to who Harlan is. He was, is, and forever will be a true outlaw and a loyal brother. In some books, the MC may feature heavily, as per Child's Play, and in some, like I Need You, they will be on the periphery. But what I can reveal now, is there is a stand-alone Satan's Security book coming out after the third Harlan instalment! I won't give too much away yet, but what I will say is that it's going to put the MC on the map.

Are the books being well received so far by the real-life MCs?

I must say I have come across some of the nicest men around, writing these stories. Everyone we have reached out to in the real MCs has embraced the book with open arms, from reading the Advance Reader Copies (ARCs) to spending time with me in their clubhouse discussing the true outlaw lifestyle. The *book* world isn't as friendly as you would think, whereas bikers are *far more friendly* than people perceive. Funny, huh? Book and cover springs to mind (pardon the pun!)

ALSO IN THIS SERIES

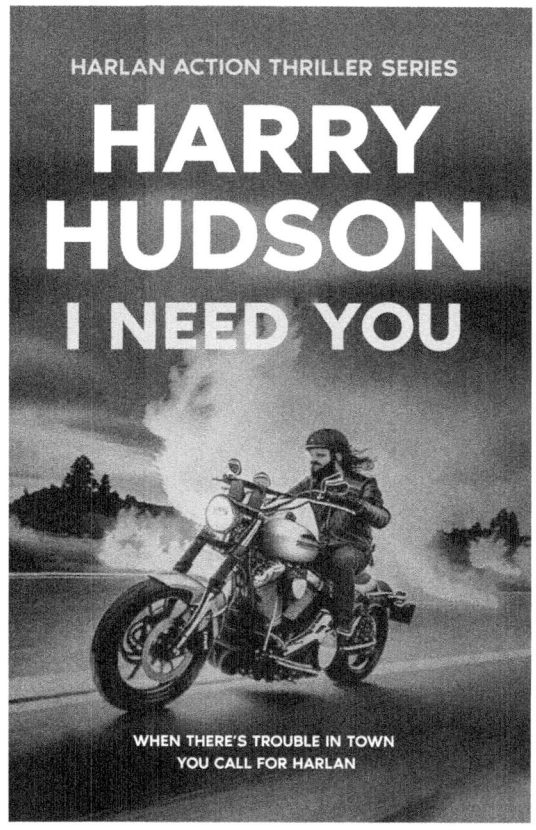

I Need You by Harry Hudson

THE NEXT HARLAN ADVENTURE

DOG EAT DOG

COMING SUMMER 2023

EBOOK AND PAPERBACK

Register for an advance copy here:

www.harlan.store

EXTRACT FROM DOG EAT DOG

The dogs were already barking way before the black 4x4 with its tinted windows and black wheels pulled up to the padlocked gates. The location of the derelict building put it away from prying eyes and engaging ears so as not to cause too much concern from inquisitive neighbours and any local law enforcement. The building was listed online as being *generously spacious* but *in need of slight modernization*. The reality was different. Very different. It was a disgusting, desolate and dangerous dump of a place but it served the operation well. The two men in the two-tonne car looked exactly what they were. Thugs. The 4x4 was black. The window tints were black. The interior was black. Their bomber jackets were black. They weren't. The vehicle came to a stop just a few feet away from the gate and headlights gave the much-needed illumination to the lock. It was an unearthly hour of the day for daylight to make an appearance. The padlocked gates served as a further deterrent to the already uninviting perimeter fencing, which had aggressive anti-climb spikes at the top and with barbed wire coarsely woven through. The crudely improvised security system was proving more than enough to protect the building from thieves, truant teenagers or worse, those people in uniform who carried metal bracelets. The barking from the other side of the gates and originating inside the building, was reaching near fever pitch and needed to be silenced quickly, as even though this rural location was perfect for such an unlawful business, life wasn't always so. What went on inside needed to be kept a secret so a pack of hungry dogs barking was adding extra stress to what was an already stressful situation. They needed to shut up. And fast. In the business they were in, silence was not just golden, silence was imperative. Which meant silence was needed. Which meant silence *would* be achieved. And no matter *what* it took to achieve it.

The passenger pulled on the door handle and started to get out and in doing so the suffocated black leather seat began to come up for air from where his fat ass had sat and suffocated it. The bulky frame underneath the tattooed haven head and fuzzy beard further continued the image that these weren't a couple of choir boy's turning up for church. Manhandling the cumbersome chain and lock wasn't easy at the best of times, even less so when it was dark, drizzly and cold. The padlock itself was an industrial one, not the cheap layman type lock that could be disjointed with a sufficient strike from a suitably sized hammer. This padlock, fastened through one-inch chained ringlets, was made to keep people out. Period.

'Fucking thing,' said Eddie. He was not known for either his elocution or his innate grasp of the English language. Shakespeare he wasn't but a bruiser he most certainly was.

The driver's window came down a few inches.

'Hurry up, the dogs are doing my head in,' Brad barked. His instruction to Eddie was said in a tone of equal annoyance but with the aid of authority. Brad was certainly more menacing to look at and a lot less amenable to deal with. With a marine styled crew haircut, a tribal tattoo around his eye, Turkish teeth and some minor scars across his forehead and a deep one on his right cheek, told even the most trusting of folk that Brad was a '*think with his fists*' type of guy.

'Chrissake, Ed, just get it open. NOW.' Brad bellowed.

Eddie, for all his size, over twenty stone and touching six four in his steel toe caps, was intimidated not only by Brad's love of extreme violence and hair trigger temper, but also of the fact that Brad's status as Jerry's number two meant he was as much his boss as the main man himself. The chain split into two as the U-section of the lock popped up and Eddie pushed the heavy gates open for Brad to drive through and make his way over to the apparently abandoned building. The vehicle pulled up slowly outside the paint-stricken roller shutter door that looked like it too had also seen its fair share of bruising in the past, probably from clumsy forklift drivers banging into it with their wooden pallets. The motion-detector lights that were screwed high up on the corners of the wall that once provided light across the four faces of the building were now permanently turned off so as not to give a bright shout-out to the world that criminality may be taking place. The dogs were making a din so loud now it could wake the dead as the saying goes and that wasn't good for business. And *nothing* can be allowed to get in the way of business. Mark got out and with a face like thunder, stormed the few paces needed and slammed the palm of his hand into the galvanized steel shutter doors, causing even more paint flakes to fall to the floor and through gritted teeth he hissed the word 'Enough.'

Eddie made his way back to the car

'Let's get these dogs sorted and get gone Brad, mate.'

Brad grunted his agreement however the stare told Eddie he was a subordinate, not a *mate*. The reason for such an early start was that in a few days there was a big event with big egos and even bigger money being held in this big building. In this chosen industry notoriety was everything and the boss man was as notorious as they came but right now, for Mark and Eddie, this wasn't glamorous organized crime, it was simply 5am, misty and in Eddie's words, 'Fucking freezing.'

Twenty miles away the gates were very different. For a start they were electric. Secondly, they were silent, no manhandling required and no creaking as they did so. Thirdly, no one-inch crude chain was entwined through them and clasped together with a padlock that was impervious to pain. The gates were fabricated in high-spec, high-grade steel and finished in rich, black gloss. When the time came for the gates to open, they would smoothly reverse and nestle behind a pair of perfectly-pointed brick walls and upon each wall stood a high-spec security camera with its red light staring intently at any new arrival. These gates acted as a fortress to the faux Belgravia mansion that spoke of affluence and grandeur. You would be forgiven in thinking that a celebrity couple, who would be draped over one another, with the look of love in their eyes whilst simultaneously trying to hide the fact they have had to sell their very souls on a regular basis to reality-based programs and publications to actually afford it, actually lived happily here. The house, a vast monument to wealth, had all the aesthetics needed to shout its worth from the rooftops; tall oak trees and Japanese maples sitting on top of the manicured lawn, a half-naked woman water fountain and a fleet of luxury cars living in the garage. But for all its opulence, the house couldn't shake off the fact that there was just the faintest feeling to the near-by neighbours that it was villainy, not celebrity, that paid the bills. The house had additional security to that of both motion and thermal image cameras and although a little less high-tech, it more than made up for it with ferocity and physical presence, serving to protect the perimeter and the person who lived within it. But for now, there was no need for the steel cage to open, allowing instead for the three male Pit Bulls, all of which were super-sized with steroids, to stay sleeping peacefully and loudly in their metal home. The law told him it was a banned breed but the dogs don't belong to a law-abiding citizen. The difference in the two buildings, just twenty miles apart was abundant, however they shared a connection in that they belonged to the same man. And that man went by the name of Jerry Flanagan. It was a name that was said only by a few, but the few knew what the man could do. The reach that he had. The fear he could evoke. It was a career that started off in debt collecting and through the course of meeting, and beating his clients, it opened up young Jerry's natural entrepreneurial mind to the fact that the common customer to collect from, was a gambler and that gamblers *needed* to gamble. The skill, he decided, was constantly finding new sports to gamble on. He set about devising a sport punter could gamble on; but with a difference as instead of collecting debts he would instead be collecting his winnings. And one thing Jerry always wanted to do... was win.

The skyline was a beautiful blend of dark blue and vibrant orange. The high-rise buildings had started to cast their shadows and the early morning silence was about to be broken. The view from where he was stood afforded him a look out across the city. A different city. The same problem. His life had become a Ferris wheel, only with no end to the ride. Or maybe, he didn't want the ride to stop. He wasn't sure which it was. He had got used to his introverted thoughts in the early hours. That time of day before the smog had settled and the rat race began. This was a city he was familiar with. He had been here before on club business, sent up by Jim to settle a dispute. The row had escalated over a pricing issue, one in which the seller thought it would be a good idea to try and fleece the club of its cash. It was a bad idea. Two shattered knee caps had told the fella that. Its position in the country made it a perfect middle ground for the thoroughfare of criminal activity. Scotland was one side; London the other, Manchester was a rose between two thorns. The city was awash with firms. Some, just local scallies, wanting to be the next up and coming. The others, the ones with criminal CVs, were a force to be reckoned with and it was these gangsters that the MC had a lot of time, and respect, for. Manchester was an industrial city and the view of the old factories and cotton mills from the balcony reiterating that fact, there was now money about. Foreign investment had paved the way for the two football teams to start winning everything and buying everyone and it so badly wanted to ditch the grime and replace it with glitter. But underneath the rebranding bracket that it had so cleverly constructed, it was still very much a working-class place with working-class issues. The crime rate here was high and intrinsically linked to poverty. But Harlan wasn't here to be swayed by the bright lights or saddened by the boarded-up windows, he was here to do a job. Nothing more; nothing less. A different city; the same problem. It was money that brought him here. Not to the city; to this apartment. The coded message had come the week before. Harlan had told the sender he would need to wait as he wasn't finished with his current problem. The sender didn't want to wait and offered to double his fee. Again, Harlan had said no. Money wasn't his god. He would be there when he was ready. And *if* he was ready. Harlan answered to no-one outside of the MC. If they wanted him; they waited for him. It really was that simple.

FOLLOW HARLAN

Website: www.harlan.store

Facebook: Meet Harlan

Instagram: meet_harlan

Twitter: meet_harlan

TikTok: meet_harlan

JOIN THE CLUB

Satan's Security MC © is a fictional motorcycle club.

To make the Harlan experience as real and immersive as possible, the club has its own online clubhouse and private members' group.

In the clubhouse you will find interviews with the author, member-only offers, bonus content and more.

All are welcome but, as with a real MC, rules must be respected.

To find out more, head to: www.harlan.store

OFFICIAL MERCHANDISE

Read the book? Now get the t-shirt!

For a range of official Satan's Security© and Harlan merchandise, from t-shirts and hoodies to mugs and phone cases., please visit our website.

Go on, be a little bit badass.

You know you want to.

www.harlan.store

Printed in Great Britain
by Amazon

23535649R00202